Augustine Birrell, James Boswell

Boswell's Life of Johnson

Vol. 2

Augustine Birrell, James Boswell

Boswell's Life of Johnson
Vol. 2

ISBN/EAN: 9783337333409

Printed in Europe, USA, Canada, Australia, Japan

Cover: Foto ©Raphael Reischuk / pixelio.de

More available books at **www.hansebooks.com**

BOSWELL'S
LIFE OF JOHNSON

EDITED BY

AUGUSTINE BIRRELL

IN SIX VOLUMES

VOL. II

𝔚𝔢𝔰𝔱𝔪𝔦𝔫𝔰𝔱𝔢𝔯

ARCHIBALD CONSTABLE AND CO

1896

THE LIFE OF
SAMUEL JOHNSON, LL.D.

In 1758 we find him, it should seem, in as easy and pleasant a state of existence, as constitutional unhappiness ever permitted him to enjoy.

TO BENNET LANGTON, ESQ., AT LANGTON, LINCOLNSHIRE

'Dearest Sir,—I must have indeed slept very fast, not to have been awakened by your letter. None of your suspicions are true; I am not much richer than when you left me; and, what is worse, my omission of an answer to your first letter will prove that I am not much wiser. But I go on as I formerly did, designing to be some time or other both rich and wise; and yet cultivate neither mind nor fortune. Do you take notice of my example, and learn the danger of delay. When I was as you are now, towering in confidence of twenty-one, little did I suspect that I should be at forty-nine what I now am.

'But you do not seem to need my admonition. You are busy in acquiring and in communicating knowledge, and while you are studying, enjoy the end of study by making others wiser and happier. I was much pleased with the tale that you told me of being tutor to your sisters. I, who have no sisters nor brothers, look with some degree of innocent envy on those who may be said to be born to friends; and cannot see, without wonder, how rarely that native union is afterwards regarded. It sometimes, indeed, happens that some supervenient cause of discord may overpower this original amity;

but it seems to me more frequently thrown away with levity, or lost by negligence, than destroyed by injury or violence. We tell the ladies that good wives make good husbands; I believe it is a more certain position that good brothers make good sisters.

'I am satisfied with your stay at home, as Juvenal with his friend's retirement to Cumæ: I know that your absence is best, though it be not best for me.

> ' "Quamvis digressu veteris confusus amici,
> Laudo tamen vacuis quod sedem figere Cumis
> Destinet, atque unum civem donare Sibyllæ."—iii. 2.

'*Langton* is a good *Cumæ*, but who must be Sibylla? Mrs. Langton is as wise as Sibyl, and as good; and will live, if my wishes can prolong life, till she shall in time be as old. But she differs in this, that she has not scattered her precepts in the wind, at least not those which she bestowed upon you.

'The two Wartons just looked into the town, and were taken to see *Cleone*, where, David[1] says, they were starved, for want of company to keep them warm. David and Doddy[2] have had a new quarrel, and, I think, cannot conveniently quarrel any more. *Cleone* was well acted by all their characters, but Bellamy left nothing to be desired. I went the first night and supported it as well as I might; for Doddy, you know, is my patron, and I would not desert him. The play was very well received. Doddy, after the danger was over, went every night to the stage-side, and cried at the distress of poor Cleone.

'I have left off housekeeping, and therefore made presents of the game which you were pleased to send me. The pheasant I gave to Mr. Richardson,[3] the bustard to Dr. Lawrence, and the pot I placed with Miss Williams, to be eaten by myself. She desires that her compliments and good wishes may be accepted by the family; and I make the same request for myself.

'Mr. Reynolds has within these few days raised his price to twenty guineas a head, and Miss is much employed in

---

[1] Mr. Garrick.   [2] Mr. Dodsley, the Author of *Cleone*.
[3] Mr. Samuel Richardson, author of *Clarissa*.

miniatures. I know not anybody [else] whose prosperity has increased since you left them.

'Murphy is to have his *Orphan of China* acted next month; and is therefore, I suppose, happy. I wish I could tell you of any great good to which I was approaching, but at present my prospects do not much delight me; however, I am always pleased when I find that you, dear sir, remember your affectionate, humble servant,   SAM. JOHNSON.

'*Jan.* 9, 1758.'

TO MR. BURNEY, AT LYNNE, NORFOLK

'SIR,—Your kindness is so great, and my claim to any particular regard from you so little, that I am at a loss how to express my sense of your favours;[1] but I am, indeed, much pleased to be thus distinguished by you.

'I am ashamed to tell you that my Shakespeare will not be out so soon as I promised my subscribers: but I did not promise them more than I promised myself. It will, however, be published before summer.

'I have sent you a bundle of proposals, which, I think, do not profess more than I have hitherto performed. I have printed many of the plays, and have hitherto left very few passages unexplained; where I am quite at a loss, I confess my ignorance, which is seldom done by commentators.

'I have, likewise, enclosed twelve receipts; not that I impose upon you the trouble of pushing them, with more importunity than may seem proper, but that you may rather have more than fewer than you shall want. The proposals you will disseminate as there shall be an opportunity. I once printed them at length in the *Chronicle*, and some of my friends (I believe Mr. Murphy, who formerly wrote the *Gray's Inn Journal*) introduced them with a splendid encomium.

'Since the *Life of Browne*, I have been a little engaged, from time to time, in the *Literary Magazine*, but not very lately. I have not the collection by me, and therefore cannot draw out a catalogue of my own parts, but will do it, and send it. Do not buy them, for I will gather all those that

---

[1] This letter was an answer to one in which was enclosed a draft for the payment of some subscriptions to his Shakespeare.

have anything of mine in them, and send them to Mrs.
Burney, as a small token of gratitude for the regard which
she is pleased to bestow upon me.—I am, sir, your most
obliged and most humble servant,   SAM. JOHNSON.
    '*London, March* 8, 1758.'

Dr. Burney has kindly favoured me with the following memorandum, which I take the liberty to insert in
his own genuine easy style.   I love to exhibit sketches
of my illustrious friend by various eminent hands :

'Soon after this, Mr. Burney, during a visit to the capital,
had an interview with him in Gough Square, where he dined
and drank tea with him, and was introduced to the acquaintance of Mrs. Williams.   After dinner, Mr. Johnson proposed
to Mr. Burney to go up with him into his garret, which being
accepted, he there found about five or six Greek folios, a deal
writing-desk, and a chair and a half.   Johnson, giving to his
guest the entire seat, tottered himself on one with only three
legs and one arm.   Here he gave Mr. Burney Mrs. Williams's
history, and showed him some volumes of his Shakespeare
already printed, to prove that he was in earnest.   Upon Mr.
Burney's opening the first volume, at the "Merchant of Venice,"
he observed to him, that he seemed to be more severe on
Warburton than Theobald.   "O poor Tib. ! (said Johnson)
he was ready knocked down to my hands; Warburton stands
between me and him."   "But, sir (said Mr. Burney), you'll
have Warburton upon your bones, won't you?"   'No, sir;
he'll not come out: he'll only growl in his den."   "But you
think, sir, that Warburton is a superior critic to Theobald?"
"O, sir, he'd make two-and-fifty Theobalds, cut into slices!
The worst of Warburton is, that he has a rage for saying
something, when there's nothing to be said."   Mr. Burney
then asked him whether he had seen the letter which Warburton had written in answer to a pamphlet addressed "To
the most impudent man alive."   He answered in the negative.
Mr. Burney told him it was supposed to be written by Mallet.
The controversy now raged between the friends of Pope and
Bolingbroke; and Warburton and Mallet were the leaders of

the several parties. Mr. Burney asked him then if he had
seen Warburton's book against Bolingbroke's Philosophy.
"No, sir; I have never read Bolingbroke's impiety, and therefore am not interested about its confutation."'

On the 15th of April he began a new periodical
paper, entitled the *Idler,* which came out every
Saturday in a weekly newspaper called the *Universal
Chronicle or Weekly Gazette,* published by Newbery.
These essays were continued till April 5, 1760. Of
one hundred and three, their total number, twelve
were contributed by his friends; of which, Nos. 33,
93, and 96 were written by Mr. Thomas Warton;
No. 67 by Mr. Langton; and Nos. 76, 79, and 82
by Sir Joshua Reynolds: the concluding words of
No. 82, 'and pollute his canvas with deformity,' being
added by Johnson; as Sir Joshua informed me.

The *Idler* is evidently the work of the same mind
which produced the *Rambler,* but has less body and
more spirit. It has more variety of real life, and
greater facility of language. He describes the miseries
of idleness, with the lively sensations of one who has
felt them; and in his private memorandums while
engaged in it, we find 'This year I hope to learn
diligence.'[1] Many of these excellent essays were
written as hastily as an ordinary letter. Mr. Langton
remembers Johnson, when on a visit at Oxford, asking him one evening how long it was till the post went
out; and on being told about half an hour, he exclaimed, 'Then we shall do very well.' He upon
this instantly sat down and finished an *Idler,* which
it was necessary should be in London the next day.

---

[1] *Prayers and Meditations.*

Mr. Langton having signified a wish to read it, 'Sir
. (said he), you shall do no more than I have done
myself.' He then folded it up, and sent it off.

Yet there are in the *Idler* several papers which show
as much profundity of thought, and labour of language as any of this great man's writings. No. 14,
'Robbery of Time'; No. 24, 'Thinking'; No. 41, 'Death
of a Friend'; No. 43, 'Flight of Time'; No. 51, 'Domestic greatness unattainable'; No. 52, 'Self-Denial';
No. 58, 'Actual, how short of fancied, excellence'; No.
89, 'Physical evil moral good'; and his concluding
paper on 'The Horror of the last,' will prove the assertion. I know not why a motto, the usual trapping of
periodical papers, is prefixed to very few of the *Idlers*,
as I have heard Johnson commend the custom : and
he never could be at a loss for one, his memory being
stored with innumerable passages of the classics. In
this series of essays he exhibits admirable instances of
grave humour, of which he had an uncommon share.
Nor on some occasions has he repressed that power of
sophistry which he possessed in so eminent a degree.
In No. 11, he treats with the utmost contempt the
opinion that our mental faculties depend, in some degree, upon the weather ; an opinion which they who
have never experienced its truth are not to be envied,
and of which he himself could not but be sensible, as
the effects of weather upon him were very visible. Yet
thus he declaims :

'Surely, nothing is more reproachful to a being endowed
with reason, than to resign its powers to the influence of the
air, and live in dependence on the weather and the wind for
the only blessings which nature has put into our power,
tranquillity and benevolence. This distinction of seasons is

produced only by imagination operating on luxury. To temperance, every day is bright; and every hour is propitious to diligence. He that shall resolutely excite his faculties, or exert his virtues, will soon make himself superior to the seasons; and may set at defiance the morning mist and the evening damp, the blasts of the east, and the clouds of the south.'

Alas! it is too certain, that where the frame has delicate fibres, and there is a fine sensibility, such influences of the air are irresistible. He might as well have bid defiance to the ague, the palsy, and all other bodily disorders. Such boasting of the mind is false elevation.

> 'I think the Romans call it Stoicism.'

But in this number of his *Idler* his spirits seem to run riot; for in the wantonness of his disquisition he forgets, for a moment, even the reverence for that which he held in high respect; and describes 'the attendant on a *Court*' as one 'whose business is to watch the looks of a being weak and foolish as himself.'

His unqualified ridicule of rhetorical gesture or action is not, surely, a test of truth; yet we cannot help admiring how well it is adapted to produce the effect which he wished:

> 'Neither the judges of our laws, nor the representatives of our people, would be much affected by laboured gesticulations, or believe any man the more because he rolled his eyes, or puffed his cheeks, or spread abroad his arms, or stamped the ground, or thumped his breast; or turned his eyes sometimes to the ceiling and sometimes to the floor.'

A casual coincidence with other writers, or an

adoption of a sentiment or image which has been found in the writings of another, and afterwards appears in the mind as one's own, is not unfrequent. The richness of Johnson's fancy, which could supply his page abundantly on all occasions, and the strength of his memory, which at once detected the real owner of any thought, made him less liable to the imputation of plagiarism than, perhaps, any of our writers. In the *Idler*, however, there is a paper, in which conversation is assimilated to a bowl of punch, where there is the same train of comparison as in a poem by Blacklock, in his collection published in 1756; in which a parallel is ingeniously drawn between human life and that liquor.   It ends :

> ' Say, then, physicians of each kind,
> Who cure the body or the mind,
> What harm in drinking can there be,
> Since punch and life so well agree ?'

To the *Idler*, when collected in volumes, he added, beside the Essay on Epitaphs, and the Dissertation on those of Pope, an Essay on the Bravery of the English Common Soldiers.   He, however, omitted one of the original papers, which, in the folio copy, is No. 22.[1]

TO THE REV. MR. THOMAS WARTON

' DEAR SIR,—Your notes upon my poet were very acceptable. I beg that you will be so kind as to continue your searches. It will be reputable to my work, and suitable to your professorship, to have something of yours in the notes. As you have given no directions about your name, I shall

---

[1] This paper may be found in Stockdale's supplemental volume of Johnson's *Miscellaneous Pieces.*

therefore put it. I wish your brother would take the same trouble. A commentary must arise from the fortuitous discoveries of many men in devious walks of literature. Some of your remarks are on plays already printed: but I purpose to add an Appendix of Notes, so that nothing comes too late.

'You give yourself too much uneasiness, dear sir, about the loss of the papers.[1] The loss is nothing, if nobody has found them; nor even then, perhaps, if the numbers be known. You are not the only friend that has had the same mischance. You may repair your want out of a stock, which is deposited with Mr. Allen, of Magdalen Hall; or out of a parcel which I have just sent to Mr. Chambers[2] for the use of anybody that will be so kind as to want them. Mr. Langtons are well; and Miss Roberts, whom I have at last brought to speak, upon the information which you gave me, that she had something to say.—I am, etc.,   SAM. JOHNSON.

'*London, April* 14, 1758.'

TO THE SAME

'DEAR SIR,—You will receive this by Mr. Baretti, a gentleman particularly entitled to the notice and kindness of the Professor of poesy. He has time but for a short stay, and will be glad to have it filled up with as much as he can hear and see.

'In recommending another to your favour, I ought not to omit thanks for the kindness which you have shown to myself. Have you any more notes on Shakespeare? I shall be glad of them.

'I see your pupil sometimes:[3] his mind is as exalted as his stature. I am half afraid of him; but he is no less amiable than formidable. He will, if the forwardness of his spring be not blasted, be a credit to you, and to the University. He brings some of my plays[4] with him, which he has my

---

1 'Receipts for Shakespeare.'
2 'Then of Lincoln College. Now Sir Robert Chambers, one of the Judges in India.'
3 'Mr. Langton.'
4 'Part of the impression of the Shakespeare which Dr. Johnson conducted alone and published by subscription. This edition came out in 1765.'

permission to show you, on condition you will hide them from
everybody else.—I am, dear sir, etc.,

'SAM. JOHNSON.

'[*London*,] *June* 1, 1758.'

TO BENNET LANGTON, ESQ., OF TRINITY COLLEGE
OXFORD

'DEAR SIR,—Though I might have expected to hear from
you, upon your entrance into a new state of life at a new
place, yet recollecting (not without some degree of shame)
that I owe you a letter upon an old account, I think it my
part to write first. This, indeed, I do not only from com-
plaisance but from interest; for living on in the old way, I
am very glad of a correspondent so capable as yourself to
diversify the hours. You have, at present, too many novelties
about you to need any help from me to drive along your time.

'I know not anything more pleasant, or more instructive,
than to compare experience with expectation, or to register
from time to time the difference between idea and reality. It
is by this kind of observation that we grow daily less liable to
be disappointed. You, who are very capable of anticipating
futurity, and raising phantoms before your own eyes, must
often have imagined to yourself an academical life, and have
conceived what would be the manners, the views, and the
conversation, of men devoted to letters; how they would
choose their companions, how they would direct their studies,
and how they would regulate their lives. Let me know what
you expected, and what you have found. At least record it
to yourself before custom has reconciled you to the scenes
before you, and the disparity of your discoveries to your hopes
has vanished from your mind. It is a rule never to be forgotten, that whatever strikes strongly should be described
while the first impression remains fresh upon the mind.

'I love, dear sir, to think on you, and, therefore, should
willingly write more to you, but that the post will not now
give me leave to do more than send my compliments to Mr.
Warton, and tell you that I am, dear sir, most affectionately,
your very humble servant   SAM. JOHNSON.

'*June* 28, 1758.'

TO BENNET LANGTON, ESQ., AT LANGTON, NEAR SPILSBY,
LINCOLNSHIRE

'DEAR SIR,—I should be sorry to think that what engrosses
the attention of my friend, should have no part of mine.
Your mind is now full of the fate of Dury;[1] but his fate
is past, and nothing remains but to try what reflection will
suggest to mitigate the terrors of a violent death, which is
more formidable at the first glance, than on a nearer and more
steady view. A violent death is never very painful; the only
danger is, lest it should be unprovided. But if a man can be
supposed to make no provision for death in war, what can be
the state that would have awakened him to the care of
futurity? When would that man have prepared himself to
die, who went to seek death without preparation? What, then,
can be the reason why we lament more him that dies of a
wound, than him that dies of a fever? A man that languishes
with disease, ends his life with more pain, but with less
virtue: he leaves no example to his friends, nor bequeaths
any honour to his descendants. The only reason why we
lament a soldier's death, is, that we think he might have lived
longer; yet this cause of grief is common to many other kinds
of death, which are not so passionately bewailed. The truth
is, that every death is violent which is the effect of accident;
every death which is not gradually brought on by the
miseries of age, or when life is extinguished for any other
reason than that it is burnt out. He that dies before sixty,
of a cold or consumption, dies, in reality, by a violent death;
yet his death is borne with patience, only because the cause
of his untimely end is silent and invisible. Let us endeavour
to see things as they are, and then inquire whether we ought
to complain. Whether to see life as it is, will give us much
consolation, I know not; but the consolation which is drawn
from truth, if any there be, is solid and durable: that which

---

[1] Major-General Alexander Dury, of the First Regiment of Foot
Guards, who fell in the gallant discharge of his duty, near St. Cas,
in the well-known unfortunate expedition against France, in 1758. His
lady and Mr. Langton's mother were sisters. He left an only son,
Lieutenant-Colonel Dury, who has a company in the same regiment.

may be derived from error, must be, like its original, fallacious and fugitive.—I am, dear, dear sir, your most humble servant,

'SAM. JOHNSON.

'*Sept.* 21, 1758.'

In 1759, in the month of January, his mother died, at the great age of ninety, an event which deeply affected him; not that 'his mind had acquired no firmness by the contemplation of mortality;[1] but that his reverential affection for her was not abated by years, as indeed he retained all his tender feelings even to the latest period of his life. I have been told that he regretted much his not having gone to visit his mother for several years previous to her death. But he was constantly engaged in literary labours which confined him to London; and though he had not the comfort of seeing his aged parent, he contributed liberally to her support.

TO MRS. JOHNSON, AT LICHFIELD [2]

'HONOURED MADAM,—The account which Miss [Porter] gives me of your health, pierces my heart. God comfort and preserve you, and save you, for the sake of Jesus Christ.

'I would have Miss read to you from time to time the Passion of our Saviour, and sometimes the sentences in the communion service, beginning—*Come unto me all that travail and are heavy laden, and I will give you rest.*

'I have just now read a physical book, which inclines me to think that a strong infusion of the bark would do you good. Do, dear mother, try it.

'Pray send me your blessing, and forgive all that I have

---

[1] Hawkins's *Life of Johnson*, p. 395.
[2] [Since the publication of the third edition of this work, the following letters of Dr. Johnson, occasioned by the last illness of his mother, were obligingly communicated to Mr. Malone by the Rev. Dr. Vyse. They are placed here agreeably to the chronological order almost uniformly observed by the author; and so strongly evince Dr. Johnson's piety and tenderness of heart, that every reader must be gratified by their insertion.—M.]

done amiss to you. And whatever you would have done, and what debts you would have paid first, or anything else that you would direct, let Miss put it down; I shall endeavour to obey you.

'I have got twelve guineas [1] to send you, but unhappily am at a loss how to send it to-night. If I cannot send it to-night, it will come by the next post.

'Pray, do not admit anything mentioned in this letter. God bless you for ever and ever. I am, your dutiful son,

'SAM. JOHNSON.

'*Jan.* 13, 1758.' [2]

TO MISS PORTER, AT MRS. JOHNSON'S, IN LICHFIELD

'MY DEAR MISS,—I think myself obliged to you beyond all expression of gratitude for your care of my dear mother. God grant it may not be without success. Tell Kitty [3] that I shall never forget her tenderness for her mistress. Whatever you can do, continue to do. My heart is very full.

'I hope you received twelve guineas on Monday. I found a way of sending them by means of the postmaster, after I had written my letter, and hope they came safe. I will send you more in a few days. God bless you all.—I am, my dear, your most obliged and most humble servant,

'SAM. JOHNSON.

'*Jan.* 16, 1759.
'Over the leaf is a letter to my mother.'

'DEAR HONOURED MOTHER,—Your weakness afflicts me beyond what I am willing to communicate to you. I do not

---

[1] [Six of these twelve guineas Johnson appears to have borrowed from Mr. Allen, the printer. See Hawkins's *Life of Johnson*, p. 266, n. —M.]

[2] [Written by mistake for 1759, as the subsequent letters show. In the next letter, he had inadvertently fallen into the same error, but corrected it. On the *outside* of the letter of the 13th was written by another hand—'Pray acknowledge the receipt of this by return of post without fail.'—M.]

[3] [Catharine Chambers, Mrs. Johnson's maid-servant. She died in October 1767. See Dr. Johnson's *Prayers and Meditations* : 'Sunday, Oct. 18, 1767. Yesterday, Oct. 17, I took my leave for ever of my dear old friend, Catharine Chambers, who came to live with my mother about 1724, and has been but little parted from us since. She buried my father, my brother, and my mother. She is now fifty-eight years old.'—M.]

think you unfit to face death, but I know not how to bear the thought of losing you. Endeavour to do all you [can] for yourself. Eat as much as you can.

'I pray often for you; do you pray for me.—I have nothing to add to my last letter.—I am, dear, dear mother, your dutiful son,   SAM JOHNSON.
'*Jan.* 16, 1759.'

TO MRS. JOHNSON, IN LICHFIELD

'DEAR HONOURED MOTHER,—I fear you are too ill for long letters; therefore I will only tell you, you have from me all the regard that can possibly subsist in the heart. I pray God to bless you for evermore, for Jesus Christ's sake. Amen.

'Let Miss write to me every post, however short.—I am, dear mother, your dutiful son,   SAM. JOHNSON.
'*Jan.* 18, 1759.'

TO MISS PORTER, AT MRS. JOHNSON'S, IN LICHFIELD

'DEAR MISS,—I will, if it be possible, come down to you. God grant I may yet [find] my dear mother breathing and sensible. Do not tell her, lest I disappoint her. If I miss to write next post, I am on the road.—I am, my dearest Miss, your most humble servant,   SAM. JOHNSON.
'*Jan.* 20, 1759.

On the other side.

'DEAR HONOURED MOTHER,[1]—Neither your condition nor your character make it fit for me to say much. You have been the best mother, and I believe the best woman in the world. I thank you for your indulgence to me, and beg forgiveness of all that I have done ill, and all that I have omitted to do well.[2] God grant you his Holy Spirit, and

---

[1] [This letter was written on the second leaf of the preceding, addressed to Miss Porter.—M.]

[2] [So, in the prayer which he composed on this occasion : 'Almighty God, merciful Father, in whose hands are life and death, sanctify unto me the sorrow which I now feel. *Forgive me whatever I have done unkindly to my mother, and whatever I have omitted to do kindly.* Make me to remember her good precepts and good example, and to reform my life according to thy holy word,' etc.—*Prayers and Meditations.*—M.]

receive you to everlasting happiness, for Jesus Christ's sake. Amen. Lord Jesus receive your spirit. Amen.—I am, dear, dear mother, your dutiful son, SAM. JOHNSON.
    '*Jan.* 20, 1759.'

TO MISS PORTER, IN LICHFIELD

'You will conceive my sorrow for the loss of my mother, of the best mother. If she were to live again, surely I should behave better to her. But she is happy, and what is past is nothing to her; and for me, since I cannot repair my faults to her, I hope repentance will efface them. I return you and all those that have been good to her my sincerest thanks, and pray God to repay you all with infinite advantage. Write to me, and comfort me, dear child. I shall be glad likewise, if Kitty will write to me. I shall send a bill of £20 in a few days, which I thought to have brought to my mother; but God suffered it not. I have not power or composure to say much more. God bless you, and bless us all.—I am, dear Miss, your affectionate humble servant, SAM. JOHNSON.
    '*Jan.* 23, 1759.' [1]

Soon after this event he wrote his *Rasselas, Prince of Abyssinia*; concerning the publication of which Sir John Hawkins guesses vaguely and idly, instead of having taken the trouble to inform himself with authentic precision. Not to trouble my readers with a repetition of the Knight's reveries, I have to mention that the late Mr. Strahan the printer told me, that Johnson wrote it, that with the profits he might defray the expense of his mother's funeral, and pay some little debts which she had left. He told Sir Joshua Reynolds that he composed it in the evenings of one week,[2] sent it to the press in portions as it was

---

[1] [Mrs. Johnson probably died on the 20th or 21st of January, and was buried on the day this letter was written.—M.]

[2] *Rasselas* was published in two duodecimo volumes, price five shillings. The title was got of *Lobo* (p. 102). *Ras* means head or chief.—A. B.]

written, and had never since read it over.[1]   Mr.
Strahan, Mr. Johnson, and Mr. Dodsley, purchased
it for £100, but afterwards paid him £25 more, when
it came to a second edition.

Considering the large sums which have been received
for compilations, and works requiring not much more
genius than compilations, we cannot but wonder at the
very low price which he was content to receive for this
admirable performance ; which, though he had written
nothing else, would have rendered his name immortal
in the world of literature.   None of his writings has
been so extensively diffused over Europe ; for it has
been translated into most, if not all, of the modern
languages.   This tale, with all the charms of oriental
imagery, and all the force and beauty of which the
English language is capable, leads us through the
most important scenes of human life, and shows us
that this stage of our being is full of 'vanity and
vexation of spirit.'   To those who look no further than
the present life, or who maintain that human nature
has not fallen from the state in which it was created,
the instruction of this sublime story will be of no avail.
But they who think justly, and feel with strong
sensibility, will listen with eagerness and admiration
to its truth and wisdom.   Voltaire's *Candide,* written
to refute the system of Optimism, which it has accomplished with brilliant success, is wonderfully similar
in its plan and conduct to Johnson's *Rasselas* ; inso-
much, that I have heard Johnson say, that if they
had not been published so closely one after the other

---

[1] [See vol. iv. under June 2, 1781. Finding it then accidentally in
a chaise with Mr. Boswell, he read it eagerly. This was doubtless
long after his declaration to Sir Joshua Reynolds.—M.]

that there was not time for imitation, it would have
been in vain to deny that the scheme of that which
came latest was taken from the other. Though the
proposition illustrated by both these works was the
same, namely, that in our present state there is more
evil than good, the intention of the writers was very
different. Voltaire, I am afraid, meant only by wanton
profaneness to obtain a sportive victory over religion,
and to discredit the belief of a superintending Providence : Johnson meant, by showing the unsatisfactory
nature of things temporal, to direct the hopes of man
to things eternal. *Rasselas*, as was observed to me by
a very accomplished lady, may be considered as a
more enlarged and more deeply philosophical discourse
in prose, upon the interesting truth, which in his
Vanity of Human Wishes he had so successfully enforced in verse.

The fund of thinking which this work contains is
such, that almost every sentence of it may furnish a
subject of long meditation. I am not satisfied if a
year passes without my having read it through ; and
at every perusal, my admiration of the mind which
produced it is so highly raised, that I can scarcely
believe that I had the honour of enjoying the intimacy
of such a man.

I restrain myself from quoting passages from this
excellent work, or even referring to them, because I
should not know what to select, or rather what to
omit. I shall, however, transcribe one, as it shows
how well he could state the arguments of those who
believe in the appearance of departed spirits ; a doctrine which it is a mistake to suppose that he himself
ever positively held :

'If all your fear be of apparitions (said the Prince) I will promise you safety : there is no danger from the dead : he that is once buried will be seen no more.

'That the dead are seen no more (said Imlac), I will not undertake to maintain, against the concurrent and unvaried testimony of all ages, and of all nations. There is no people, rude or learned, among whom apparitions of the dead are not related and believed. This opinion, which prevails as far as human nature is diffused, could become universal only by its truth ; those that never heard of one another, would not have agreed in a tale which nothing but experience can make credible. That it is doubted by single cavillers, can very little weaken the general evidence ; and some who deny it with their tongues, confess it by their fears.'

Notwithstanding my high admiration of *Rasselas,* I will not maintain that the 'morbid melancholy' in Johnson's constitution may not, perhaps, have made life appear to him more insipid and unhappy than it generally is ; for I am sure that he had less enjoyment from it than I have. Yet, whatever additional shade his own particular sensations may have thrown on his representation of life, attentive observation and close inquiry have convinced me that there is too much reality in the gloomy picture. The truth, however, is, that we judge of the happiness and misery of life differently at different times, according to the state of our changeable frame. I always remember a remark made to me by a Turkish lady, educated in France :— '*Ma foi, Monsieur, notre bonheur depend de la façon que notre sang circule.*' This have I learned from a pretty hard course of experience, and would, from sincere benevolence, impress upon all who honour this book with a perusal, that until a steady conviction is obtained that the present life is an imperfect state, and only a passage to a better, if we comply with the

divine scheme of progressive improvement; and also
that it is a part of the mysterious plan of Providence
that intellectual beings must 'be made perfect through
suffering'; there will be a continual recurrence of
disappointment and uneasiness. But if we walk with
hope in 'the midday sun' of revelation, our temper
and disposition will be such that the comforts and
enjoyments in our way will be relished, while we
patiently support the inconveniences and pains. After
much speculation and various reasonings, I acknowledge myself convinced of the truth of Voltaire's conclusion, '*Apres tout, c'est un monde passable.*' But we
must not think too deeply;

> '*where ignorance is bliss,*
> '*Tis folly to be wise,*'

is, in many respects, more than poetically just. Let
us cultivate, under the command of good principles,
'*la théorie des sensations agréables*'; and, as Mr. Burke
once admirably counselled a grave and anxious gentleman, 'live pleasant.'

The effect of *Rasselas*, and of Johnson's other moral
tales, is thus beautifully illustrated by Mr. Courtenay :

> '*Impressive truth, in splendid fiction drest,*
> *Checks the vain wish, and calms the troubled breast;*
> *O'er the dark mind a light celestial throws,*
> *And soothes the angry passions to repose;*
> *As oil effused illumes and smooths the deep,*
> *When round the bark the swelling surges sweep.*'[1]

It will be recollected that during all this year he
carried on his *Idler*,[2] and, no doubt, was proceeding,

---

[1] *Literary and Moral Character of Johnson.*
[2] This paper was in such high estimation before it was collected into
volumes that it was seized on with avidity by various publishers of

though slowly, in his edition of Shakespeare. He, however, from that liberality which never failed, when called upon to assist other labourers in literature, found time to translate for Mrs. Lenox's English version of Brumoy, 'A Dissertation on the Greek Comedy,' and 'The General Conclusion of the Book.'

An inquiry into the state of foreign countries was an object that seems at all times to have interested Johnson. Hence Mr. Newbery found no great difficulty in persuading him to write the Introduction to a collection of voyages and travels published by him under the title of *The World Displayed*: the first volume of which appeared this year, and the remaining volumes in subsequent years.

newspapers and magazines to enrich their publications. Johnson, to put a stop to this unfair proceeding, wrote for the *Universal Chronicle* the following advertisement; in which there is, perhaps, more pomp of words than the occasion demanded:

'*London, Jan.* 5, 1759. ADVERTISEMENT.—The proprietors of the paper entitled the *Idler*, having found that those essays are inserted in the newspapers and magazines with so little regard to justice or decency that the *Universal Chronicle*, in which they first appear, is not always mentioned, think it necessary to declare to the publishers of those collections, that however patiently they have hitherto endured these injuries, made yet more injurious by contempt, they have now determined to endure them no longer. They have already seen essays, for which a very large price is paid, transferred, with the most shameless rapacity, into the weekly or monthly compilations, and their right, at least for the present, alienated from them, before they could themselves be said to enjoy it. But they would not willingly be thought to want tenderness, even for men by whom no tenderness hath been shown. The past is without remedy, and shall be without resentment. But those who have been thus busy with their sickles in the fields of their neighbours are henceforth to take notice that the time of impunity is at an end. Whoever shall, without our leave, lay the hand of rapine upon our papers is to expect that we shall vindicate our due, by the means which justice prescribes, and which are warranted by the immemorial prescriptions of honourable trade. We shall lay hold, in our turn, on their copies, degrade them from the pomp of wide margin and diffuse typography, contract them into a narrow space, and sell them at an humble price; yet not with a view of growing rich by confiscations, for we think not much better of money got by punishment than by crimes. We shall, therefore, when our losses are repaid, give what profit shall remain to the Magdalens; for we know not who can be more properly taxed for the support of penitent prostitutes, than prostitutes in whom there yet appears neither penitence nor shame.'

I would ascribe to this year the following letter to
a son of one of his early friends at Lichfield, Mr.
Joseph Simpson, Barrister, and author of a tract
entitled, *Reflections on the Study of the Law.*

TO JOSEPH SIMPSON, ESQ.

'Dear Sir,—Your father's inexorability not only grieves
but amazes me: he is your father; he was always accounted
a wise man; nor do I remember anything to the disadvantage
of his good nature; but in his refusal to assist you there
is neither good nature, fatherhood, nor wisdom. It is the
practice of good nature to overlook faults which have already,
by the consequences, punished the delinquent. It is natural
for a father to think more favourably than others of his
children; and it is always wise to give assistance, while a
little help will prevent the necessity of greater.

'If you married imprudently, you miscarried at your own
hazard, at an age when you had a right of choice. It would
be hard if the man might not choose his own wife, who has a
right to plead before the judges of his country.

'If your imprudence has ended in difficulties and inconveniences, you are yourself to support them; and, with the
help of a little better health, you would support them and
conquer them. Surely, that want which accident and sickness produces is to be supported in every region of humanity,
though there were neither friends nor fathers in the world.
You have certainly from your father the highest claim of
charity, though none of right: and therefore I would counsel
you to omit no decent nor manly degree of importunity.
Your debts in the whole are not large, and of the whole but
a small part is troublesome. Small debts are like small shot;
they are rattling on every side, and can scarcely be escaped
without a wound: great debts are like cannon; of loud noise
but little danger. You must, therefore, be enabled to discharge petty debts, that you may have leisure, with security,
to struggle with the rest. Neither the great nor the little
debts disgrace you. I am sure you have my esteem for the
courage with which you contracted them, and the spirit with

which you endure them. I wish my esteem could be of more use. I have been invited, or have invited myself, to several parts of the kingdom ; and will not incommode my dear Lucy by coming to Lichfield, while her present lodging is of any use to her. I hope in a few days to be at leisure, and to make visits. Whither I shall fly is matter of no importance. A man unconnected is at home everywhere ; unless he may be said to be at home nowhere. I am sorry, dear sir, that where you have parents, a man of your merits should not have a home. I wish I could give it you. I am, my dear sir, affectionately yours,   SAM. JOHNSON.'

He now refreshed himself by an excursion to Oxford, of which the following short characteristical notice, in his own words, is preserved :

'. . . is now making tea for me. I have been in my gown ever since I came here. It was, at my first coming, quite new and handsome. I have swum thrice, which I had disused for many years. I have proposed to Vansittart [1] climbing over the wall, but he has refused me. And I have clapped my hands till they are sore at Dr. King's speech.' [2]

His negro servant, Francis Barber, having left him, and been some time at sea, not pressed as has been supposed, but with his own consent, it appears from a letter to John Wilkes, Esq., from Dr. Smollett, that his master kindly interested himself in procuring his release from a state of life of which Johnson always expressed the utmost abhorrence. He said, ' No man will be a sailor who has contrivance enough to get himself into a jail ; for being in a ship is being in a

---

[1] Dr. Robert Vansittart of the ancient and respectable family of that name in Berkshire. He was eminent for learning and worth, and much esteemed by Dr. Johnson.
[2] *Gentleman's Magazine*, April 1785.

jail, with the chance of being drowned.'[1] And at
another time, 'A man in a jail has more room, better
food, and commonly better company.'[2] The letter
was as follows:

Chelsea, March 16, 1759.

'DEAR SIR,—I am again your petitioner, in behalf of that
great Cham[3] of literature, Samuel Johnson. His black
servant, whose name is Francis Barber, has been pressed on
board the *Stag* frigate, Captain Angel, and our lexicographer
is in great distress. He says the boy is a sickly lad, of a
delicate frame, and particularly subject to a malady in his
throat, which renders him very unfit for his Majesty's service.
You know what matter of animosity the said Johnson has
against you: and I dare say you desire no other opportunity
of resenting it, than that of laying him under an obligation.
He was humble enough to desire my assistance on this
occasion, though he and I were never cater-cousins; and I
gave him to understand that I would make application to my
friend Mr. Wilkes, who, perhaps, by his interest with Dr.
Hay and Mr. Elliott, might be able to procure the discharge
of his lacquey. It would be superfluous to say more on the
subject, which I leave to your own consideration; but I cannot
let slip this opportunity of declaring that I am, with the most
inviolable esteem and attachment, dear sir, your affectionate
obliged humble servant, T. SMOLLETT.'

---

[1] *Journal of a Tour to the Hebrides*, 3rd edit., p. 126.
[2] *Ibid.*, p. 251.
[3] In my first edition this word was printed *Chum*, as it appears in
one of Mr. Wilkes's *Miscellanies*, and I animadverted on Dr. Smollett's
ignorance; for which let me propitiate the *manes* of that ingenious and
benevolent gentleman. Chum was certainly a mistaken reading for
Cham, the title of the sovereign of Tartary, which is well applied to
Johnson, the Monarch of Literature: and was an epithet familiar to
Smollett. See *Roderick Random*, chap. lvi. For this correction I
am indebted to Lord Palmerston, whose talents and literary acquire-
ments accord well with his respectable pedigree of Temple.
[After the publication of the second edition of this work, the author
was furnished by Mr. Abercrombie of Philadelphia, with the copy of a
letter written by Dr. John Armstrong, the poet, to Dr. Smollett at
Legborn, containing the following paragraph:
'As to the K. Bench patriot, it is hard to say from what motive he
published a letter of yours asking some trifling favour of him in behalf
of somebody for whom the great Cham of literature, Mr. Johnson, had
interested himself.'—M.]

Mr. Wilkes, who upon all occasions has acted as a private gentleman, with most polite liberality, applied to his friend Sir George Hay, then one of the Lords Commissioners of the Admiralty ; and Francis Barber was discharged, as he has told me, without any wish of his own.   He found his old master in chambers in the Inner Temple, and returned to his service.

What particular new scheme of life Johnson had in view this year I have not discovered ; but that he meditated one of some sort, is clear from his private devotions, in which we find,[1] 'the change of outward things which I am now to make'; and, 'Grant me the grace of thy Holy Spirit, that the course which I am now beginning may proceed according to thy laws, and end in the enjoyment of thy favour.'   But he did not, in fact, make any external or visible change.

At this time there being a competition among the architects of London to be employed in the building of Blackfriars Bridge, a question was very warmly agitated whether semicircular or elliptical arches were preferable.   In the design offered by Mr. Mylne the elliptical form was adopted, and therefore it was the great object of his rivals to attack it.   Johnson's regard for his friend Mr. Gwyn, induced him to engage in this controversy against Mr. Mylne;[2] and after

---

[1] *Prayers and Meditations.*
[2] Sir John Hawkins has given a long detail of it, in that manner vulgarly, but significantly, called *rigmarole*; in which, amidst an ostentatious exhibition of arts and artists, he talks of 'proportions of a column being taken from that of the human figure, and *adjusted by Nature*—masculine and feminine—in a man, *sesquioctave* of the head, and in a woman *sesquional*'; nor has he failed to introduce a jargon of musical terms, which do not seem much to correspond with the subject, but serve to make up the heterogeneous mass.   To follow the knight through all this would be a useless fatigue to myself, and not a little disgusting to my readers.   I shall, therefore, only make a few remarks upon his statement.—He seems to exult in having detected

being at considerable pains to study the subject, he wrote three several letters in the *Gazetteer*, in opposition to his plan.

If it should be remarked that this was a controversy which lay quite out of Johnson's way, let it be remembered, that after all, his employing his powers of reasoning and eloquence upon a subject which he had studied on the moment, is not more strange than what we often observe in lawyers, who, as *Quicquid agunt*

Johnson in procuring 'from a person eminently skilled in mathematics and the principles of architecture, answers to a string of questions drawn up by himself, touching the comparative strength of semicircular and elliptical arches.' Now I cannot conceive how Johnson could have acted more wisely. Sir John complains that the opinion of that excellent mathematician, Mr. Thomas Simpson, did not preponderate in favour of the semicircular arch. But he should have known, that however eminent Mr. Simpson was in the higher parts of abstract mathematical science, he was little versed in mixed and practical mechanics. Mr. Muller of Woolwich Academy, the scholastic father of all the great engineers which this country has employed for forty years, decided the question by declaring clearly in favour of the elliptical arch.

It is ungraciously suggested, that Johnson's motive for opposing Mr. Mylne's scheme may have been his prejudice against him as a native of North Britain; when, in truth, as has been stated, he gave the aid of his able pen to a friend, who was one of the candidates; and so far was he from having any illiberal antipathy to Mr. Mylne that he afterwards lived with that gentleman upon very agreeable terms of acquaintance, and dined with him at his house. Sir John Hawkins, indeed, gives full vent to his own prejudice in abusing Blackfriars Bridge, calling it 'an edifice, in which beauty and symmetry are in vain sought for; by which the citizens of London have perpetuated their own disgrace, and subjected a whole nation to the reproach of foreigners.' Whoever has contemplated, *placido lumine*, this stately, elegant, and airy structure, which has so fine an effect, especially on approaching the capital of that quarter, must wonder at such unjust and ill-tempered censure; and I appeal to all foreigners of good taste, whether this bridge be not one of the most distinguished ornaments of London. As to the stability of the fabric, it is certain that the city of London took every precaution to have the best Portland stone for it; but as this is to be found in the quarries belonging to the public, under the direction of the Lords of the Treasury, it so happened that Parliamentary interests, which is often the bane of fair pursuits, thwarted their endeavours. Notwithstanding this disadvantage, it is well known that not only has Blackfriars Bridge never sunk either in its foundation or in its arches, which were so much the subject of contest, but any injuries which it has suffered from the effects of severe frosts have been already, in some measure, repaired with sounder stone, and every necessary renewal can be completed at a moderate expense.—BOSWELL.

homines is the matter of lawsuits, are sometimes obliged to pick up a temporary knowledge of an art or science, of which they understood nothing till their brief was delivered, and appear to be much masters of it. In like manner, members of the legislature frequently introduce and expatiate upon subjects of which they have informed themselves for the occasion.

In 1760 he wrote *An Address of the Painters to George III. on his Accession to the Throne of these Kingdoms,* which no monarch ever ascended with more sincere congratulations from his people. Two generations of foreign princes had prepared their minds to rejoice in having again a king who gloried in being 'born a Briton.' He also wrote for Mr. Baretti the Dedication of his *Italian and English Dictionary,* to the Marquis of Abreu, then Envoy-Extraordinary from Spain at the court of Great Britain.

Johnson was now either very idle, or very busy with his Shakespeare; for I can find no other public composition by him except an Introduction to the Proceedings of the Committee for Clothing the French Prisoners; one of the many proofs that he was ever awake to the calls of humanity; and an account which he gave in the *Gentleman's Magazine* of Mr. Tytler's acute and able vindication of Mary Queen of Scots. The generosity of Johnson's feeling shines forth in the following sentence :

'It has now been fashionable, for near half a century, to defame and vilify the house of Stuart, and to exalt and magnify the reign of Elizabeth. The Stuarts have found few apologists, for the dead cannot pay for praise; and who will, without reward, oppose the tide of popularity? Yet there remains still among us, not wholly extinguished, a zeal for truth, a desire of establishing right in opposition to fashion.'

In this year I have not discovered a single private
letter written by him to any of his friends. It should
seem, however, that he had at this period a floating
intention of writing a history of the recent and
wonderful successes of the British arms in all quarters
of the globe; for among his resolutions or memorandums, September 18, there is, 'Send for books for
Hist. of War.'[1] How much is it to be regretted
that this intention was not fulfilled! His majestic
expression would have carried down to the latest
posterity the glorious achievements of his country,
with the same fervent glow which they produced on
the mind at the time. He would have been under no
temptation to deviate in any degree from truth which
he held very sacred, or to take a licence, which a
learned divine told me he once seemed in a conversation jocularly to allow to historians. 'There are
(said he) inexcusable lies, and consecrated lies. For
instance, we are told that on the arrival of the
news of the unfortunate battle of Fontenoy, every
heart beat and every eye was in tears. Now we
know that no man eat his dinner the worse, but
there *should* have been all this concern; and to say
there was (smiling), may be reckoned a consecrated
lie.'

This year Mr. Murphy, having thought himself ill-
treated by the Reverend Dr. Franklin, who was one
of the writers of the *Critical Review,* published an indignant vindication in 'A Poetical Epistle to Samuel
Johnson, A.M.,' in which he compliments Johnson in
a just and elegant manner:

---

[1] *Prayers and Meditations.*

'Transcendent Genius! whose prolific vein
Ne'er knew the frigid poet's toil and pain;
To whom Apollo opens all his store,
And every Muse presents her sacred lore;
Say, powerful Johnson, whence thy verse is fraught
With so much grace, such energy of thought;
Whether thy Juvenal instructs the age
In chaster numbers, and new-points his rage;
Or faire Irene sees, alas! too late,
Her innocence exchanged for guilty state;
Whate'er you write, in every golden line
Sublimity and elegance combine;
Thy nervous phrase impresses every soul,
While harmony gives rapture to the whole.'

Again, towards the conclusion :

Thou then, my friend, who see'st the dang'rous strife
In which some demon bids me plunge my life,
To the Aonian fount direct my feet,
Say, where the Nine thy lonely musings meet?
Where warbles to thy ear the sacred throng,
Thy moral sense, thy dignity of song?
Tell, for you can, by what unerring art
You wake to finer feelings every heart;
In each bright page some truth important give,
And bid to future times thy *Rambler* live.'

I take this opportunity to relate the manner in which
an acquaintance first commenced between Dr. Johnson
and Mr. Murphy. During the publication of the
Gray's Inn Journal, a periodical paper which was
successfully carried on by Mr. Murphy alone, when a
very young man, he happened to be in the country
with Mr. Foote; and having mentioned that he was
obliged to go to London in order to get ready for the
press one of the numbers of that Journal, Foote said
to him, ' You need not go on that account. Here is
a French magazine, in which you will find a very

pretty oriental tale; translate that, and send it to
your printer.' Mr. Murphy having read the tale, was
highly pleased with it, and followed Foote's advice.
When he returned to town this tale was pointed out
to him in the *Rambler*, from whence it had been translated into the French magazine. Mr. Murphy then
waited upon Johnson to explain this curious incident.
His talents, literature, and gentleman-like manners
were soon perceived by Johnson, and a friendship was
formed which was never broken.[1]

TO BENNET LANGTON, ESQ., AT LANGTON, NEAR SPILSBY,
LINCOLNSHIRE

'DEAR SIR,—You that travel about the world have more
materials for letters, than I who stay at home: and should,
therefore, write with frequency equal to your opportunities.
I should be glad to have all England surveyed by you, if you
would impart your observations in narratives as agreeable as
your last. Knowledge is always to be wished to those who
can communicate it well. While you have been riding and
running, and seeing the tombs of the learned, and the camps
of the valiant, I have only stayed at home and intended to do
great things, which I have not done. Beau[2] went away to
Cheshire, and has not yet found his way back. Chambers
passed the vacation at Oxford.

' I am very sincerely solicitous for the preservation or curing
of Mr. Langton's sight, and am glad that the chirurgeon at
Coventry gives him so much hope. Mr. Sharpe is of opinion
that the tedious maturation of the cataract is a vulgar error,
and that it may be removed as soon as it is formed. This
notion deserves to be considered; I doubt whether it be
universally true; but if it be true in some cases, and those

---

[1] [When Mr. Murphy first became acquainted with Dr. Johnson he
was about thirty-one years old. He died at Knightsbridge, June 18,
1805, it is believed in his eighty-second year.—M.]
[2] Topham Beauclerk, Esq.

cases can be distinguished, it may save a long and uncomfortable delay.

'Of dear Mrs. Langton you gave me no account; which is the less friendly, as you know how highly I think of her, and how much I interest myself in her health. I suppose you told her of my opinion, and likewise suppose it was not followed; however, I still believe it to be right.

'Let me hear from you again; wherever you are, or whatever you are doing; whether you wander or sit still, plant trees or make *Rustics*,[1] play with your sisters or muse alone; and in return I will tell you the success of Sheridan, who at this instant is playing Cato, and has already played Richard twice. He had more company the second than the first night, and will make, I believe, a good figure in the whole, though his faults seem to be very many; some of natural deficience, and some of laborious affectation. He has, I think, no power of assuming either that dignity or elegance which some men, who have little of either in common life, can exhibit on the stage. His voice when strained is unpleasing, and when low is not always heard. He seems to think too much on the audience, and turns his face too often to the galleries.

'However, I wish him well; and among other reasons, because I like his wife.[2]—Make haste to write to, dear sir, your most affectionate servant,   SAM. JOHNSON.

'*Oct.* 18, 1760.'

In 1761, Johnson appears to have done little. He was still, no doubt, proceeding in his edition of Shakespeare; but what advances he made in it cannot be ascertained. He certainly was at this time not active; for in his scrupulous examination of himself on Easter eve, he laments, in his too rigorous mode of censuring his own conduct, that his life, since the communion of the preceding Easter, had been 'dis-

---

[1] Essays with that title, written about this time by Mr. Langton, but not published.
[2] Mrs. Sheridan was author of *Memoirs of Miss Sydney Biddulph*, a novel of great merit, and of some other pieces.

sipated and useless.'[1] He, however, contributed this
year the Preface to Rolt's *Dictionary of Trade and
Commerce*, in which he displayed such a clear and
comprehensive knowledge of the subject, as might
lead the reader to think that its author had devoted
all his life to it. I asked him whether he knew much
of Rolt and of his work. 'Sir (said he), I never saw
the man, and never read the book. The booksellers
wanted a Preface to a Dictionary of Trade and Commerce. I knew very well what such a Dictionary
should be, and I wrote a Preface accordingly.' Rolt,
who wrote a great deal for the booksellers, was, as
Johnson told me, a singular character. Though not
in the least acquainted with him, he used to say, 'I
am just come from Sam. Johnson.' This was a
sufficient specimen of his vanity and impudence. But
he gave a more eminent proof of it in our sister kingdom, as Dr. Johnson informed me. When Akenside's
Pleasures of the Imagination first came out he did not
put his name to the poem. Rolt went over to Dublin,
published an edition of it, and put his own name to
it. Upon the fame of this he lived for several months,
being entertained at the best tables as 'the ingenious
Mr. Rolt.'[2] His conversation, indeed, did not discover
much of the fire of a poet; but it was recollected that
both Addison and Thomson were equally dull till
excited by wine. Akenside having been informed

---

[1] *Prayers and Meditations.*
[2] I have had inquiry made in Ireland as to this story, but do not
find it recollected there. I give it on the authority of Dr. Johnson, to
which may be added that of the *Biographical Dictionary*, and *Bio-
graphia Dramatica*; in both of which it has stood many years. Mr.
Malone observes, that the truth probably is, not that an edition was
published with Rolt's name in the title-page, but that the poem being
thus anonymous, Rolt acquiesced in its being attributed to him in
conversation.

of this imposition, vindicated his right by publishing the poem with its real author's name. Several instances of such literary fraud have been detected. The Reverend Dr. Campbell, of St. Andrews, wrote *An Inquiry into the original of Moral Virtue*, the manuscript of which he sent to Mr. Innes, a clergyman in England, who was his countryman and acquaintance. Innes published it with his own name to it; and before the imposition was discovered, obtained considerable promotion as a reward of his merit.[1]   The celebrated Dr. Hugh Blair, and his cousin, Mr. George Bannatine, when students in divinity, wrote a poem, entitled *The Resurrection*, copies of which were handed about in manuscript. They were at length very much surprised to see a pompous edition of it in folio, dedicated to the Princess Dowager of Wales, by a Dr. Douglas as his own.   Some years ago a little novel, entitled *The Man of Feeling*, was assumed by Mr. Eccles, a young Irish clergyman, who was afterwards drowned near Bath. He had been at the pains to transcribe the whole book, with blottings, interlineations, and corrections, that it might be shown to several people as an original. It was, in truth, the production of Mr. Henry Mackenzie, an attorney in the Exchequer at Edinburgh, who is the author of several other ingenious pieces; but the belief with regard to Mr. Eccles became so general, that it was thought necessary for Messieurs Strahan and Cadell to publish an advertisement in the newspapers contradicting the report, and

---

[1] I have both the books. Innes was the clergyman who brought Psalmanazar to England, and was an accomplice in his extraordinary fiction.

mentioning that they purchased the copyright of Mr.
Mackenzie. I can conceive this kind of fraud to be
very easily practised with successful effrontery. The
Filiation of a literary performance is difficult of proof ;
seldom is there any witness present at its birth. A
man either in confidence or by improper means
obtains possession of a copy of it in manuscript, and
boldly publishes it as his own. The true author, in
many cases, may not be able to make his title clear.
Johnson, indeed, from the peculiar features of his
literary offspring, might bid defiance to an attempt
to appropriate them to others :

> 'But Shakespeare's magic could not copied be,
> Within that circle none durst walk but he.'

He this year lent his friendly assistance to correct
and improve a pamphlet written by Mr. Gwyn the
architect, entitled *Thoughts on the Coronation of
George III.*

Johnson had now for some years admitted Mr.
Baretti to his intimacy ; nor did their friendship cease
upon their being separated by Baretti's revisiting his
native country, as appears from Johnson's letters to
him.

TO MR. JOSEPH BARETTI, AT MILAN [1]

'You reproach me very often with parsimony of writing ;
but you may discover by the extent of my paper that I design
to recompense rarity by length. A short letter to a distant
friend is, in my opinion, an insult like that of a slight bow or

---

[1] The originals of Dr. Johnson's three letters to Mr. Baretti, which
are among the very best he ever wrote, were communicated to the
proprietors of that instructive and elegant monthly miscellany, *The
European Magazine,* in which they first appeared.

cursory salutation;—a proof of unwillingness to do much, even where there is a necessity of doing something. Yet it must be remembered, that he who continues the same course of life in the same place will have little to tell. One week and one year are very like one another. The silent changes made by him are not always perceived, and if they are not perceived cannot be recounted. I have risen and lain down, talked and mused, while you have roved over a considerable part of Europe; yet I have not envied my Baretti any of his pleasures, though, perhaps, I have envied others his company; and I am glad to have other nations made acquainted with the character of the English, by a traveller who has so nicely inspected our manners, and so successfully studied our literature. I received your kind letter from Falmouth, in which you gave me notice of your departure for Lisbon; and another from Lisbon, in which you told me that you were to leave Portugal in a few days. To either of these how could any answer be returned? I have had a third from Turin, complaining that I have not answered the former. Your English style still continues in its purity and vigour. With vigour your genius will supply it; but its purity must be continued by close attention. To use two languages familiarly, and without contaminating one by the other, is very difficult: and to use more than two is hardly to be hoped. The praises which some have received for their multiplicity of languages may be sufficient to excite industry, but can hardly generate confidence.

'I know not whether I can heartily rejoice at the kind reception which you have found, or at the popularity to which you are exalted. I am willing that your merit should be distinguished; but cannot wish that your affections may be gained. I would have you happy wherever you are: yet I would have you wish to return to England. If ever you visit us again you will find the kindness of your friends undiminished. To tell you how many inquiries are made after you would be tedious, or if not tedious, would be vain; because you may be told in a very few words, that all who knew you wish you well; and that all you embraced at your departure will caress you at your return: therefore do not let Italian academicians nor Italian ladies drive us from your thoughts.

You may find among us what you will leave behind, soft smiles and easy sonnets. Yet I shall not wonder if all our invitations should be rejected : for there is a pleasure in being considerable at home which is not easily resisted.

'By conducting Mr. Southwell to Venice you fulfilled, I know, the original contract : yet I would wish you not wholly to lose him from your notice, but to recommend him to such acquaintance as may best secure him from suffering by his own follies, and to take such general care both of his safety and his interest as may come within your power. His relations will thank you for any such gratuitous attention : at least they will not blame you for any evil that may happen, whether they thank you or not for any good.

'You know that we have a new King and a new Parliament. Of the new Parliament Fitzherbert is a member. We were so weary of our old King, that we are much pleased with his successor ; of whom we are so much inclined to hope great things, that most of us begin already to believe them. The young man is hitherto blameless ; but it would be unreasonable to expect much from the immaturity of juvenile years, and the ignorance of princely education. He has been long in the hands of the Scots, and has already favoured them more than the English will contentedly endure. But, perhaps, he scarcely knows whom he has distinguished, or whom he has disgusted.

'The artists have instituted a yearly Exhibition of pictures and statues, in imitation, as I am told, of foreign academies. This year was the second Exhibition. They please themselves much with the multitude of spectators, and imagine that the English school will rise in reputation. Reynolds is without a rival, and continues to add thousands to thousands, which he deserves, among other excellencies, by retaining his kindness for Baretti. This Exhibition has filled the heads of the artists and lovers of art. Surely life, if it be not long, is tedious, since we are forced to call in the assistance of so many trifles to rid us of our time, of that time which never can return.

'I know my Baretti will not be satisfied with a letter in which I give him no account of myself ; yet what account shall I give him ? I have not, since the day of our separation, suffered or done anything considerable. The only change in my way of life is that I have frequented the theatre more than in former seasons. But I have gone thither only to escape from myself. We have had many new farces, and the comedy called *The Jealous Wife*, which, though not written with much genius, was yet so well adapted to the stage, and so well exhibited by the actors, that it was crowded for near twenty nights. I am digressing from myself to the play-house; but a barren plan must be filled with episodes. Of myself I have nothing to say, but that I have hitherto lived without the concurrence of my own judgment; yet I continue to flatter myself that, when you return, you will find me mended. I do not wonder that, where the monastic life is permitted, every order finds votaries, and every monastery inhabitants. Men will submit to any rule, by which they may be exempted from the tyranny of caprice and of chance. They are glad to supply by external authority their own want of constancy and resolution, and court the government of others, when long experience has convinced them of their own inability to govern themselves. If I were to visit Italy, my curiosity would be more attracted by convents than by palaces; though I am afraid that I should find expectation in both places equally disappointed, and life in both places supported with impatience and quitted with reluctance. That it must be so soon quitted is a powerful remedy against impatience; but what shall free us from reluctance? Those who have endeavoured to teach us to die well have taught few to die willingly; yet I cannot but hope that a good life might end at last in a contented death.

'You see to what a train of thought I am drawn by the mention of myself. Let me now turn my attention upon you. I hope you take care to keep an exact journal, and to register all occurrences and observations; for your friends here expect such a book of travels as has not been often seen. You have given us good specimens in your letters from Lisbon. I wish you had stayed longer in Spain, for no country is less known to the rest of Europe; but the quickness of your discernment must make amends for the celerity of your motions. He that knows which way to direct his view sees much in a little time.

'Write to me very often, and I will not neglect to write to you ; and I may, perhaps, in time, get something to write : at least, you will know by my letters, whatever else they may have or want, that I continue to be your most affectionate friend, SAM. JOHNSON.

'[*London*,] *June* 10, 1761.'

In 1762 he wrote for the Reverend Dr. Kennedy, Rector of Bradley in Derbyshire, in a strain of very courtly elegance, a Dedication to the King of that gentleman's work, entitled *A Complete System of Astronomical Chronology, unfolding the Scriptures.* He had certainly looked at this work before it was printed : for the concluding paragraph is undoubtedly of his composition, of which let my readers judge :

'Thus have I endeavoured to free Religion and History from the darkness of a disputed and uncertain chronology ; from difficulties which have hitherto appeared insuperable, and darkness which no luminary of learning has hitherto been able to dissipate. I have established the truth of the Mosaical account, by evidence which no transcription can corrupt, no negligence can lose, and no interest can pervert. I have shown that the universe bears witness to the inspiration of its historian, by the revolution of its orbs and the succession of its seasons: *that the stars in their courses fight against* incredulity, that the works of God give hourly confirmation to the *law*, the *prophets*, and the *gospel*, of which *one day telleth another, and one night certifieth another* ; and that the validity of the sacred writings never can be denied, while the moon shall increase and wane, and the sun shall know his going down.'

He this year wrote also the Dedication to the Earl of Middlesex of Mrs. Lenox's *Female Quixote*, and the Preface to the *Catalogue of the Artists' Exhibition.*

The following letter, which, on account of its intrinsic merit, it would have been unjust both to Johnson and the public to have withheld, was obtained for me by the solicitation of my friend Mr. Seward :

TO DR. STAUNTON (NOW SIR GEORGE STAUNTON, BARONET)

'DEAR SIR,—I make haste to answer your kind letter, in hope of hearing again from you before you leave us. I cannot but regret that a man of your qualifications should find it necessary to seek an establishment in Guadaloupe, which if a peace should restore to the French, I shall think it some alleviation of the loss, that it must restore likewise Dr. Staunton to the English.

' It is a melancholy consideration, that so much of our time is necessarily to be spent upon the care of living, and that we can seldom obtain ease in one respect but by resigning it in another ; yet I suppose we are by this dispensation not less happy in the whole than if the spontaneous bounty of Nature poured all that we want into our hands. A few, if they were left thus to themselves, would, perhaps, spend their time in laudable pursuits : but the greater part would prey upon the quiet of each other, or, in the want of other subjects, would prey upon themselves.

'This, however, is our condition, which we must improve and solace as we can ; and though we cannot choose always our place of residence, we may in every place find rational amusements, and possess in every place the comforts of piety and a pure conscience.

' In America there is little to be observed except natural curiosities. The new world must have many vegetables and animals with which philosophers are but little acquainted. I hope you will furnish yourself with some books of natural history, and some glasses and other instruments of observation. Trust as little as you can to report : examine all you can by your own senses. I do not doubt but you will be able to add much to knowledge, and, perhaps, to medicine. Wild nations trust to simples ; and, perhaps, the Peruvian bark is not the only specific which those extensive regions may afford us.

'Wherever you are, and whatever be your fortune, be certain, dear sir, that you carry with you my kind wishes ;

and that whether you return hither, or stay in the other hemisphere, to hear that you are happy will give pleasure to, sir,
your most affectionate humble servant,

                                      'SAM. JOHNSON.

    '*June* 1, 1762.'

A lady having at this time solicited him to obtain
the Archbishop of Canterbury's patronage to have her
son sent to the University, one of those solicitations
which are too frequent, where people, anxious for a
particular object, do not consider propriety, or the opportunity which the persons whom they solicit have to
assist them, he wrote to her the following answer,
with a copy of which I am favoured by the Reverend
Dr. Farmer, Master of Emanuel College, Cambridge :

    'MADAM,—I hope you will believe that my delay in answer-
ing your letter could proceed only from my unwillingness to
destroy any hope that you had formed. Hope is itself a
species of happiness, and, perhaps, the chief happiness which
this world affords : but, like all other pleasures immoderately
enjoyed, the excesses of hope must be expiated by pain ; and
expectations improperly indulged must end in disappointment. If it be asked, what is the improper expectation which
it is dangerous to indulge, experience will quickly answer, that
it is such expectation as is dictated not by reason, but by
desire ; expectation raised, not by the common occurrences of
life, but by the wants of the expectant ; an expectation that
requires the common course of things to be changed, and the
general rules of action to be broken.
    'When you made your request to me, you should have con-
sidered, Madam, what you were asking. You ask me to
solicit a great man, to whom I never spoke, for a young person
whom I had never seen, upon a supposition which I had no
means of knowing to be true. There is no reason why,
amongst all the great, I should choose to supplicate the Archbishop, nor why, among all the possible objects of his bounty,
the Archbishop should choose your son. I know, madam,

how unwillingly conviction is admitted, when interest opposes it; but surely, madam, you must allow, that there is no reason why that should be done by me which every other man may do with equal reason, and which, indeed, no man can do properly, without some very particular relation both to the Archbishop and to you. If I could help you in this exigence by any proper means, it would give me pleasure; but this proposal is so very remote from usual methods, that I cannot comply with it, but at the risk of such answer and suspicions as I believe you do not wish me to undergo.

'I have seen your son this morning; he seems a pretty youth, and will, perhaps, find some better friend than I can procure him; but though he should at last miss the University he may still be wise, useful, and happy.—I am, madam, your most humble servant,   SAM. JOHNSON.

'*June* 8, 1762.'

TO MR. JOSEPH BARETTI, AT MILAN

'*London, July* 20, 1762.

'SIR,—However justly you may accuse me for want of punctuality in correspondence, I am not so far lost in negligence as to omit the opportunity of writing to you, which Mr. Beauclerk's passage through Milan affords me.

'I suppose you received the *Idlers*, and I intend that you shall soon receive *Shakespeare*, that you may explain his works to the ladies of Italy, and tell them the story of the editor, among the other strange narratives with which your long residence in this unknown region has supplied you.

'As you have now been long away, I suppose your curiosity may pant for some news of your old friends. Miss Williams and I live much as we did. Miss Cotterell still continues to cling to Mrs. Porter, and Charlotte is now big of the fourth child. Mr. Reynolds gets six thousand a year. Levet is lately married, not without much suspicion that he has been wretchedly cheated in his match. Mr. Chambers is gone this day, for the first time, the circuit with the Judges. Mr. Richardson[1] is dead of an apoplexy, and his second daughter has married a merchant.

---

[1] [Samuel Richardson, the author of *Clarissa, Sir Charles Grandison*, etc. He died July 4, 1761, aged 72.—M.]

'My vanity or my kindness makes me flatter myself that
you would rather hear of me than of those whom I have mentioned; but of myself I have very little which I care to tell.
Last winter I went down to my native town, where I found the
streets much narrower and shorter than I thought I had left
them, inhabited by a new race of people, to whom I was very
little known. My playfellows were grown old, and forced me
to suspect that I was no longer young. My only remaining
friend has changed his principles, and was become the tool of
the predominant faction. My daughter-in-law, from whom
I expected most, and whom I met with sincere benevolence,
has lost the beauty and gaiety of youth, without having gained
much of the wisdom of age. I wandered about for five days,
and took the first convenient opportunity of returning to a
place where, if there is not much happiness, there is at least
such a diversity of good and evil that slight vexations do not
fix upon the heart.

'I think in a few weeks to try another excursion; though
to what end? Let me know, my Baretti, what has been the
result of your return to your own country: whether time has
made any alteration for the better, and whether, when the
first raptures of salutation were over, you did not find your
thoughts confessed their disappointment.

'Moral sentences appear ostentatious and tumid, when they
have no greater occasions than the journey of a wit to his own
town; yet such pleasures and such pains make up the general
mass of life; and as nothing is little to him that feels it with
great sensibility, a mind able to see common incidents in
their real state is disposed by very common incidents to very
serious contemplations. Let us trust that a time will come
when the present moment shall be no longer irksome; when
we shall not borrow all our happiness from hope, which at
last is to end in disappointment.

'I beg that you will show Mr. Beauclerk all the civilities which
you have in your power, for he has always been kind to me.

'I have lately seen Mr. Stratico, Professor of Padua, who
has told me of your quarrel with an abbot of the Celestine
order; but had not the particulars very ready in his memory.
When you write to Mr. Marsili, let him know that I remember
him with kindness.

'May you, my Baretti, be very happy at Milan, or some other place nearer to, sir, your most affectionate humble servant,   SAM. JOHNSON.'

The accession of George the Third to the throne of these kingdoms opened a new and brighter prospect to men of literary merit, who had been honoured with no mark of royal favour in the preceding reign. His present Majesty's education in this country, as well as his taste and beneficence, prompted him to be the patron of science and the arts; and early this year, Johnson having been represented to him as a very learned and good man, without any certain provision, his Majesty was pleased to grant him a pension of three hundred pounds a year. The Earl of Bute, who was then Prime Minister, had the honour to announce this instance of his Sovereign's bounty, concerning which many and various stories, all equally erroneous, have been propagated; maliciously representing it as a political bribe to Johnson to desert his avowed principles, and become the tool of a government which he held to be founded in usurpation. I have taken care to have it in my power to refute them from the most authentic information. Lord Bute told me that Mr. Wedderburne, now Lord Loughborough, was the person who first mentioned this subject to him. Lord Loughborough told me that the pension was granted to Johnson solely as the reward of his literary merit, without any stipulation whatever, or even tacit understanding that he should write for administration. His Lordship added, that he was confident the political tracts which Johnson afterwards did write, as they were entirely consonant with his own opinions, would have been written by him though no pension had been granted to him.

Mr. Thomas Sheridan and Mr. Murphy, who then lived a good deal both with him and Mr. Wedderburne, told me, that they previously talked with Johnson upon this matter, and that it was perfectly understood by all parties that the pension was merely honorary. Sir Joshua Reynolds told me that Johnson called on him after his Majesty's intention had been notified to him, and said he wished to consult his friends as to the propriety of his accepting this mark of the royal favour, after the definitions which he had given in his *Dictionary* of *pension* and *pensioners.* He said he should not have Sir Joshua's answer till the next day, when he would call again, and desired he might think of it. Sir Joshua answered that he was clear to give his opinion then, that there could be no objection to his receiving from the King a reward for literary merit; and that certainly the definitions in his *Dictionary* were not applicable to him. Johnson, it should seem, was satisfied, for he did not call again till he had accepted the pension, and waited on Lord Bute to thank him. He then told Sir Joshua that Lord Bute said to him expressly, ' It is not given you for anything you are to do, but for what you have done.'[1] His Lordship, he said, behaved in the handsomest manner. He repeated the words twice, that he might be sure Johnson heard them, and thus set his mind perfectly at ease. This nobleman, who has

[1] [This was said by Lord Bute, as Dr. Burney was informed by Johnson himself, in answer to a question which he put, previously to his acceptance of the intended bounty : 'Pray, my Lord, what am I expected to do for this pension?'—M.]

been so virulently abused, acted with great honour in this instance, and displayed a mind truly liberal. A minister of a more narrow and selfish disposition would have availed himself of such an opportunity to fix an implied obligation on a man of Johnson's powerful talents to give him his support.

Mr. Murphy and the late Mr. Sheridan severally contended for the distinction of having been the first who mentioned to Mr. Wedderburne that Johnson ought to have a pension. When I spoke of this to Lord Loughborough, wishing to know if he recollected the prime mover in the business, he said, 'All his friends assisted': and when I told him that Mr. Sheridan strenuously asserted his claim to it, his Lordship said, 'He rang the bell.' And it is but just to add, that Mr. Sheridan told me, that when he communicated to Dr. Johnson that a pension was to be granted him he replied in a fervour of gratitude, 'The English language does not afford me terms adequate to my feelings on this occasion. I must have recourse to the French. I am *pénétré* with his Majesty's goodness.' When I repeated this to Dr. Johnson he did not contradict it.

His definitions of *pension* and *pensioner*, partly founded on the satirical verses of Pope, which he quotes, may be generally true; and yet everybody must allow that there may be, and have been, instances of pensions given and received upon liberal and honourable terms. Thus, then, it is clear, that there was nothing inconsistent or humiliating in Johnson's accepting of a pension so unconditionally and so honourably offered to him.

But I shall not detain my readers longer by any

words of my own, on a subject on which I am happily
enabled, by the favour of the Earl of Bute, to present
them with what Johnson himself wrote ; his Lordship
having been pleased to communicate to me a copy of
the following letter to his late father, which does
great honour both to the writer and to the noble
person to whom it is addressed :—

TO THE RIGHT HONOURABLE THE EARL OF BUTE

' MY LORD,—When the bills were yesterday delivered to me
by Mr. Wedderburne, I was informed by him of the future
favours which his Majesty has, by your Lordship's recommendation, been induced to intend for me.

'Bounty always receives part of its value from the manner
in which it is bestowed; your Lordship's kindness includes
every circumstance that can gratify delicacy or enforce
obligation. You have conferred your favours on a man who
has neither alliance nor interest, who has not merited them
by services, nor courted them by officiousness ; you have spared
him the shame of solicitation and the anxiety of suspense.

'What has been thus elegantly given will, I hope, not be
reproachfully enjoyed ; I shall endeavour to give your Lordship the only recompense which generosity desires, — the
gratification of finding that your benefits are not improperly
bestowed.—I am, my Lord, your Lordship's most obliged,
most obedient, and most humble servant, SAM. JOHNSON.

' *July 20, 1762.*'

This year his friend Sir Joshua Reynolds paid a
visit of some weeks to his native county, Devonshire,
in which he was accompanied by Johnson, who was
much pleased with this jaunt, and declared he had derived from it a great accession of new ideas. He was
entertained at the seats of several noblemen and gentlemen in the west of England ;[1] but the greatest

---

[1] At one of these seats Dr. Amyat, physician in London, told me he
happened to meet him. In order to amuse him till dinner should be

part of this time was passed at Plymouth, where the magnificence of the navy, the shipbuilding, and all its circumstances, afforded him a grand subject of contemplation. The Commissioner of the Dockyard paid him the compliment of ordering the yacht to convey him and his friend to the Eddystone, to which they accordingly sailed. But the weather was so tempestuous that they could not land.

Reynolds and he were at this time the guests of Dr. Mudge, the celebrated surgeon, and now physician of that place, not more distinguished for quickness of parts and variety of knowledge than loved and esteemed for his amiable manners; and here Johnson formed an acquaintance with Dr. Mudge's father, that very eminent divine, the Reverend Zachariah Mudge, Prebendary of Exeter, who was idolised in the west, both for his excellence as a preacher and the uniform perfect propriety of his private conduct. He preached a sermon purposely that Johnson might hear him; and we shall see afterwards that Johnson honoured his memory by drawing his character. While Johnson was at Plymouth he saw a great many of its inhabitants, and was not sparing of his very entertaining conversation. It was here that he made that frank and truly original confession, that 'ignorance, pure ignorance,' was the cause of a wrong definition in his *Dictionary* of the word *pastern*,[1] to the no small surprise of a lady who put the question to him; who having

---

ready, he was taken out to walk in the garden. The master of the house, thinking it proper to introduce something scientific into the conversation, addressed him thus: 'Are you a botanist, Dr. Johnson?' 'No, sir (answered Johnson), I am not a botanist; and (alluding, no doubt, to his near-sightedness) should I wish to become a botanist, I must first turn myself into a reptile.'

[1] See vol. i. p. 242.

the most profound reverence for his character, so as
almost to suppose him endowed with infallibility,
expected to hear an explanation (of what, to be sure,
seemed strange to a common reader) drawn from some
deep-learned source with which she was unacquainted.

Sir Joshua Reynolds, to whom I was obliged for
my information concerning this excursion, mentions
a very characteristical anecdote of Johnson while at
Plymouth. Having observed, that in consequence of
the Dockyard a new town had arisen about two miles
off as a rival to the old, and knowing from his
sagacity, and just observation of human nature, that
it is certain if a man hates at all he will hate his next
neighbour, he concluded that this new and rising
town could not but excite the envy and jealousy of
the old, in which conjecture he was very soon confirmed; he therefore set himself resolutely on the
side of the old town, the *established* town, in which his
lot was cast, considering it as a kind of duty to *stand
by* it. He accordingly entered warmly into its interests,
and upon every occasion talked of the *dockers*, as the
inhabitants of the new town were called, as upstarts
and aliens. Plymouth is very plentifully supplied
with water by a river brought into it from a great
distance, which is so abundant that it runs to waste
in the town. The Dock, or new town, being totally
destitute of water, petitioned Plymouth that a small
portion of the conduit might be permitted to go to
them, and this was now under consideration. Johnson,
affecting to entertain the passions of the place, was
violent in opposition ; and half laughing at himself
for his pretended zeal, where he had no concern, exclaimed, ' No, no ! I am against the *dockers* ; I am a

Plymouth man. Rogues! let them die of thirst. They shall not have a drop!'[1]

Lord Macartney obligingly favoured me with a copy of the following letter, in his own handwriting, from the original, which was found, by the present Earl of Bute, among his father's papers :—

TO THE RIGHT HONOURABLE THE EARL OF BUTE

'MY LORD,—That generosity, by which I was recommended to the favour of his Majesty, will not be offended at a solicitation necessary to make that favour permanent and effectual.

'The pension appointed to be paid me at Michaelmas I have not received, and know not where or from whom I am to ask it. I beg, therefore, that your Lordship will be pleased to supply Mr. Wedderburne with such directions as may be necessary, which, I believe, his friendship will make him think it no trouble to convey to me.

'To interrupt your Lordship, at a time like this, with such petty difficulties, is improper and unseasonable ; but your knowledge of the world has long since taught you, that every man's affairs, however little, are important to himself. Every man hopes that he shall escape neglect ; and, with reason, may every man, whose vices do not preclude his claim, expect favour from that beneficence which has been extended to, my Lord, your Lordship's most obliged and most humble servant,   SAM. JOHNSON.

'*Temple Lane, Nov.* 3, 1762.'

TO MR. JOSEPH BARETTI, AT MILAN

'*London, Dec.* 21, 1762.

'SIR,—You are not to suppose, with all your conviction of my idleness, that I have passed all this time without writing to my Baretti. I gave a letter to Mr. Beauclerk, who in my opinion, and in his own, was hastening to Naples for the recovery of his health ; but he has stopped at Paris, and I know not when he will proceed. Langton is with him.

---

[1] [A friend of mine once heard him, during this visit, exclaim with the utmost vehemence, 'I HATE a docker.'—J. BLAKEWAY.]

'I will not trouble you with speculations about peace and war. The good or ill success of battles and embassies extends itself to a very small part of domestic life: we all have good and evil, which we feel more sensibly than our petty part of public miscarriage or prosperity. I am sorry for your disappointment, with which you seem more touched than I should expect a man of your resolution and experience to have been, did I not know that general truths are seldom applied to particular occasions; and that the fallacy of our self-love extends itself as wide as our interest or affections. Every man believes that mistresses are unfaithful and patrons capricious: but he excepts his own mistress and his own patron. We have all learned that greatness is negligent and contemptuous, and that in courts life is often languished away in ungratified expectation; but he that approaches greatness, or glitters in a court, imagines that destiny has at last exempted him from the common lot.

'Do not let such evils overwhelm you as thousands have suffered, and thousands have surmounted; but turn your thoughts with vigour to some other plan of life, and keep always in your mind, that, with due submission to Providence, a man of genius has been seldom ruined but by himself. Your patron's weakness or insensibility will finally do you little hurt, if he is not assisted by your own passions. Of your love I know not the propriety, nor can estimate the power; but in love, as in every other passion of which hope is the essence, we ought always to remember the uncertainty of events. There is, indeed, nothing that so much seduces reason from vigilance as the thought of passing life with an amiable woman; and if all would happen that a lover fancies, I know not what other terrestrial happiness would deserve pursuit. But love and marriage are different states. Those who are to suffer the evils together,[1] and to suffer often for the sake of one another, soon lose that tenderness of look, and that benevolence of mind, which arose from the participation of unmingled pleasure and successive amuse-

---

1 [Johnson probably wrote 'the evils *of life* together.' The words in italics, however, are not found in Baretti's original edition of this letter, but they may have been omitted inadvertently, either in his transcript or at the press.—M.]

ment. A woman, we are sure, will not be always fair; we
are not sure she will always be virtuous; and man cannot
retain through life that respect and assiduity by which he
pleases for a day or for a month. I do not, however, pretend
to have discovered that life has anything more to be desired
than a prudent and virtuous marriage: therefore know not
what counsel to give you.

'If you can quit your imagination of love and greatness,
and leave your hopes of preferment and bridal raptures to try
once more the fortune of literature and industry, the way
through France is now open. We flatter ourselves that we
shall cultivate, with great diligence, the arts of peace; and
every man will be welcome among us who can teach us anything we do not know. For your part, you will find all your
old friends willing to receive you.

'Reynolds still continues to increase in reputation and in
riches. Miss Williams, who very much loves you, goes on in
the old way. Miss Cotterell is still with Mrs. Porter. Miss
Charlotte is married to Dean Lewis, and has three children.
Mr. Levet has married a street-walker. But the gazette of my
narration must now arrive to tell you that Bathurst went
physician to the army, and died at the Havannah.

'I know not whether I have not sent you word that Huggins
and Richardson are both dead. When we see our enemies
and friends gliding away before us, let us not forget that we
are subject to the general law of mortality, and shall soon be
where our doom will be fixed for ever. I pray God to bless
you, and am, sir, your most affectionate humble servant,

'SAM. JOHNSON.

'Write soon.'

In 1763 he furnished to *The Poetical Calendar*, published by Fawkes and Woty, a character of Collins,
which he afterwards ingrafted into his entire life of
that admirable poet, in the collection of lives which
he wrote for the body of English poetry, formed and
published by the booksellers of London. His account
of the melancholy depression with which Collins was

severely afflicted, and which brought him to his grave, is, I think, one of the most tender and interesting passages in the whole series of his writings.   He also favoured Mr. Hoole with the Dedication of his translation of Tasso to the Queen, which is so happily conceived and elegantly expressed, that I cannot but point it out to the peculiar notice of my readers.[1]

This is to me a memorable year ; for in it I had the happiness to obtain the acquaintance of that extraordinary man whose memoirs I am now writing ; an acquaintance which I shall ever esteem as one of the most fortunate circumstances in my life.   Though then but two-and-twenty, I had for several years read his works with delight and instruction, and had the highest reverence for their author, which had grown up in my fancy into a kind of mysterious veneration, by figuring to myself a state of solemn elevated abstraction, in which I supposed him to live in the immense metropolis of London.   Mr. Gentleman, a native of Ireland, who passed some years in Scotland

---

[1] 'MADAM,—To approach the high and illustrious has been in all ages the privilege of Poets ; and though translators cannot justly claim the same honour, yet they naturally follow their authors as attendants ; and I hope that in return for having enabled Tasso to diffuse his fame through the British dominions, I may be introduced by him to the presence of Your Majesty.

'Tasso has a peculiar claim to Your Majesty's favour, as follower and panegyrist of the House of Este, which has one common ancestor with the House of Hanover ; and in reviewing his life it is not easy to forbear a wish that he had lived in a happier time, when he might among the descendants of that illustrious family have found a more liberal and potent patronage.

'I cannot but observe, Madam, how unequally reward is proportioned to merit, when I reflect that the happiness which was withheld from Tasso is reserved for me ; and that the poem which once hardly procured to its author the countenance of the Princes of Ferrara, has attracted to its translator the favourable notice of a British Queen.

' Had this been the fate of Tasso, he would have been able to have celebrated the condescension of Your Majesty in nobler language, but could not have felt it with more ardent gratitude, than, Madam, Your Majesty's most faithful and devoted servant.'

as a player, and as an instructor in the English language, a man whose talents and worth were depressed by misfortunes, had given me a representation of the figure and manner of DICTIONARY JOHNSON! as he was then generally called;[1] and during my first visit to London, which was for three months in 1760, Mr. Derrick the poet, who was Gentleman's friend and countryman, flattered me with hopes that he would introduce me to Johnson, an honour of which I was very ambitious. But he never found an opportunity; which made me doubt that he had promised to do what was not in his power; till Johnson some years afterwards told me, ' Derrick, sir, might very well have introduced you. I had a kindness for Derrick, and am sorry he is dead.'

In the summer of 1761 Mr. Thomas Sheridan was at Edinburgh, and delivered lectures upon the English Language and Public Speaking to large and respectable audiences. I was often in his company, and heard him frequently expatiate on Johnson's extraordinary knowledge, talents, and virtues, repeat his pointed sayings, describe his particularities, and boast of his being his guest sometimes till two or three in the morning. At his house I hoped to have many opportunities of seeing the sage, as Mr. Sheridan obligingly assured me I should not be disappointed.

When I returned to London in the end of 1762, to my surprise and regret I found an irreconcilable

---

[1] As great men of antiquity, such as Scipio *Africanus*, had an epithet added to their names, in consequence of some celebrated action, so my illustrious friend was often called Dictionary Johnson, from that wonderful achievement of genius and labour, his *Dictionary of the English Language*; the merit of which I contemplate with more and more admiration.

difference had taken place between Johnson and Sheridan. A pension of two hundred pounds a year had been given to Sheridan. Johnson, who, as has been already mentioned, thought slightingly of Sheridan's art, upon hearing that he was also pensioned, exclaimed, ' What ! have they given *him* a pension ? Then it is time for me to give up mine.' Whether this proceeded from a momentary indignation, as if it were an affront to his exalted merit that a player should be rewarded in the same manner with him, or was the sudden effect of a fit of peevishness, it was unluckily said, and, indeed, cannot be justified. Mr. Sheridan's pension was granted to him not as a player, but as a sufferer in the cause of Government, when he was manager of the Theatre Royal in Ireland, when parties ran high in 1753. And it must also be allowed that he was a man of literature, and had considerably improved the arts of reading and speaking with distinctness and propriety.

Besides, Johnson should have recollected that Mr. Sheridan taught pronunciation to Mr. Alexander Wedderburne, whose sister was married to Sir Harry Erskine, an intimate friend of Lord Bute, who was the favourite of the King ; and surely the most outrageous Whig will not maintain that, whatever ought to be the principle in the disposal of *offices*, a *pension* ought never to be granted from any bias of court connection. Mr. Macklin, indeed, shared with Mr. Sheridan the honour of instructing Mr. Wedderburne ; and though it was too late in life for a Caledonian to acquire the genuine English cadence, yet so successful were Mr. Wedderburne's instructors, and his own unabating endeavours, that he got rid of the coarse part of the

Scotch accent, retaining only as much of the 'native wood-note wild' as to mark his country; which, if any Scotchman should affect to forget, I should heartily despise him. Nowithstanding the difficulties which are to be encountered by those who have not had the advantage of an English education, he by degrees formed a mode of speaking, to which Englishmen do not deny the praise of elegance. Hence his distinguished oratory, which he exerted in his own country as an advocate in the Court of Session, and a ruling elder of the *Kirk*, has had its fame and ample reward in much higher spheres. When I look back on this noble person at Edinburgh, in situations so unworthy of his brilliant powers, and behold Lord Loughborough at London, the change seems almost like one of the metamorphoses in Ovid; and as his two preceptors, by refining his utterance, gave currency to his talents, we may say in the words of that poet, ' *Nam vos mutastis.*'

I have dwelt the longer upon this remarkable instance of successful parts and assiduity; because it affords animating encouragement to other gentlemen of North Britain to try their fortunes in the southern part of the island, where they may hope to gratify their utmost ambition; and now that we are one people by the Union, it would surely be illiberal to maintain that they have not an equal title with the natives of any other part of his Majesty's dominions.

Johnson complained that a man who disliked him repeated his sarcasm to Mr. Sheridan, without telling him what followed, which was, that after a pause he added, ' However, I am glad that Mr. Sheridan has a pension, for he is a very good man.' Sheridan coulp

never forgive this hasty contemptuous expression. It
rankled in his mind ; and though I informed him of
all that Johnson said, and that he would be very glad
to meet him amicably, he positively declined repeated
offers which I made, and once went off abruptly from
a house where he and I were engaged to dine, because
he was told that Dr. Johnson was to be there. I
have no sympathetic feeling with such persevering
resentment. It is painful when there is a breach
between those who have lived together socially and
cordially ; and I wonder there is not, in all such cases,
a mutual wish that it should be healed. I could perceive that Mr. Sheridan was by no means satisfied
with Johnson's acknowledging him to be a good man.
That could not soothe his injured vanity. I could
not but smile, at the same time that I was offended,
to observe Sheridan in the *Life of Swift*, which he
afterwards published, attempting, in the writhings of
his resentment, to depreciate Johnson, by character-
ising him as ' a writer of gigantic fame in these days
of little men ' ; that very Johnson whom he once so
highly admired and venerated.

This rupture with Sheridan deprived Johnson of
one of his most agreeable resources for amusement in
his lonely evenings ; for Sheridan's well-informed,
animated, and bustling mind never suffered conversation to stagnate ; and Mrs. Sheridan was a most
agreeable companion to an intellectual man. She was
sensible, ingenious, unassuming, yet communicative.
I recollect, with satisfaction, many pleasing hours
which I passed with her under the hospitable roof of
her husband, who was to me a very kind friend. Her
novel, entitled *Memoirs of Miss Sydney Biddulph*, con-

tains an excellent moral while it inculcates a future
state of retribution ;[1] and what it teaches is impressed
upon the mind by a series of as deep distress as can
affect humanity, in the amiable and pious heroine who
goes to her grave unrelieved, but resigned, and full
of hope of ' Heaven's mercy.' Johnson paid her this
high compliment upon it: ' I know not, madam, that
you have a right upon moral principles to make your
readers suffer so much.'

Mr. Thomas Davies the actor, who then kept a
bookseller's shop in Russel Street, Covent Garden,[2]

---

[1] My position has been very well illustrated by Mr. Belsham of
Bedford, in his Essay on Dramatic Poetry. ' The fashionable doctrine
(says he) both of moralists and critics in these times is, that virtue and
happiness are constant concomitants; and it is regarded as a kind of
dramatic impiety to maintain that virtue should not be rewarded, nor
vice punished, in the last scene of the last act of every tragedy. This
conduct in our modern poets is, however, in my opinion, extremely
injudicious; for it labours in vain to inculcate a doctrine in theory,
which every one knows to be false in fact, viz., that virtue in real life
is always productive of happiness, and vice of misery. Thus Congreve
concludes the Tragedy of *The Mourning Bride* with the following
foolish couplet :—

" For blessings ever wait on virtuous deeds,
And, though a late, a sure reward succeeds."

'When a man eminently virtuous, a Brutus, a Cato, or a Socrates,
finally sinks under the pressure of accumulated misfortune, we are not
only led to entertain a more indignant hatred of vice than if he rose
from his distress, but we are inevitably induced to cherish the sublime
idea that a day of future retribution will arrive when he shall receive
not merely poetical, but real and substantial justice.'—*Essays Philosophical, Historical, and Literary*, London, 1791, vol. ii. 8vo, p. 317.
This is well reasoned and well expressed. I wish, indeed, that the
ingenious author had not thought it necessary to introduce any *instance*
of ' a man eminently virtuous '; as he would then have avoided mentioning such a ruffian as Brutus under that description. Mr. Belsham
discovers in his *Essays* so much reading and thinking and good composition, that I regret his not having been fortunate enough to be
educated a member of our excellent national establishment. Had he
not been nursed in nonconformity, he probably would not have been
tainted with those heresies (as I sincerely, and on no slight investiga-
tion, think them) both in religion and politics, which, while I read, I
am sure, with candour, I cannot read without offence.

[2] No. 8. The very place where I was fortunate enough to be introduced to the illustrious subject of this work deserves to be particularly
marked. I never pass by it without feeling reverence and regret.

told me that Johnson was very much his friend, and
came frequently to his house, where he more than
once invited me to meet him; but by some unlucky
accident or other he was prevented from coming to us.

Mr. Thomas Davies was a man of good understanding
and talents, with the advantage of a liberal education.
Though somewhat pompous, he was an entertaining
companion; and his literary performances have no
inconsiderable share of merit. He was a friendly and
very hospitable man. Both he and his wife (who has
been celebrated for her beauty), though upon the
stage for many years, maintained a uniform decency
of character: and Johnson esteemed them, and lived
in as easy an intimacy with them as with any family
he used to visit. Mr. Davies recollected several of
Johnson's remarkable sayings, and was one of the
best of the many imitators of his voice and manner
while relating them. He increased my impatience
more and more to see the extraordinary man whose
works I highly valued, and whose conversation was
reported to be so peculiarly excellent.

At last, on Monday the 16th of May, when I was
sitting in Mr. Davies's back parlour, after having
drunk tea with him and Mrs. Davies, Johnson unexpectedly came into the shop;[1] and Mr. Davies

---

[1] Mr. Murphy, in his *Essay on the Life and Genius of Dr. Johnson*,
has given an account of this meeting considerably different from mine,
I am persuaded without any consciousness of error. His memory, at
the end of near thirty years, has undoubtedly deceived him, and he
supposes himself to have been present at a scene, which he has probably heard inaccurately described by others. In my note, *taken on the
very day*, in which I am confident I marked everything material that
passed, no mention is made of this gentleman; and I am sure that I
should not have omitted one so well known in the literary world. It
may easily be imagined that this my first interview with Dr. Johnson,
with all its circumstances, made a strong impression on my mind, and
would be registered with peculiar attention.

having perceived him through the glass door in the
room in which we were sitting, advancing towards us,
—he announced his awful approach to me, somewhat
in the manner of an actor in the part of Horatio,
when he addresses Hamlet on the appearance of his
father's ghost, ' Look, my Lord, it comes.' I found
that I had a very perfect idea of Johnson's figure,
from the portrait of him painted by Sir Joshua
Reynolds soon after he had published his *Dictionary*,
in the attitude of sitting in his easy-chair in deep
meditation; which was the first picture his friend did
for him, which Sir Joshua very kindly presented to
me, and from which an engraving has been made for
this work.   Mr. Davies mentioned my name, and
respectfully introduced me to him.   I was much
agitated; and recollecting his prejudice against the
Scotch, of which I had heard much, I said to Davies,
' Don't tell where I come from.'   ' From Scotland,'
cried Davies roguishly.   ' Mr. Johnson (said I), I do
indeed come from Scotland, but I cannot help it.'
I am willing to flatter myself that I meant this as
light pleasantry to soothe and conciliate him, and not
as a humiliating abasement at the expense of my
country.   But however that might be, this speech
was somewhat unlucky; for with that quickness of
wit for which he was so remarkable, he seized the
expression ' come from Scotland,' which I used in
the sense of being of that country; and, as if I had
said that I had come away from it, or left it, retorted,
' That, sir, I find, is what a very great many of your
countrymen cannot help.'   This stroke stunned me a
good deal; and when we had sat down I felt myself
not a little embarrassed and apprehensive of what

might come next. He then addressed himself to
Davies : ' What do you think of Garrick? He has
refused me an order for the play for Miss Williams,
because he knows the house will be full, and that an
order would be worth three shillings.' Eager to take
any opening to get into conversation with him, I
ventured to say, ' O, sir, I cannot think Mr. Garrick
would grudge such a trifle to you.' ' Sir (said he,
with a stern look) I have known David Garrick longer
than you have done : and I know no right you have
to talk to me on the subject.' Perhaps I deserved
this check ; for it was rather presumptuous in me, an
entire stranger, to express any doubt of the justness
of the animadversion upon his old acquaintance and
pupil.[1] I now felt myself much mortified, and began
to think that the hope which I had long indulged of
obtaining his acquaintance was blasted. And, in
truth, had not my ardour been uncommonly strong,
and my resolution uncommonly persevering, so rough
a reception might have deterred me for ever from
making any further attempts. Fortunately, however,
I remained upon the field not wholly discomfited ;
and was soon rewarded by hearing some of his conversation, of which I preserved the following short
minute, without marking the questions and observations by which it was produced.

' People (he remarked) may be taken in once, who

---

[1] That this was a momentary sally against Garrick there can be no
doubt ; for at Johnson's desire he had, some years before, given a
benefit night at his theatre to this very person, by which she had got
two hundred pounds. Johnson, indeed, upon all other occasions, when
I was in his company, praised the very liberal charity of Garrick.
I once mentioned to him, ' It is observed, sir, that you attack Garrick
yourself, but will suffer nobody else to do it.' JOHNSON (smiling),
' Why, sir, that is very true.'

imagine that an author is greater in private file than other men.   Uncommon parts require uncommon opportunities for their exertion.

'In barbarous society, superiority of parts is of real consequence.   Great strength or great wisdom is of much value to an individual.   But in more polished times there are people to do everything for money; and then there are a number of other superiorities, such as those of birth and fortune and rank, that dissipate men's attention, and leave no extraordinary share of respect for personal and intellectual superiority.   This is wisely ordered by Providence, to preserve some equality among mankind.'

'Sir, this book (*The Elements of Criticism*, which he had taken up) is a pretty essay, and deserves to be held in some estimation, though much of it is chimerical.'

Speaking of one who with more than ordinary boldness attacked public measures and the royal family, he said, 'I think he is safe from the law, but he is an abusive scoundrel; and instead of applying to my Lord Chief-Justice to punish him I would send half a dozen footmen and have him well ducked.'

'The notion of liberty amuses the people of England, and helps to keep off the *tædium vitæ*.   When a butcher tells you that *his heart bleeds for his country*, he has, in fact, no uneasy feeling.'

'Sheridan will not succeed at Bath with his oratory. Ridicule has gone down before him, and, I doubt, Derrick is his enemy.[1]

'Derrick may do very well, as long as he can out-

---

[1] Mr. Sheridan was then reading lectures upon Oratory at Bath, where Derrick was Master of the Ceremonies; or, as the phrase is, King.

run his character ; but the moment his character gets
up with him, it is all over.'

It is, however, but just to record, that some years
afterwards, when I reminded him of this sarcasm, he
said, ' Well, but Derrick has now got a character that
he need not run away from.'

I was highly pleased with the extraordinary vigour
of his conversation, and regretted that I was drawn
away from it by an engagement at another place.   I
had, for a part of the evening, been left alone with him,
and had ventured to make an observation now and
then, which he received very civilly ; so that I was
satisfied that though there was a roughness in his
manner there was no ill-nature in his disposition.
Davies followed me to the door, and when I complained to him a little of the hard blows which the
great man had given me, he kindly took upon him to
console me by saying, ' Don't be uneasy.   I can see
he likes you very well.'

A few days afterwards I called on Davies, and asked
him if he thought I might take the liberty of waiting
on Mr. Johnson at his chambers in the Temple.   He
said I certainly might, and that Mr. Johnson would
take it as a compliment.   So upon Tuesday the 24th
of May, after having been enlivened by the witty
sallies of Messieurs Thornton, Wilkes, Churchill, and
Lloyd, with whom I had passed the morning, I boldly
repaired to Johnson.   His chambers were on the first
floor of No. 1 Inner Temple Lane, and I entered them
with an impression given me by the Rev. Dr. Blair
of Edinburgh, who had been introduced to him not
long before, and described his having ' found the
Giant in his den '; an expression which, when I came

to be pretty well acquainted with Johnson, I repeated
to him, and he was diverted at this picturesque account
of himself. Dr. Blair had been presented to him by
Dr. James Fordyce. At this time the controversy
concerning the pieces published by Mr. James Mac-
pherson as translations of Ossian was at its height.
Johnson had all along denied their authenticity ; and,
what was still more provoking to their admirers,
maintained that they had no merit. The subject
having been introduced by Dr. Fordyce, Dr. Blair,
relying on the internal evidence of their antiquity,
asked Dr. Johnson whether he thought any man of a
modern age could have written such poems ? Johnson
replied, ' Yes, sir, many men, many women, and
many children.' Johnson, at this time, did not know
that Dr. Blair had just published a Dissertation, not
only defending their authenticity, but seriously
ranking them with the poems of Homer and Virgil ;
and when he was afterwards informed of this circumstance, he expressed some displeasure at Dr. Fordyce's
having suggested the topic, and said, ' I am not sorry
that they got thus much for their pains. Sir, it was
like leading one to talk of a book when the author is
concealed behind the door.'

He received me very courteously ; but it must be
confessed that his apartment, and furniture, and
morning dress were sufficiently uncouth. His brown
suit of clothes looked very rusty ; he had on a little
old shrivelled unpowdered wig, which was too small
for his head ; his shirt-neck and knees of his breeches
were loose ; his black worsted stockings ill drawn up ;
and he had a pair of unbuckled shoes by way of
slippers. But all these slovenly particularities were

forgotten the moment that he began to talk. Some
gentlemen, whom I do not recollect, were sitting with
him; and when they went away I also rose; but he
said to me, 'Nay, don't go.' 'Sir (said I), I am
afraid that I intrude upon you. It is benevolent to
allow me to sit and hear you.' He seemed pleased
with this compliment, which I sincerely paid him, and
answered, 'Sir, I am obliged to any man who visits
me.' I have preserved the following short minute of
what passed this day.

'Madness frequently discovers itself merely by unnecessary deviation from the usual modes of the world.
My poor friend Smart showed the disturbance of his
mind by falling upon his knees and saying his prayers
in the street, or in any other unusual place. Now
although, rationally speaking, it is greater madness
not to pray at all than to pray as Smart did, I am
afraid there are so many who do not pray that their
understanding is not called in question.'

Concerning this unfortunate poet, Christopher
Smart, who was confined in a madhouse, he had, at
another time, the following conversation with Dr.
Burney. BURNEY : 'How does poor Smart do, sir?
is he likely to recover?' JOHNSON : It seems as if his
mind had ceased to struggle with the disease ; for he
grows fat upon it.' BURNEY: 'Perhaps, sir, that
may be from want of exercise.' JOHNSON : 'No, sir ;
he has partly as much exercise as he used to have, for
he digs in the garden. Indeed, before his confinement,
he used for exercise to walk to the ale-house ; but he
was *carried* back again. I did not think he ought
to be shut up. His infirmities were not noxious to
society. He insisted on people praying with him;

and I'd as lief pray with Kit Smart as any one else. Another charge was, that he did not love clean linen ; and I have no passion for it.'

Johnson continued. 'Mankind had a great aversion to intellectual labour ; but even supposing knowledge to be easily attainable, more people would be content to be ignorant than would take even a little trouble to acquire it.

'The morality of an action depends on the motive from which we act. If I fling half a crown to a beggar with intention to break his head, and he picks it up and buys victuals with it, the physical effect is good ; but with respect to me the action is very wrong. So, religious exercises, if not performed with an intention to please God, avail us nothing. As our Saviour says of those who perform them from other motives, "Verily they have their reward."

'The Christian religion has very strong evidences. It, indeed, appears in some degree strange to reason ; but in history we have undoubted facts, against which, in reasoning *à priori*, we have more arguments than we have for them ; but then, testimony has great weight, and casts the balance. I would recommend to every man whose faith is yet unsettled, Grotius, Dr. Pearson, and Dr. Clarke.'

Talking of Garrick, he said, 'He is the first man in the world for sprightly conversation.'

When I rose a second time he again pressed me to stay, which I did.

He told me that he generally went abroad at four in the afternoon, and seldom came home till two in the morning. I took the liberty to ask if he did not think it wrong to live thus, and not make more use of his great talents. He owned it was a bad habit. On reviewing, at the distance of many years, my journal of this period, I wonder how, at my first visit, I ventured to talk to him so freely, and that he bore it with so much indulgence.

Before we parted he was so good as to promise to favour me with his company one evening at my lodgings; and as I took my leave, shook me cordially by the hand. It is almost needless to add, that I felt no little elation at having now so happily established an acquaintance of which I had been so long ambitious.

My readers will, I trust, excuse me for being thus minutely circumstantial, when it is considered that the acquaintance of Dr. Johnson was to me a most valuable acquisition, and laid the foundation of whatever instruction and entertainment they may receive from my collections concerning the great subject of the work which they are now perusing.

I did not visit him again till Monday, June 13, at which time I recollect no part of his conversation, except that when I told him I had been to see Johnson ride upon three horses, he said, ' Such a man, sir, should be encouraged; for his performances show the extent of the human powers in one instance, and thus tend to raise our opinion of the faculties of man. He shows what may be attained by persevering application; so that every man may hope that by giving as much application, although perhaps he may never ride three horses at a time, or dance upon a wire, yet he may be equally expert in whatever profession he has chosen to pursue.'

He again shook me by the hand at parting, and asked me why I did not come oftener to him. Trusting that I was now in his good graces, I answered, that he had not given me much encouragement, and reminded him of the check I had received from him at our first interview. 'Poh, poh! (said he, with a complacent smile), never mind these things. Come to me as often as you can. I shall be glad to see you.'

I had learnt that his place of frequent resort was the Mitre tavern in Fleet Street, where he loved to sit up late, and I begged I might be allowed to pass an evening with him there soon, which he promised I should. A few days afterwards I met him near Temple Bar about one o'clock in the morning, and asked if he would then go to the Mitre. 'Sir (said he), it is too late; they won't let us in. But I'll go with you another night with all my heart.'

A revolution of some importance in my plan of life had just taken place; for instead of procuring a commission in the foot-guards, which was my own inclination, I had, in compliance with my father's wishes, agreed to study the law, and was soon to set out for Utrecht, to hear the lectures of an excellent Civilian in that University, and then to proceed on my travels. Though very desirous of obtaining Dr. Johnson's advice and instruction on the mode of pursuing my studies, I was at this time so occupied, shall I call it? or so dissipated, by the amusements of London, that our next meeting was not till Saturday, June 25, when, happening to dine at Clifton's eating-house in Butcher Row, I was surprised to perceive Johnson come in and take his seat at another table. The mode of dining, or rather being fed, at such houses in London is well known to many to be particularly unsocial, as there

is no Ordinary, or united company, but each person
has his own mess, and is under no obligation to hold
any intercourse with any one. A liberal and full-
minded man, however, who loves to talk will break
through this churlish and unsocial restraint. Johnson and an Irish gentleman got into a dispute concerning the cause of some part of mankind being
black. 'Why, sir (said Johnson), it has been accounted for in three ways: either by supposing that
they are the posterity of Ham, who was cursed ; or
that God at first created two kinds of men, one black
and another white; or that by the heat of the sun the
skin is scorched, and so acquires a sooty hue. This
matter has been much canvassed among naturalists,
but has never been brought to any certain issue.'
What the Irishman said is totally obliterated from my
mind ; but I remember that he became very warm
and intemperate in his expressions, upon which
Johnson rose and quietly walked away. When he
had retired, his antagonist took his revenge, as he
thought, by saying, 'He has a most ungainly figure,
and an affectation of pomposity unworthy of a man
of genius.'

Johnson had not observed that I was in the room.
I followed him, however, and he agreed to meet me
in the evening at the Mitre. I called on him, and we
went thither at nine. We had a good supper, and
port wine, of which he then sometimes drank a bottle.
The orthodox high-church sound of the Mitre,—the
figure and manner of the celebrated Samuel Johnson,
—the extraordinary power and precision of his conversation, and the pride·arising from finding myself
admitted as his companion, produced a variety of

sensations, and a pleasing elevation of mind beyond what I had ever before experienced. I find in my Journal the following minute of our conversation, which, though it will give but a very faint notion of what passed, is, in some degree, a valuable record; and it will be curious in this view as showing how habitual to his mind were some opinions which appear in his works.

'Colley Cibber, sir, was by no means a blockhead; but by arrogating to himself too much, he was in danger of losing that degree of estimation to which he was entitled. His friends give out that he *intended* his birthday Odes should be bad : but that was not the case, sir ; for he kept them many months by him, and a few years before he died he showed me one of them, with great solicitude to render it as perfect as might be, and I made some corrections, to which he was not very willing to submit. I remember the following couplet in allusion to the King and himself :

> "Perch'd on the eagle's soaring wing,
> The lowly linnet loves to sing."

Sir, he had heard something of the fabulous tale of the wren sitting upon the eagle's wing, and he had applied it to a linnet. Cibber's familiar style, however, was better than that which Whitehead has assumed. *Grand* nonsense is insupportable. Whitehead is but a little man to inscribe verses to players.'

I did not presume to controvert this censure, which was tinctured with his prejudice against players, but I could not help thinking that a dramatic poet might with propriety pay a compliment to an eminent per-

former, as Whitehead has very happily done in his
verses to Mr. Garrick.

'Sir, I do not think Gray a first-rate poet. He has
not a bold imagination, nor much command of words.
The obscurity in which he has involved himself will
not persuade us that he is sublime. His "Elegy in a
Churchyard" has a happy selection of images, but I
don't like what are called his great things. His Ode
which begins

> "Ruin seize thee, ruthless King,
> Confusion on thy banners wait!"

has been celebrated for its abruptness, and plunging
into the subject all at once. But such arts as these
have no merit, unless when they are original. We
admire them only once; and this abruptness has
nothing new in it. We have had it often before.
Nay, we have it in the old song of Johnny Armstrong:

> "Is there ever a man in all Scotland,
> From the highest estate to the lowest degree," etc.

And then, sir,

> "Yes, there is a man in Westmoreland,
> And Johnny Armstrong they do him call."

There, now, you plunge at once into the subject.
You have no previous narration to lead you to it.—
The two next lines in that Ode are, I think, very
good:

> "Though fann'd by conquest's crimson wing,
> They mock the air with idle state."'[1]

---

[1] My friend Mr. Malone, in his valuable comments on Shakespeare,
has traced in that great poet the *disjecta membra* of these lines.

Here let it be observed, that although his opinion
of Gray's poetry was widely different from mine, and
I believe from that of most men of taste, by whom it
is with justice highly admired, there is certainly much
absurdity in the clamour which has been raised, as if
he had been culpably injurious to the merit of that
bard, and had been actuated by envy.   Alas ! ye little
short-sighted critics, could Johnson be envious of the
talents of any of his contemporaries?   That his
opinion on this subject was what in private and in
public he uniformly expressed, regardless of what
others might think, we may wonder, and perhaps
regret ; but it is shallow and unjust to charge him
with expressing what he did not think.

Finding him in a placid humour, and wishing to
avail myself of the opportunity which I fortunately
had of consulting a sage, to hear whose wisdom, I
conceived in the ardour of youthful imagination, that
men filled with a noble enthusiasm for intellectual
improvement would gladly have resorted from distant
lands, I opened my mind to him ingenuously, and
gave him a little sketch of my life, to which he was
pleased to listen with great attention.

I acknowledged, that though educated very strictly
in the principles of religion, I had for some time been
misled into a certain degree of infidelity ; but that I
was come now to a better way of thinking, and was
fully satisfied of the truth of the Christian revelation,
though I was not clear as to every point considered
to be orthodox.   Being at all times a curious examiner
of the human mind, and pleased with an undisguised
display of what had passed in it, he called to me with
warmth, ' Give me your hand ; I have taken a liking

to you.' He then began to descant upon the force
of testimony, and the little we could know of final
causes; so that the objections of, Why was it so?
or, Why was it not so? ought not to disturb us:
adding, that he himself had at one period been guilty
of a temporary neglect of religion, but that it was
not the result of argument, but mere absence of
thought.

After having given credit to reports of his bigotry,
I was agreeably surprised when he expressed the following very liberal sentiment, which has the additional value of obviating an objection to our holy
religion, founded upon the discordant tenets of Christians themselves: 'For my part, sir, I think all
Christians, whether Papists or Protestants, agree in
the essential articles, and that their differences are
trivial, and rather political than religious.'

We talked of belief in ghosts. He said, 'Sir, I
make a distinction between what a man may experience by the mere strength of his imagination, and
what imagination cannot possibly produce. Thus,
suppose I should think that I saw a form, and heard
a voice cry, "Johnson, you are a very wicked fellow,
and unless you repent you will certainly be punished";
my own unworthiness is so deeply impressed upon my
mind that I might *imagine* I thus saw and heard, and
therefore I should not believe that an external communication had been made to me. But if a form
should appear, and a voice should tell me that a particular man had died at a particular place, and a particular hour, a fact which I had no apprehension of,
nor any means of knowing, and this fact, with all its
circumstances, should afterwards be unquestionably

proved, I should, in that case, be persuaded that I had supernatural intelligence imparted to me.'

Here it is proper, once for all, to give a true and fair statement of Johnson's way of thinking upon the question, whether departed spirits are ever permitted to appear in this world, or in any way to operate upon human life.   He has been ignorantly misrepresented as weakly credulous upon that subject; and therefore, though I feel an inclination to disdain and treat with silent contempt so foolish a notion concerning my illustrious friend, yet, as I find it has gained ground, it is necessary to refute it.   The real fact then is, that Johnson had a very philosophical mind, and such a rational respect for testimony as to make him submit his understanding to what was authentically proved, though he could not comprehend why it was so.   Being thus disposed, he was willing to inquire into the truth of any relation of supernatural agency, a general belief of which has prevailed in all nations and ages.   But so far was he from being the dupe of implicit faith, that he examined the matter with a jealous attention, and no man was more ready to refute its falsehood when he had discovered it. Churchill, in his poem entitled 'The Ghost,' availed himself of the absurd credulity imputed to Johnson, and drew a caricature of him under the name of 'Pomposo,' representing him as one of the believers of the story of a Ghost in Cock Lane, which, in the year 1762, had gained very general credit in London. Many of my readers, I am convinced, are to this hour under an impression that Johnson was thus foolishly deceived.   It will therefore surprise them a good dela when they are informed, upon undoubted authority, that Johnson was one of those by whom the imposture was detected. The story had become so popular, that he thought it should be investigated; and in this research he was assisted by the Reverend Dr. Douglas, now Bishop of Salisbury, the great detecter of impostures, who informs me that after the gentlemen who went and examined into the evidence were satisfied of its falsity, Johnson wrote in their presence an account of it, which was published in the newspapers and *Gentleman's Magazine,* and undeceived the world.[1]

---

[1] The account was as follows: 'On the night of the 1st of February, many gentlemen, eminent for their rank and character, were, by the invitation of the Reverend Mr. Aldrich, of Clerkenwell, assembled at his house, for the examination of the noises supposed to be made by a departed spirit, for the detection of some enormous crime.

'About ten at night the gentlemen met in the chamber in which the girl supposed to be disturbed by a spirit, had, with proper caution, been put to bed by several ladies. They sat rather more than an hour, and, hearing nothing, went downstairs, when they interrogated the father of the girl, who denied, in the strongest terms, any knowledge or belief of fraud.

'The supposed spirit had before publicly promised, by an affirmative knock, that it would attend one of the gentlemen into the vault under the church of St. John, Clerkenwell, where the body is deposited, and give a token of her presence there by a knock upon her coffin; it was therefore determined to make this trial of the existence or veracity of the supposed spirit.

'While they were inquiring and deliberating, they were summoned into the girl's chamber by some ladies who were near her bed, and who had heard knocks and scratches. When the gentlemen entered, the girl declared that she felt the spirit like a mouse upon her back, and was required to hold her hands out of bed. From that time, though the spirit was very solemnly required to manifest its existence by appearance, by impression on the hand or body of any present, by scratches, knocks, or any other agency, no evidence of any preternatural power was exhibited.

'The spirit was then very seriously advertised that the person to whom the promise was made of striking the coffin was then about to visit the vault, and that the performance of the promise was then claimed. The company at one o'clock went into the church, and the gentleman to whom the promise was made went with another into the vault. The spirit was solemnly required to perform its promise, but nothing more than silence ensued: the person supposed to be accused by the spirit then went down with several others, but no effect was perceived. Upon their return they examined the girl, but could draw

Our conversation proceeded. 'Sir (said he), I am a friend to subordination, as most conducive to the happiness of society. There is a reciprocal pleasure in governing and being governed.'

'Dr. Goldsmith is one of the first men we now have as an author, and he is a very worthy man too. He has been loose in his principles, but he is coming right.'

I mentioned Mallet's tragedy of *Elvira*, which had been acted the preceding winter at Drury Lane, and that the Honourable Andrew Erskine, Mr. Dempster, and myself, had joined in writing a pamphlet, entitled 'Critical Strictures,' against it;[1] that the mildness of Dempster's disposition had, however, relented, and he candidly said, 'We have hardly a right to abuse this tragedy; for, bad as it is, how vain should either of us be to write one not near so good.' JOHNSON: 'Why, no, sir; this is not just reasoning. You *may* abuse a tragedy, though you cannot write one. You may scold a carpenter who has made you a bad table, though you cannot make a table. It is not your trade to make tables.'

When I talked to him of the paternal estate to which I was heir, he said, 'Sir, let me tell you, that to be a Scotch landlord, where you have a number of families dependent upon you, and attached to you, is, perhaps, as high a situation as humanity can arrive at.

no confession from her. Between two and three she desired and was permitted to go home with her father.
'It is, therefore, the opinion of the whole assembly, that the child has some art of making or counterfeiting a particular noise, and that there is no agency of any higher cause.'
[1] The *Critical Review*, in which Mallet himself sometimes wrote, characterised this pamphlet as 'the crude efforts of envy, petulance, and self-conceit.' There being thus three epithets, we the three authors had a humorous contention how each should be appropriated.

A merchant upon the 'Change of London, with
£100,000, is nothing; an English Duke, with an
immense fortune, is nothing; he has no tenants who
consider themselves as under his patriarchal care, and
who will follow him to the field upon an emergency.'

His notion of the dignity of a Scotch landlord had
been formed upon what he had heard of the Highland
Chiefs; for it is long since a Lowland landlord has
been so curtailed in his feudal authority that he has
little more influence over his tenants than an English
landlord; and of late years most of the Highland
Chiefs have destroyed, by means too well known, the
princely power which they once enjoyed.

He proceeded: 'You are going abroad, sir, and
breaking off idle habits may be of great importance to
you. I would go where there are courts and learned
men. There is a good deal of Spain that has not been
perambulated. I would have you go thither. A man
of inferior talents to yours may furnish us with useful
observations upon that country.' His supposing me,
at that period of life, capable of writing an account of
my travels that would deserve to be read, elated me
not a little.

I appeal to every impartial reader whether this
faithful detail of his frankness, complacency, and
kindness to a young man, a stranger and a Scotchman,
does not refute the unjust opinion of the harshness of
his general demeanour. His occasional reproofs of
folly, impudence, or impiety, and even the sudden
sallies of his constitutional irritability of temper,
which have been preserved for the poignancy of their
wit, have produced that opinion among those who have
not considered that such instances, though collected

by Mrs. Piozzi into a small volume, and read over in a few hours, were, in fact, scattered through a long series of years; years in which his time was chiefly spent in instructing and delighting mankind by his writings and conversation, in acts of piety to God and good-will to men.

I complained to him that I had not yet acquired much knowledge, and asked his advice as to my studies. He said, 'Don't talk of study now. I will give you a plan; but it will require some time to consider of it.' 'It is very good in you (I replied) to allow me to be with you thus. Had it been foretold to me some years ago that I should pass an evening with the author of the *Rambler*, how should I have exulted!' What I then expressed was sincerely from the heart. He was satisfied that it was, and cordially answered, 'Sir, I am glad we have met. I hope we shall pass many evenings, and mornings too, together.' We finished a couple of bottles of port, and sat till between one and two in the morning.

He wrote this year in the *Critical Review* the account of 'Telemachus, a Mask,' by the Reverend George Graham, of Eton College. The subject of this beautiful poem was particularly interesting to Johnson, who had much experience of 'the conflict of opposite principles,' which he describes as 'the contention between pleasure and virtue, a struggle which will always be continued while the present system of nature shall subsist; nor can history or poetry exhibit more than pleasure triumphing over virtue, and virtue subjugating pleasure.'

As Dr. Oliver Goldsmith will frequently appear in this narrative, I shall endeavour to make my readers in some degree acquainted with his singular character. He was a native of Ireland, and a contemporary with Mr. Burke at Trinity College, Dublin, but did not then give much promise of future celebrity.[1] He, however, observed to Mr. Malone, that 'though he made no great figure in mathematics, which was a study in much repute there, he could turn an Ode of Horace into English better than any of them.' He afterwards studied physic at Edinburgh, and upon the Continent, and, I have been informed, was enabled to pursue his travels on foot, partly by demanding at Universities to enter the lists as a disputant, by which, according to the custom of many of them, he was entitled to the premium of a crown, when luckily for him his challenge was not accepted; so that, as I once observed to Dr. Johnson, he *disputed* his passage through Europe. He then came to England, and was employed successively in the capacities of an usher to an academy, a corrector of the press, a reviewer, and a writer for a newspaper. He had sagacity enough to cultivate assiduously the acquaintance of Johnson, and his faculties were gradually enlarged by the contemplation of such a model. To me and many others it appeared that he studiously copied the manner of Johnson, though, indeed, upon a smaller scale.

At this time I think he had published nothing with

---

[1] [Goldsmith got a premium at a Christmas examination in Trinity College, Dublin, which I have seen.—K.]

[A premium obtained at the Christmas examination is generally more honourable than any other, because it ascertains the person who receives it to be the first in literary merit. At the other examinations, the person thus distinguished may be only the second in merit; he who has previously obtained the same honorary reward sometimes receiving a written certificate that *he* was the best answerer, it being a rule that no more than one premium should be adjudged to the same person in one year. See vol. i. p. 261.—M.]

his name, though it was pretty generally known that
one Dr. Goldsmith was the author of *An Inquiry into
the Present State of Polite Learning in Europe,* and of
The Citizen of the World—a series of letters supposed
to be written from London by a Chinese.[1] No man
had the art of displaying with more advantage as a
writer whatever literary acquisitions he made.   *'Nihil
quod tetigit non ornavit.'*[2]   His mind resembled a
fertile, but thin soil.   There was a quick, but not a
strong vegetation, of whatever chanced to be thrown
upon it. No deep root could be struck.   The oak of
the forest did not grow there ; but the elegant shrub-
bery and the fragrant parterre appeared in gay succession.   It has been generally circulated and believed
that he was a mere fool in conversation ;[3] but in truth
this has been greatly exaggerated. He had, no doubt,
a more than common share of that hurry of ideas
which we often find in his countrymen, and which
sometimes produces a laughable confusion in expressing them.   He was very much what the French call
un étourdi, and from vanity and an eager desire of

---

[1] [He had also published, in 1759, '*The Bee,* being Essays on the
most interesting subjects.'—M.]

[2] See his Epitaph in Westminster Abbey, written by Dr. Johnson.

[3] In allusion to this, Mr. Horace Walpole, who admired his writings,
said he was 'an inspired idiot '; and Garrick described him as one,

> ' for shortness call'd Noll,
> Who wrote like an angel, and talk'd like poor Poll.'

Sir Joshua Reynolds mentioned to me that he frequently heard Goldsmith talk warmly of the pleasure of being liked, and observe how hard
it would be if literary excellence should preclude a man from that
satisfaction, which he perceived it often did, from the envy which
attended it ; and therefore Sir Joshua was convinced that he was
intentionally more absurd, in order to lessen himself in social intercourse, trusting that his character would be sufficiently supported by
his work. If it indeed was his intention to appear absurd in company,
he was often very successful. But with due deference to Sir Joshua's
ingenuity, I think the conjecture too refined.

being conspicuous wherever he was, he frequently
talked carelessly without knowledge of the subject, or
even without thought. His person was short, his
countenance coarse and vulgar, his deportment that
of a scholar awkwardly affecting the easy gentleman.
Those who were in any way distinguished excited
envy in him to so ridiculous an excess that the
instances of it are hardly credible. When accompany-
ing two beautiful young ladies[1] with their mother on
a tour in France, he was seriously angry that more
attention was paid to them than to him ; and once at
the exhibition of the *Fantoccini* in London, when
those who sat next him observed with what dexterity
a puppet was made to toss a pike, he could not bear
that it should have such praise, and exclaimed with
some warmth, 'Pshaw ! I can do it better myself.'[2]

He, I am afraid, had no settled system of any sort,
so that his conduct must not be strictly scrutinised ;
but his affections were social and generous, and when
he had money he gave it away very liberally. His
desire of imaginary consequence predominated over
his attention to truth. When he began to rise into
notice, he said he had a brother who was Dean of
Durham,[3] a fiction so easily detected, that it was
wonderful how he should have been so inconsiderate
as to hazard it. He boasted to me at this time of
the power of his pen in commanding money, which I

---

[1] Miss Hornecks, one of whom is now married to Henry Bunbury,
Esq., and the other to Colonel Gwyn.

[2] He went home with Mr. Burke to supper ; and broke his shin by
attempting to exhibit to the company how much better he could jump
over a stick than the puppets.

[3] I am willing to hope that there may have been some mistake as to
this anecdote, though I had it from a dignitary of the Church. Dr.
Isaac Goldsmith, his near relation, was Dean of Cloyne, in 1747.

believe was true in a certain degree, though in the
instance he gave he was by no means correct. He told
me that he had sold a novel for four hundred pounds.
This was his *Vicar of Wakefield*. But Johnson informed me, that he had made the bargain for Goldsmith, and the price was sixty pounds. 'And, sir
(said he), a sufficient price too, when it was sold; for
then the fame of Goldsmith had not been elevated, as
it afterwards was, by his *Traveller*; and the bookseller
had such faint hopes of profit by his bargain, that he
kept the manuscript by him a long time, and did not
publish it till after the *Traveller* had appeared. Then,
to be sure, it was accidentally worth more money.'

Mrs. Piozzi [1] and Sir John Hawkins [2] have strangely
mis-stated the history of Goldsmith's situation and
Johnson's friendly interference, when this novel was
sold. I shall give it authentically from Johnson's own
exact narration :—

'I received one morning a message from poor Goldsmith
that he was in great distress, and as it was not in his power
to come to me, begging that I would come to him as soon as
possible. I sent him a guinea, and promised to come to him
directly. I accordingly went as soon as I was drest, and found
that his landlady had arrested him for his rent, at which he
was in a violent passion. I perceived that he had already
changed my guinea, and had got a bottle of Madeira and a
glass before him. I put the cork into the bottle, desired he
would be calm, and began to talk to him of the means by
which he might be extricated. He then told me that he had
a novel ready for the press, which he produced to me. I
looked into it, and saw its merit; told the landlady I should
soon return, and, having gone to a bookseller, sold it for sixty
pounds. I brought Goldsmith the money, and he discharged

---

1 *Anecdotes of Johnson.*   2 *Life of Johnson*, p. 420.

his rent, not without rating his landlady in a high tone for having used him so ill.'[1]

My next meeting with Johnson was on Friday the 1st of July, when he and I and Dr. Goldsmith supped at the Mitre. I was before this time pretty well acquainted with Goldsmith, who was one of the brightest ornaments of the Johnsonian school. Goldsmith's respectful attachment to Johnson was then at its height; for his own literary reputation had not yet distinguished him so much as to excite a vain desire of competition with his great Master. He had increased my admiration of the goodness of Johnson's heart by incidental remarks in the course of conversation; such as, when I mentioned Mr. Levet, whom he entertained under his roof, 'He is poor and honest, which is recommendation enough to Johnson'; and when I wondered that he was very kind to a man of whom I had heard a very bad character, 'He is now become miserable, and that ensures the protection of Johnson.'

Goldsmith attempting this evening to maintain, I suppose from an affectation of paradox, 'that know-

---

[1] It may not be improper to annex here Mrs. Piozzi's account of this transaction, in her own words, as a specimen of the extreme inaccuracy with which all her anecdotes of Dr. Johnson are related, or rather discoloured and distorted: 'I have forgotten the year, but it could scarcely, I think, be later than 1765 or 1766, that he was *called abruptly from our house after dinner*, and returning *in about three hours*, said he had been with an enraged author, whose landlady pressed him for payment within doors, while the bailiffs beset him without; that he was *drinking himself drunk* with Madeira, to drown care, and fretting over a novel, which, when *finished*, was to be his *whole fortune*, but *he could not get it done for distraction*, nor could he step out of doors to offer it for sale. Mr. Johnson, therefore, sent away the bottle, and went to the bookseller, recommending the performance, and *desiring some immediate relief*; which when he brought back to the writer, *he called the woman of the house directly to partake of punch, and pass their time in merriment.*'—*Anecdotes of Dr. Johnson.*

ledge was not desirable on its own account, for it often was a source of unhappiness.' JOHNSON: 'Why, sir, that knowledge may in some cases produce unhappiness, I allow. But, upon the whole, knowledge, *per se,* is certainly an object which every man would wish to attain, although, perhaps, he may not take the trouble necessary for attaining it.'

Dr. John Campbell, the celebrated political and biographical writer, being mentioned, Johnson said, 'Campbell is a man of much knowledge, and has a good share of imagination. His *Hermippus Redivivus* is very entertaining, as an account of the Hermetic philosophy, and as furnishing a curious history of the extravagances of the human mind. If it were merely imaginary it would be nothing at all. Campbell is not always rigidly careful of truth in his conversation; but I do not believe there is anything of this carelessness in his books. Campbell is a good man, a pious man. I am afraid he has not been in the inside of a church for many years;[1] but he never passes a church without pulling off his hat. This shows that he has good principles. I used to go pretty

---

[1] I am inclined to think that he was misinformed as to this circumstance. I own I am jealous for my worthy friend Dr. John Campbell. For though Milton could without remorse absent himself from public worship, I cannot. On the contrary, I have the same habitual impressions upon my mind with those of a truly venerable Judge, who said to Mr. Langton, 'Friend Langton, if I have not been at church on a Sunday, I do not feel myself easy.' Dr. Campbell was a sincerely religious man. Lord Macartney, who is eminent for his variety of knowledge and attention to men of talents, and knew him well, told me that when he called on him in a morning he found him reading a chapter in the Greek New Testament, which he informed his Lordship was his constant practice. The quantity of Dr. Campbell's composition is almost incredible, and his labours brought him large profits. Dr. Joseph Warton told me that Johnson said of him, 'He is the richest author that ever grazed the common of literature.' [Prices in the last century for Histories and compilations were very high. Hawkesworth was paid £6000 for his collection of *Travels.*—A. B.]

often to Campbell's on a Sunday evening, till I began
to consider that the shoals of Scotchmen who flocked
about him might probably say, when anything of
mine was well done, " Ay, ay, he has learnt this of
Cawmell ! " '

He talked very contemptuously of Churchill's
poetry, observing that ' it had a temporary currency
only from its audacity of abuse, and being filled with
living names, and that it would sink into oblivion.'
I ventured to hint that he was not quite a fair judge,
as Churchill had attacked him violently. JOHNSON :
'Nay, sir, I am a very fair judge. He did not attack
me violently till he found I did not like his poetry ;
and his attack on me shall not prevent me from con-
tinuing to say what I think of him, from an apprehension that it may be ascribed to resentment. No,
sir, I called the fellow a blockhead at first, and I will
call him a blockhead still. However, I will acknowledge that I have a better opinion of him now than
I once had, for he has shown more fertility than I
expected. To be sure, he is a tree that cannot produce good fruit : he only bears crabs. But, sir, a
tree that produces a great many crabs is better than
a tree which produces only a few.'

In this depreciation of Churchill's poetry I could
not agree with him. It is very true that the greatest
part of it is upon the topics of the day, on which
account, as it brought him great fame and profit at
the time, it must proportionably slide out of the
public attention as other occasional objects succeed.
But Churchill had extraordinary vigour both of
thought and expression. His portraits of the players
will ever be valuable to the true lovers of the drama,

and his strong caricatures of several eminent men of his age will not be forgotten by the curious. Let me add, that there is in his works many passages which are of a general nature ; and his ' Prophecy of Famine' is a poem of no ordinary merit. It is, indeed, falsely injurious to Scotland ; but therefore may be allowed a greater share of invention.

Bonnell Thornton had just published a burlesque 'Ode on St. Cecilia's Day,' adapted to the ancient British music, viz., the salt-box, the Jew's harp, the marrow-bones and cleaver, the hum-strum or hurdy-gurdy, etc. Johnson praised its humour, and seemed much diverted with it. He repeated the following passage :

> 'In strains more exalted the salt-box shall join,
>   And clattering and battering and clapping combine ;
>   With a rap and a tap while the hollow side sounds,
>   Up and down leaps the flap, and with rattling rebounds.'[1]

I mentioned the periodical paper called *The Connoisseur*. He said it wanted matter. No doubt it had not the deep thinking of Johnson's writings. But surely it has just views of the surface of life, and in a very sprightly manner. His opinion of *The World* was not much higher than that of *The Connoisseur*.

Let me here apologise for the imperfect manner in which I am obliged to exhibit Johnson's conversation

---

[1] [In 1769 I set for Smart and Newbery Thornton's burlesque ' Ode on St. Cecilia's Day.' It was performed at Ranelagh in masks, to a very crowded audience, as I was told ; for I then resided in Norfolk. Beard sung the salt-box song, which was admirably accompanied on that instrument by Brent, the fencing-master, and father of Miss Brent, the celebrated singer ; Skeggs on the broom-stick, as bassoon ; and a remarkable performer on the Jew's harp,—' Buzzing twangs the iron lyre.' Cleavers were cast in bell-metal for this entertainment. All the performers of the old woman's Oratory, employed by Foote, were, I believe, employed at Ranelagh on this occasion.—B.]

at this period. In the early part of my acquaintance
with him, I was so rapt in admiration of his extraordinary colloquial talents, and so little accustomed to
his peculiar mode of expression, that I found it extremely difficult to recollect and record his conversation with its genuine vigour and vivacity. In progress
of time, when my mind was, as it were, *strongly impregnated with the Johnsonian æther*, I could with
much facility and exactness carry in my memory and
commit to paper the exuberant variety of his wisdom
and wit.

At this time *Miss* Williams,[1] as she was then called,
though she did not reside with him in the Temple
under his roof, but had lodgings in Bolt Court, Fleet
Street, had so much of his attention that he every
night drank tea with her before he went home, however late it might be, and she always sat up for him.
This, it may be fairly conjectured, was not alone a
proof of his regard for *her*, but of his own unwillingness to go into solitude, before that unseasonable
hour at which he had habituated himself to expect
the oblivion of repose. Dr. Goldsmith, being a
privileged man, went with him this night, strutting
away, and calling to me with an air of superiority,
like that of an esoteric over an exoteric disciple of
a sage of antiquity, ‘I go to Miss Williams.’ I confess I then envied him this mighty privilege, of which
he seemed so proud; but it was not long before I
obtained the same mark of distinction.

On Tuesday the 5th of July I again visited John-

---

1 [See vol. i. p. 247. This lady resided in Dr. Johnson's house in Gough
Square from about 1753 to 1758; and in that year, on his removing to
Gray's Inn, she went into lodgings. At a subsequent period she again
became an inmate with Johnson in Johnson's Court.—M.]

son. He told me he had looked into the poems of
a pretty voluminous writer, Mr. (now Dr.) John
Ogilvie, one of the Presbyterian ministers of Scotland, which had lately come out, but could find no
thinking in them. BOSWELL: 'Is there not imagination in them, sir?' JOHNSON: 'Why, sir, there is
in them what *was* imagination, but it is no more
imagination in *him* than sound is sound in the echo.
And his diction, too, is not his own. We have long
ago seen *white-robed innocence* and *flower-bespangled
meads.*'

Talking of London, he observed, 'Sir, if you wish
to have a just notion of the magnitude of this city, you
must not be satisfied with seeing its great streets and
squares, but must survey the innumerable little lanes
and courts. It is not in the showy evolutions of
buildings, but in the multiplicity of human habitations which are crowded together, that the wonderful
immensity of London consists.' I have often amused
myself with thinking how different a place London is
to different people. They whose narrow minds are
contracted to the consideration of some one particular
pursuit, view it only through that medium. A politician thinks of it merely as the seat of government in
its different departments; a grazier, as a vast market
for cattle; a mercantile man, as a place where a
prodigious deal of business is done upon 'Change;
a dramatic enthusiast, as the grand scene of theatrical
entertainments; a man of pleasure, as an assemblage
of taverns, and the great emporium for ladies of easy
virtue. But the intellectual man is struck with it,
as comprehending the whole of human life in all its
variety, the contemplation of which is inexhaustible.

On Wednesday, July 6, he was engaged to sup with
me at my lodgings in Downing Street, Westminster.
But on the preceding night my landlord having
behaved very rudely to me and some company who
were with me, I had resolved not to remain another
night in his house. I was exceedingly uneasy at the
awkward appearance I supposed I should make to
Johnson and the other gentlemen whom I had invited,
not being able to receive them at home, and being
obliged to order supper at the Mitre. I went to
Johnson in the morning, and talked of it as of a
serious distress. He laughed, and said, 'Consider,
sir, how insignificant this will appear a twelvemonth
hence.' Were this consideration to be applied to
most of the little vexatious incidents of life, by which
our quiet is too often disturbed, it would prevent
many painful sensations. I have tried it frequently
with good effect. 'There is nothing (continued he)
in this mighty misfortune ; nay, we shall be better at
the Mitre.' I told him that I had been at Sir John
Fielding's office, complaining of my landlord, and had
been informed, that though I had taken my lodgings
for a year, I might, upon proof of his bad behaviour,
quit them when I pleased, without being under an
obligation to pay rent for any longer time than while
I possessed them. The fertility of Johnson's mind
could show itself even upon so small a matter as this.
'Why, sir (said he), I suppose this must be the law,
since you have been told so in Bow Street. But, if
your landlord could hold you to your bargain, and the
lodging should be yours for a year, you may certainly
use them as you think fit. So, sir, you may quarter
two life-guardmen upon him ; or you may send the

greatest scoundrel you can find into your apartments; or you may say that you want to make some experiments in natural philosophy, and may burn a large quantity of assafœtida in his house.'

I had as my guests this evening at the Mitre tavern, Dr. Johnson, Dr. Goldsmith, Mr. Thomas Davies, Mr. Eccles, an Irish gentleman, for whose agreeable company I was obliged to Mr. Davies, and the Reverend Mr. John Ogilvie,[1] who was desirous of being in company with my illustrious friend, while I, in my turn, was proud to have the honour of showing one of my countrymen upon what easy terms Johnson permitted me to live with him.

Goldsmith, as usual, endeavoured, with too much eagerness, to *shine*, and disputed very warmly with Johnson against the well-known maxim of the British constitution, 'The King can do no wrong,' affirming, that 'what was morally false could not be politically true; and as the King might, in the exercise of his regal power, command and cause the doing of what was wrong, it certainly might be said, in sense and in reason, that he could do wrong.' JOHNSON: 'Sir, you are to consider, that in our constitution, according to its true principles, the King is the head; he is supreme; he is above everything, and there is no power by which he can be tried. Therefore it is, sir, that we hold the King can do no wrong; that whatever may happen to be wrong in government may not be above our

---

[1] The Northern bard mentioned p. 86. When I asked Dr. Johnson's permission to introduce him, he obligingly agreed; adding, however, with a sly pleasantry, 'but he must give us none of his poetry.' It is remarkable that Johnson and Churchill, however much they differed in other points, agreed on this subject. See Churchill's *Journey*. It is, however, but justice to Dr. Ogilvie to observe that his *Day of Judgment* has no inconsiderable share of merit.

reach by being ascribed to majesty. Redress is always to be had against oppression, by punishing the immediate agents. The King, though he should command, cannot force a judge to condemn a man unjustly; therefore it is the judge whom we prosecute and punish. Political institutions are formed upon the consideration of what will most frequently tend to the good of the whole, although now and then exceptions may occur. Thus it is better in general that a nation should have a supreme legislative power, although it may at times be abused. And then, sir, there is this consideration, that *if the abuse be enormous, Nature will rise up, and, claiming her original rights, overturn a corrupt political system.*' I mark this animated sentence with peculiar pleasure, as a noble instance of that truly dignified spirit of freedom which ever glowed in his heart, though he was charged with slavish tenets by superficial observers; because he was at all times indignant against that false patriotism, that pretended love of freedom, that unruly restlessness, which is inconsistent with the stable authority of any good government.

This generous sentiment, which he uttered with great fervour, struck me exceedingly, and stirred my blood to that pitch of fancied resistance, the possibility of which I am glad to keep in mind, but to which I trust I never shall be forced.

'Great abilities (said he) are not requisite for an historian; for in historical composition all the greatest powers of the human mind are quiescent. He has facts ready to his hand; so there is no exercise of invention. Imagination is not required in any high degree; only about as much as is used in the lower kinds of poetry. Some penetration, accuracy, and colouring will fit a man for the task, if he can give the application which is necessary.'

'Bayle's *Dictionary* is a very useful work for those to consult who love the biographical part of literature, which is what I love most.'

Talking of the eminent writers in Queen Anne's reign, he observed, 'I think Dr. Arbuthnot the first man among them. He was the most universal genius, being an excellent physician, a man of deep learning, and a man of much humour. Mr. Addison was, to be sure, a great man; his learning was not profound; but his morality, his humour, and his elegance of writing, set him very high.'

Mr. Ogilvie was unlucky enough to choose for the topic of his conversation the praises of his native country. He began with saying that there was very rich land around Edinburgh. Goldsmith, who had studied physic there, contradicted this, very untruly, with a sneering laugh. Disconcerted a little by this, Mr. Ogilvie then took new ground, where I suppose he thought himself perfectly safe; for he observed that Scotland had a great many noble wild prospects. JOHNSON: 'I believe, sir, you have a great many. Norway, too, has noble wild prospects; and Lapland is remarkable for prodigious noble wild prospects. But, sir, let me tell you, the noblest prospect which a Scotchman ever sees is the high road that leads him to England!' This unexpected and pointed sally produced a roar of applause. After all, however, those who admire the rude grandeur of Nature cannot deny it to Caledonia.

On Saturday, July 9, I found Johnson surrounded

with a numerous levee, but have not preserved any
part of his conversation. On the 14th we had another
evening by ourselves at the Mitre. It happening to
be a very rainy night, I made some commonplace
observations on the relaxation of nerves and depression
of spirits which such weather occasioned ;[1] adding,
however, that it was good for the vegetable creation.
Johnson, who, as we have already seen, denied that
the temperature of the air had any influence on the
human frame, answered, with a smile of ridicule,
'Why, yes, sir, it is good for vegetables, and for the
animals who eat those vegetables, and for the animals
who eat those animals.' This observation of his aptly
enough introduced a good supper ; and I soon forgot
in Johnson's company the influence of a moist
atmosphere.

Feeling myself now quite at ease as his companion,
though I had all possible reverence for him, I expressed
a regret that I could not be so easy with my father,
though he was not much older than Johnson, and
certainly, however respectable, had not more learning
and greater abilities to depress me. I asked him the
reason of this. JOHNSON: 'Why, sir, I am a man of
the world. I live in the world, and I take, in some
degree, the colour of the world as it moves along.
Your father is a judge in a remote part of the island,
and all his notions are taken from the old world.
Besides, sir, there must always be a struggle between
a father and son, while one aims at power and the
other at independence.' I said, I was afraid my father

---

1 [Johnson would suffer none of his friends to fill up chasms in
conversation with remarks on the weather : 'Let us not talk of the
weather.'—B.]

would force me to be a lawyer. JOHNSON: 'Sir, you need not be afraid of his forcing you to be a laborious practising lawyer; that is not in his power. For, as the proverb says, "One man may lead a horse to the water, but twenty cannot make him drink." He may be displeased that you are not what he wishes you to be; but that displeasure will not go far. If he insists only on your having as much law as is necessary for a man of property, and then endeavours to get you into Parliament, he is quite in the right.'

He enlarged very convincingly upon the excellence of rhyme over blank verse in English poetry. I mentioned to him that Dr. Adam Smith, in his lectures upon composition, when I studied under him in the College of Glasgow, had maintained the same opinion strenuously, and I repeated some of his arguments. JOHNSON: 'Sir, I was once in company with Smith, and we did not take to each other; but had I known that he loved rhyme as much as you tell me he does, I should have hugged him.'

Talking of those who denied the truth of Christianity, he said, 'It is always easy to be on the negative side. If a man were now to deny that there is salt upon the table, you could not reduce him to an absurdity. Come, let us try this a little further. I deny that Canada is taken, and I can support my denial by pretty good arguments. The French are a much more numerous people than we; and it is not likely that they would allow us to take it. "But the ministry have assured us, in all the formality of the Gazette, that it is taken." Very true. But the ministry have put us to an enormous expense by the war in America, and it is their interest to persuade us that we have got something for our money. "But the fact is confirmed by thousands of men who were at the taking of it." Ay, but these men have still more interest in deceiving us. They don't want that you should think the French have beat them, but that they have beat the French. Now suppose you should go over and find that it is really taken, that would only satisfy yourself; for when you come home we will not believe you. We will say you have been bribed. Yet, sir, notwithstanding all these plausible objections, we have no doubt that Canada is really ours. Such is the weight of common testimony. How much stronger are the evidences of the Christian religion?'

'Idleness is a disease which must be combated; but I would not advise a rigid adherence to a particular plan of study. I myself have never persisted in any plan for two days together. A man ought to read just as inclination leads him; for what he reads as a task will do him little good. A young man should read five hours in a day, and so may acquire a great deal of knowledge.'

To a man of vigorous intellect and ardent curiosity like his own, reading without a regular plan may be beneficial; though even such a man must submit to it, if he would attain a full understanding of any of the sciences.

To such a degree of unrestrained frankness had he now accustomed me, that in the course of this evening I talked of the numerous reflections which had been thrown out against him on account of his having accepted a pension from his present Majesty. 'Why, sir (said he, with a hearty laugh), it is a mighty foolish noise that they make.[1] I have accepted of a pension as a reward which has been thought due to my literary merit; and now that I have this pension, I am the same man in every respect that I have ever been; I retain the same principles. It is true that I cannot now curse (smiling) the House of Hanover; nor would it be decent for me to drink King James's health in the wine that King George gives me money to pay for. But, sir, I think that the pleasure of cursing the House of Hanover, and drinking King James's health, are amply overbalanced by £300 a year.'

There was here, most certainly, an affectation of more Jacobitism than he really had; and indeed an intention of admitting, for the moment, in a much greater extent than it really existed, the charge of disaffection imputed to him by the world, merely for the purpose of showing how dexterously he could repel an attack, even though he were placed in the most disadvantageous position; for I have heard him declare, that if holding up his right hand would have secured victory at Culloden to Prince Charles's army, he was not sure he would have held it up; so little confidence had he in the right claimed by the House of Stuart, and so fearful was he of the consequences of another revolution on the throne of Great Britain; and Mr. Topham Beauclerk assured me he had heard him say this before he had his pension. At another time he said to Mr. Langton, 'Nothing has ever offered that has made it worth my while to consider the question fully.' He, however, also said to the

---

[1] When I mentioned the same idle clamour to him several years afterwards, he said, with a smile, 'I wish my pension were twice as large, that they might make twice as much noise.'

same gentleman, talking of King James the Second,
'It was become impossible for him to reign any longer
in this country.' He no doubt had an early attachment to the House of Stuart; but his zeal had cooled
as his reason strengthened. Indeed, I heard him once
say, 'that after the death of a violent Whig, with
whom he used to contend with great eagerness, he
felt his Toryism much abated.'[1] I suppose he meant
Mr. Walmsley.

Yet there is no doubt that at earlier periods he
was wont often to exercise both his pleasantry and
ingenuity in talking Jacobitism. My much respected
friend, Dr. Douglas, now Bishop of Salisbury, has
favoured me with the following admirable instance
from his Lordship's own recollection. One day when
dining at old Mr. Langton's, where Miss Roberts, his
niece, was one of the company, Johnson, with his
usual complacent attention to the fair sex, took her
by the hand and said, 'My dear, I hope you are a
Jacobite.' Old Mr. Langton, who, though a high and
steady Tory, was attached to the present Royal Family,
seemed offended, and asked Johnson, with great
warmth, what he could mean by putting such a
question to his niece? 'Why, sir (said Johnson), I
meant no offence to your niece; I meant her a great
compliment. A Jacobite, sir, believes in the divine
right of kings. He that believes in the divine right
of kings believes in a Divinity. A Jacobite believes
in the divine right of bishops. He that believes in
the divine right of bishops believes in the divine
authority of the Christian religion. Therefore, Sir,
a Jacobite is neither an Atheist nor a Deist. That

---

[1] *Journal of a Tour to the Hebrides,* 3d edit., p. 420.

cannot be said of a Whig; for *Whiggism is a negation of all principle.*'[1]

He advised me, when abroad, to be as much as I could with the Professors in the Universities, and with the clergy; for from their conversation I might expect the best accounts of everything in whatever country I should be, with the additional advantage of keeping my learning alive.

It will be observed, that when giving me advice as to my travels, Dr. Johnson did not dwell upon cities, and palaces, and pictures, and shows, and Arcadian scenes. He was of Lord Essex's opinion, who advises his kinsman Roger Earl of Rutland, 'rather to go a hundred miles to speak with one wise man than five miles to see a fair town.'[2]

I described to him an impudent fellow from Scotland, who affected to be a savage, and railed at all established systems. JOHNSON: 'There is nothing surprising in this, sir. He wants to make himself conspicuous. He would tumble in a hog-sty, as long as you looked at him and called to him to come out. But let him alone, never mind him, and he'll soon give it over.'

I added, that the same person maintained that there was no distinction between virtue and vice. JOHNSON: 'Why, sir, if the fellow does not think as he speaks, he is lying; and I see not what honour he can propose

---

1 He used to tell, with great humour, from my relation to him, the following little story of my early years, which was literally true: 'Boswell, in the year 1745, was a fine boy, wore a white cockade, and prayed for King James, till one of his uncles (General Cochran) gave him a shilling on condition that he would pray for King George, which he accordingly did. So you see (says Boswell) that *Whigs of all ages are made the same way.*'
2 *Letter to Rutland on Travel,* 16mo, 1596.

to himself from having the character of a liar. But if he does really think that there is no distinction between virtue and vice, why, sir, when he leaves our houses let us count our spoons.'

Sir David Dalrymple, now one of the Judges of Scotland by the title of Lord Hailes, had contributed much to increase my high opinion of Johnson, on account of his writings, long before I attained to a personal acquaintance with him ; I, in return, had informed Johnson of Sir David's eminent character for learning and religion ; and Johnson was so much pleased that at one of our evening meetings he gave him for his toast. I at this time kept up a very frequent correspondence with Sir David ; and I read to Dr. Johnson to-night the following passage from the letter which I had last received from him :

'It gives me pleasure to think that you have obtained the friendship of Mr. Samuel Johnson. He is one of the best moral writers which England has produced. At the same time, I envy you the free and undisguised converse with such a man. May I beg you to present my best respects to him, and to assure him of the veneration which I entertain for the author of the *Rambler* and of *Rasselas*? Let me recommend this last work to you ; with the *Rambler* you certainly are acquainted. In *Rasselas* you will see a tender-hearted operator, who probes the wound only to heal it. Swift, on the contrary, mangles human nature. He cuts and slashes, as if he took pleasure in the operation, like the tyrant who said, *Ita feri, ut se sentiat emori.*'

Johnson seemed to be much gratified by this just and well-turned compliment.

He recommended to me to keep a journal of my life, full and unreserved. He said it would be a very good exercise, and would yield me great satisfaction when the particulars were faded from my remembrance. I was uncommonly fortunate in having had a previous coincidence of opinion with him upon this subject, for I had kept such a journal for some time; and it was no small pleasure to me to have this to tell him, and to receive his approbation. He counselled me to keep it private, and said I might surely have a friend who would burn it in case of my death. From this habit I have been enabled to give the world so many anecdotes which would otherwise have been lost to posterity. I mentioned that I was afraid I put into my journal too many little incidents. JOHNSON: 'There is nothing, sir, too little for so little a creature as man. It is by studying little things that we attain the great art of having as little misery and as much happiness as possible.'

Next morning Mr. Dempster happened to call on me, and was so much struck even with the imperfect account which I gave him of Dr. Johnson's conversation, that, to his honour be it recorded, when I complained that drinking port and sitting up late with him affected my nerves for some time after, he said, 'One had better be palsied at eighteen than not keep company with such a man.'

On Tuesday, July 18, I found tall Sir Thomas Robinson sitting with Johnson. Sir Thomas said that the King of Prussia valued himself upon three things; —upon being a hero, a musician, and an author. JOHNSON: Pretty well, sir, for one man. As to his being an author, I have not looked at his poetry; but his prose is poor stuff. He writes just as you would suppose Voltaire's footboy to do, who has been his amanuensis. He has such parts as the valet might

have, and about as much of the colouring of the style
as might be got by transcribing his works.' When I
was at Ferney I repeated this to Voltaire, in order to
reconcile him somewhat to Johnson, whom he, in
affecting the English mode of expression, had previously characterised as 'a superstitious dog'; but
after hearing such a criticism on Frederick the Great,
with whom he was then on bad terms, he exclaimed,
'An honest fellow !'

But I think the criticism much too severe ; for the
Memoirs of the House of Brandenburgh are written as
well as many works of that kind.   His poetry, for the
style of which he himself makes a frank apology,
'*Jargonnant un François barbare,*' though fraught with
pernicious ravings of infidelity, has, in many places,
great animation, and in some a pathetic tenderness.

Upon this contemptuous animadversion on the King
of Prussia, I observed to Johnson, 'It would seem
then, sir, that much less parts are necessary to make
a king than to make an author; for the King of
Prussia is confessedly the greatest king now in
Europe, yet you think he makes a very poor figure as
an author.'

Mr. Levet this day showed me Dr. Johnson's library,
which was contained in two garrets over his chambers,
where Lintot, son of the celebrated bookseller of that
name, had formerly his warehouse. I found a number
of good books, but very dusty and in great confusion.
The floor was strewed with manuscript leaves, in Johnson's own handwriting, which I beheld with a degree
of veneration, supposing they perhaps might contain
portions of the *Rambler* or of *Rasselas*.   I observed an
apparatus for chemical experiments, of which Johnson

was all his life very fond. The place seemed to be very favourable for retirement and meditation. Johnson told me that he went up thither without mentioning it to his servant, when he wanted to study secure from interruption ; for he would not allow his servant to say he was not at home when he really was. 'A servant's strict regard for truth (said he) must be weakened by such a practice. A philosopher may know that it is merely a form of denial ; but few servants are such nice distinguishers. If I accustom a servant to tell a lie for *me*, have I not reason to apprehend that he will tell many lies for *himself*?' I am, however, satisfied that every servant, of any degree of intelligence, understands saying his master is not at home, not at all as the affirmation of a fact, but as customary words, intimating that his master wishes not to be seen ; so that there can be no bad effect from it.

Mr. Temple, now vicar of St. Gluvias, Cornwall, who had been my intimate friend for many years, had at this time chambers in Farrar's Buildings, at the bottom of Inner Temple Lane, which he kindly lent me upon quitting my lodgings, he being to return to Trinity Hall, Cambridge. I found them particularly convenient for me, as they were so near Dr. Johnson's.

On Wednesday, July 20, Dr. Johnson, Mr. Dempster, and my uncle Dr. Boswell, who happened to be now in London, supped with me at these chambers. JOHNSON : 'Pity is not natural to man. Children are always cruel. Savages are always cruel. Pity is acquired and improved by the cultivation of reason. We may have uneasy sensations from seeing

a creature in distress, without pity; for we have not
pity unless we wish to relieve them. When I am on
my way to dine with a friend, and finding it late, have
bid the coachman make haste, if I happen to attend
when he whips his horses, I may feel unpleasantly
that the animals are put to pain, but I do not wish
him to desist. No, sir, I wish him to drive on.'

Mr. Alexander Donaldson, bookseller, of Edinburgh,
had for some time opened a shop in London, and sold
his cheap editions of the most popular English books,
in defiance of the supposed common-law right of
Literary Property. Johnson, though he concurred in
the opinion which was afterwards sanctioned by a
judgment of the House of Lords, that there was no
such right, was at this time very angry that the booksellers of London, for whom he uniformly professed
much regard, should suffer from an invasion of what
they had ever considered to be secure, and he was
loud and violent against Mr. Donaldson. 'He is a
fellow who takes advantage of the law to injure his
brethren; for notwithstanding that the statute secures
only fourteen years of exclusive right, it has always
been understood by *the trade* that he who buys the
copyright of a book from the author obtains a perpetual property; and upon that belief numberless
bargains are made to transfer that property after the
expiration of the statutory term. Now Donaldson, I
say, takes advantage here of people who have really
an equitable title from usage; and if we consider how
few of the books, of which they buy the property,
succeed so well as to bring profit, we should be of
opinion that the term of fourteen years is too short;
it should be sixty years.' DEMPSTER: 'Donaldson,

sir, is anxious for the encouragement of literature.
He reduces the price of books, so that poor students
may buy them.'   JOHNSON (laughing): 'Well, sir,
allowing that to be his motive, he is no better than
Robin Hood, who robbed the rich in order to give to
the poor.'[1]

It is remarkable, that when the great question concerning literary property came to be ultimately tried
before the supreme tribunal of this country, in consequence of the very spirited exertions of Mr.
Donaldson,[2] Dr. Johnson was zealous against a per-
petuity; but he thought that the term of exclusive
right of authors should be considerably enlarged.   He
was then for granting a hundred years.

The conversation now turned upon Mr. David
Hume's style.   JOHNSON: 'Why, sir, his style is not
English; the structure of his sentences is French.
Now the French structure and the English structure,
may, in the nature of things, be equally good.   But if
you allow that the English language is established,
he is wrong.   My name might originally have been
Nicholson, as well as Johnson; but were you to call
me Nicholson now, you would call me very absurdly.'

Rousseau's treatise on the inequality of mankind
was at this time a fashionable topic.   It gave rise to
an observation by Mr. Dempster, that the advantages
of fortune and rank were nothing to a wise man, who
ought to value only merit.   JOHNSON: 'If man were
a savage, living in the woods by himself, this might be

---

[1] [Donaldson's Hospital in Edinburgh represents the fortune of this
larcenous bookseller.—A. B.]

[2] [In Donaldson v. Becket, in 1774, the House of Lords decided,
after hearing the Judges, that the Statute of Queen Anne destroyed
perpetual copyright, and substituted a term of years.—A. B.]

true ; but in civilised society we all depend upon each other, and our happiness is very much owing to the good opinion of mankind.   Now, sir, in civilised society, external advantages make us more respected. A man with a good coat upon his back meets with a better reception than he who has a bad one.   Sir, you may analyse this, and say what is there in it ?   But that will avail you nothing, for it is a part of a general system.   Pound St. Paul's church into atoms, and consider any single atom ; it is, to be sure, good for nothing : but, put all these atoms together, and you have St. Paul's church.   So it is with human felicity, which is made up of many ingredients, each of which may be shown to be very insignificant.   In civilised society personal merit will not serve you so much as money will.   Sir, you may make the experiment. Go into the street and give one man a lecture on morality, and another a shilling, and see which will respect you most.   If you wish only to support nature, Sir William Petty fixes your allowance at £3 a year ; but as times are much altered, let us call it £6.   This sum will fill your belly, shelter you from the weather, and even get you a strong lasting coat, supposing it to be made of good bull's hide.   Now, sir, all beyond this is artificial, and is desired in order to obtain a greater degree of respect from our fellow-creatures. And, sir, if £600 a year procure a man more consequence, and, of course, more happiness, than £6 a year, the same proportion will hold as to £6000, and so on, as far as opulence can be carried.   Perhaps he who has a large fortune may not be so happy as he who has a small one ; but that must proceed from other causes than from his having the large fortune ;

for, *cæteris paribus*, he who is rich in a civilised society must be happier than he who is poor; as riches, if properly used (and it is a man's own fault if they are not), must be productive of the highest advantages. Money, to be sure, of itself, is of no use; for its only use is to part with it. Rousseau, and all those who deal in paradoxes, are led away by a childish desire of novelty.[1] When I was a boy I used always to choose the wrong side of a debate, because most ingenious things, that is to say, most new things, could be said upon it. Sir, there is nothing for which you may not muster up more plausible arguments than those which are urged against wealth and other external advantages. Why, now, there is stealing: why should it be thought a crime? When we consider by what unjust methods property has been often acquired, and that what was unjustly got it must be unjust to keep, where is the harm in one man's taking the property of another from him? Besides, sir, when we consider the bad use that many people make of their property, and how much better use the thief may make of it, it may be defended as a very allowable practice. Yet, sir, the experience of mankind has discovered stealing to be so very bad a thing that they make no scruple to hang a man for it. When I was running about this town a very poor fellow, I was a great arguer for the advantages of poverty; but I was, at the same time, very sorry to be poor. Sir, all the arguments which are brought to represent

---

[1] [Johnson told Mr. Burney that Goldsmith said, when he first began to write, he determined to commit to paper nothing but what was *new*; but he afterwards found that what was *new* was generally false, and from that time was no longer solicitous about novelty.—B.]

poverty as no evil, show it to be evidently a great evil. You never find people labouring to convince you that you may live very happily upon a plentiful fortune. So you hear people talking how miserable a king must be; and yet they all wish to be in his place.'

It was suggested that kings must be unhappy, because they are deprived of the greatest of all satisfactions, easy and unreserved society. JOHNSON: 'That is an ill-founded notion. Being a king does not exclude a man from such society. Great kings have always been social. The King of Prussia, the only great king at present, is very social. Charles the Second, the last King of England who was a man of parts, was social; and our Henrys and Edwards were all social.'

Mr. Dempster having endeavoured to maintain that intrinsic merit *ought* to make the only distinction amongst mankind :—JOHNSON: 'Why, sir, mankind have found that this cannot be. How shall we determine the proportion of intrinsic merit? Were that to be the only distinction amongst mankind, we should soon quarrel about the degrees of it. Were all distinctions abolished, the strongest would not long acquiesce, but would endeavour to obtain a superiority by their bodily strength. But, sir, as subordination is very necessary for society, and contentions for superiority very dangerous, mankind, that is to say, all civilised nations, have settled it upon a plain invariable principle. A man is born to hereditary rank; or his being appointed to certain offices gives him a certain rank. Subordination tends greatly to human happiness. Were we all upon an equality, we should have no other enjoyment than mere animal pleasures.'

I said I considered distinction or rank to be of so much importance in civilised society, that if I were asked on the same day to dine with the first duke in England, and with the first man in Britain for genius, I should hesitate which to prefer. JOHNSON: 'To be sure, sir, if you were to dine only once, and it were never to be known where you dined, you would choose rather to dine with the first man of genius; but to gain most respect you should dine with the first duke in England. For nine people in ten that you meet with would have a higher opinion of you for having dined with a duke; and the great genius himself would receive you better, because you had been with the great duke.'

He took care to guard himself against any possible suspicion that his settled principles of reverence for rank and respect for wealth were at all owing to mean or interested motives; for he asserted his own independence as a literary man. 'No man (said he) who ever lived by literature has lived more independently than I have done.' He said he had taken longer time than he needed to have done in composing his *Dictionary*. He received our compliments upon that great work with complacency, and told us that the *Academia della Crusca* could scarcely believe that it was done by one man.

Next morning I found him alone, and have preserved the following fragments of his conversation. Of a gentleman who was mentioned, he said, 'I have not met with any man for a long time who has given me such general displeasure. He is totally unfixed in his principles, and wants to puzzle other people.' I said his principles had been poisoned by a noted infidel writer, but that he was, nevertheless, a benevolent good man. JOHNSON: 'We can have no dependence upon that instinctive, that constitutional goodness which is not founded upon principle. I grant you that such a man may be a very amiable member of society. I can conceive him placed in such a situation that he is not much tempted to deviate from what is right; and as every man prefers virtue, when there is not some strong incitement to transgress its precepts, I can conceive him doing nothing wrong. But if such a man stood in need of money I should not like to trust him; and I should certainly not trust him with young ladies, for *there* there is always temptation. Hume, and other sceptical innovators, are vain men, and will gratify themselves at any expense. Truth will not afford sufficient food to their vanity; so they have betaken themselves to error. Truth, sir, is a cow which will yield such people no more milk, and so they are gone to milk the bull. If I could have allowed myself to gratify my vanity at the expense of truth, what fame might I have acquired! Everything which Hume has advanced against Christianity had passed through my mind long before he wrote. Always remember this, that after a system is well settled upon positive evidence, a few partial objections ought not to shake it. The human mind is so limited that it cannot take in all the parts of a subject, so that there may be objections raised against anything. There are objections against a *plenum*, and objections against a *vacuum*; yet one of them must certainly be true.'

I mentioned Hume's argument against the belief of miracles, that it is more probable that the witnesses to the truth of them are mistaken, or speak falsely, than that the miracles should be true. JOHNSON: 'Why, sir, the great difficulty of proving miracles should make us very cautious in believing them. But let us consider: although God has made Nature to operate by certain fixed laws, yet it is not unreasonable to think that He may suspend those laws in order to establish a system highly advantageous to mankind. Now the Christian religion is a most beneficial system, as it gives us light and certainty where we were before in darkness and doubt. The miracles which prove it are attested by men who had no interest in deceiving us; but who, on the contrary, were told that they should suffer persecution, and did actually lay down their lives in confirmation of the truth of the facts which they asserted. Indeed, for some centuries the heathens did not pretend to deny the miracles; but said they were performed by the aid of evil spirits. This is a circumstance of great weight. Then, sir, when we take the proofs derived from the prophecies which have been so exactly fulfilled, we have most satisfactory evidence. Supposing a miracle possible, as to which in my opinion there can be no doubt, we have as strong evidence for the miracles in support of Christianity as the nature of the thing admits.'

At night Mr. Johnson and I supped in a private room at the Turk's Head coffee-house, in the Strand. 'I encourage this house (said he), for the mistress of it is a good civil woman, and has not much business.'

'Sir, I love the acquaintance of young people; because, in the first place, I don't like to think myself growing old. In the next place, young acquaintances must last longest, if they do last; and then, sir, young men have more virtue than old men ; they have more generous sentiments in every respect. I love the young dogs of this age, they have more wit and humour and knowledge of life than we had ; but then the dogs are not so good scholars. Sir, in my early years I read very hard. It is a sad reflection, but a true one, that I knew almost as much at eighteen as I do now. My judgment, to be sure, was not so good ; but I had all the facts. I remember very well, when I was at Oxford, an old gentleman said to me, " Young man, ply your book diligently now, and acquire a stock of knowledge ; for when years come unto you, you will find that poring upon books will be but an irksome task." '

This account of his reading, given by himself in plain words, sufficiently confirms what I have already advanced upon the disputed question as to his application. It reconciles any seeming inconsistency in his way of talking upon it at different times ; and shows that idleness and reading hard were with him relative terms, the import of which, as used by him, must be gathered from a comparison with what scholars of different degrees of ardour and assiduity have been known to do. And let it be remembered that he was now talking spontaneously, and expressing his genuine sentiments ; whereas at other times he might be induced from his spirit of contradiction, or more properly from his love of argumentative contest, to speak lightly of his own application to study. It is pleasing to consider that the old gentleman's gloomy prophecy as to the irksomeness of books to men of an advanced age, which is too often fulfilled, was so far from being verified in Johnson that his ardour for literature never failed, and his last writings had more ease and vivacity than any of his earlier productions.

He mentioned to me now, for the first time, that he had been distressed by melancholy, and for that reason had been obliged to fly from study and meditation to the dissipating variety of life. Against melancholy he recommended constant occupation of mind, a great deal of exercise, moderation in eating and drinking, and especially to shun drinking at night. He said melancholy people were apt to fly to intemperance for relief, but that it sunk them much deeper in misery. He observed that labouring men, who work hard and live sparingly, are seldom or never troubled with low spirits.

He again insisted on the duty of maintaining subordination of rank. 'Sir, I would no more deprive a nobleman of his respect than of his money. I consider myself as acting a part in the great system of society, and I do to others as I would have them do to me. I would behave to a nobleman as I should expect he would behave to me, were I a nobleman and he Sam. Johnson. Sir, there is one Mrs. Macaulay[1] in this town, a great republican. One day when I was at her house I put on a very grave countenance, and said to her, "Madam, I am now become a convert to your way of thinking. I am convinced that all mankind are upon an equal footing; and to give you an unquestionable proof, madam, that I am in earnest,

---

[1] This *one* Mrs. Macaulay was the same personage who afterwards made herself so much known as 'the celebrated female historian.'— BOSWELL. [And whose History of England is well worth reading.— A. B.]

here is a very sensible, civil, well-behaved fellow-citizen, your footman; I desire that he may be allowed to sit down and dine with us." I thus, sir, showed her the absurdity of the levelling doctrine. She has never liked me since. Sir, your levellers wish to level *down* as far as themselves; but they cannot bear levelling *up* to themselves. They would all have some people under them; why not then have some people above them?' I mentioned a certain author who disgusted me by his forwardness, and by showing no deference to noblemen into whose company he was admitted. JOHNSON: 'Suppose a shoe-maker should claim an equality with him, as he does with a lord: how he would stare! "Why, sir, do you stare? (says the shoemaker); I do great service to society. 'Tis true, I am paid for doing it; but so are you, sir: and I am sorry to say it, better paid than I am, for doing something not so necessary. For man-kind could do better without your books than without my shoes." Thus, sir, there would be a perpetual struggle for precedence, were there no fixed invariable rules for the distinction of rank, which creates no jealousy, as it is allowed to be accidental.'

He said Dr. Joseph Warton was a very agreeable man, and his *Essay on the Genius and Writings of Pope* a very pleasing book. I wondered that he delayed so long to give us the continuation of it. JOHNSON: 'Why, sir, I suppose he finds himself a little disappointed in not having been able to persuade the world to be of his opinion as to Pope.'

We have now been favoured with the concluding volume, in which, to use a parliamentary expression, he has *explained*, so as not to appear quite so adverse to the opinion of the world, concerning Pope, as was at first thought; and we must all agree that his work is a most valuable accession to English literature.

A writer of deserved eminence being mentioned, Johnson said, ' Why, sir, he is a man of good parts, but, being originally poor, he has got a love of mean company and low jocularity; a very bad thing, sir. To laugh is good, as to talk is good. But you ought no more to think it enough if you laugh, than you are to think it enough if you talk. You may laugh in as many ways as you talk; and surely *every* way of talking that is practised cannot be esteemed.'

I spoke of a Sir James Macdonald as a young man of most distinguished merit, who united the highest reputation at Eton and Oxford with the patriarchal spirit of a great Highland chieftain. I mentioned that Sir James had said to me that he.had never seen Mr. Johnson, but he had a great respect for him, though at the same time it was mixed with some degree of terror. Johnson: 'Sir, if he were to be acquainted with me it might lessen both.'

The mention of this gentleman led us to talk of the Western Islands of Scotland, to visit which he expressed a wish that then appeared to me a very romantic fancy, which I little thought would be afterward realised. He told me that his father had put Martin's account of those islands into his hands when he was very young, and that he was highly pleased with it; that he was particularly struck with the St. Kilda man's notion that the High Church of Glasgow had been hollowed out of a rock; a circumstance to which old Mr. Johnson had directed his attention. He said he would go to the Hebrides with me when I returned from my travels, unless some very good companion should offer when I was absent, which he did not think probable : adding, 'There are few people to whom I take so much to as to you.'   And when I talked of my leaving England, he said, with a very affectionate air, 'My dear Boswell, I should be very unhappy at parting, did I think we were not to meet again.'   I cannot too often remind my readers, that although such instances of his kindness are doubtless very flattering to me, yet I hope my recording them will be ascribed to a better motive than to vanity ; for they afford unquestionable evidence of his tenderness and complacency, which some, while they were forced to acknowledge his great powers, have been so strenuous to deny.

He maintained that a boy at school was the happiest of human beings.   I supported a different opinion, from which I have never yet varied, that a man is happier : and I enlarged upon the anxiety and sufferings which are endured at school.   JOHNSON : 'Ah ! sir, a boy's being flogged is not so severe as a man's having the hiss of the world against him.   Men have a solicitude about fame ; and the greater share they have of it the more afraid they are of losing it.';   I silently asked myself, 'Is it possible that the great Samuel Johnson really entertains any such apprehension, and is not confident that his exalted fame is established upon a foundation never to be shaken?'

He this evening drank a bumper to Sir David Dalrymple, 'as a man of worth, a scholar, and a wit.' 'I have (said he) never heard of him, except from you ; but let him know my opinion of him : for as he does not show himself much in the world, he should have the praise of the few who hear of him.'

On Tuesday, July 26, I found Mr. Johnson alone. It was a very wet day, and I again complained of the disagreeable effects of such weather. JOHNSON : 'Sir, this is all imagination, which physicians encourage ; for man lives in air, as a fish lives in water ; so that if the atmosphere press heavy from above, there is an equal resistance from below. To be sure, bad weather is hard upon people who are obliged to be abroad ; and men cannot labour so well in the open air in bad weather as in good : but, sir, a smith or a tailor, whose work is within-doors, will surely do as much in rainy weather as in fair. Some very delicate frames, indeed, may be affected by wet weather ; but not common constitutions.'

We talked of the education of children ; and I asked him what he thought was best to teach them first. JOHNSON : 'Sir, it is no matter what you teach them first, any more than what leg you shall put into your breeches first. Sir, you may stand disputing which is best to put in first, but in the meantime your breech is bare. Sir, while you are considering which of two things you should teach your child first, another boy has learnt them both.'

On Thursday, July 28, we again supped in private at the Turk's Head coffee-house. JOHNSON : 'Swift has a higher reputation than he deserves. His excellence is strong sense ; for his humour, though very well, is not remarkably good. I doubt whether the *Tale of a Tub* be his, for he never owned it, and it is much above his usual manner.[1]

'Thomson, I think, has as much of the poet about

---

[1] [An extraordinary bit of prejudice. There can be no doubt about Swift's authorship. See Scott's *Life of Swift.*—A. B.]

him as most writers. Everything appeared to him
through the medium of his favourite pursuit.   He
could not have viewed those two candles burning but
with a poetical eye.'

'Has not ——[1] a great deal of wit, sir?' JOHNSON:
'I do not think so, sir. He is indeed continually
attempting wit, but he fails. And I have no more
pleasure in hearing a man attempting wit and failing,
than in seeing a man trying to leap over a ditch and
tumbling into it.'

He laughed heartily when I mentioned to him a
saying of his concerning Mr. Thomas Sheridan, which
Foote took a wicked pleasure to circulate. 'Why, sir,
Sherry is dull, naturally dull; but it must have taken
him a great deal of pains to become what we now see
him. Such an excess of stupidity, sir, is not in
Nature.' 'So (said he), I allowed him all his own
merit.'

He now added, 'Sheridan cannot bear me. I bring
his declamation to a point. I ask him a plain question,
"What do you mean to teach?" Besides, sir, what
influence can Mr. Sheridan have upon the language of
this great country by his narrow exertions? Sir, it is
burning a farthing candle at Dover to show light at
Calais.'

Talking of a young man who was uneasy from
thinking that he was very deficient in learning and
knowledge, he said, 'A man has no reason to complain who holds a middle place, and has many below
him; and perhaps he has not six of his years above

---

[1] [This blank may be filled with the name of Burke, to whom Johnson very properly denied both wit and humour. Burke's strong points
were imagination and the illuminative faculty.—A. B.]

him;—perhaps not one. Though he may not know anything perfectly, the general mass of knowledge that he has acquired is considerable. Time will do for him all that is wanting.'

The conversation then took a philosophical turn. JOHNSON: 'Human experience, which is constantly contradicting theory, is the great test of truth. A system built upon the discoveries of a great many minds is always of more strength than what is produced by the mere workings of any one mind, which, of itself, can do little. There is not so poor a book in the world that would not be a prodigious effort were it wrought out entirely by a single mind, without the aid of prior investigators. The French writers are superficial, because they are not scholars, and so proceed upon the mere power of their own minds; and we see how very little power they have.'

'As to the Christian religion, sir, besides the strong evidence which we have for it, there is a balance in its favour from the number of great men who have been convinced of its truth, after a serious consideration of the question. Grotius was an acute man, a lawyer, a man accustomed to examine evidence, and he was convinced. Grotius was not a recluse, but a man of the world, who certainly had no bias to the side of religion. Sir Isaac Newton set out an infidel, and came to be a very firm believer.'

He this evening again recommended to me to perambulate Spain.[1] I said it would amuse him to get a

---

[1] I fully intended to have followed advice of such weight ; but having stayed much longer both in Germany and Italy than I proposed to do, and having also visited Corsica, I found that I had exceeded the time allowed me by my father, and hastened to France in my way homewards.

letter from me dated at Salamanca. JOHNSON : ‘I love
the University of Salamanca ; for when the Spaniards
were in doubt as to the lawfulness of their conquering
America, the University of Salamanca gave it as their
opinion that it was not lawful.’ He spoke this with
great emotion, and with that generous warmth which
dictated the lines in his ‘London,’ against Spanish
encroachment.

I expressed my opinion of my friend Derrick as but
a poor writer. JOHNSON : ‘To be sure, sir, he is :
but you are to consider that his being a literary man
has got for him all that he has. It has made him
King of Bath. Sir, he has nothing to say for himself
but that he is a writer. Had he not been a writer,
he must have been sweeping the crossings in the
streets, and asking halfpence from everybody that
passed.’

In justice, however, to the memory of Mr. Derrick,
who was my first tutor in the ways of London, and
showed me the town in all its variety of departments,
both literary and sportive, the particulars of which Dr.
Johnson advised me to put in writing, it is proper to
mention what Johnson, at a subsequent period, said
of him both as a writer and an editor : ‘Sir, I have
often said that if Derrick’s letters had been written
by one of a more established name, they would have
been thought very pretty letters.’[1] And, ‘I sent
Derrick to Dryden’s relations to gather materials for
his life ; and I believe he got all that I myself should
have got.’[2]

Poor Derrick ! I remember him with kindness.

---

[1] *Journal of a Tour to the Hebrides*, 2nd edition, p. 104.
[2] *Ibid.* p. 142.

Yet I cannot withhold from my readers a pleasant
humorous sally which could not have hurt him had
he been alive, and now is perfectly harmless.   In his
collection of poems there is one upon entering the
harbour of Dublin, his native city, after a long absence.   It begins thus:

> 'Eblana! much loved city, hail!
>   Where first I saw the light of day.'

, And after a solemn reflection on his being 'num-
bered with forgotten dead,' there is the following
stanza:

> 'Unless my lines protract my fame,
>   And those who chance to read them, cry,
> I knew him! Derrick was his name,
>   In yonder tomb his ashes lie,'—

which was thus happily parodied by Mr. John Home,
to whom we owe the beautiful and pathetic tragedy of
Douglas:

> 'Unless my *deeds* protract my fame,
>   *And he who passes sadly sings,*
> I knew him! Derrick was his name,
>   *On yonder tree his carcass swings!*'

I doubt much whether the amiable and ingenious
author of these burlesque lines will recollect them;
for they were produced extempore one evening while
he and I were walking together in the dining-room at
Eglintoune Castle, in 1760, and I have never mentioned them to him since.

Johnson said once to me, 'Sir, I honour Derrick
for his presence of mind.   One night, when Floyd,[1]

---

[1] He published a biographical work, containing an account of eminent
writers, in 3 vols. 8vo.

another poor author, was wandering about the streets
in the night, he found Derrick fast asleep upon a
bulk; upon being suddenly waked, Derrick started
up, "My dear Floyd, I am sorry to see you in this
destitute state: will you go home with me to *my
lodgings?*"'

I again begged his advice as to my method of study
at Utrecht. 'Come (said he), let us make a day of it.
Let us go down to Greenwich and dine, and talk of it
there.' The following Saturday was fixed for this
excursion.

As we walked along the Strand to-night, arm in
arm, a woman of the town accosted us, in the usual
enticing manner. 'No, no, my girl (said Johnson),
it won't do.'[1] He, however, did not treat her
with harshness; and we talked of the wretched life
of such women, and agreed that much more misery
than happiness, upon the whole, is produced by illicit
commerce between the sexes.

On Saturday, July 30, Dr. Johnson and I took a
sculler at the Temple stairs, and set out for Greenwich. I asked him if he really thought a knowledge
of the Greek and Latin languages an essential requisite
to a good education. JOHNSON: 'Most certainly, sir;
for those who know them have a very great advantage
over those who do not. Nay, sir, it is wonderful
what a difference learning makes upon people even in
the common intercourse of life, which does not appear
to be much connected with it.' 'And yet (said I),
people go through the world very well, and carry on
the business of life to good advantage, without learn-

---

[1] [This is another passage that powerfully affected the imagination
of Carlyle.—A. B.]

ing.' JOHNSON: 'Why, sir, that may be true in cases where learning cannot possibly be of any use; for instance, this boy rows us as well without learning as if he could sing the song of Orpheus to the Argonauts, who were the first sailors.' He then called to the boy, 'What would you give, my lad, to know about the Argonauts?' 'Sir (said the boy), I would give what I have.' Johnson was much pleased with his answer, and we gave him a double fare. Dr. Johnson then turning to me, 'Sir (said he), a desire of knowledge is the natural feeling of mankind; and every human being, whose mind is not debauched, will be willing to give all that he has to get knowledge.'

We landed at the Old Swan, and walked to Billingsgate, where we took oars and moved smoothly along the silver Thames. It was a very fine day. We were entertained with the immense number and variety of ships that were lying at anchor, and with the beautiful country on each side of the river.

I talked of preaching and of the great success which those called Methodists[1] have. JOHNSON: 'Sir, it is

---

[1] All who are acquainted with the history of religion (the most important, surely, that concerns the human mind) know that the appellation of *Methodists* was first given to a society of students in the University of Oxford, who, about the year 1730, were distinguished by an earnest and *methodical* attention to devout exercises. This disposition of mind is not a novelty, or peculiar to any sect, but has been, and still may be, found in many Christians of every denomination. Johnson himself was, in a dignified manner, a Methodist. In his *Rambler*, No. 110, he mentions with respect 'the whole discipline of regulated piety,' and in his *Prayers and Meditations* many instances occur of his anxious examination into his spiritual state. That this religious earnestness, and in particular an observation of the influence of the Holy Spirit, has sometimes degenerated into folly, and sometimes been counterfeited for base purposes, cannot be denied. But it is not, therefore, fair to decry it when genuine. The principal argument in reason and good sense against Methodism is, that it tends to debase human nature, and prevent the generous exertions of goodness, by an unworthy supposition that God will pay no regard to them; although it is positively said in the Scriptures that he 'will reward

owing to their expressing themselves in a plain and familiar manner, which is the only way to do good to the common people, and which clergymen of genius and learning ought to do from a principle of duty, when it is suited to their congregation; a practice for which they will be praised by men of sense. To insist against drunkenness as a crime, because it debases reason, the noblest faculty of man, would be of no service to the common people: but to tell them that they may die in a fit of drunkenness, and show them how dreadful that would be, cannot fail to make a deep impression. Sir, when your Scotch clergy give up their homely manner, religion will soon decay in that country.' Let this observation, as Johnson meant it, be ever remembered.

I was much pleased to find myself with Johnson at Greenwich, which he celebrates in his ' London ' as a favourite scene. I had the poem in my pocket, and read the lines aloud with enthusiasm :

> ' On Thames's banks in silent thought we stood,
> Where Greenwich smiles upon the silver flood :
> Pleased with the seat which gave Eliza birth,
> We kneel, and kiss the consecrated earth.'

---

every man according to his works.' But I am happy to have it in my power to do justice to those whom it is the fashion to ridicule, without any knowledge of their tenets ; and this I can do by quoting a passage from one of their best apologists, Mr. Milner, who thus expresses their doctrine upon this subject : ' Justified by faith, renewed in his faculties, and constrained by the love of Christ, the believer moves in the sphere of love and gratitude, and all his *duties* flow more or less from this principle. And though *they are accumulating for him in heaven a treasure of bliss proportioned to his faithfulness and activity, and it is by no means inconsistent with his principles to feel the force of this consideration,* yet love itself sweetens every duty to his mind ; and he thinks there is no absurdity in his feeling the love of GOD as the grand commanding principle of his life.'—*Essays on several Religious Subjects, etc.,* by Joseph Milner, A.M., Master of the Grammar School of Kingston-upon-Hull, 1789, p. 11.—BOSWELL.

He remarked that the structure of Greenwich hospital was too magnificent for a place of charity, and that its parts were too much detached to make one great whole.

Buchanan, he said, was a very fine poet; and observed that he was the first who complimented a lady, by ascribing to her the different perfections of the heathen goddesses;[1] but that Johnson improved upon this by making his lady at the same time free from their defects.

He dwelt upon Buchanan's elegant verses to Mary Queen of Scots, *Nympha Caledoniæ*, etc., and spoke with enthusiasm of the beauty of Latin verse. 'All the modern languages (said he) cannot furnish so melodious a line as

"Formosam resonare doces Amaryllida silvas."'[2]

Afterwards he entered upon the business of the day, which was to give me his advice as to a course of study. And here I am to mention with much regret that my record of what he said is miserably scanty. I recollect with admiration an animating blaze of eloquence, which roused every intellectual power in me to the highest pitch, but must have dazzled me so much that my memory could not preserve the substance of his discourse; for the note which I find of it is no more than this: 'He ran over the grand scale of human knowledge; advised me to select some particular branch to excel in, but to acquire a little

---

[1] [*Epigram.* Lib. ii. 'In Elizabeth. Angliæ Reg.' I suspect that the author's memory here deceived him, and that Johnson said, 'the first *modern* poet,' for there is a well-known Epigram in the *Anthologia* containing this kind of eulogy.—M.]
[2] Virgil, *Ecl.* i. v. 5.

of every kind.' The defect of my minutes will be fully supplied by a long letter upon the subject, which he favoured me with after I had been some time at Utrecht, and which my readers will have the pleasure to peruse in its proper place.

We walked in the evening to Greenwich Park. He asked me, I suppose by way of trying my disposition, 'Is not this very fine?' Having no exquisite relish of the beauties of Nature, and being more delighted with 'the busy hum of men,' I answered, 'Yes, sir, but not equal to Fleet Street.' JOHNSON : 'You are right, sir.'

I am aware that many of my readers may censure my want of taste. Let me, however, shelter myself under the authority of a very fashionable Baronet [1] in the brilliant world, who, on his attention being called to the fragrance of a May evening in the country, observed, 'This may be very well ; but for my part I prefer the smell of a flambeau at the playhouse.'

We stayed so long at Greenwich that our sail up the river, in our return to London, was by no means so pleasant as in the morning ; for the night air was so cold that it made me shiver. I was the more sensible of it from having sat up all the night before recollecting and writing in my Journal what I thought worthy of preservation,—an exertion which, during the first part of my acquaintance with Johnson, I

---

[1] My friend Sir Michael Le Fleming. This gentleman, with all his experience of sprightly and elegant life, inherits, with the beautiful family domain, no inconsiderable share of that love of literature which distinguished his venerable grandfather, the Bishop of Carlisle. He one day observed to me of Dr. Johnson, in a felicity of phrase, ' There is a blunt dignity about him on every occasion.'

[Sir Michael Le Fleming died of an apoplectic fit while conversing at the Admiralty with Lord Howick, May 19, 1806.—M.]

frequently made.   I remember having sat up four nights in one week, without being much incommoded in the daytime.

Johnson, whose robust frame was not in the least affected by the cold, scolded me, as if my shivering had been a paltry effeminacy, saying, 'Why do you shiver?' Sir William Scott of the Commons told me that when he complained of a headache in the post-chaise, as they were travelling together to Scotland, Johnson treated him in the same manner: 'At your age, sir, I had no headache.' It is not easy to make allowance for sensations in others which we ourselves have not at the time.   We must all have experienced how very differently we are affected by the complaints of our neighbours when we are well and when we are ill.   In full health we can scarcely believe that they suffer much; so faint is the image of pain upon our imagination: when softened by sickness we readily sympathise with the sufferings of others.

We concluded the day at the Turk's Head coffee-house very socially.   He was pleased to listen to a particular account which I gave him of my family, and of its hereditary estate, as to the extent and population of which he asked questions and made calculations; recommending at the same time a liberal kindness to the tenantry, as people over whom the proprietor was placed by Providence.   He took delight in hearing my description of the romantic seat of my ancestors.   'I must be there, sir (said he), and we will live in the old castle; and if there is not room in it remaining we will build one.'   I was highly flattered, but could scarcely indulge a hope that Auchinleck would indeed be honoured by his presence, and celebrated by a description, as it afterwards was, in his *Journey to the Western Islands.*

After he had again talked of my setting out for Holland, he said, 'I must see thee out of England; I will accompany you to Harwich.' I could not find words to express what I felt upon this unexpected and very great mark of his affectionate regard.

Next day, Sunday, July 31, I told him I had been that morning at a meeting of the people called Quakers, where I had heard a woman preach. JOHNSON: 'Sir, a woman's preaching is like a dog's walking on his hind legs. It is not done well; but you are surprised to find it done at all.'

On Tuesday, August 2 (the day of my departure from London having been fixed for the 5th), Dr. Johnson did me the honour to pass a part of the morning with me at my chambers. He said that 'he always felt an inclination to do nothing.' I observed that it was strange to think that the most indolent man in Britain had written the most laborious work, *The English Dictionary.*

I mentioned an imprudent publication,[1] by a certain friend of his, at an early period of life, and asked him if he thought it would hurt him. JOHNSON: 'No, sir, not much. It may, perhaps, be mentioned at an election.'

I had now made good my title to be a privileged man, and was carried by him in the evening to drink tea with Miss Williams,[2] whom, though under the

---

[1] [This is generally supposed to refer to Burke's ironical *Vindication of Natural Society,* published when its author was twenty-six years of age.—A. B.]

[2] [In a paper already referred to (see vol. i. p. 64), a lady who appears to have been well acquainted with Mrs. Williams thus speaks of her:—
'Mrs. Williams was a person extremely interesting. She had an un-

misfortune of having lost her sight, I found to be agreeable in conversation; for she had a variety of literature, and expressed herself well: but her peculiar value was the intimacy in which she had long lived with Johnson, by which she was acquainted with his habits, and knew how to lead him on to talk.

After tea he carried me to what he called his walk, which was a long narrow paved court in the neighbourhood, overshadowed by some trees. There we sauntered a considerable time; and I complained to

common firmness of mind, a boundless curiosity, retentive memory, and strong judgment. She had various powers of pleasing. Her personal afflictions and slender fortune she seemed to forget when she had the power of doing an act of kindness: she was social, cheerful, and active, in a state of body that was truly deplorable. Her regard to Dr. Johnson was formed with such strength of judgment and firm esteem that her voice never hesitated when she repeated his maxims or recited his good deeds; though upon many other occasions her want of sight had led her to make so much use of her ear as to affect her speech.

'Mrs. Williams was blind before she was acquainted with Dr. Johnson. She had many resources, though none very great. With the Miss Wilkinsons she generally passed a part of the year, and received from them presents, and from the first who died a legacy of clothes and money. The last of them, Mrs. Jane, left her an annual rent; but from the blundering manner of the will I fear she never reaped the benefit of it. That lady left money to erect a hospital for ancient maids: but the number she had allotted being too great for the donation, the Doctor [Johnson] said, it would be better to expunge the word *maintain*, and put in to *starve* such a number of old maids. They asked him, "What name should be given it?" he replied, "Let it be called Jenny's Whim." [The name of a well-known tavern near Chelsea, in former days.]

'Lady Philips made her a small annual allowance, and some other Welsh ladies, to all of whom she was related. Mrs. Montagu, on the death of Mr. Montagu, settled upon her [by deed] ten pounds per annum. As near as I can calculate, Mrs. Williams had about thirty-five or forty pounds a year. The furniture she used [in her apartment in Dr. Johnson's house] was her own; her expenses were small, tea and bread and butter being at least half of her nourishment. Sometimes she had a servant or charwoman to do the ruder offices of the house: but she was herself active and industrious. I have frequently seen her at work. Upon remarking one day her facility in moving about the house, searching into drawers, and finding books, without the help of sight, "Believe me (said she), persons who cannot do those common offices without sight did but little while they enjoyed that blessing." Scanty circumstances, bad health, and blindness, are surely a sufficient apology for her being sometimes impatient: her natural disposition was good, friendly, and humane.'—M.]

him that my love of London and of his company was
such that I shrunk almost from the thought of going
away even to travel, which is generally so much
desired by young men. He roused me by manly and
spirited conversation. He advised me, when settled
in any place abroad, to study with an eagerness after
knowledge, and to apply to Greek an hour every day;
and when I was moving about, to read diligently the
great book of mankind.

On Wednesday, August 3, we had our last social
evening at the Turk's Head coffee-house, before my
setting out for foreign parts. I had the misfortune,
before we parted, to irritate him unintentionally. I
mentioned to him how common it was in the world to
tell absurd stories of him, and to ascribe to him very
strange sayings. JOHNSON : 'What do they make me
say, sir?' BOSWELL : 'Why, sir, as an instance very
strange indeed (laughing heartily as I spoke), David
Hume told me you said that you would stand before
a battery of cannon to restore the Convocation to its
full powers.' Little did I apprehend that he had
actually said this : but I was soon convinced of my
error ; for, with a determined look, he thundered out,
'And would I not, sir? Shall the Presbyterian *Kirk*
of Scotland have its General Assembly, and the Church
of England be denied its Convocation?' He was
walking up and down the room while I told him the
anecdote ; but when he uttered this explosion of high-
church zeal he had come close to my chair, and his
eyes flashed with indignation. I bowed to the storm,
and diverted the force of it, by leading him to expatiate
on the influence which religion derived from maintaining the church with great external respectability.

I must not omit to mention that he this year wrote *The Life of Ascham* and the Dedication to the Earl of Shaftesbury prefixed to the edition of that writer's English works, published by Mr. Bennet.

On Friday, August 5, we set out early in the morning in the Harwich stage-coach. A fat elderly gentlewoman, and a young Dutchman, seemed the most inclined among us to conversation. At the inn where we dined the gentlewoman said that she had done her best to educate her children; and particularly, that she had never suffered them to be a moment idle. JOHNSON: 'I wish, madam, you would educate me too: for I have been an idle fellow all my life.' 'I am sure, sir (said she), you have not been idle.' JOHNSON: 'Nay, madam, it is very true; and that gentleman there (pointing to me) has been idle. He was idle at Edinburgh. His father sent him to Glasgow, where he continued to be idle. He then came to London, where he has been very idle; and now he is going to Utrecht, where he will be as idle as ever.' I asked him privately how he could expose me so. JOHNSON: 'Poh, poh! (said he), they knew nothing about you, and will think of it no more.' In the afternoon the gentlewoman talked violently against the Roman Catholics, and of the horrors of the Inquisition. To the utter astonishment of all the passengers but myself who knew that he could talk upon any side of a question, he defended the Inquisition, and maintained that 'false doctrine should be checked on its first appearance; that the civil power should unite with the church in punishing those who dared to attack the established religion, and that such only were punished by the Inquisition.' He had in his pocket *Pomponius*

Mela de Situ Orbis, in which he read occasionally, and
seemed very intent upon ancient geography. Though
by no means niggardly, his attention to what was
generally right was so minute, that having observed
at one of the stages that I ostentatiously gave a shilling
to the coachman, when the custom was for each
passenger to give only sixpence, he took me aside and
scolded me, saying that what I had done would make
the coachman dissatisfied with all the rest of the
passengers who gave him no more than his due. This
was a just reprimand ; for in whatever way a man may
indulge his generosity or his vanity in spending his
money, for the sake of others he ought not to raise
the price of any article for which there is a constant
demand.

He talked of Mr. Blacklock's poetry, so far as it
was descriptive of visible objects ; and observed, that
'as its author had the misfortune to be blind, we may
be absolutely sure that such passages are combinations
of what he has remembered of the works of other
writers who could see. That foolish fellow, Spence,
has laboured to explain philosophically how Blacklock may have done, by means of his own faculties,
what it is impossible he should do. The solution, as I
have given it, is plain. Suppose I know a man to be
so lame that he is absolutely incapable to move him
self, and I find him in a different room from that in
which I left him ; shall I puzzle myself with idle con-
jectures, that perhaps his nerves have by some unknown change all at once become effective ? No, sir,
it is clear how he got into a different room : he was
carried.'

Having stopped a night at Colchester, Johnson

talked of that town with veneration, for having stood a siege for Charles the First. The Dutchman alone now remained with us. He spoke English tolerably well; and thinking to recommend himself to us by expatiating on the superiority of the criminal jurisprudence of this country over that of Holland, he inveighed against the barbarity of putting an accused person to the torture in order to force a confession. But Johnson was as ready for this as for the Inquisition. 'Why, sir, you do not, I find, understand the law of your own country. To torture in Holland is considered as a favour to an accused person; for no man is put to the torture there unless there is as much evidence against him as would amount to conviction in England. An accused person among you, therefore, has one chance more to escape punishment than those who are tried among us.'

At supper this night he talked of good eating with uncommon satisfaction. 'Some people (said he) have a foolish way of not minding, or pretending not to mind, what they eat. For my part, I mind my belly very studiously, and very carefully; for I look upon it that he who does not mind his belly will hardly mind anything else.' He now appeared to me *Jean Bull philosophe*, and he was for the moment not only serious but vehement. Yet I have heard him, upon other occasions, talk with great contempt of people who were anxious to gratify their palates; and the 206th number of his *Rambler* is a masterly essay against gulosity. His practice, indeed, I must acknowledge, may be considered as casting the balance of his different opinions upon this subject: for I never knew any man who relished good eating more than he did.

When at table he was totally absorbed in the business
of the moment; his looks seemed riveted to his
plate; nor would he, unless when in very high company, say one word, or even pay the least attention
to what was said by others, till he had satisfied his
appetite, which was so fierce, and indulged with such
intenseness, that while in the act of eating the veins
of his forehead swelled, and generally a strong per-
spiration was visible. To those whose sensations were
delicate this could not but be disgusting; and it was
doubtless not very suitable to the character of a
philosopher, who should be distinguished by self-
command. But it must be owned that Johnson,
though he could be rigidly *abstemious*, was not a
temperate man either in eating or drinking. He could
refrain, but he could not use moderately. He told
me that he had fasted two days without inconvenience,
and that he had never been hungry but once. They
who beheld with wonder how much he ate upon all
occasions when his dinner was to his taste, could not
easily conceive what he must have meant by hunger;
and not only was he remarkable for the extraordinary
quantity which he ate, but he was, or affected to be, a
man of very nice discernment in the science of cookery.
He used to descant critically on the dishes which had
been at table where he had dined or supped, and to
recollect very minutely what he had liked. I remember, when he was in Scotland, his praising
'Gordon's palates' (a dish of palates at the Honourable Alexander Gordon's), with a warmth of expression
which might have done honour to more important
subjects. 'As for Maclaurin's imitation of a *made dish*,
it was a wretched attempt.' He about the same time

was so much displeased with the performance of a nobleman's French cook that he exclaimed with vehemence, 'I'd throw such a rascal into the river'; and he then proceeded to alarm a lady at whose house he was to sup, by the following manifesto of his skill: 'I, madam, who live at a variety of good tables, am a much better judge of cookery than any person who has a very tolerable cook, but lives much at home; for his palate is gradually adapted to the taste of his cook, whereas, madam, in trying by a wider range I can more exquisitely judge.' When invited to dine, even with an intimate friend, he was not pleased if something better than a plain dinner was not prepared for him. I have heard him say on such an occasion, 'This was a good dinner enough, to be sure; but it was not a dinner to *ask* a man to.' On the other hand, he was wont to express with great glee his satisfaction when he had been entertained quite to his mind. One day when he had dined with his neighbour and landlord in Bolt Court, Mr. Allen the printer, whose old housekeeper had studied his taste in everything, he pronounced this eulogy: 'Sir, we could not have had a better dinner had there been a *Synod of Cooks.*'

While we were left by ourselves after the Dutchman had gone to bed, Dr. Johnson talked of that studied behaviour which many have recommended and practised. He disapproved of it: and said, 'I never considered whether I should be a grave man or a merry man, but just let inclination for the time have its course.'

He flattered me with some hopes that he would, in the course of the following summer, come over to

Holland, and accompany me in a tour through the
Netherlands.

I teased him with fanciful apprehensions of unhappiness. A moth having fluttered round the candle,
and burnt itself, he laid hold of this little incident to
admonish me, saying, with a sly look, and in a solemn
but a quiet tone, 'That creature was its own tor-
mentor, and I believe its name was Boswell.'

Next day we got to Harwich to dinner ; and my
passage in the packet-boat to Helvoetsluys being
secured, and my baggage put on board, we dined at
our inn by ourselves. I happened to say it would be
terrible if he should not find a speedy opportunity of
returning to London, and be confined in so dull a
place. JOHNSON : 'Don't, sir, accustom yourself to
use big words for little matters. It would *not* be
terrible though I *were* to be detained some time here.'
The practice of using words of disproportionate magnitude is, no doubt, too frequent everywhere ; but I
think most remarkable among the French, of which
all who have travelled in France must have been
struck with innumerable instances.

We went and looked at the church, and having
gone into it and walked up to the altar, Johnson,
whose piety was constant and fervent, sent me to my
knees, saying, 'Now that you are going to leave your
native country, recommend yourself to the protection
of your Creator and Redeemer.'

After we came out of the church we stood talking
for some time together of Bishop Berkeley's ingenious
sophistry to prove the non-existence of matter, and
that everything in the universe is merely ideal. I
observed, that though we are satisfied his doctrine is

not true, it is impossible to refute it. I never shall forget the alacrity with which Johnson answered, striking his foot with mighty force against a large stone, till he rebounded from it, 'I refute it *thus.*'[1] This was a stout exemplification of the *first truths* of *Père Bouffier*, or the *original principles* of Reid and of Beattie; without admitting which we can no more argue in metaphysics than we can argue in mathematics without axioms. To me it is not conceivable how Berkeley can be answered by pure reasoning; but I know that the nice and difficult task was to have been undertaken by one of the most luminous minds of the present age, had not politics 'turned him from calm philosophy aside.' What an admirable display of subtilty, united with brilliance, might his contending with Berkeley have afforded us! How must we, when we reflect on the loss of such an intellectual feast, regret that he should be characterised as the man,

> 'Who born for the universe narrow'd his mind,
> And to party gave up what was meant for mankind'?

My revered friend walked down with me to the beach, where we embraced and parted with tenderness, and engaged to correspond by letters. I said, 'I hope, sir, you will not forget me in my absence.'

---

[1] [Dr. Johnson seems to have been imperfectly acquainted with Berkeley's doctrine: as his experiment only proves that we have the sensation of solidity, which Berkeley did not deny. He admitted that we had sensations or ideas that are usually called sensible qualities, one of which is solidity: he only denied the existence of *matter*, i.e. an inert senseless substance, in which they are supposed to subsist. Johnson's exemplification concurs with the vulgar notion that solidity is matter.—KEARNEY.] [Dr. Birkbeck Hill appositely quotes a saying of Turgot's: 'He who had never doubted of the existence of matter might be assured he had no turn for metaphysical disquisitions.'—A. B.]

JOHNSON : 'Nay, sir, it is more likely you should forget me than I should forget you.' As the vessel put out to sea I kept my eyes upon him for a considerable time, while he remained rolling his majestic frame in his usual manner ; and at last I perceived him walk back into the town, and he disappeared.

Utrecht seeming at first very dull to me, after the animated scenes of London, my spirits were grievously affected ; and I wrote to Johnson a plaintive and desponding letter, to which he paid no regard. Afterwards, when I had acquired a firmer tone of mind, I wrote him a second letter, expressing much anxiety to hear from him. At length I received the following epistle, which was of important service to me, and, I trust, will be so to many others :—

À MR. MR. BOSWELL, À LA COUR DE L'EMPEREUR,
UTRECHT

'DEAR SIR,—You are not to think yourself forgotten, or criminally neglected, that you have had yet no letter from me. I love to see my friends, to hear from them, to talk to them, and to talk of them ; but it is not without a considerable effort of resolution that I prevail upon myself to write. I would not, however, gratify my own indolence by the omission of any important duty, or any office of real kindness.

'To tell you that I am or am not well, that I have or have not been in the country, that I drank your health in the room in which we last sat together, and that your acquaintance continue to speak of you with their former kindness, topics with which those letters are commonly filled which are written only for the sake of writing, I seldom shall think worth communicating ; but if I can have it in my power to calm any harassing disquiet, to excite any virtuous desire, to rectify any important opinion, or fortify any generous resolution, you need not doubt but I shall at least wish to prefer the pleasure of gratifying a friend much less esteemed than your-

self, before the gloomy calm of idle vacancy. Whether I
shall easily arrive at an exact punctuality of correspondence
I cannot tell. I shall, at present, expect that you will receive
this in return for two which I have had from you. The first,
indeed, gave me an account so hopeless of the state of your
mind, that it hardly admitted or deserved an answer; by the
second I was much better pleased; and the pleasure will still
be increased by such a narrative of the progress of your
studies, as may evince the continuance of an equal and
rational application of your mind to some useful inquiry.

'You will, perhaps, wish to ask what study I would recommend. I shall not speak of theology, because it ought not to
be considered as a question whether you shall endeavour to
know the will of God.

'I shall, therefore, consider only such studies as we are at
liberty to pursue or to neglect; and of these I know not how
you will make a better choice than by studying the civil law
as your father advises, and the ancient languages, as you had
determined for yourself; at least resolve, while you remain
in any settled residence, to spend a certain number of hours
every day amongst your books. The dissipation of thought of
which you complain is nothing more than the vacillation of a
mind suspended between different motives, and changing its
direction as any motive gains or loses strength. If you can
but kindle in your mind any strong desire, if you can but keep
predominant any wish for some particular excellence or attain-
ment, the gusts of imagination will break away without any
effect upon your conduct, and commonly without any traces
left upon the memory.

'There lurks, perhaps, in every human heart a desire of
distinction, which inclines every man first to hope, and then
to believe, that nature has given him something peculiar to
himself. This vanity makes one mind nurse aversion, and
another actuate desires, till they rise by art much above their
original state of power; and as affectation in time improves
to habit, they at last tyrannise over him who at first encouraged them only for show. Every desire is a viper in the
bosom, who, while he was chill, was harmless; but when
warmth gave him strength, exerted it in poison. You know a
gentleman, who, when first he set his foot in the gay world,

as he prepared himself to whirl in the vortex of pleasure, imagined a total indifference and universal negligence to be the most agreeable concomitants of youth, and the strongest indication of an airy temper and a quick apprehension. Vacant to every object, and sensible of every impulse, he thought that all appearance of diligence would deduct something from the reputation of genius; and hoped that he should appear to attain, amidst all the ease of carelessness, and all the tumult of diversion, that knowledge and those accomplishments which mortals of the common fabric obtain only by mute abstraction and solitary drudgery. He tried this scheme of life a while, was made weary of it by his sense and his virtue; he then wished to return to his studies; and finding long habits of idleness and pleasure harder to be cured than he expected, still willing to retain his claim to some extraordinary prerogatives, resolved the common consequences of irregularity into an unalterable decree of destiny, and concluded that Nature had originally formed him incapable of rational employment.

'Let all such fancies, illusive and destructive, be banished henceforward from your thoughts for ever. Resolve, and keep your resolution; choose, and pursue your choice. If you spend this day in study, you will find yourself still more able to study to-morrow; not that you are to expect that you shall at once obtain a complete victory. Depravity is not very easily overcome. Resolution will sometimes relax, and diligence will sometimes be interrupted; but let no accidental surprise or deviation, whether short or long, dispose you to despondency. Consider these failings as incident to all mankind. Begin again where you left off, and endeavour to avoid the seducements that prevailed over you before.

'This, my dear Boswell, is advice which, perhaps, has been often given you, and given you without effect. But this advice, if you will not take from others, you must take from your own reflections, if you purpose to do the duties of the station to which the bounty of Providence has called you.

'Let me have a long letter from you as soon as you can. I hope you continue your Journal, and enrich it with many observations upon the country in which you reside. It will be a favour if you can get me any books in the Frisic lan-

guage, and can inquire how the poor are maintained in the
Seven Provinces.—I am, dear sir, your most affectionate servant,   SAM. JOHNSON.

'*London, Dec.* 8, 1763.'

I am sorry to observe, that neither in my own
minutes, nor in my letters to Johnson which have
been preserved by him, can I find any information
how the poor are maintained in the Seven Provinces.
But I shall extract from one of my letters what I
learnt concerning the other subject of his curiosity:

'I have made all possible inquiry with respect to the Frisic
language, and find that it has been less cultivated than any
other of the northern dialects; a certain proof of which is
their deficiency of books.   Of the old Frisic there are no
remains, except some ancient laws preserved by Schotanus in
his *Beschryvinge van die Heerlykheid van Friesland,* and his
Historia Frisica. I have not yet been able to find these
books.   Professor Trotz, who formerly was of the University
of Vranyken, in Friesland, and is at present preparing an
edition of all the Frisic laws, gave me this information.   Of
the modern Frisic, or what is spoken by the boors of this
day, I have procured a specimen.   It is Gisbert Japix's
Rymelerie, which is the only book that they have.   It is
amazing that they have no translation of the Bible, no treatises
of devotion, nor even any of the ballads and story-books which
are so agreeable to country people.   You shall have Japix by
the first convenient opportunity.   I doubt not to pick up
Schotanus.   Mynheer Trotz has promised me his assistance.'

Early in 1764 Johnson paid a visit to the Langton
family, at their seat of Langton in Lincolnshire, where
he passed some time, much to his satisfaction.   His
friend Bennet Langton, it will not be doubted, did
everything in his power to make the place agreeable
to so illustrious a guest: and the elder Mr. Langton
and his lady, being fully capable of understanding his
value, were not wanting in attention.   He, however,

told me, that old Mr. Langton, though a man of considerable learning, had so little allowance to make for his occasional 'laxity of talk,' that because in the course of discussion he sometimes mentioned what might be said in favour of the peculiar tenets of the Romish Church, he went to his grave believing him to be of that communion.

Johnson, during his stay at Langton, had the advantage of a good library, and saw several gentlemen of the neighbourhood. I have obtained from Mr. Langton the following particulars of this period.

He was now fully convinced that he could not have been satisfied with a country living; for talking of a respectable clergyman in Lincolnshire, he observed, 'This man, sir, fills up the duties of his life well. I approve of him, but could not imitate him.'

To a lady who endeavoured to vindicate herself from blame for neglecting social attention to worthy neighbours, by saying 'I would go to them if it would do them any good,' he said, 'What good, madam, do you expect to have in your power to do them? It is showing them respect, and that is doing them good.'

So socially accommodating was he, that once, when Mr. Langton and he were driving together in a coach, and Mr. Langton complained of being sick, he insisted that they should go out and sit on the back of it in the open air, which they did. And being sensible how strange the appearance must be, observed, that a countryman whom they saw in a field would probably be thinking, 'If these two madmen should come down, what would become of me?'

Soon after his return to London, which was in February, was founded that Club which existed long without a name, but at Mr. Garrick's funeral became distinguished by the title of The Literary Club. Sir Joshua Reynolds had the merit of being the proposer of it, to which Johnson acceded, and the original members were, Sir Joshua Reynolds, Dr. Johnson, Mr. Edmund Burke, Dr. Nugent, Mr. Beauclerk, Mr. Langton, Dr. Goldsmith, Mr. Chamier, and Sir John Hawkins. They met at the Turk's Head, in Gerrard Street, Soho, one evening in every week, at seven, and generally continued their conversation till a pretty late hour. This club has been gradually increased to its present number, thirty-five. After about ten years, instead of supping weekly, it was resolved to dine together once a fortnight during the meeting of Parliament. Their original tavern having been converted into a private house, they moved first to Prince's in Sackville Street, then to Le Telier's in Dover Street, and now meet at Parsloe's, St. James's Street. Between the time of its formation and the time at which this work is passing through the press (June 1792),[1] the following persons, now dead, were members of it: Mr. Dunning (afterwards Lord Ashburton), Mr. Samuel Dyer, Mr. Garrick, Dr. Shipley, Bishop of St. Asaph, Mr. Vesey, Mr. Thomas Warton, and Dr. Adam Smith. The present members are, Mr. Burke, Mr. Langton, Lord Charlemont, Sir Robert Chambers, Dr. Percy Bishop of Dromore, Dr. Barnard Bishop of Killaloe, Dr. Marlay Bishop of Clonfert, Mr. Fox, Dr. George Fordyce, Sir William Scott, Sir Joseph Banks, Sir Charles Bunbury, Mr. Windham of Norfolk, Mr. Sheridan, Mr. Gibbon, Sir William Jones, Mr. Colman, Mr. Steevens, Dr. Burney, Dr. Joseph

1 [The second edition is here spoken of.—M.]

Warton, Mr. Malone, Lord Ossory, Lord Spencer,
Lord Lucan, Lord Palmerston, Lord Eliot, Lord
Macartney, Mr. Richard Burke junior, Sir William
Hamilton, Dr. Warren, Mr. Courtenay, Dr. Hinch-
liffe Bishop of Peterborough, the Duke of Leeds,
Dr. Douglas Bishop of Salisbury, and the writer of
this account.

Sir John Hawkins [1] represents himself as a '*seceder*'
from this society, and assigns as the reason of his
'*withdrawing*' himself from it, that its late hours were
inconsistent with his domestic arrangements. In this
he is not accurate ; for the fact was that he one evening attacked Mr. Burke in so rude a manner that all
the company testified their displeasure ; and at their
next meeting his reception was such that he never
came again. [2]

He is equally inaccurate with respect to Mr. Garrick,
of whom he says, 'he trusted that the least intimation
of a desire to come among us would procure him a
ready admission, but, in this he was mistaken. Johnson consulted me upon it ; and when I could find no
objection to receiving him, exclaimed, "He will disturb us by his buffoonery"; and afterwards so managed
matters that he was never formally proposed, and, by
consequence, never admitted.' [3]

In justice both to Mr. Garrick and Dr. Johnson, I
think it necessary to rectify this mis-statement. The
truth is, that not very long after the institution of our
club, Sir Joshua Reynolds was speaking of it to

---

[1] *Life of Johnson*, p. 425.
[2] From Sir Joshua Reynolds. [The Knight having refused to pay
his portion of the reckoning for the supper, because he usually ate no
supper at home, Johnson observed, 'Sir John, sir, is a very *unclubable*
man.'—BURNEY.] [3] *Life of Johnson*, p. 425.

Garrick. 'I like it much (said he), I think I shall be of you.' When Sir Joshua mentioned this to Dr. Johnson he was much displeased with the actor's conceit. 'He'll be of us (said Johnson), how does he know we will *permit* him ? The first duke in England has no right to hold such language.' However, when Garrick was regularly proposed some time afterwards, Johnson, though he had taken a momentary offence at his arrogance, warmly and kindly supported him, and he was accordingly elected,[1] was a most agreeable member, and continued to attend our meetings to the time of his death.

Mrs. Piozzi[2] has also given a similar misrepresentation of Johnson's treatment of Garrick in this particular, as if he had used these contemptuous expressions : 'If Garrick *does* apply, I'll blackball him.   Surely, one ought to sit in a society like ours,

"Unelbow'd by a gamester, pimp, or player."'

I am happy to be enabled by such unquestionable authority as that of Sir Joshua Reynolds, as well as from my own knowledge, to vindicate at once the heart of Johnson and the social merit of Garrick.

In this year, except what he may have done in revising Shakespeare, we do not find that he laboured much in literature.   He wrote a review of Grainger's 'Sugar Cane,' a poem, in the *London Chronicle*.   He told me that Dr. Percy wrote the greatest part of this review ; but I imagine he did not recollect it distinctly, for it appears to be mostly, if not altogether,

---

1 [Mr. Garrick was elected in March 1773.—M.]
2 *Letters to and from Dr. Johnson*, vol. ii. p. 278.

his own. He also wrote in the *Critical Review* an
account of Goldsmith's excellent poem, 'The Traveller.'

The ease and independence to which he had at last
attained by royal munificence increased his natural
indolence. In his *Meditations* he thus accuses himself:
'Good Friday, April 20, 1764.—I have made no reformation ; I have lived totally useless, more sensual in
thought, and more addicted to wine and meat.'[1] And
next morning he thus feelingly complains : 'My indolence, since my last reception of the sacrament, has
sunk into grosser sluggishness, and my dissipation
spread into wilder negligence. My thoughts have
been clouded with sensuality ; and, except that from
the beginning of this year I have, in some measure,
forborne excess of strong drink, my appetites have
predominated over my reason. A kind of strange
oblivion has overspread me, so that I know not what
has become of the last year ; and perceive that incidents and intelligence pass over me without leaving
any impression.' He then solemnly says, 'This is
not the life to which heaven is promised,'[2] and he
earnestly resolves an amendment.

It was his custom to observe certain days with a
pious abstraction, viz., New Year's Day, the day of his
wife's death, Good Friday, Easter Day, and his own
birthday. He this year says : 'I have now spent fifty-
five years in resolving, having, from the earliest time
almost that I can remember, been forming schemes of
a better life. I have done nothing. The need of doing,
therefore, is pressing, since the time of doing is short.
O God, grant me to resolve aright, and to keep my

---

[1] *Prayers and Meditations*, p. 53.   [2] *Ibid.* p. 51.

resolutions, for Jesus Christ's sake. Amen.'[1] Such a
tenderness of conscience, such a fervent desire of
improvement, will rarely be found. It is surely not
decent in those who are hardened in indifference to
spiritual improvement, to treat this pious anxiety of
Johnson with contempt.

About this time he was afflicted with a very severe
return of the hypochondriac disorder which was ever
lurking about him. He was so ill as, notwithstanding
his remarkable love of company, to be entirely averse
to society—the most fatal symptom of that malady.
Dr. Adams told me that, as an old friend, he was
admitted to visit him, and that he found him in a
deplorable state, sighing, groaning, talking to himself,
and restlessly walking from room to room. He then
used this emphatical expression of the misery which
he felt : ' I would consent to have a limb amputated
to recover my spirits.'

Talking to himself was, indeed, one of his singularities ever since I knew him. I was certain that he
was frequently uttering pious ejaculations ; for fragments of the Lord's Prayer have been distinctly over-
heard.[2] His friend, Mr. Thomas Davies—of whom
Churchill says,

'That Davies hath a very pretty wife':

---

[1] *Prayers and Meditations*, p. 584.

[2] [It used to be imagined at Mr. Thrale's, when Johnson retired to a
window or corner of the room, by perceiving his lips in motion, and
hearing a murmur without audible articulation, that he was praying :
but this was not *always* the case, for I was once, perhaps unperceived
by him, writing at a table, so near the place of his retreat that I heard
him repeat some lines in an ode of Horace, over and over again, as if
by iteration, to exercise the organs of speech, and fix the ode in his
memory :

Audiet cives acuisse ferrum,
Quo graves *Persæ* melius perirent ;
Audiet pugnas . . .
                    Carm. L. 1. Od. ii. 21.

It was during the American war.—BURNEY.]

when Dr. Johnson muttered, 'Lead us not into temptation'—used with waggish and gallant humour to whisper Mrs. Davies: 'You, my dear, are the cause of this.'

He had another particularity, of which none of his friends ever ventured to ask an explanation. It appeared to me some superstitious habit, which he had contracted early, and from which he had never called upon his reason to disentangle him. This was his anxious care to go out or in at a door or passage by a certain number of steps from a certain point, or at least so as that either his right or his left foot (I am not certain which) should constantly make the first actual movement when he came close to the door or passage. Thus I conjecture: for I have, upon innumerable occasions, observed him suddenly stop, and then seem to count his steps with a deep earnestness; and when he had neglected or gone wrong in this sort of magical movement, I have seen him go back again, put himself in a proper posture to begin the ceremony, and, having gone through it, break from his abstraction, walk briskly on, and join his companion. A strange instance of something of this nature, even when on horseback, happened when he was in the isle of Skye.[1] Sir Joshua Reynolds has observed him to go a good way about rather than cross a particular alley in Leicester-fields; but this Sir Joshua imputed to his having had some disagreeable recollection associated with it.

That the most minute singularities which belonged to him, and made very observable parts of his appear-

---

[1] *Journal of a Tour to the Hebrides*, 3rd edition, p. 315.

ance and manner, may not be omitted, it is requisite to mention, that while talking, or even musing as he sat in his chair, he commonly held his head to one side towards his right shoulder, and shook it in a tremulous manner, moving his body backwards and forwards, and rubbing his left knee in the same direction with the palm of his hand. In the intervals of articulating he made various sounds with his mouth, sometimes as if ruminating, or what is called chewing the cud, sometimes giving half a whistle, sometimes making his tongue play backwards from the roof of his mouth, as if clucking like a hen, and sometimes protruding it against his upper gums in front, as if pronouncing quickly under his breath, *too, too, too* : all this accompanied sometimes with a thoughtful look, but more frequently with a smile. Generally when he had concluded a period, in the course of a dispute, by which time he was a good deal exhausted by violence and vociferation, he used to blow out his breath like a whale. This I suppose was a relief to his lungs ; and seemed in him to be a contemptuous mode of expression, as if he had made the arguments of his opponent fly like chaff before the wind.

I am fully aware how very obvious an occasion I here give for the sneering jocularity of such as have no relish of an exact likeness, which, to render complete, he who draws it must not disdain the slightest strokes. But if witlings should be inclined to attack this account, let them have the candour to quote what I have offered in my defence.

He was for some time in the summer at Easton Maudit, Northamptonshire, on a visit to the Reverend Dr. Percy, now Bishop of Dromore. Whatever dis-

satisfaction he felt at what he considered as a slow
progress in intellectual improvement, we find that his
heart was tender, and his affections warm, as appears
from the following very kind letter :

TO JOSHUA REYNOLDS, ESQ., IN LEICESTER-FIELDS,
LONDON

'DEAR SIR,—I did not hear of your sickness till I heard
likewise of your recovery, and therefore escape that part of
your pain, which every man must feel, to whom you are
known as you are known to me.

'Having had no particular account of your disorder, I know
not in what state it has left you. If the amusement of my
company can exhilarate the languor of a slow recovery, I will
not delay a day to come to you ; for I know not how I can so
effectually promote my own pleasure as by pleasing you, or
my own interest as by preserving you, in whom, if I should
lose you, I should lose almost the only man whom I call a
friend.

'Pray let me hear of you from yourself, or from dear Miss
Reynolds.[1] Make my compliments to Mr. Mudge.—I am,
dear sir, your most affectionate and most humble servant,

'SAM. JOHNSON.

'At the Rev. Mr. Percy's at Easton-
Maudit, Northamptonshire (by
Castle Ashby), *Aug.* 19, 1764.'

Early in the year 1765 he paid a short visit to the
University of Cambridge, with his friend Mr. Beauclerk. There is a lively picturesque account of his
behaviour on this visit, in the *Gentleman's Magazine*
for March 1785, being an extract of a letter from the
late Dr. John Sharp. The two following sentences are

---

1 Sir Joshua's sister, for whom Johnson had a particular affection,
and to whom he wrote many letters, which I have seen, and which I
am sorry her too nice delicacy will not permit to be published.

very characteristical : 'He drank his large potations of tea with me, interrupted by many an indignant contradiction and many a noble sentiment.' 'Several persons got into his company the last evening at Trinity, where, about twelve, he began to be very great; stripped poor Mrs. Macaulay to the very skin, then gave her for his toast, and drank her in two bumpers.'

The strictness of his self-examination, and scrupulous Christian humility, appear in his pious meditation on Easter Day this year : 'I purpose again to partake of the blessed sacrament; yet when I considered how vainly I have hitherto resolved, at this annual commemoration of my Saviour's death, to regulate my life by his laws, I am almost afraid to renew my resolutions.'

The concluding words are very remarkable, and show that he laboured under a severe depression of spirits. 'Since the last Easter I have reformed no evil habit; my time has been unprofitably spent, and seems as a dream that has left nothing behind. *My memory grows confused, and I know not how the days pass over me.* Good Lord, deliver me !'[1]

No man was more gratefully sensible of any kindness done to him than Johnson. There is a little circumstance in his diary this year which shows him in a very amiable light :

'July 2. I paid Mr. Simpson ten guineas, which he had formerly lent me in my necessity, and for which Tetty expressed her gratitude.'
'July 8. I lent Mr. Simpson ten guineas more.'

Prayers and Meditations, p. 61.

Here he had a pleasing opportunity of doing the same kindness to an old friend which he had formerly received from him. Indeed, his liberality as to money was very remarkable. The next article in his diary is:

'July 16th. I received £75. Lent Mr. Davies £25.'

Trinity College, Dublin, at this time surprised Johnson with a spontaneous compliment of the highest academical honours by creating him Doctor of Laws. The diploma, which is in my possession, is as follows:

'Omnibus, ad quos præsentes literæ pervenerint, salutem. Nos, Præpositus et Socii Seniores Collegii sacrosanctæ et individuæ Trinitatis Reginæ Elizabethæ juxta Dublin, testamur, Samueli Johnson, Armigero, ob egregiam scriptorum elegantiam et utilitatem, gratiam concessam fuisse pro gradu Doctoratûs in utroque Jure, octavo die Julii, Anno Domini millesimo septingentesimo sexagesimo-quinto. In cujus rei testimonium singulorum manus et sigillum quo in hisce utimur apposuimus, vicesimo tertio die Julii, Anno Domini millesimo septingentesimo sexagesimo-quinto.

'Gul. Clement.	Fran. Andrews.	R. Murray.
Tho. Wilson.	Præp⁹.	Rob^tus Law.
Tho. Leland.		Mich. Kearney.'

This unsolicited mark of distinction, conferred on so great a literary character, did much honour to the judgment and liberal spirit of that learned body. Johnson acknowledged the favour in a letter to Dr. Leland, one of their number; but I have not been able to obtain a copy of it.[1]

---

[1] [Since the publication of the edition in 1804 a copy of this letter has been obligingly communicated to me by John Leland, Esq., son to the learned historian to whom it is addressed:

TO THE REV. DR. LELAND

'Sir,—Among the names subscribed to the degree which I have had the honour of receiving from the University of Dublin, I find none of

He appears this year to have been seized with a temporary fit of ambition, for he had thoughts both of studying law and of engaging in politics.   His 'Prayer before the Study of Law' is truly admirable :

'*Sept.* 26, 1765.

'Almighty God, the giver of wisdom, without whose help resolutions are vain, without whose blessing study is ineffectual; enable me, if it be Thy will, to attain such knowledge as may qualify me to direct the doubtful and instruct the ignorant; to prevent wrongs and terminate contentions; and grant that I may use that knowledge which I shall attain to Thy glory and my own salvation, for Jesus Christ's sake. Amen.'[1]

His prayer in the view of becoming a politician is entitled, 'Engaging in Politics with H——n,'—no doubt his friend the Right Honourable William Gerard Hamilton, for whom, during a long acquaintance, he had a great esteem, and to whose conversation he once paid this high compliment: 'I am very unwilling to be left alone, sir, and therefore I go with my company down the first pair of stairs, in some hopes that they may, perhaps, return again; I go

---

which I have any personal knowledge but those of Dr. Andrews and yourself.

'Men can be estimated by those who know them not, only as they are represented by those who know them; and therefore I flatter myself that I owe much of the pleasure which this distinction gives me to your concurrence with Dr. Andrews in recommending me to the learned society.

'Having desired the Provost to return my general thanks to the University, I beg that you, sir, will accept my particular and immediate acknowledgments.—I am, sir, your most obedient and most humble servant,   SAM. JOHNSON.

'*Johnson's Court, Fleet Street,*
    London, Oct. 17, 1765.'

I have not been able to recover the letter which Johnson wrote to Dr. Andrews on this occasion.—M.]

[1] *Prayers and Meditations*, p. 66.

with you, sir, as far as the street door.' In what
particular department he intended to engage does
not appear, nor can Mr. Hamilton explain. His
prayer is in general terms : 'Enlighten my understanding with the knowledge of right, and govern my
will by thy laws, that no deceit may mislead me nor
temptation corrupt me ; that I may always endeavour
to do good, and hinder evil.' There is nothing upon
the subject in his diary.

This year was distinguished by his being introduced
into the family of Mr. Thrale, one of the most eminent
brewers in England, and member of Parliament for
the borough of Southwark. Foreigners are not a little
amazed when they hear of brewers, distillers, and men
in similar departments of trade, held forth as persons
of considerable consequence. In this great commer-
cial country it is natural that a situation which produces much wealth should be considered as very
respectable ; and, no doubt, honest industry is entitled
to esteem. But perhaps the too rapid advances of
men of low extraction tends to lessen the value of
that distinction by birth and gentility, which has ever
been found beneficial to the grand scheme of subordination. Johnson used to give this account of the rise
of Mr. Thrale's father :

'He worked at six shillings a week for twenty years in the
great brewery which afterwards was his own. The proprietor
of it [2] had an only daughter, who was married to a nobleman.

---

1 *Prayers and Meditations*, p. 67.
2 [The predecessor of old Thrale was Edmund Halsey, Esq. ; the
nobleman who married his daughter was Lord Cobham, great-uncle of
the Marquis of Buckingham. But I believe Dr. Johnson was mistaken
in assigning so very low an origin to Mr. Thrale. The Clerk of St.
Alban's, a very aged man, told me that he (the elder Thrale) married a

It was not fit that a peer should continue the business. On the old man's death, therefore, the brewery was to be sold. To find a purchaser for so large a property was a difficult matter; and, after some time, it was suggested that it would be advisable to treat with Thrale, a sensible, active, honest man, who had been employed in the house, and to transfer the whole to him for £30,000 security being taken upon the property. This was accordingly settled. In eleven years Thrale paid the purchase-money. He acquired a large fortune, and lived to be a member of Parliament for Southwark.[1] But what was most remarkable was the liberality with which he used his riches. He gave his son and daughters the best education. The esteem which his good conduct procured him from the nobleman who had married his master's daughter made him be treated with much affection; and his son, both at school and at the University of Oxford, associated with young men of the first rank. His allowance from his father, after he left college, was splendid,—not less than a thousand a year. This, in a man who had risen as old Thrale did, was a very extraordinary instance of generosity. He used to say, "If this young dog does not find so much after I am gone as he expects, let him remember that he has had a great deal in my own time."'

The son, though in affluent circumstances, had good sense enough to carry on his father's trade, which was of such extent that I remember he once told me he would not quit it for an annuity of ten thousand a year, 'Not (said he) that I get ten thousand a year by it, but it is an estate to a family.' Having left daughters

---

sister of Mr. Halsey. It is at least certain that the family of Thrale was of some consideration in that town : in the abbey church is a handsome monument to the memory of Mr. John Thrale, late of London, merchant, who died in 1704, aged 54, Margaret his wife, and three of their children, who died young between the years 1676 and 1690. The arms upon this monument are, paly of eight, gules and or, impaling, ermine, on a chief indented vert, three wolves' (or gryphons') heads, or, couped at the neck:—Crest on a ducal coronet, a tree, vert.—J. BLAKEWAY.]

[1] [In 1733 he served the office of High Sheriff for Surrey, and died April 9, 1758.—A. C.]

only, the property was sold for the immense sum of £135,000, a magnificent proof of what may be done by fair trade in a long period of time.

There may be some who think that a new system of gentility[1] might be established, upon principles totally different from what have hitherto prevailed. Our present heraldry, it may be said, is suited to the barbarous times in which it had its origin. It is chiefly founded upon ferocious merit, upon military excellence. Why, in civilised times, we may be asked, should there not be rank and honours, upon principles which, independent of long custom, are certainly not less worthy, and which, when once allowed to be connected with elevation and precedency, would obtain the same dignity in our imagination? Why should not the knowledge, the skill, the expertness, the assiduity, and the spirited hazards, of trade and commerce, when crowned with success, be entitled to give those flattering distinctions by which mankind are so universally captivated?

Such are the specious, but false, arguments for a proposition which always will find numerous advocates, in a nation where men are every day starting up from obscurity to wealth. To refute them is needless. The general sense of mankind cries out, with irre-

---

[1] Mrs. Burney informs me that she heard Dr. Johnson say, 'An English merchant is a new species of gentleman.' He, perhaps, had in his mind the following ingenious passage in *The Conscious Lovers*, Act iv. Scene 2, where Mr. Sealand thus addresses Sir John Bevil: 'Give me leave to say that we merchants are a species of gentry that have grown into the world this last century, and are as honourable, and almost as useful, as you landed folks, that have always thought yourselves so much above us; for your trading, forsooth, is extended no further than a load of hay or a fat ox. You are pleasant people indeed! because you are generally bred up to be lazy, therefore, I warrant you, industry is dishonourable.' *The Conscious Lovers* is by Steele.

sistible force, ' *Un gentilhomme est toujours gentil-homme.*'

Mr. Thrale had married Miss Hesther Lynch Salus-bury, of good Welsh extraction, a lady of lively talents, improved by education. That Johnson's introduction into Mr. Thrale's family, which contributed so much to the happiness of his life, was owing to her desire for his conversation, is a very probable and the general supposition : but it is not the truth. Mr. Murphy, who was intimate with Mr. Thrale, having spoken very highly of Dr. Johnson, he was requested to make them acquainted. This being mentioned to Johnson, he accepted an invitation to dinner at Thrale's, and was so much pleased with his reception, both by Mr. and Mrs. Thrale, and they so much pleased with him, that his invitations to their house were more and more frequent, till at last he became one of the family, and an apartment was appropriated to him, both in their house at Southwark and in their villa at Streatham.

Johnson had a very sincere esteem for Mr. Thrale, as a man of excellent principles, a good scholar, well skilled in trade, of a sound understanding, and of manners such as presented the character of a plain independent English 'Squire. As this family will fre-quently be mentioned in the course of the following pages, and as a false notion has prevailed that Mr. Thrale was inferior, and in some degree insignificant, compared with Mrs. Thrale, it may be proper to give a true state of the case from the authority of Johnson himself in his own words.

' I know no man (said he) who is more master of his wife and family than Thrale. If he but holds up a finger he is obeyed. It is a great mistake to suppose that she is above him in literary attainments. She is more flippant; but he has ten times her learning: he is a regular scholar; but her learning is that of a school-boy in one of the lower forms.' My readers may naturally wish for some representation of the figures of this couple. Mr. Thrale was tall, well-proportioned, and stately. As for *Madam*, or *my Mistress*, by which epithets Johnson used to mention Mrs. Thrale, she was short, plump, and brisk. She has herself given us a lively view of the idea which Johnson had of her person, on her appearing before him in a dark-coloured gown: ' You little creatures should never wear those sort of clothes, however; they are unsuitable in every way. What! have not all insects gay colours?'[1] Mr. Thrale gave his wife a liberal indulgence, both in the choice of their company, and in the mode of entertaining them. He understood and valued Johnson, without remission, from their first acquaintance to the day of his death. Mrs. Thrale was enchanted with Johnson's conversation for its own sake, and had also a very allowable vanity in appearing to be honoured with the attention of so celebrated a man.

Nothing could be more fortunate for Johnson than this connection. He had at Mr. Thrale's all the comforts, and even luxuries, of life; his melancholy was diverted, and his irregular habits lessened by association with an agreeable and well-ordered family. He was treated with the utmost respect, and even affection. The vivacity of Mrs. Thrale's literary talk roused him to cheerfulness and exertion, even when

---

[1] Mrs. Piozzi's *Anecdotes*, p. 279.

they were alone. But this was not often the case; for he found here a constant succession of what gave him the highest enjoyment, the society of the learned, the witty, and the eminent in every way, who were assembled in numerous companies, called forth his wonderful powers, and gratified him with admiration, to which no man could be insensible.

In the October of this year[1] he at length gave to the world his edition of Shakespeare, which, if it had no other merit but that of producing his Preface, in which the excellencies and defects of that immortal bard are displayed with a masterly hand, the nation would have had no reason to complain. A blind, indiscriminate admiration of Shakespeare had exposed the British nation to the ridicule of foreigners. Johnson, by candidly admitting the faults of his poet, had the more credit in bestowing on him deserved and indisputable praise ; and doubtless none of all his panegyrists have done him half so much honour. Their praise was like that of a counsel, upon his own side of the cause ; Johnson's was like the grave, well-considered, and impartial opinion of the judge, which falls from his lips with weight, and is received with reverence. What he did as a commentator has no

---

[1] [From a letter written by Dr. Johnson to Dr. Joseph Warton, the day after the publication of his Shakespeare, Oct. 9, 1765 (see Wool's *Memoirs of Dr. Warton*, 4to, 1806), it appears that Johnson spent some time with that gentleman at Winchester in this year. In a letter written by Dr. Warton to Mr. Thomas Warton, not long afterwards (January 28, 1766), is a paragraph which may throw some light on various passages in Dr. Warton's edition of Pope, relative to Johnson : —'I only dined with Johnson, who seemed cold and indifferent, and scarce said anything to me : perhaps he has heard what I said of his Shakespeare, or rather was offended at what I wrote to him :—as he pleases.' The letter here alluded to, it is believed, has not been preserved : at least it does not appear in the collection above referred to. —M.]

small share of merit, though his researches were not
so ample, and his investigations so acute as they might
have been, which we now certainly know from the
labours of other able and ingenious critics who have
followed him. He has enriched his edition with a
concise account of each play, and of its characteristic
excellence. Many of his notes have illustrated obscurities in the text, and placed passages eminent for
beauty in a more conspicuous light; and he has in
general exhibited such a mode of annotation as may
be beneficial to all subsequent editors.

His Shakespeare was virulently attacked by Mr.
William Kenrick, who obtained the degree of LL.D.
from a Scotch University, and wrote for the booksellers in a great variety of branches. Though he
certainly was not without considerable merit, he wrote
with so little regard to decency, and principles, and
decorum, and in so hasty a manner, that his reputation was neither extensive nor lasting. I remember
one evening, when some of his works were mentioned,
Dr. Goldsmith said he had never heard of them; upon
which Dr. Johnson observed, 'Sir, he is one of the
many who have made themselves *public*, without
making themselves *known*.'

A young student of Oxford, of the name of Barclay,
wrote an answer to Kenrick's review of Johnson's
Shakespeare. Johnson was at first angry that Kenrick's attack should have the credit of an answer.
But afterwards, considering the young man's good intention, he kindly noticed him, and probably would
have done more had not the young man died.

In his Preface to Shakespeare, Johnson treated
Voltaire very contemptuously, observing, upon some

of his remarks, 'These are the petty cavils of petty minds.' Voltaire, in revenge, made an attack upon Johnson in one of his numerous literary sallies, which I remember to have read; but there being no general index to his voluminous works, I have searched in vain, and therefore cannot quote it.[1]

Voltaire was an antagonist with whom I thought Johnson should not disdain to contend. I pressed him to answer. He said he perhaps might; but he never did.

Mr. Burney having occasion to write to Johnson for some receipts for subscriptions to his Shakespeare, which Johnson had omitted to deliver when the money was paid, he availed himself of that opportunity of thanking Johnson for the great pleasure which he had received from the perusal of his Preface to Shakespeare; which, although it excited much clamour against him at first, is now justly ranked among the most excellent of his writings. To this letter Johnson returned the following answer:

TO CHARLES BURNEY, ESQ., IN POLAND STREET

'Sir,—I am sorry that your kindness to me has brought upon you so much trouble, though you have taken care to abate that sorrow by the pleasure which I receive from your approbation. I defend my criticism in the same manner with you. We must confess the faults of our favourite, to gain credit to our praise of his excellencies. He that claims, either

---

[1] [See *Dictionnaire Philosophique* under title *Art Dramatique du Théâtre Anglais*: 'J'ai jeté les yeux sur une édition de Shakespeare donnée par le Sieur Johnson. . . . Je ne veux point soupçonner le Sieur Johnson d'être un mauvais plaisant, et d'aimer trop le vin, mais je trouve un peu extraordinaire qu'il compte la bouffonnerie et l'ivrognerie parmi les beautés du théâtre tragique.'—A. B.]

in himself or for another, the honours of perfection, will surely injure the reputation which he designs to assist.

'Be pleased to make my compliments to your family.—I am, sir, your most obliged and most humble servant,

'SAM. JOHNSON.

'*Oct.* 16, 1765.'

From one of his journals I transcribe what follows :—

'At church, Oct.—65.

'To avoid all singularity; *Bonaventura*.[1]

'To come in before service, and compose my mind by meditation, or by reading some portions of Scripture.   *Tetty*.

'If I can hear the sermon, to attend it, unless attention be more troublesome than useful.

'To consider the act of prayer as a reposal of myself upon God, and a resignation of all into his holy hand.'

In 1764 and 1765 it should seem that Dr. Johnson was so busily employed with his edition of Shakespeare as to have had little leisure for any other literary exertion, or, indeed, even for private correspondence. He did not favour me with a single letter for more than two years, for which it will appear that he afterward apologised.

He was, however, at all times ready to give assistance to his friends, and others, in revising their works, and in writing for them, or greatly improving, their Dedications. In that courtly species of composition no man excelled Dr. Johnson. Though the loftiness of his mind prevented him from ever dedicating in his own person, he wrote a very great number of Dedications for others. Some of these, the persons who

---

[1] He was probably proposing to himself the model of this excellent person, who for his piety was named 'The Seraphic Doctor.'

were favoured with them are unwilling should be
mentioned, from a too anxious apprehension, as I
think, that they might be suspected of having received
larger assistance; and some, after all the diligence I
have bestowed, have escaped my inquiries. He told
me, a great many years ago, 'he believed he had
dedicated to all the Royal Family round'; and it was
indifferent to him what was the subject of the work
dedicated, provided it were innocent. He once dedicated some Music for the German Flute to Edward,
Duke of York. In writing Dedications for others, he
considered himself as by no means speaking his own
sentiments.

Notwithstanding his long silence, I never omitted
to write to him, when I had anything worthy of com-
municating. I generally kept copies of my letters to
him, that I might have a full view of our correspondence, and never be at a loss to understand any reference in his letters. He kept the greater part of mine
very carefully; and a short time before his death was
attentive enough to seal them up in bundles, and order
them to be delivered to me, which was accordingly
done. Amongst them I found one, of which I had
not made a copy, and which I own I read with pleasure
at the distance of almost twenty years. It is dated
November 1765, at the palace of Pascal de Paoli, in
Corte, the capital of Corsica, and is full of generous
enthusiasm. After giving a sketch of what I had
seen and heard in that island, it proceeded thus: 'I
dare to call this a spirited tour. I dare to challenge
your approbation.'

This letter produced the following answer, which I
found on my arrival at Paris:

À MR. MR. BOSWELL, CHEZ MR. WATERS, BANQUIER

À PARIS

'DEAR SIR,—Apologies are seldom of any use. We will delay till your arrival the reasons, good or bad, which have made me such a sparing and ungrateful correspondent. Be assured, for the present, that nothing has lessened either the esteem or love with which I dismissed you at Harwich. Both have been increased by all that I have been told of you by yourself or others; and when you return you will return to an unaltered, and, I hope, unalterable friend.

'All that you have to fear from me is the vexation of disappointing me. No man loves to frustrate expectations which have been formed in his favour; and the pleasure which I promise myself from your journals and remarks is so great, that perhaps no degree of attention or discernment will be sufficient to afford it.

'Come home, however, and take your chance. I long to see you, and to hear you; and hope that we shall not be so long separated again. Come home, and expect such welcome as is due to him whom a wise and noble curiosity has led where perhaps no native of this country ever was before.

'I have no news to tell you that can deserve your notice, nor would I willingly lessen the pleasure that any novelty may give you at your return. I am afraid we shall find it difficult to keep among us a mind which has been so long feasted with variety. But let us try what esteem and kindness can effect.

'As your father's liberality has indulged you with so long a ramble, I doubt not but you will think his sickness, or even his desire to see you, a sufficient reason for hastening your return. The longer we live, and the more we think, the higher value we learn to put on the friendship and tenderness of parents and of friends. Parents we can have but once: and he promises himself too much who enters life with the expectation of finding many friends. Upon some motive, I hope that you will be here soon; and am willing to think that it will be an inducement to your return, that it is sincerely desired by, dear sir, your affectionate humble servant,

'SAM. JOHNSON.

Johnson's Court, Fleet Street,
January 14, 1766.'

I returned to London in February, and found Dr. Johnson in a good house in Johnson's Court, Fleet Street, in which he had accommodated Miss Williams with an apartment on the ground-floor, while Mr. Levet occupied his post in the garret: his faithful Francis was still attending upon him. He received me with much kindness. The fragments of our first conversation, which I have preserved, are these: I told him that Voltaire, in a conversation with me, had distinguished Pope and Dryden thus:—'Pope drives a handsome chariot, with a couple of neat trim nags; Dryden a coach, and six stately horses!' JOHNSON: 'Why, sir, the truth is, they both drive coaches and six; but Dryden's horses are either galloping or stumbling: Pope's go at a steady, even trot.'[1] He said of Goldsmith's 'Traveller,' which had been published in my absence, 'There has not been so fine a poem since Pope's time.'

And here it is proper to settle, with authentic precision, what has long floated in public report, as to Johnson's being himself the author of a considerable part of that poem. Much, no doubt, both of the

---

[1] It is remarkable that Mr. Gray has employed somewhat the same image to characterise Dryden. He, indeed, furnishes his car with but two horses; but they are of 'ethereal race':

'Behold where Dryden's less presumptuous car,
Wide o'er the fields of glory bear
Two coursers of ethereal race,
With necks in thunder clothed, and long resounding pace.'
Ode on the Progress of Poesy.

sentiments and expression, were derived from conversation with him ; and it was certainly submitted to his
friendly revision : but in the year 1783, he, at my
request, marked with a pencil the lines which he had
furnished, which are only line 420th,

> 'To stop too fearful, and too faint to go';

and the concluding ten lines, except the last couplet
but one, which I distinguish by the Italic character :

> 'How small of all that human hearts endure,
> That part which kings or laws can cause or cure.
> Still to ourselves in every place consign'd,
> Our own felicity we make or find ;
> With secret course, which no loud storms annoy,
> Glides the smooth current of domestic joy :
> *The lifted axe, the agonising wheel,*
> *Luke's iron crown, and Damien's bed of steel,*
> To men remote from power, but rarely known,
> Leave reason, faith, and conscience all our own.'

He added, 'These are all of which I can be sure.'
They bear a small proportion to the whole, which
consists of four hundred and thirty-eight verses.
Goldsmith, in the couplet which he inserted, mentions
Luke as a person well known, and superficial readers
have passed it over quite smoothly; while those of
more attention have been as much perplexed by *Luke*
as by *Lydiat*, in *The Vanity of Human Wishes.* The
truth is, that Goldsmith himself was in a mistake. In
the *Respublica Hungarica* there is an account of a
desperate rebellion in the year 1514, headed by two
brothers of the name of *Zeck*,[1] George and Luke.

---

1 [Their real name was Dosa. Zeck signifies that they were Zecklers
or Szeklers, one of the native races of Transylvania.—A. B.]

When it was quelled, *George*, not *Luke*, was punished by his head being encircled with a red-hot iron crown: '*corona candescente ferrca coronatur.*' The same severity of torture was exercised on the Earl of Athol, one of the murderers of King James I. of Scotland.

Dr. Johnson at the same time favoured me by marking the lines which he furnished to Goldsmith's 'Deserted Village,' which are only the last four :

> 'That trade's proud empire hastes to swift decay,
> As ocean sweeps the labour'd mole away :
> While self-dependent power can time defy,
> As rocks resist the billows and the sky.'

Talking of education, 'People have now-a-days (said he) got a strange opinion that everything should be taught by lectures. Now, I cannot see that lectures can do so much good as reading the books from which the lectures are taken. I know nothing that can be best taught by lectures, except where experiments are to be shown. You may teach chemistry by lectures. —You might teach making of shoes by lectures !' [1]

At night I supped with him at the Mitre tavern, that we might renew our social intimacy at the original place of meeting. But there was now a considerable difference in his way of living. Having had an illness, in which he was advised to leave off wine, he had, from that period, continued to abstain from it, and drank only water, or lemonade.

I told him that a foreign friend of his, whom I had met with abroad, was so wretchedly perverted to infidelity that he treated the hopes of immortality with brutal levity, and said, 'As man dies like a dog,

---

[1] [Lecturers are very fond of this quotation—but they go on lecturing all the same.—A. B.]

let him lie like a dog.' JOHNSON : '*If* he dies like a dog, *let* him lie like a dog.' I added, that this man said to me, 'I hate mankind, for I think myself one of the best of them, and I know how bad I am.' JOHNSON : 'Sir, he must be very singular in his opinion, if he thinks himself one of the best of men ; for none of his friends think him so.' He said, 'No honest man could be a Deist ; for no man could be so after a fair examination of the proofs of Christianity.' I named Hume. JOHNSON : 'No, sir ; Hume owned to a clergyman in the bishopric of Durham that he had never read the New Testament with attention.' I mentioned Hume's notion, that all who are happy are equally happy ; a little miss with a new gown at a dancing-school ball, a general at the head of a victorious army, and an orator, after having made an eloquent speech in a great assembly. JOHNSON : 'Sir, that all who are happy are equally happy is not true. A peasant and a philosopher may be equally *satisfied*, but not equally *happy*. Happiness consists in the multiplicity of agreeable consciousness. A peasant has not capacity for having equal happiness with a philosopher.' I remember this very question very happily illustrated in opposition to Hume, by the Reverend Mr. Robert Brown, at Utrecht. 'A small drinking-glass and a large one (said he) may be equally full ; but the large one holds more than the small.'[1]

Dr. Johnson was very kind this evening, and said to me, 'You have now lived five-and-twenty years,

---

[1] [Bishop Hall, in discussing this subject, has the same image : 'Yet so conceive of these heavenly degrees that the least is glorious. *So do these vessels differ that all are full.'—Epistles*, Dec. iii. cp. 6. 'Of the different degrees of heavenly glory,' etc.—M.]

and you have employed them well.' 'Alas, sir (said I), I fear not. Do I know history? Do I know mathematics? Do I know law?' JOHNSON: 'Why, sir, though you may know no science so well as to be able to teach it, and no profession so well as to be able to follow it, your general mass of knowledge of books and men renders you very capable to make yourself master of any science or fit yourself for any profession.' I mentioned that a gay friend had advised me against being a lawyer, because I should be excelled by plodding blockheads. JOHNSON: 'Why, sir, in the formulary and statutory part of law a plodding blockhead may excel; but in the ingenious and rational part of it a plodding blockhead can never excel.'

I talked of the mode adopted by some to rise in the world, by courting great men, and asked him whether he had ever submitted to it. JOHNSON: 'Why, sir, I never was near enough to great men to court them. You may be prudently attached to great men, and yet independent. You are not to do what you think wrong; and, sir, you are to calculate, and not pay too dear for what you get. You must not give a shilling's worth of court for sixpence worth of good. But if you can get a shilling's worth of good for sixpence worth of court, you are a fool if you do not pay court.'

He said, 'If convents should be allowed at all, they should only be retreats for persons unable to serve the public, or who have served it. It is our first duty to serve society; and, after we have done that, we may attend wholly to the salvation of our own souls. A youthful passion for abstracted devotion should not be encouraged.'

I introduced the subject of second-sight, and other mysterious manifestations, the fulfilment of which, I suggested, might happen by chance. JOHNSON: 'Yes, sir, but they have happened so often that mankind have agreed to think them not fortuitous.'

I talked to him a great deal of what I had seen in Corsica, and of my intention to publish an account of it. He encouraged me by saying, 'You cannot go to the bottom of the subject; but all that you tell us will be new to us. Give us as many anecdotes as you can.'

Our next meeting at the Mitre was on Saturday the 15th of February, when I presented to him my old and most intimate friend the Reverend Mr. Temple, then of Cambridge. I having mentioned that I had passed some time with Rousseau in his wild retreat, and having quoted some remark made by Mr. Wilkes, with whom I had spent many pleasant hours in Italy, Johnson said (sarcastically), 'It seems, sir, you have kept very good company abroad, Rousseau and Wilkes!' Thinking it enough to defend one at a time, I said nothing as to my gay friend, but answered with a smile, 'My dear sir, you don't call Rousseau bad company. Do you really think *him* a bad man?' JOHNSON: 'Sir, if you are talking jestingly of this, I don't talk with you. If you mean to be serious, I think him one of the worst of men; a rascal, who ought to be hunted out of society, as he has been. Three or four nations have expelled him; and it is a shame that he is protected in this country.' BOSWELL: 'I don't deny, sir, but that his novel may, perhaps, do harm; but I cannot think his intention was bad.' JOHNSON: 'Sir, that will not do. We cannot prove any man's intention to be bad. You may shoot a man through the head and say you intended to miss him; but the judge will order you to be hanged. An alleged want of intention, when evil is committed, will not be allowed in a court of justice. Rousseau, sir, is a very bad man. I would sooner sign a sentence for his transportation than that of any felon who has gone from the Old Bailey these many years. Yes, I should like to have him work in the plantations.' BOSWELL: 'Sir, do you think him as bad a man as Voltaire?' JOHNSON: 'Why, sir, it is difficult to settle the proportion of iniquity between them.'

This violence seemed very strange to me, who had read many of Rousseau's animated writings with great pleasure, and even edification; had been much pleased with his society, and was just come from the Continent, where he was very generally admired. Nor can I yet allow that he deserves the very severe censure which Johnson pronounced upon him. His absurd preference of savage to civilised life, and other singularities, are proofs rather of a defect in his understanding than of any depravity in his heart. And notwithstanding the unfavourable opinion which many worthy men have expressed of his *Profession de Foi du Vicaire Savoyard*, I cannot help admiring it as the performance of a man full of sincere reverential submission to Divine Mystery, though beset with perplexing doubts: a state of mind to be viewed with pity rather than with anger.

On his favourite subject of subordination, Johnson said, 'So far is it from being true that men are naturally equal, that no two people can be half an hour together but one shall acquire an evident superiority over the other.'

I mentioned the advice given us by philosophers, to console ourselves, when distressed or embarrassed, by thinking of those who are in a worse situation than ourselves. This, I observed, could not apply to all, for there must be some who have nobody worse than they are. JOHNSON: 'Why, to be sure, sir, there are; but they don't know it. There is no being so poor and so contemptible, who does not think there is somebody still poorer and still more contemptible.'

As my stay in London at this time was very short, I had not many opportunities of being with Dr. Johnson; but I felt my veneration for him in no degree lessened by my having seen *multorum hominum mores et urbes*. On the contrary, by having it in my power to compare him with many of the most celebrated persons of other countries, my admiration of his extraordinary mind was increased and confirmed.

The roughness, indeed, which sometimes appeared in his manners was more striking to me now, from my having been accustomed to the studied smooth complying habits of the Continent; and I clearly recognised in him, not without respect for his honest conscientious zeal, the same indignant and sarcastical mode of treating every attempt to unhinge or weaken good principles.

One evening, when a young gentleman teased him with an account of the infidelity of his servant, who, he said, would not believe the Scriptures, because he could not read them in the original tongues, and be sure that they were not invented:—'Why, foolish fellow (said Johnson), has he any better authority for almost everything that he believes?' BOSWELL: 'Then the vulgar, sir, never can know they are right, but must submit themselves to the learned.' JOHNSON: 'To be sure, sir. The vulgar are the children of the State, and must be taught like children.' BOSWELL: 'Then, sir, a poor Turk must be a Mahometan, just as a poor Englishman must be a Christian?' JOHNSON: 'Why, yes, sir; and what then? This now is such stuff as I used to talk to my mother, when I first began to think myself a clever fellow; and she ought to have whipped me for it.'

Another evening Dr. Goldsmith and I called on him, with the hope of prevailing on him to sup with us at the Mitre. We found him indisposed, and resolved not to go abroad. 'Come, then (said Goldsmith), we will not go to the Mitre to-night, since we cannot have the big man with us.' Johnson then called for a bottle of port, of which Goldsmith and I partook, while our friend, now a water-drinker, sat by us. GOLDSMITH: 'I think, Mr. Johnson, you don't go near the theatres now. You give yourself no more concern about a new play than if you had never had anything to do with the stage.' JOHNSON: 'Why, sir, our tastes greatly alter. The lad does not care for the child's rattle, and the old man does not care for the young man's whore.' GOLDSMITH: 'Nay, sir; but your Muse was not a whore.' JOHNSON: 'Sir, I do not think she was. But as we advance in the journey of life we drop some of the things which have pleased us; whether it be that we are fatigued, and don't choose to carry so many things any farther, or that we find other things which we like better.' BOSWELL: 'But, sir, why don't you give us something in some other way?' GOLDSMITH: 'Ay, sir, we have a claim upon you.' JOHNSON: 'No, sir, I am not

obliged to do any more. No man is obliged to do as
much as he can do. A man is to have part of his
life to himself. If a soldier has fought a good many
campaigns, he is not to be blamed if he retires to ease
and tranquillity. A physician, who has practised long
in a great city, may be excused if he retires to a small
town and takes less practice. Now, sir, the good I
can do by my conversation bears the same proportion
to the good I can do by my writings that the practice
of a physician, retired to a small town, does to his
practice in a great city.' BOSWELL: 'But I wonder,
sir, you have not more pleasure in writing than in not
writing.' JOHNSON: 'Sir, you *may* wonder.'

He talked of making verses, and observed, 'The
great difficulty is, to know when you have made good
ones. When composing, I have generally had them
in my mind, perhaps fifty at a time, walking up and
down in my room; and then I have written them
down, and often, from laziness, have written only half
lines. I have written a hundred lines in a day. I
remember I wrote a hundred lines of "The Vanity of
Human Wishes" in a day. Doctor (turning to Goldsmith), I am not quite idle; I made one line t'other
day; but I made no more.' GOLDSMITH: 'Let us
hear it; we'll put a bad one to it.' JOHNSON: 'No,
sir; I have forgot it.'

Such specimens of the easy and playful conversation
of the great Dr. Samuel Johnson are, I think, to be
prized, as exhibiting the little varieties of a mind so
enlarged and so powerful when objects of consequence
required its exertions, and as giving us a minute
knowledge of his character and modes of thinking.

TO BENNET LANGTON, ESQ., AT LANGTON, NEAR SPILSBY,
LINCOLNSHIRE

'DEAR SIR,—What your friends have done, that from your
departure till now nothing has been heard of you, none of us
are able to inform the rest; but as we are all neglected alike,
no one thinks himself entitled to the privilege of complaint.

'I should have known nothing of you or of Langton, from
the time that dear Miss Langton left us. had not I met Mr.
Simpson, of Lincoln, one day in the street, by whom I was
informed that Mr. Langton, your mamma, and yourself, had
been all ill, but that you were all recovered.

'That sickness should suspend your correspondence I did
not wonder, but hoped that it would be renewed at your
recovery.

'Since you will not inform us where you are, or how you
live, I know not whether you desire to know anything of us.
However, I will tell you that the Club subsists; but we have
the loss of Burke's company since he has been engaged in
public business, in which he has gained more reputation than
perhaps any man at his [first] appearance ever gained before.
He made two speeches in the House for repealing the Stamp
Act, which were publicly commended by Mr. Pitt, and have
filled the town with wonder.

'Burke is a great man by nature, and is expected soon to
attain civil greatness. I am grown greater too, for I have
maintained the newspapers these many weeks; and, what is
greater still, I have risen every morning since New Year's
Day at about eight: when I was up I have indeed done but
little; yet it is no slight advancement to obtain for so many
hours more the consciousness of being.

'I wish you were in my new study; I am now writing the
first letter in it. I think it looks very pretty about me.

'Dyer [1] is constant at the Club; Hawkins is remiss; I am

---

[1] [Samuel Dyer, Esq., a most learned and ingenious member of the
Literary Club, for whose understanding and attainments Dr. Johnson
had great respect. He died Sept. 14, 1772. A more particular account
of this gentleman may be found in a Note on the Life of Dryden,
p. 186, prefixed to the edition of that great writer's prose works, in four
volumes 8vo, 1800, in which his character is vindicated, and the very
unfavourable representation of it given by Sir John Hawkins in his
Life of Johnson, pp. 222-232, is minutely examined.—M.]

not over diligent. Dr. Nugent, Dr. Goldsmith, and Mr. Reynolds are very constant. Mr. Lye is printing his Saxon and Gothic Dictionary; all the Club subscribes.

'You will pay my respects to all my Lincolnshire friends.— I am, dear sir, most affectionately yours,   SAM. JOHNSON.

'*March* 9, 1766,
'*Johnson's Court, Fleet Street.*'

TO BENNET LANGTON, ESQ., AT LANGTON, NEAR SPILSBY, LINCOLNSHIRE

'DEAR SIR,—In supposing that I should be more than commonly affected by the death of Peregrine Langton,[1] you were not mistaken; he was one of those whom I loved at once by instinct and by reason. I have seldom indulged more hope of anything than of being able to improve our acquaintance to friendship. Many a time have I placed myself again at Langton, and imagined the pleasure with which I should walk to Partney[2] in a summer morning; but this is no longer possible. We must now endeavour to preserve what is left us,— his example of piety and economy. I hope you make what inquiries you can, and write down what is told you. The little things which distinguish domestic characters are soon forgotten: if you delay to inquire you will have no information; if you neglect to write, information will be vain.[3]

---

[1] Mr. Langton's uncle.
[2] The place of residence of Mr. Peregrine Langton.
[3] Mr. Langton did not disregard this counsel, but wrote the following account, which he has been pleased to communicate to me :—
'The circumstances of Mr. Peregrine Langton were these. He had an annuity for life of two hundred pounds per annum. He resided in a village in Lincolnshire : the rent of his house, with two or three small fields, was twenty-eight pounds ; the county he lived in was not more than moderately cheap : his family consisted of a sister, who paid him eighteen pounds annually for her board, and a niece. The servants were two maids, and two men in livery. His common way of living at his table was three or four dishes ; the appurtenances to his table were neat and handsome : he frequently entertained company at dinner, and then his table was well served with as many dishes as were usual at the tables of the other gentlemen in the neighbourhood. His own appearance as to clothes was genteelly neat and plain. He had always a post-chaise, and kept three horses.
'Such, with the resources I have mentioned, was his way of living, which he did not suffer to employ his whole income ; for he had always

'His art of life certainly deserves to be known and studied. He lived in plenty and elegance upon an income which to many would appear indigent, and to most scanty. How he lived, therefore, every man has an interest in knowing. His death, I hope, was peaceful; it was surely happy.

'I wish I had written sooner, lest, writing now, I should renew your grief; but I would not forbear saying what I have now said.

'This loss is, I hope, the only misfortune of a family to whom no misfortune at all should happen, if my wishes could avert it. Let me know how you all go on. Has Mr. Langton got him the little horse that I recommended? It would do him good to ride about his estate in fine weather.

---

a sum of money lying by him for any extraordinary expenses that might arise. Some money he put into the stocks; at his death the sum he had there amounted to one hundred and fifty pounds. He purchased out of his income his household furniture and linen, of which latter he had a very ample store: and, as I am assured by those that had very good means of knowing, not less than the tenth part of his income was set apart for charity; at the time of his death the sum of twenty-five pounds was found, with a direction to be employed in such uses.

'He had laid down a plan of living proportioned to his income, and did not practise any extraordinary degree of parsimony, but endeavoured that in his family there should be plenty without waste. As an instance that this was his endeavour it may be worth while to mention a method he took in regulating a proper allowance of malt liquor to be drunk in his family, that there might not be a deficiency or any intemperate profusion. On a complaint made that his allowance of a hogshead in a month was not enough for his own family, he ordered the quantity of a hogshead to be put into bottles, had it locked up from the servants, and distributed out, every day, eight quarts, which is the quantity each day at one hogshead in a month; and told his servants that if that did not suffice he would allow them more; but by this method it appeared at once that the allowance was much more than sufficient for his small family; and this proved a clear conviction, that could not be answered, and saved all future dispute. He was in general very diligently and punctually attended and obeyed by his servants: he was very considerate as to the injunctions he gave, and explained them distinctly; and at their first coming to his service steadily exacted a close compliance with them, without any remission: and the servants finding this to be the case, soon grew habitually accustomed to the practice of their business, and then very little further attention was necessary. On extraordinary instances of good behaviour or diligent service he was not wanting in particular encouragements and presents above their wages: it is remarkable that he would permit their relations to visit them, and stay at his house two or three days at a time.

'The wonder with most that hear an account of his economy will be how he was able, with such an income, to do so much, especially when it is considered that he paid for everything he had. He had no land,

'Be pleased to make my compliments to Mrs. Langton, and to dear Miss Langton, and Miss Di, and Miss Juliet, and to everybody else.

'The Club holds very well together. Monday is my night.[1] I continue to rise tolerably well, and read more than I did. I hope something will yet come on it.—I am, sir, your most affectionate servant,   SAM. JOHNSON.

'*May* 10, 1766,

'*Johnson's Court, Fleet Street.*'

After I had been some time in Scotland I mentioned to him in a letter that 'on my first return to my

---

except the two or three small fields which I have said he rented ; and, instead of gaining anything by their produce, I have reason to think he lost by them ; however, they furnished him with no further assistance towards his housekeeping than grass for his horses (not hay, for that I know he bought) and for two cows. Every Monday morning he settled his family accounts, and so kept up a constant attention to the confining his expenses within his income ; and to do it more exactly, compared those expenses with a computation he had made how much that income would afford him every week and day of the year. One of his economical practices was, as soon as any repair was wanting in or about his house, to have it immediately performed. When he had money to spare he chose to lay in a provision of linen or clothes, or any other necessaries ; as then, he said, he could afford it, which he might not be so well able to do when the actual want came ; in consequence of which method he had a considerable supply of necessary articles lying by him, beside what was in use.

'But the main particular that seems to have enabled him to do so much with his income, was that he paid for everything as soon as he had it, except alone what were current accounts, such as rent for his house and servants' wages, and these he paid at the stated times with the utmost exactness. He gave notice to the tradesmen of the neighbouring market towns that they should no longer have his custom if they let any of his servants have anything without their paying for it. Thus he put it out of his power to commit those imprudences to which those are liable that defer their payments by using their money some other way than where it ought to go. And whatever money he had by him he knew that it was not demanded elsewhere, but that he might safely employ it as he pleased.

'His example was confined, by the sequestered place of his abode, to the observation of few, though his prudence and virtue would have made it valuable to all who could have known it. These few particulars, which I knew myself, or have obtained from those who lived with him, may afford instruction, and be an incentive to that wise art of living, which he so successfully practised.'

[1] Of his being in the chair of the Literary Club, which at this time met once a week in the evening.

native country, after some years of absence, I was told of a vast number of my acquaintance who were all gone to the land of forgetfulness, and I found myself like a man stalking over a field of battle, who every moment perceives some one lying dead.' I complained of irresolution, and mentioned my having made a vow as a security for good conduct. I wrote to him again without being able to move his indolence; nor did I hear from him till he had received a copy of my inaugural exercise, or Thesis in Civil Law, which I published at my admission as an advocate, as is the custom in Scotland. He then wrote to me as follows *

TO JAMES BOSWELL, ESQ.

'DEAR SIR,—The reception of your Thesis put me in mind of my debt to you. Why did you . . .[1] I will punish you for it, by telling you that your Latin wants correction.[2] In the beginning, *Spei alteræ*, not to urge that it should be *primæ*, is not grammatical: *alteræ* should be *alteri*. In the next line you seem to use *genus* absolutely, for what we call *family*, that is, for *illustrious extraction*, I doubt without authority. *Homines nullius originis*, for *Nullis orti majoribus*, or,

---

[1] The passage omitted alluded to a private transaction.
[2] This censure of my Latin relates to the Dedication, which was as follows :—

VIRO NOBILISSIMO, ORNATISSIMO,
JOANNI
VICECOMITI MOUNTSTUART,
ATAVIS EDITO REGIBUS,
EXCELSÆ FAMILIÆ DE BUTE SPEI ALTERÆ;
LABENTE SECULO,
QUUM HOMINES NULLIUS ORIGINIS
GENUS ÆQUARE OPIBUS AGGREDIUNTUR,
SANGUINIS ANTIQUI ET ILLUSTRIS
SEMPER MEMORI,
NATALIUM SPLENDOREM VIRTUTIBUS AUGENTI :
AD PUBLICA POPULI COMITIA
JAM LEGATO;
IN OPTIMATIUM VERO MAGNÆ BRITANNIÆ SENATU,
JURE HÆREDITARIO,

Nullo loco nati, is, as I am afraid, barbarous.—Ruddiman is dead.

'I have now vexed you enough, and will try to please you. Your resolution to obey your father I sincerely approve ; but do not accustom yourself to enchain your volatility by vows ; they will sometime leave a thorn in your mind, which you will, perhaps, never be able to extract or eject. Take this warning ; it is of great importance.

'The study of the law is what you very justly term it, copious and generous : [1] and in adding your name to its professors you have done exactly what I always wished, when I wished you best. I hope that you will continue to pursue it vigorously and constantly. You gain, at least, what is no small advantage, security from those troublesome and wearisome discontents, which are always obtruding themselves upon a mind vacant, unemployed, and undetermined.

'You ought to think it no small inducement to diligence and perseverance, that they will please your father. We all live upon the. hope of pleasing somebody ; and the pleasure of pleasing ought to be greatest, and at last always will be greatest, when our endeavours are exerted in consequence of our duty.

'Life is not long, and too much of it must not pass in idle deliberation how it shall be spent : deliberation, which those who begin it by prudence, and continue it with subtilty, must, after long expense of thought, conclude by chance. To prefer

---

OLIM CONCESSURO :
VIM INSITAM VARIA DOCTRINA PROMOVENTE,
NEC TAMEN SE VENDITANTE :
PRÆDITO
PRISCA FIDE, ANIMO LIBERRIMO,
ET MORUM ELEGANTIA
INSIGNI :
IN ITALIÆ VISITANDÆ ITINERE,
SOCIO SUO HONORATISSIMO,
HASCE JURISPRUDENTIÆ PRIMITIAS,
DEVINCTISSIMÆ AMICITIÆ ET OBSERVANTIÆ
MONUMENTUM,
D. D. C. Q.
JACOBUS BOSWELL.

1 This alludes to the first sentence of the *Prœmium* of my Thesis. Jurisprudentiæ *studio nullum uberius, nullum generosius: in legibus enim agitandis, populorum mores variasque fortunæ vices, ex quibus leges oriuntur, contemplari simul solemus.*'

one future mode of life to another, upon just reasons, requires faculties which it has not pleased our Creator to give us.

'If therefore the profession you have chosen has some unexpected inconveniences, console yourself by reflecting that no profession is without them; and that all the importunities and perplexities of business are softness and luxury compared with the incessant cravings of vacancy and the unsatisfactory expedients of idleness.

> " Hæc sunt, quæ nostra potui te voce monere ;
>   Vade, age."

'As to your History of Corsica, you have no materials which others have not, or may not have.   You have, somehow or other, warmed your imagination.   I wish there were some cure, like the lover's leap, for all heads of which some single idea has obtained an unreasonable and irregular possession. Mind your own affairs, and leave the Corsicans to theirs.—I am, dear sir, your most humble servant,

' SAM. JOHNSON.

'*London, Aug.* 21, 1766.'

TO DR. SAMUEL JOHNSON

'*Auchinleck, Nov.* 6, 1766

'MUCH ESTEEMED AND DEAR SIR,—I plead not guilty to[1] . . .

'Having thus, I hope, cleared myself of the charge brought against me, I presume you will not be displeased if I escape the punishment which you have decreed for me unheard. If you have discharged the arrows of criticism against an innocent man you must rejoice to find they have missed him, or have not been pointed so as to wound him.

'To talk no longer in allegory, I am, with all deference, going to offer a few observations in defence of my Latin, which you have found fault with.

'You think I should have used *spei primæ* instead of *spei alteræ*.   *Spes* is, indeed, often used to express something on

---

[1] The passage omitted explained the transaction to which the preceding letter had alluded.

which we have a future dependence, as in Virg. *Eclog*. i.
l. 14:

> "modo namque gemellos,
> *Spem* gregis, ah! silice in nuda connixa reliquit,"

and in *Georg*. iii. l. 473:

> "*Spemque* gregemque simul,"

for the lambs and the sheep. Yet it is also used to express
anything on which we have a present dependence, and is well
applied to a man of distinguished influence,—our support, our
refuge, our *præsidium*, as Horace calls Mæcenas. So, in
Æneid xii. l. 57, Queen Amata addresses her son-in-law
Turnus: "Spes *tu nunc una*": and he was then no future
hope, for she adds,

> "decus imperiumque Latini
>   Te penes,"

which might have been said of my Lord Bute some years ago.
Now I consider the present Earl of Bute to be "*Excelsæ
familiæ de Bute* spes prima"; and my Lord Mountstuart, as
his eldest son, to be "*spes altera*." So in *Æneid* xii. l. 168,
after having mentioned "Pater Æneas," who was the *present*
"spes," the *reigning* "spes," as my German friends would
say, the *spes prima*, the poet adds,

> "Et juxta Ascanius, magnæ *spes altera* Romæ."

'You think *alteræ* ungrammatical, and you tell me it should
have been *alteri*. You must recollect that in old times *alter*
was declined regularly; and when the ancient fragments preserved in the *Juris Civilis Fontes* were written, it was
certainly declined in the way that I use it. This, I should
think, may protect a lawyer who writes *alteræ* in a dissertation upon part of his own science. But as I could hardly
venture to quote fragments of old law to so classical a man as
Mr. Johnson, I have not made an accurate search into these
remains, to find examples of what I am able to produce in
poetical composition. We find in Plaut. *Rudens*, Act iii.
scene 4, line 45:

> "Nam huic *alteræ* patria quæ sit profecto nescio.'

Plautus is, to be sure, an old comic writer; but in the days
of Scipio and Lælius we find Terent. *Heautontim.* Act ii. scene
3, line 30 :

> "hoc ipsa in itinere *alteræ*
> Dum narrat, forte audivi."

'You doubt my having authority for using *genus* absolutely,
for what we call *family*, that is, for *illustrious extraction.*
Now I take *genus* in Latin to have much the same signification with *birth* in English ; both in their primary meaning expressing simply descent, but both made to stand κατ' ἐξοχὴν, for
noble descent.   *Genus* is thus used in Hor. lib. ii. *Sat.* v. l. 8 :

> "Et *genus*, et virtus, nisi cum re, vilior alga est."

And in lib. i. *Epist.* vi. l. 37 :

> 'Et *genus* et formam Regina pecunia donat."

And in the celebrated contest between Ajax and Ulysses,
Ovid's *Metamorph.* lib. xiii. l. 140 :

> "Nam *genus*, et proavos, et quæ non fecimus ipsi,
> Vix ea nostra voco."

'*Homines nullius originis*, for *nullis orti majoribus*, or
nullo loco nati, is, "you are afraid, barbarous."
'*Origo* is used to signify extraction, as in Virg. *Æneid* i.
l. 286 :

> "Nascetur pulcra Trojanus *origine* Cæsar,"

and in *Æneid* x. l. 618 :

> "Ille tamen nostra deducit *origine* nomen " ;

and as *nullus* is used for obscure, is it not in the genius of
the Latin language to write *nullius origini.* for obscure
extraction ?
'I have defended myself as well as I could.
'Might I venture to differ from you with regard to the
utility of vows?   I am sensible that it would be very dangerous
to make vows rashly, and without a due consideration.   But
I cannot help thinking that they may often be of great
advantage to one of a variable judgment and irregular inclina-
tions.   I always remember a passage in one of your letters to

our Italian friend Baretti, where, talking of the monastic life, you say you do not wonder that serious men should put themselves under the protection of a religious order, when they have found how unable they are to take care of themselves. For my own part, without affecting to be a Socrates, I am sure I have a more than ordinary struggle to maintain with *the Evil Principle*; and all the methods I can devise are little enough to keep me tolerably steady in the paths of rectitude.

—I am ever, with the highest veneration, your affectionate humble servant,   JAMES BOSWELL.'

It appears from Johnson's Diary that he was this year at Mr. Thrale's from before Midsummer till after Michaelmas, and that he afterwards passed a month at Oxford. He had then contracted a great intimacy with Mr. Chambers of that University, afterwards Sir Robert Chambers, one of the Judges in India.

He published nothing this year in his own name; but the noble dedication to the King of Gwyn's 'London and Westminster Improved' was written by him; and he furnished the Preface and several of the pieces which compose a volume of Miscellanies by Mrs. Anna Williams, the blind lady who had an asylum in his house.[1] Of these, there are his 'Epitaph

---

[1] [In a paper already mentioned (see vol. i. p. 64, and near the end of the year 1763), the following account of this publication is given by a lady well acquainted with Mrs. Williams:
'As to her poems, she many years attempted to publish them: the half-crowns she had got towards the publication, she confessed to me, went for necessaries, and that the greatest pain she ever felt was from the appearance of defrauding her subscribers: " But what can I do? the Doctor (Johnson) always puts me off with ' Well, we 'll think about it,' and Goldsmith says, ' Leave it to me.' " However, two of her friends, under her directions, made a new subscription at a crown, the whole price of the work, and in a very little time raised sixty pounds. Mrs. Carter was applied to by Mrs. Williams's desire, and she, with the utmost activity and kindness, procured a long list of names. At length the work was published, in which is a fine written but gloomy tale of Dr. Johnson. The money Mrs. Williams had various uses for, and a part of it was funded.'
By this publication Mrs. Williams got £150.—*Ibid.*—M.]

on Philips'; 'Translation of a Latin Epitaph on Sir Thomas Hanmer'; 'Friendship, an Ode'; and 'The Ant,' a paraphrase from the Proverbs, of which I have a copy in his own handwriting; and, from internal evidence, I ascribe to him, 'To Miss —— on her giving the Author a gold and silk net-work Purse of her own weaving'; and 'The happy Life.' Most of the pieces of this volume have evidently received additions from his superior pen, particularly 'Verses to Mr. Richardson on his Sir Charles Grandison'; 'The Excursion'; 'Reflections on a Grave digging in Westminster Abbey.' There is in this collection a poem, 'On the death of Stephen Grey, the Electrician,' which, on reading it, appeared to me to be undoubtedly Johnson's. I asked Mrs. Williams whether it was not his. 'Sir (said she, with some warmth), I wrote that poem before I had the honour of Dr. Johnson's acquaintance.' I, however, was so much impressed with my first notion that I mentioned it to Johnson, repeating at the same time what Mrs. Williams had said. His answer was, 'It is true, sir, that she wrote it before she was acquainted with me; but she has not told you that I wrote it all over again, except two lines.' 'The Fountains,' a beautiful little fairy tale in prose, written with exquisite simplicity, is one of Johnson's productions; and I cannot withhold from Mrs. Thrale the praise of being the author of that admirable poem, 'The Three Warnings.'

He wrote this year a letter, not intended for publication, which has, perhaps, as strong marks of his sentiment and style as any of his compositions. The original is in my possession. It is addressed to the late Mr. William Drummond, bookseller in Edin-

burgh, a gentleman of good family, but small estate,
who took arms for the house of Stuart in 1745; and
during his concealment in London till the Act of
general pardon came out, obtained the acquaintance
of Dr. Johnson, who justly esteemed him as a very
worthy man.   It seems some of the members of the
Society in Scotland for Propagating Christian Knowledge had opposed the scheme of translating the Holy
Scriptures into the Erse or Gaelic language, from
political considerations of the disadvantage of keeping
up the distinction between the Highlanders and the
other inhabitants of North Britain.   Dr. Johnson
being informed of this, I suppose by Mr. Drummond,
wrote with a generous indignation as follows:

TO MR. WILLIAM DRUMMOND

'Sir,—I did not expect to hear that it could be, in an
assembly convened for the propagation of Christian knowledge, a question whether any nation uninstructed in religion
should receive instruction; or whether that instruction should
be imparted to them by a translation of the holy books into
their own language.   If obedience to the will of God be
necessary to happiness, and knowledge of his will be necessary
to obedience, I know not how he that withholds this knowledge, or delays it, can be said to love his neighbour as himself.   He that voluntarily continues ignorance is guilty of all
the crimes which ignorance produces; as to him that should
extinguish the tapers of a lighthouse might justly be imputed
the calamities of shipwreck.   Christianity is the highest
perfection of humanity; and as no man is good but as he
wishes the good of others, no man can be good in the highest
degree who wishes not to others the largest measures of the
greatest good.   To omit for a year, or for a day, the most
efficacious method of advancing Christianity, in compliance
with any purposes that terminate on this side of the grave, is
a crime of which I know not that the world has yet had an
example, except in the practice of the planters of America,

a race of mortals whom, I suppose, no other man wishes to resemble.

'The Papists have, indeed, denied to the laity the use of the Bible; but this prohibition, in few places now very rigorously enforced, is defended by arguments which have for their foundation the care of souls. To obscure, upon motives merely political, the light of revelation, is a practice reserved for the reformed; and, surely, the blackest midnight of Popery is meridian sunshine to such a reformation. I am not very willing that any language should be totally extinguished. The similitude and derivation of languages afford the most indubitable proof of the traduction of nations and the genealogy of mankind. They add often physical certainty to historical evidence; and often supply the only evidence of ancient migrations, and of the revolution of ages which left no written monuments behind them.

'Every man's opinions, at least his desires, are a little influenced by his favourite studies. My zeal for languages may seem, perhaps, rather over-heated, even to those by whom I desire to be well esteemed. To those who have nothing in their thoughts but trade or policy, present power, or present money, I should not think it necessary to defend my opinions; but with men of letters I would not unwillingly compound, by wishing the continuance of every language, however narrow in its extent, or however incommodious for common purposes, till it is reposited in some version of a known book, that it may be always hereafter examined and compared with other languages, and then permitting its disuse. For this purpose the translation of the Bible is most to be desired. It is not certain that the same method will not preserve the Highland language, for the purposes of learning, and abolish it from daily use. When the Highlanders read the Bible they will naturally wish to have its obscurities cleared, and to know the history, collateral or appendant. Knowledge always desires increase; it is like fire, which must first be kindled by some external agent, but which will afterward propagate itself. When they once desire to learn, they will naturally have recourse to the nearest language by which that desire can be gratified; and one will tell another that if he would attain knowledge he must learn English.

'This speculation may, perhaps, be thought more subtle than the grossness of real life will easily admit. Let it, however, be remembered that the efficacy of ignorance has long been tried, and has not produced the consequence expected. Let knowledge, therefore, take its turn; and let the patrons of privation stand a while aside, and admit the operation of positive principles.

'You will be pleased, sir, to assure the worthy man who is employed in the new translation,[1] that he has my wishes for his success; and if here or at Oxford I can be of any use, that I shall think it more than honour to promote his undertaking.

'I am sorry that I delayed so long to write.—I am, sir, your most humble servant, SAM. JOHNSON.

'*Johnson's Court, Fleet Street,*
 Aug. 13, 1766.'

The opponents of this pious scheme being made ashamed of their conduct, the benevolent undertaking was allowed to go on.

The following letters, though not written till the year after, being chiefly upon the same subject, are here inserted:

TO MR. WILLIAM DRUMMOND

'DEAR SIR,—That my letter should have had such effects as you mention gives me great pleasure. I hope you do not flatter me by imputing to me more good than I have really

---

[1] The Rev. Mr. John Campbell, minister of the parish of Kippen, near Stirling, who has lately favoured me with a long, intelligent, and very obliging letter upon this work, makes the following remark:—'Dr. Johnson has alluded to the worthy man employed in the translation of the New Testament. Might not this have afforded you an opportunity of paying a proper tribute of respect to the memory of the Rev. Mr. James Stuart, late minister of Killin, distinguished by his eminent piety, learning, and taste? The amiable simplicity of his life, his warm benevolence, his indefatigable and successful exertions for civilising and improving the parish of which he was minister for upwards of fifty years, entitle him to the gratitude of his country and the veneration of all good men. It certainly would be a pity if such a character should be permitted to sink into oblivion.'

done. Those whom my arguments have persuaded to change their opinion show such modesty and candour as deserve great praise.

'I hope the worthy translator goes diligently forward. He has a higher reward in prospect than any honours which this world can bestow. I wish I could be useful to him.

'The publication of my letter, if it could be of use in a cause to which all other causes are nothing, I should not prohibit. But, first, I would have you to consider whether the publication will really do any good; next, whether by printing and distributing a very small number, you may not attain all that you propose; and, what perhaps I should have said first, whether the letter, which I do not now perfectly remember, be fit to be printed.

'If you can consult Dr. Robertson, to whom I am a little known, I shall be satisfied about the propriety of whatever he shall direct. If he thinks that it should be printed, I entreat him to revise it; there may, perhaps, be some negligent lines written, and whatever is amiss, he knows very well how to rectify.[1]

'Be pleased to let me know, from time to time, how this excellent design goes forward.

'Make my compliments to young Mr. Drummond, whom I hope you will live to see such as you desire him.

'I have not lately seen Mr. Elphinston, but believe him to be prosperous. I shall be glad to hear the same of you, for I am, sir, your affectionate humble servant,

'SAM. JOHNSON.

'*Johnson's Court, Fleet Street,*
     April 21, 1767.'

TO MR. WILLIAM DRUMMOND

'SIR,—I returned this week from the country, after an absence of near six months, and found your letter with many others, which I should have answered sooner, if I had sooner seen them.

'Dr. Robertson's opinion was surely right. Men should

---

[1] This paragraph shows Johnson's real estimation of the character and abilities of the celebrated Scottish historian, however lightly, in a moment of caprice, he may have spoken of his works.

not be told of the faults which they have mended. I am glad
the old language is taught, and honour the translator as a man
whom God has distinguished by the high office of propagating
his word.

'I must take the liberty of engaging you in an office of
charity. Mrs. Heely, the wife of Mr. Heely, who had lately
some office in your theatre, is my near relation, and now in
great distress. They wrote me word of their situation some
time ago, to which I returned them an answer which raised
hopes of more than it is proper for me to give them. Their
representation of their affairs I have discovered to be such as
cannot be trusted; and at this distance, though their case
requires haste, I know not how to act. She, or her daughters,
may be heard of at Canongate Head. I must beg, sir, that
you will inquire after them, and let me know what is to be
done. I am willing to go to ten pounds, and will transmit
you such a sum if upon examination you find it likely to be
of use. If they are in immediate want, advance them what
you think proper. What I could do, I would do for the
woman, having no great reason to pay much regard to Heely
himself.[1]

'I believe you may receive some intelligence from Mrs.
Baker, of the theatre, whose letter I received at the same
time with yours; and to whom, if you see her, you will make
my excuse for the seeming neglect of answering her.

'Whatever you advance within ten pounds shall be immediately returned to you, or paid as you shall order. I trust
wholly to your judgment.—I am, sir, etc.,

'SAM. JOHNSON.

'*London, Johnson's Court, Fleet Street,*
Oct. 24, 1767.'

Mr. Cuthbert Shaw,[2] alike distinguished by his
genius, misfortunes, and misconduct, published this
year a poem, called 'The Race, by Mercurius Spur,
Esq.,' in which he whimsically made the living poets

---

[1] This is the person concerning whom Sir John Hawkins has thrown
out very unwarrantable reflections both against Dr. Johnson and Mr.
Francis Barber.
[2] See an account of him in *The European Magazine*, Jan. 1786.

of England contend for pre-eminence of fame by
running :

> 'Prove by their heels the prowess of their head.'

In this poem there was the following portrait of
Johnson :

> 'Here Johnson comes,—unblest with outward grace,
> His rigid morals stamp'd upon his face.
> While strong conceptions struggle in his brain ;
> (For even wit is brought to bed with pain :)
> To view him, porters with their loads would rest,
> And babes cling frighted to the nurse's breast.
> With looks convulsed he roars in pompous strain,
> And, like an angry lion, shakes his mane.
> The Nine, with terror struck, who ne'er had seen
> Aught human with so terrible a mien,
> Debating whether they should stay or run,
> Virtue steps forth, and claims him for her son.
> With gentle speech she warns him now to yield,
> Nor stain his glories in the doubtful field ;
> But wrapt in conscious worth, content sit down,
> Since Fame, resolved his various pleas to crown,
> Though forced his present claim to disavow,
> Had long reserved a chaplet for his brow.
> He bows, obeys ; for Time shall first expire,
> Ere Johnson stay, when Virtue bids retire.'

The Honourable Thomas Hervey [1] and his lady having
unhappily disagreed, and being about to separate,
Johnson interfered as their friend, and wrote him a
letter of expostulation, which I have not been able to
find ; but the substance of it is ascertained by a letter
to Johnson in answer to it, which Mr. Hervey printed.

---

[1] [The Honourable Thomas Hervey, whose letter to Sir Thomas
Hanmer in 1742 was much read at that time.   He was the second son
of John, the first Earl of Bristol, and one of the brothers of Johnson's
early friend, Henry Hervey.   He married in 1744, Anne, daughter of
Francis Coughlan, Esq., and died Jan. 20, 1775.—M.]

The occasion of this correspondence between Dr. Johnson and Mr. Hervey was thus related to me by Mr. Beauclerk : 'Tom Hervey had a great liking for Johnson, and in his will had left him a legacy of fifty pounds. One day he said to me, "Johnson may want this money now, more than afterward. I have a mind to give it him directly. Will you be so good as to carry a fifty-pound note from me to him?" This I positively refused to do, as he might, perhaps, have knocked me down for insulting him, and have afterward put the note in his pocket. But I said if Hervey would write him a letter, and enclose a fifty-pound note, I should take care to deliver it. He accordingly did write him a letter, mentioning that he was only paying a legacy a little sooner. To his letter he added, "*P.S. I am going to part with my wife.*" Johnson then wrote to him, saying nothing of the note, but remonstrating with him against parting with his wife.'

When I mentioned to Johnson this story, in as delicate terms as I could, he told me that the fifty-pound note was given to him by Mr. Hervey in consideration of his having written for him a pamphlet against Sir Charles Hanbury Williams, who, Mr. Hervey imagined, was the author of an attack upon him ; but that it was afterwards discovered to be the work of a garreteer, who wrote *The Fool* : the pamphlet, therefore, against Sir Charles was not printed.

In February 1767 there happened one of the most remarkable incidents of Johnson's life, which gratified his monarchical enthusiasm, and which he loved to relate with all its circumstances, when requested by his friends. This was his being honoured by a private conversation with his Majesty, in the library at the Queen's house.   He had frequently visited those splendid rooms and noble collection of books,[1] which he used to say was more numerous and curious than he supposed any person could have made in the time which the King had employed.   Mr. Barnard, the librarian, took care that he should have every accommodation that could contribute to his ease and convenience, while indulging his literary taste in that place, so that he had here a very agreeable resource at leisure hours.

His Majesty having been informed of his occasional visits, was pleased to signify a desire that he should be told when Dr. Johnson came next to the library. Accordingly, the next time that Johnson did come, as soon as he was fairly engaged with a book, on which, while he sat by the fire, he seemed quite intent, Mr. Barnard stole round to the apartment where the King was, and, in obedience to his Majesty's commands, mentioned that Dr. Johnson was then in the library.   His Majesty said he was at leisure, and would go to him; upon which Mr. Barnard took one of the candles that stood on the King's table, and lighted his Majesty through a suite of rooms, till they came to a private door into the library, of which his Majesty had the key.   Being entered, Mr. Barnard stepped forward hastily to Dr. Johnson, who was still in a profound study, and whispered him, 'Sir, here is

---

[1] Dr. Johnson had the honour of contributing his assistance towards the formation of this library ; for I have read a long letter from him to Mr. Barnard, giving the most masterly instructions on the subject.   I wished much to have gratified my readers with the perusal of this letter, and have reason to think that his Majesty would have been graciously pleased to permit its publication ; but Mr. Barnard, to whom I applied, declined it, ' on his own account.'

the King.' Johnson started up, and stood still. His Majesty approached him, and at once was courteously easy.[1]

His Majesty began by observing that he understood he came sometimes to the library ; and then mentioned his having heard that the Doctor had been lately at Oxford, and asked him if he was not fond of going thither. To which Johnson answered, that he was indeed fond of going to Oxford sometimes, but was likewise glad to come back again. The King then asked him what they were doing at Oxford. Johnson answered, he could not much commend their diligence, but that in some respects they were mended, for they had put their press under better regulations, and were at that time printing Polybius. He was then asked whether there were better libraries at Oxford or Cambridge. He answered, he believed the Bodleian was larger than any they had at Cambridge ; at the same time adding : ' I hope, whether we have more books or not than they have at Cambridge, we shall

---

1 The particulars of this conversation I have been at great pains to collect with the utmost authenticity from Dr. Johnson's own detail to myself : from Mr. Langton, who was present when he gave an account of it to Dr. Joseph Warton, and several other friends at Sir Joshua Reynolds's ; from Mr. Barnard ; from the copy of a letter written by the late Mr. Strahan the printer to Bishop Warburton ; and from a minute, the original of which is among the papers of the late Sir James Caldwell, and a copy of which was most obligingly obtained for me from his son, Sir John Caldwell, by Sir Francis Lumm. To all these gentlemen I beg leave to make my grateful acknowledgments, and particularly to Sir Francis Lumm, who was pleased to take a great deal of trouble, and even had the minute laid before the King by Lord Caer-marthen, now Duke of Leeds, then one of his Majesty's Principal Secretaries of State, who announced to Sir Francis the royal pleasure concerning it by a letter, in these words : ' I have the King's commands to assure you, sir, how sensible his Majesty is of your attention in com-municating the minute of conversation previous to its publication. As there appears no objection to your complying with Mr. Boswell's wishes on the subject, you are at full liberty to deliver it to that gentleman, to make such use of in his *Life of Dr. Johnson* as he may think proper.'

make as good use of them as they do.' Being asked
whether All-Souls or Christ Church Library was the
largest, he answered : 'All-Souls Library is the largest
we have, except the Bodleian.' 'Ay (said the King),
that is the public library.'

His Majesty inquired if he was then writing anything. He answered, he was not, for he had pretty
well told the world what he knew, and must now read
to acquire more knowledge. The King, as it should
seem with a view to urge him to rely on his own
stores as an original writer, and to continue his
labours, then said : ' I do not think you borrow much
from anybody.' Johnson said, he thought he had
already done his part as a writer. 'I should have
thought so too (said the King), if you had not written
so well.' Johnson observed to me upon this, that 'no
man could have paid a handsomer compliment; and
it was fit for a king to pay. It was decisive.' When
asked by another friend at Sir Joshua Reynolds's,
whether he made any reply to this high compliment,
he answered : ' No, sir. When the King had said it,
it was to be so. It was not for me to bandy civilities
with my Sovereign.' Perhaps no man who had spent
his whole life in courts could have shown a more nice
and dignified sense of true politeness than Johnson
did in this instance.

His Majesty having observed to him that he supposed he must have read a great deal, Johnson
answered, that he thought more than he read ; that
he had read a great deal in the early part of his life,
but having fallen into ill health, he had not been able
to read much compared with others : for instance, he
said he had not read much compared with Dr. Warbur-

ton. Upon which the King said that he heard Dr.
Warburton was a man of such general knowledge
that you could scarce talk with him on any subject on
which he was not qualified to speak ; and that his
learning resembled Garrick's acting in its universality.[1]
His Majesty then talked of the controversy between
Warburton and Lowth, which he seemed to have read,
and asked Johnson what he thought of it. Johnson
answered : ' Warburton has most general, most scholastic learning ; Lowth is the more correct scholar. I
do not know which of them calls names best.' The
King was pleased to say he was of the same opinion,
adding : ' You do not think then, Dr. Johnson, that
there was much argument in the case ? ' Johnson said
he did not think there was. ' Why, truly (said the
King), when once it comes to calling names, argument
is pretty well at an end.'

His Majesty then asked him what he thought of
Lord Lyttelton's history, which was then just published. Johnson said he thought his style pretty
good, but that he had blamed Henry the Second
rather too much. ' Why (said the King), they seldom do these things by halves.' ' No, sir (answered
Johnson), not to kings.' But fearing to be mis-
understood, he procceded to explain himself ; and
immediately subjoined, ' That for those who spoke
worse of kings than they deserved, he could find no
excuse ; but that he could more easily conceive how
some might speak better of them than they deserved,

---

[1] The Reverend Mr. Strahan clearly recollects having been told by
Johnson that the King observed that Pope made Warburton a Bishop.
' True, sir (said Johnson), but Warburton did more for Pope ; he made
him a Christian,'—alluding, no doubt, to his ingenious comments on
the *Essay on Man.*

without any ill intention; for, as kings had much in their power to give, those who were favoured by them would frequently, from gratitude, exaggerate their praises : and as this proceeded from a good motive, it was certainly excusable, as far as error could be excusable.'

The King then asked him what he thought of Dr. Hill. Johnson answered, that he was an ingenious man, but had no veracity; and immediately mentioned, as an instance of it, an assertion of that writer, that he had seen objects magnified to a much greater degree by using three or four microscopes at a time than by using one. 'Now (added Johnson), every one acquainted with microscopes knows, that the more of them he looks through, the less the object will appear.' 'Why (replied the King), this is not only telling an untruth, but telling it clumsily; for, if that be the case, every one who can look through a microscope will be able to detect him.'

'I now (said Johnson to his friends, when relating what had passed), began to consider that I was depreciating this man in the estimation of his Sovereign, and thought it was time for me to say something that might be more favourable.' He added, therefore, that Dr. Hill was, notwithstanding, a very curious observer; and if he would have been contented to tell the world no more than he knew, he might have been a very considerable man, and needed not to have recourse to such mean expedients to raise his reputation.

The King then talked of literary journals, mentioned particularly the *Journal des Savans,* and asked Johnson if it was well done. Johnson said it was formerly

very well done, and gave some account of the persons
who began it, and carried it on for some years; en-
larging, at the same time, on the nature and use of
such works.   The King asked him if it was well done
now.   Johnson answered, he had no reason to think
that it was.   The King then asked him if there were
any other literary journals published in this kingdom,
except the *Monthly* and *Critical Reviews* ; and on being
answered there was no other, his Majesty asked which
of them was the best: Johnson answered that the
Monthly Review was done with most care, the *Critical*
upon the best principles; adding that the authors of
the *Monthly Review* were enemies to the Church.   This
the King said he was sorry to hear.

The conversation next turned on the Philosophical
Transactions, when Johnson observed that they had
now a better method of arranging their materials than
formerly.   'Ay (said the King), they are obliged to
Dr. Johnson for that'; for his Majesty had heard and
remembered the circumstance, which Johnson himself had forgot.

His Majesty expressed a desire to have the literary
biography of this country ably executed, and proposed
to Dr. Johnson to undertake it.   Johnson signified
his readiness to comply with his Majesty's wishes.

During the whole of this interview, Johnson talked
to his Majesty with profound respect, but still in his
firm, manly manner, with a sonorous voice, and never
in that subdued tone which is commonly used at the
levee and in the drawing-room.   After the King with-
drew, Johnson showed himself highly pleased with his
Majesty's conversation, and gracious behaviour.   He
said to Mr. Barnard, ' Sir, they may talk of the King

as they will; but he is the finest gentleman I have
ever seen.' And he afterwards observed to Mr. Langton, 'Sir, his manners are those of as fine a gentleman
as we may suppose Louis the Fourteenth or Charles
the Second.'

At Sir Joshua Reynolds's, where a circle of Johnson's friends was collected round him to hear his
account of this memorable conversation, Dr. Joseph
Warton, in his frank and lively manner, was very
active in pressing him to mention the particulars.
'Come now, sir, this is an interesting matter; do
favour us with it.' Johnson, with great good humour,
complied.

He told them, 'I found his Majesty wished I should
talk, and I made it my business to talk. I find it
does a man good to be talked to by his Sovereign. In
the first place a man cannot be in a passion——'
Here some question interrupted him, which is to be
regretted, as he certainly would have pointed out
and illustrated many circumstances of advantage,
from being in a situation where the powers of the
mind are at once excited to vigorous exertion, and
tempered by reverential awe.

During all the time in which Dr. Johnson was employed in relating to the circle at Sir Joshua Reynolds's
the particulars of what passed between the King and
him, Dr. Goldsmith remained unmoved upon a sofa
at some distance, affecting not to join in the least in
the eager curiosity of the company. He assigned as
a reason for his gloom and seeming inattention, that
he apprehended Johnson had relinquished his purpose
of furnishing him with a Prologue to his play, with
the hopes of which he had been flattered; but it was

strongly suspected that he was fretting with chagrin
and envy at the singular honour Dr. Johnson had
lately enjoyed.   At length, the frankness and simplicity of his natural character prevailed.   He sprung
from the sofa, advanced to Johnson, and in a kind of
flutter, from imagining himself in the situation which
he had just been hearing described, exclaimed, ' Well,
you acquitted yourself in this conversation better than
I should have done; for I should have bowed and
stammered through the whole of it.'

I received no letter from Johnson this year ; nor
have I discovered any of the correspondence[1] he had,
except the two letters to Mr. Drummond, which have
been inserted, for the sake of connection with that to
the same gentleman in 1766.   His diary affords no
light as to his employment at this time.   He passed
three months at Lichfield ;[2] and I cannot omit an
affecting and solemn scene there, as related by himself :

'*Sunday, Oct.* 18, 1767.—Yesterday, Oct. 17, at about ten in
the morning, I took my leave for ever of my dear old friend,
Catherine Chambers, who came to live with my mother about
1724, and has been but little parted from us since.   She buried
my father, my brother, and my mother.   She is now fifty-
eight years old.

'I desired all to withdraw, then told her that we were to
part for ever ; that as Christians we should part with prayer ;

---

[1] It is proper here to mention, that when I speak of his correspondence, I consider it independent of the voluminous collection of letters
which, in the course of many years, he wrote to Mrs. Thrale, which
forms a separate part of his works ; and, as a proof of the high estimation set on anything which came from his pen, was sold by that lady
for the sum of five hundred pounds.

[2] [In his letter to Mr. Drummond, dated October 24, 1767, he mentions that he had arrived in London, after an absence of nearly *six
months* in the country.   Probably part of that time was spent at
Oxford.—M.]

and that I would, if she was willing, say a short prayer beside
her. She expressed great desire to hear me; and held up her
poor hands, as she lay in bed, with great fervour, while I
prayed, kneeling by her, nearly in the following words:

'"Almighty and most merciful Father, whose lovingkind-
ness is over all thy works, behold, visit, and relieve this thy
servant, who is grieved with sickness. Grant that the sense
of her weakness may add strength to her faith and seriousness
to her repentance. And grant that by the help of thy Holy
Spirit, after the pains and labours of this short life, we may
all obtain everlasting happiness, through Jesus Christ our
Lord, for whose sake hear our prayers. Amen. Our Father,
etc."

'I then kissed her. She told me that to part was the
greatest pain that she had ever felt, and that she hoped we
should meet again in a better place. I expressed, with swelled
eyes, and great emotion of tenderness, the same hopes. We
kissed, and parted, I humbly hope, to meet again, and to part
no more.'[1]

By those who have been taught to look upon Johnson as a man of a harsh and stern character, let this
tender and affectionate scene be candidly read ; and
let them then judge whether more warmth of heart,
and grateful kindness, is often found in human
nature.

We have. the following notice in his devotional
record :

'*August 2*, 1767.—I have been disturbed and unsettled for
a long time, and have been without resolution to apply to
study or to business, being hindered by sudden snatches.'[2]

He, however, furnished Mr. Adams with a Dedication to the King of that ingenious gentleman's *Treatise
on the Globes,* conceived and expressed in such a manner

---

[1] *Prayers and Meditations*, pp. 77 and 78.
[2] *Ibid.* p. 73.

as could not fail to be very grateful to a monarch, distinguished for his love of the sciences.

This year was published a ridicule of his style, under the title of *Lexiphanes*. Sir John Hawkins ascribes it to Dr. Kenrick; but its author was one Campbell, a Scotch purser in the navy. The ridicule consisted in applying Johnson's 'words of large meaning' to insignificant matters, as if one should put the armour of Goliath upon a dwarf. The contrast might be laughable; but the dignity of the armour must remain the same in all considerate minds. This malicious drollery, therefore, it may easily be supposed, could do no harm to its illustrious object.

TO BENNET LANGTON, ESQ., AT MR. ROTHWELL'S,
PERFUMER IN NEW BOND STREET, LONDON

'DEAR SIR,—That you have been all summer in London is one more reason for which I regret my long stay in the country. I hope that you will not leave the town before my return. We have here only the chance of vacancies in the passing carriages, and I have bespoken one that may, if it happens, bring me to town on the fourteenth of this month : but this is not certain.

'It will be a favour if you communicate this to Mrs. Williams : I long to see all my friends.—I am, dear sir, your most humble servant,   SAM. JOHNSON.

' *Lichfield, Oct.* 10, 1767.'

It appears from his notes of the state of his mind,[1] that he suffered great perturbation and distraction in 1768. Nothing of his writing was given to the public this year, except the Prologue to his friend Goldsmith's comedy of *The Good-natured Man*. The first lines of this Prologue are strongly characteristical of

---

[1] *Prayers and Meditations*, p. 81.

the dismal gloom of his mind; which, in his case, as in the case of all who are distressed with the same malady of imagination, transfers to others its own feelings. Who could suppose it was to introduce a comedy, when Mr. Bensley solemnly began:

> 'Press'd with the load of life, the weary mind
> Surveys the general toil of human kind.'

But this dark ground might make Goldsmith's humour shine the more.

In the spring of this year, having published my *Account of Corsica, with the Journal of a Tour to that Island*, I returned to London, very desirous to see Dr. Johnson, and hear him upon the subject. I found he was at Oxford, with his friend Mr. Chambers, who was now Vinerian Professor, and lived in New Inn Hall. Having had no letter from him since that in which he criticised the Latinity of my Thesis, and having been told by somebody that he was offended at my having put into my book an extract of his letter to me at Paris, I was impatient to be with him, and therefore followed him to Oxford, where I was entertained by Mr. Chambers, with a civility which I shall ever gratefully remember. I found that Dr. Johnson had sent a letter to me to Scotland, and that I had nothing to complain of but his being more indifferent to my anxiety than I wished him to be. Instead of giving, with the circumstances of time and place, such fragments of his conversation as I preserved during this visit to Oxford, I shall throw them together in continuation.

I asked him whether, as a moralist, he did not think that the practice of the law, in some degree, hurt the

nice feeling of honesty.   JOHNSON: 'Why no, sir, if
you act properly.   You are not to deceive your clients
with false representations of your opinion; you are
not to tell lies to a judge.'   BOSWELL: 'But what do
you think of supporting a cause which you know to
be bad?'   JOHNSON: 'Sir, you do not know it to be
good or bad till the judge determines it.   I have said
that you are to state facts fairly; so that your thinking, or what you call knowing, a cause to be bad,
must be from reasoning, must be from your supposing
your arguments to be weak and inconclusive.   But,
sir, that is not enough.   An argument which does not
convince yourself, may convince the judge to whom
you urge it; and if it does convince him, why then,
sir, you are wrong, and he is right.   It is his business
to judge; and you are not to be confident in your
own opinion that a cause is bad, but to say all you
can for your client, and then hear the judge's opinion.'
BOSWELL: 'But, sir, does not affecting a warmth when
you have no warmth, and appearing to be clearly of
one opinion when you are in reality of another
opinion, does not such dissimulation impair one's
honesty?   Is there not some danger that a lawyer
may put on the same mask in common life, in the
intercourse with his friends?'   JOHNSON: 'Why no,
sir.   Everybody knows you are paid for affecting
warmth for your client;[1] and it is, therefore, properly
no dissimulation: the moment you come from the bar
you resume your usual behaviour.   Sir, a man will no
more carry the artifice of the bar into the common
intercourse of society, than a man who is paid for

---

[1] [*Iras et verba locant.*—A. B.]

tumbling upon his hands will continue to tumble upon his hands when he should walk on his feet.'

Talking of some of the modern plays, he said *False Delicacy*[1] was totally void of character. He praised Goldsmith's *Good-natured Man*; said it was the best comedy that had appeared since *The Provoked Husband*, and that there had not been of late any such character exhibited on the stage as that of Croaker. I observed it was the Suspirius of his *Rambler*. He said, Goldsmith had owned he had borrowed it from thence. 'Sir (continued he), there is all the difference in the world between characters of nature and characters of manners; and *there* is the difference between the characters of Fielding and those of Richardson. Characters of manners are very entertaining; but they are more to be understood by a superficial observer than characters of nature, where a man must dive into the recesses of the human heart.'

It always appeared to me that he estimated the compositions of Richardson too highly, and that he had an unreasonable prejudice against Fielding. In comparing those two writers he used this expression: 'That there was as great a difference between them as between a man who knew how a watch was made and a man who could tell the hour by looking on the dial-plate.' This was a short and figurative state of his distinction between drawing characters of nature and characters only of manners. But I cannot help being of opinion that the neat watches of Fielding are as well constructed as the large clocks of Richardson,

---

[1] [By Hugh Kelly. It was a great success. Johnson once declined an introduction to Kelly, observing, 'No, sir, I never desire to converse with a man who has written more than he has read.'—A. B.]

and that his dial-plates are brighter. Fielding's characters, though they do not expand themselves so widely in dissertation, are as just pictures of human nature, and I will venture to say, have more striking features, and nicer touches of the pencil ; and, though Johnson used to quote with approbation a saying of Richardson's, ' That the virtues of Fielding's heroes were the vices of a truly good man,' I will venture to add that the moral tendency of Fielding's writings, though it does not encourage a strained and rarely possible virtue, is ever favourable to honour and honesty, and cherishes the benevolent and generous affections. He who is as good as Fielding would make him, is an amiable member of society, and may be led on by more regulated instructors to a higher state of ethical perfection.

Johnson proceeded : 'Even Sir Francis Wronghead[1] is a character of manners, though drawn with great humour.' He then repeated, very happily, all Sir Francis's credulous account to Manly of his being with ' the great man,' and securing a place. I asked him if *The Suspicious Husband*[2] did not furnish a well-drawn character, that of Ranger. JOHNSON : ' No, sir; Ranger is a just rake, a mere rake, and a lively young fellow, but no *character*.'

The great Douglas Cause was at this time a very general subject of discussion. I found he had not studied it with much attention, but had only heard parts of it occasionally. He, however, talked of it, and said : ' I am of opinion that positive proof of fraud

---

1 [See *The Provoked Husband*, by Vambrugh.—A. B.]
2 [By Benjamin Hoadley, M.D., who I regret to say, in a letter to Garrick, familiarly refers to Johnson as ' Puffy Pensioner.'—A. B.]

should not be required of the plaintiff, but that the judges should decide according as probability shall appear to preponderate, granting to the defendant the presumption of filiation to be strong in his favour. And I think, too, that a good deal of weight should be allowed to the dying declarations, because they were spontaneous.   There is a great difference between what is said without our being urged to it, and what is said from a kind of compulsion.   If I praise a man's book without being asked my opinion of it, that is honest praise, to which one may trust.   But if an author asks me if I like his book, and I give him something like praise, it must not be taken as my real opinion.

'I have not been troubled for a long time with authors desiring my opinion of their works.   I used once to be sadly plagued with a man who wrote verses, but who literally had no other notion of a verse but that it consisted of ten syllables.   *Lay your knife and your fork across your plate* was to him a verse :

Lay yōur knife ānd your fŏrk acrōss your plăte.

As he wrote a great number of verses, he sometimes by chance made good ones, though he did not know it.'

He renewed his promise of coming to Scotland, and going with me to the Hebrides, but said he would now content himself with seeing one or two of the most curious of them.   He said : 'Macaulay, who writes the account of St. Kilda, set out with a prejudice against prejudice, and wanted to be a smart modern thinker ; and yet he affirms for a truth, that when a ship arrives there all the inhabitants are seized with a cold.'

Dr. John Campbell, the celebrated writer, took a

great deal of pains to ascertain this fact, and attempted
to account for it on physical principles, from the effect
of effluvia from human bodies. Johnson, at another
time, praised Macaulay for his *'magnanimity'* in
asserting this wonderful story, because it was well
attested. A lady of Norfolk, by a letter to my friend
Dr. Burney, has favoured me with the following solution : 'Now for the explication of this seeming mystery,
which is so very obvious as, for that reason, to have
escaped the penetration of Dr. Johnson and his friend,
as well as that of the author. Reading the book with
my ingenious friend, the late Reverend Mr. Christian
of Docking, after ruminating a little : "The cause
(says he) is a natural one. The situation of St. Kilda
renders a north-east wind indispensably necessary
before a stranger can land. The wind, not the
stranger, occasions an epidemic cold." If I am not
mistaken, Mr. Macaulay is dead ; if living, this
solution might please him, as I hope it will Mr.
Boswell, in return for the many agreeable hours his
works have afforded us.'

Johnson expatiated on the advantages of Oxford for
learning. 'There is here, sir (said he), such a progressive emulation. The students are anxious to appear
well to their tutors ; the tutors are anxious to have
their pupils appear well in the college ; the colleges are
anxious to have their students appear well in the
University ; and there are excellent rules of discipline
in every college. That the rules are sometimes ill
observed, may be true ; but is nothing against the
system. The members of a University may, for a
season, be unmindful of their duty. I am arguing for
the excellency of the institution.'

Of Guthrie, he said, 'Sir, he is a man of parts. He has no great regular fund of knowledge ; but by reading so long, and writing so long, he no doubt has picked up a good deal.'

He said he had lately been a long while at Lichfield, but had grown very weary before he left it. BOSWELL : 'I wonder at that, sir ; it is your native place.' JOHNSON : ' Why, so is Scotland *your* native place.'

His prejudice against Scotland appeared remarkably strong at this time. When I talked of our advancement in literature : 'Sir (said he), you have learned a little from us, and you think yourselves very great men. Hume would never have written history had not Voltaire written it before him. He is an echo of Voltaire.' BOSWELL: ' But, sir, we have Lord Kames.' JOHNSON : 'You *have* Lord Kames. Keep him ; ha, ha, ha ! We don't envy you him. Do you ever see Dr. Robertson?' BOSWELL : 'Yes, sir.' JOHNSON : 'Does the dog talk of me?' BOSWELL : ' Indeed, sir, he does, and loves you.' Thinking that I now had him in a corner, and being solicitous for the literary fame of my country, I pressed him for his opinion on the merit of Dr. Robertson's *History of Scotland*. But, to my surprise, he escaped.—'Sir, I love Robertson, and I won't talk of his book.'

It is but justice both to him and Dr. Robertson to add, that though he indulged himself in this sally of wit, he had too good taste not to be fully sensible of the merits of that admirable work.

An essay, written by Mr. Deane, a divine of the Church of England, maintaining the future life of brutes, by an explication of certain parts of the Scriptures, was mentioned, and the doctrine insisted on by a gentleman who seemed fond of curious speculation. Johnson, who did not like to hear of anything concerning a future state which was not authorised by the regular canons of orthodoxy, discouraged this talk ; and being offended at its continuation, he watched an opportunity to give the gentleman a blow of reprehension. So, when the poor speculatist, with a serious, metaphysical, pensive face, addressed him, ' But really, sir, when we see a very sensible dog, we don't know what to think of him.' Johnson, rolling with joy at the thought which beamed in his eye, turned quickly round, and replied, 'True, sir : and when we see a very foolish *fellow*, we don't know what to think of *him.*' He then rose up, strided to the fire, and stood for some time laughing and exulting.

I told him that I had several times, when in Italy, seen the experiment of placing a scorpion within a circle of burning coals ; that it ran round and round in extreme pain ; and finding no way to escape, retired to the centre, and like a true Stoic philosopher, darted its sting into its head, and thus at once freed itself from its woes. ' *This must end 'em.*' I said this was a curious fact, as it showed deliberate suicide in a reptile. Johnson would not admit the fact. He said Maupertuis[1] was of opinion that it does not kill itself,

---

[1] I should think it impossible not to wonder at the variety of Johnson's reading, however desultory it might have been. Who could have imagined that the High Church of England man would be so prompt in quoting Maupertuis, who, I am sorry to think, stands in the list of those unfortunate mistaken men who call themselves *esprits forts.* I have, however, a high respect for that philosopher whom the great Frederick of Prussia loved and honoured, and addressed pathetically in one of his poems—

'Maupertuis, cher Maupertuis,
Que notre vie est peu de chose !'

There was in Maupertuis a vigour and yet a tenderness of sentiment,

but dies of the heat; that it gets to the centre of the circle, as the coolest place; that its turning its tail in upon its head is merely a convulsion, and that it does not sting itself. He said he would be satisfied if the great anatomist Morgagni, after dissecting a scorpion on which the experiment had been tried, should certify that its sting had penetrated into its head.

He seemed pleased to talk of natural philosophy. 'That woodcocks (said he) fly over the northern countries, is proved, because they have been observed at sea. Swallows certainly sleep all the winter. A number of them conglobulate together by flying round and round, and then all in a heap throw themselves under water, and lie in the bed of a river.'[1] He told us one of his first essays was a Latin poem upon the glow-worm; I am sorry I did not ask where it was to be found.

Talking of the Russians and the Chinese, he advised me to read Bell's *Travels*. I asked him whether I should read Du Halde's *Account of China*. 'Why, yes (said he), as one reads such a book; that is to say, consult it.'

He talked of the heinousness of the crime of adultery, by which the peace of families was destroyed. He said, 'Confusion of progeny constitutes the essence of the crime; and therefore a woman who breaks her marriage vows is much more criminal than a man who does it. A man, to be sure, is criminal in the sight of

---

united with strong intellectual powers and uncommon ardour of soul. Would he had been a Christian! I cannot help earnestly venturing to hope that he is one now.

[Maupertuis died in 1759 at the age of sixty-two, in the arms of the Bernoullis, *très Chrétiennement.*—B.]

[1] [Even Gilbert White was not indisposed to believe this. See his *Selborne*, p. 37, Bohn's edition.—A. B.]

God; but he does not do his wife a material injury, if he does not insult her; if, for instance, from mere wantonness of appetite, he steals privately to her chambermaid. Sir, a wife ought not greatly to resent this. I would not receive home a daughter who had run away from her husband on that account. A wife should study to reclaim her husband by more attention to please him. Sir, a man will not, once in a hundred instances, leave his wife and go to a harlot, if his wife has not been negligent of ˉpleasing.'

Here he discovered that acute discrimination, that solid judgment, and that knowledge of human nature, for which he was upon all occasions remarkable. Taking care to keep in view the moral and religious duty, as understood in our nation, he showed clearly from reason and good sense the greater degree of culpability in the one sex deviating from it than the other ; and, at the same time, inculcated a very useful lesson as to *the way to keep him.*

I asked him if it was not hard that one deviation from chastity should so absolutely ruin a young woman. JOHNSON : 'Why no, sir ; it is the great principle which she is taught. When she has given up that principle she has given up every notion of female honour and virtue, which are all included in chastity.'

A gentleman talked to him of a lady whom he greatly admired, and wished to marry, but was afraid of her superiority of talents. ' Sir (said he), 'you need not be afraid ; marry her. Before a year goes about you 'll find that reason much weaker, and that wit not so bright.' Yet the gentleman may be justified in his apprehension by one of Dr. Johnson's admirable sentences in his life of Waller :

'He doubtless praised many whom he would have been afraid to marry ; and, perhaps, married one whom he would have been ashamed to praise. Many qualities contribute to domestic happiness, upon which poetry has no colours to bestow : and many airs and sallies may delight imagination, which he who flatters them never can approve.'

He praised Signior Baretti. 'His account of Italy is a very entertaining book ; and, sir, I know no man who carries his head higher in conversation than Baretti. There are strong powers in his mind. He has not, indeed, many hooks ; but with what hooks he has, he grapples very forcibly.'

At this time I observed upon a dial-plate of his watch a short Greek inscription, taken from the New Testament, Νὺξ γὰρ ἔρχεται, being the first words of our Saviour's solemn admonition to the improvement of that time which is allowed us to prepare for eternity : 'the night cometh when no man can work.' He, some time afterwards, laid aside this dial-plate ; and when I asked him the reason he said, 'It might do very well upon a clock which a man keeps in his closet ; but to have it upon his watch which he carries about with him, and which is often looked at by others, might be censured as ostentatious.' Mr. Steevens is now possessed of the dial-plate inscribed as above.

He remained at Oxford a considerable time ; I was obliged to go to London, where I received his letter, which had been returned from Scotland.

TO JAMES BOSWELL, ESQ.

'MY DEAR BOSWELL,—I have omitted a long time to write to you, without knowing very well why. I could now tell why I should not write; for who would write to men who publish the letters of their friends without their leave? Yet I write to you in spite of my caution, to tell you that I shall be glad to see you, and that I wish you would empty your head of Corsica, which I think has filled it rather too long. But, at all events, I shall be glad, very glad, to see you.—I am, sir, yours affectionately, SAM. JOHNSON.
'*Oxford, March* 23, 1768.'

I answered thus:

TO MR. SAMUEL JOHNSON

London, 26th April, 1768.

'MY DEAR SIR,—I have received your last letter, which, though very short, and by no means complimentary, yet gave me real pleasure, because it contains these words, "I shall be glad, very glad to see you." Surely you have no reason to complain of my publishing a single paragraph of one of your letters; the temptation to it was so strong. An irrevocable grant of your friendship, and your dignifying my desire of visiting Corsica with the epithet of "a wise and noble curiosity," are to me more valuable than many of tho grants of kings.

'But how can you bid me "empty my head of Corsica"? My noble-minded friend, do you not feel for an oppressed nation bravely struggling to be free? Consider fairly what is the case. The Corsicans never received any kindness from the Genoese. They never agreed to be subject to them. They owe them nothing, and when reduced to an abject state of slavery, by force, shall they not rise in the great cause of liberty, and break the galling yoke? And shall not every liberal soul be warm for them? Empty my head of Corsica! Empty it of honour, empty it of humanity, empty it of friendship, empty it of piety. No! while I live, Corsica and tho cause of the brave islanders shall ever employ much of my attention, shall ever interest me in the sincerest manner.

'I am, etc.,   JAMES BOSWELL.'

[TO MRS. LUCY PORTER, IN LICHFIELD

Oxford, April 18, 1768.

'MY DEAR DEAR LOVE,—You have had a very great loss. To lose an old friend is to be cut off from a great part of the little pleasure that this life allows. But such is the condition of our nature, that as we live on we must see those whom we love drop successively, and find our circle of relation grow less and less, till we are almost unconnected with the world; and then it must soon be our turn to drop into the grave. There is always this consolation, that we have one Protector who can never be lost but by our own fault, and every new experience of the uncertainty of all other comforts should determine us to fix our hearts where true joys are to be found. All union with the inhabitants of earth must in time be broken; and all the hopes that terminate here, must on [one] part or other end in disappointment.

'I am glad that Mrs. Adey and Mrs. Cobb do not leave you alone. Pay my respects to them, and the Sewards, and all my friends. When Mr. Porter comes, he will direct you. Let me know of his arrival, and I will write to him.

'When I go back to London, I will take care of your reading-glass. Whenever I can do anything for you, remember, my dear darling, that one of my greatest pleasures is to please you.

'The punctuality of your correspondence I consider as a proof of great regard. When we shall see each other, I know not, but let us often think on each other, and think with tenderness. Do not forget me in your prayers. I have for a long time back been very poorly; but of what use is it to complain?

'Write often, for your letters always give great pleasure to, my dear, your most affectionate, and most humble servant,

'SAM. JOHNSON.']

Upon his arrival in London in May, he surprised me one morning with a visit at my lodging in Half-Moon Street, was quite satisfied with my explanation, and was in the kindest and most agreeable frame of mind. As he had objected to a part of one of his letters being published, I thought it right to take this opportunity of asking him explicitly whether it would be improper to publish his letters after his death. His answer was, 'Nay, sir, when I am dead you may do as you will.'

He talked in his usual style with a rough contempt of popular liberty. 'They make a rout about *universal* liberty, without considering that all that is to be valued, or indeed can be enjoyed by individuals, is *private* liberty. Political liberty is good only so far as it produces private liberty. Now, sir, there is the liberty of the press, which you know is a constant topic. Suppose you and I and two hundred more were restrained from printing our thoughts: what then? What proportion would that restraint upon us bear to the private happiness of the nation?'

This mode of representing the inconveniences of restraint as light and insignificant, was a kind of sophistry in which he delighted to indulge himself, in opposition to the extreme laxity for which it has been fashionable for too many to argue, when it is evident, upon reflection, that the very essence of government is restraint; and certain it is, that as government produces rational happiness, too much restraint is better than too little. But when restraint is unnecessary, and so close as to gall those who are subject to it, the people may and ought to remonstrate; and, if relief is not granted, to resist. Of this manly and spirited principle, no man was more convinced than Johnson himself.

About this time Dr. Kenrick attacked him, through my sides, in a pamphlet entitled 'An Epistle to James Boswell, Esq., occasioned by his having transmitted the moral Writings of Dr. Samuel Johnson to Pascal Paoli, General of the Corsicans.' I was at first inclined to answer this pamphlet; but Johnson, who knew that my doing so would only gratify Kenrick, by keeping alive what would soon die away of itself, would not suffer me to take any notice of it.

His sincere regard for Francis Barber, his faithful negro servant, made him so desirous of his further improvement, that he now placed him at a school at Bishop-Stortford, in Hertfordshire. This humane attention does Johnson's heart much honour. Out of many letters which Mr. Barber received from his master, he has preserved three, which he kindly gave me, and which I shall insert according to their dates.

TO MR. FRANCIS BARBER

'DEAR FRANCIS,—I have been very much out of order. I am glad to hear that you are well, and design to come soon to you. I would have you stay at Mrs. Clapp's for the present, till I can determine what we shall do. Be a good boy.

'My compliments to Mrs. Clapp and to Mr. Fowler.—I am, yours affectionately,   SAM. JOHNSON.

'May 28, 1768.'

Soon afterwards he supped at the Crown and Anchor tavern in the Strand, with a company whom I collected to meet him. They were Dr. Percy, now Bishop of Dromore, Dr. Douglas, now Bishop of Salisbury, Mr. Langton, Dr. Robertson the historian, Dr. Hugh Blair, and Mr. Thomas Davies, who wished much to be introduced to these eminent Scotch *literati*; but on the present occasion he had very little opportunity of hearing them talk, for with an excess of prudence, for which Johnson afterwards found fault with them, they hardly opened their lips, and that only to say something which they were certain would not expose them to the sword of Goliath; such was their anxiety for their fame when in the presence of Johnson. He was this evening in remarkable vigour of mind, and eager to exert himself in conversation, which he did with great readiness and fluency; but I am sorry to find that I have preserved but a small part of what passed.

He allowed high praise to Thomson as a poet; but when one of the company said he was also a very good man, our moralist contested this with great warmth, accusing him of gross sensuality and licentiousness of manners. I was very much afraid that in writing Thomson's life, Dr. Johnson would have treated his private character with a stern severity, but I was agreeably disappointed; and I may claim a little merit in it, from my having been at pains to send him authentic accounts of the affectionate and generous conduct of the poet to his sisters, one of whom, the wife of Mr. Thomson, schoolmaster at Lanark, I knew, and was presented by her with three of his letters, one of which Dr. Johnson has inserted in his life.

He was vehement against old Dr. Mounsey[1] of Chelsea College, as 'a fellow who swore and talked bawdy.' 'I have been often in his company (said Dr.

---

1 [Messenger Mounsey, M.D., died at his apartments in Chelsea College, Dec. 26, 1783, at the great age of ninety-five. An extraordinary direction in his will may be found in the *Gentleman's Magazine*, vol. L. p. ii. p. 1183.—M.]

Percy), and never heard him swear or talk bawdy.'
Mr. Davies, who sat next to Dr. Percy, having after
this had some conversation aside with him, made a
discovery which, in his zeal to pay court to Dr. Johnson, he eagerly proclaimed aloud from the foot of the
table : 'O, sir, I have found out a very good reason
why Dr. Percy never heard Mounsey swear or talk
bawdy, for he tells me he never saw him but at the
Duke of Northumberland's table.' 'And so, sir (said
Dr. Johnson loudly to Dr. Percy), you would shield
this man from the charge of swearing and talking
bawdy, because he did not do so at the Duke of
Northumberland's table? Sir, you might as well tell
us that you had seen him hold up his hand at the
Old Bailey, and he neither swore nor talked bawdy ; or
that you had seen him in the cart at Tyburn, and he
neither swore nor talked bawdy. And is it thus, sir,
that you presume to controvert what I have related?'
Dr. Johnson's animadversion was uttered in such a
manner, that Dr. Percy seemed to be displeased, and
soon afterwards left the company, of which Johnson
did not at that time take any notice.

Swift having been mentioned, Johnson, as usual,
treated him with little respect as an author. Some of
us endeavoured to support the Dean of St. Patrick's,
by various arguments. One in particular praised his
Conduct of the Allies. JOHNSON : 'Sir, his *Conduct of
the Allies* is a performance of very little ability.'
'Surely, sir (said Dr. Douglas), you must allow it has
strong facts.'[1] JOHNSON : 'Why yes, sir ; but what is

---

[1] My respectable friend, upon reading this passage, observed that he
probably must have said not simply 'strong facts,' but 'strong facts
well arranged.' His Lordship, however, knows too well the value of
written documents to insist on setting his recollection against my notes

that to the merit of the composition? In the Sessions-, paper of the Old Bailey there are strong facts. House-breaking is a strong fact; robbery is a strong fact; and murder is a *mighty* strong fact: but is great praise due to the historian of those strong facts? No, sir, Swift has told what he had to tell distinctly enough, but that is all. He had to count ten, and he has counted it right.' Then recollecting that Mr. Davies, by acting as an *informer,* had been the occasion of his talking somewhat too harshly to his friend, Dr. Percy, for which, probably, when the first ebullition was over, he felt some compunction, he took an opportunity to give him a hit: so added, with a preparatory laugh, 'Why, sir, Tom Davies might have written the *Conduct of the Allies.*' Poor Tom being thus suddenly dragged into ludicrous notice in presence of the Scottish doctors, to whom he was ambitious of appearing to advantage, was grievously mortified. Nor did his punishment rest here; for upon subsequent occasions, whenever he, 'statesman all over,'[1] assumed a strutting importance, I used to hail him—'*the Author of the Conduct of the Allies.*'

When I called upon Dr. Johnson next morning, I found him highly satisfied with his colloquial prowess the preceding evening. 'Well (said he), we had good talk.' BOSWELL: 'Yes, sir; you tossed and gored several persons.'

The late Alexander Earl of Eglintoune, who loved

---

taken at the time. He does not attempt to *traverse the record.* The fact, perhaps, may have been, either that the additional words escaped me in the noise of a numerous company, or that Dr. Johnson, from his impetuosity and eagerness to seize an opportunity to make a lively retort, did not allow Dr. Douglas to finish his sentence.

[1] See the hard drawing of him in Churchill's *Rosciad.*

wit more than wine, and men of genius more than sycophants, had a great admiration of Johnson; but from the remarkable elegance of his own manners, was, perhaps, too delicately sensible of the roughness which sometimes appeared in Johnson's behaviour. One evening about this time, when his Lordship did me the honour to sup at my lodgings with Dr. Robertson and several other men of literary distinction, he regretted that Johnson had not been educated with more refinement, and lived more in polished society. 'No, no, my Lord (said Signior Baretti), do with him what you would, he would always have been a bear.' 'True (answered the Earl with a smile), but he would have been a *dancing* bear.'

To obviate all the reflections which have gone round the world to Johnson's prejudice, by applying to him the epithet of a *bear*, let me impress upon my readers a just and happy saying of my friend Goldsmith, who knew him well: 'Johnson, to be sure, has a roughness in his manner; but no man alive has a more tender heart. *He has nothing of the bear but his skin.*'

In 1769, so far as I can discover, the public was favoured with nothing of Johnson's composition, either for himself or any of his friends. His *Meditations* too strongly prove that he suffered much both in body and mind; yet was he perpetually striving against *evil,* and nobly endeavouring to advance his intellectual and devotional improvement. Every generous and grateful heart must feel for the distresses of so eminent a benefactor to mankind; and now that his unhappiness is certainly known, must respect that dignity of character which prevented him from complaining.

His Majesty having the preceding year instituted the Royal Academy of Arts in London, Johnson had now the honour of being appointed Professor in Ancient Literature.[1] In the course of the year he wrote some letters to Mrs. Thrale, passed some part of the summer at Oxford and at Lichfield, and when at Oxford he wrote the following letter :

TO THE REV. MR. THOMAS WARTON

'DEAR SIR,—Many years ago, when I used to read in the library of your College, I promised to recompense the College for that permission by adding to their books a Baskerville's Virgil. I have now sent it, and desire you to reposit it on the shelves in my name.[2]

'If you will be pleased to let me know when you have an hour of leisure I will drink tea with you. I am engaged for the afternoon, to-morrow and on Friday : all my mornings are my own.[3]—I am, etc. SAM. JOHNSON.

'*May* 31, 1769.'

I came to London in the autumn, and having informed him that I was going to be married in a few months, I wished to have as much of his conversation

---

[1] In which place he has been succeeded by Bennet Langton, Esq. When that truly religious gentleman was elected to the honorary professorship, at the same time that Edward Gibbon, Esq., noted for introducing a kind of sneering infidelity into his Historical Writings, was elected Professor in Ancient History, in the room of Dr. Goldsmith, I observed that it brought to my mind, 'Wicked Will Whiston and good Mr. Ditton.' I am now also of that admirable institution as Secretary for Foreign Correspondence, by the favour of the Academicians and the approbation of the Sovereign.

[2] 'It has this inscription in a blank leaf: "*Hunc librum D.D. Samuel Johnson, eo quod hic loci studiis interdum vacaret.*" Of this library, which is an old Gothic room, he was very fond. On my observing to him that some of the *modern* libraries of the University were more commodious and pleasant for study, as being more spacious and airy, he replied, "Sir, if a man has a mind to *prance* he must study at Christ Church and All Souls."'

[3] 'During this visit he seldom or never dined out. He appeared to be deeply engaged in some literary work. Miss Williams was now with him at Oxford.'

as I could before engaging in a state of life which would probably keep me more in Scotland, and prevent me seeing him so often as when I was a single man; but I found he was at Brighthelmstone with Mr. and Mrs. Thrale. I was very sorry that I had not his company with me at the Jubilee, in honour of Shakespeare, at Stratford-upon-Avon, the great poet's native town. Johnson's connection both with Shakespeare and Garrick founded a double claim to his presence; and it would have been highly gratifying to Mr. Garrick. Upon this occasion I particularly lamented that he had not that warmth of friendship for his brilliant pupil, which we may suppose would have had a benignant effect on both. When almost every man of eminence in the literary world was happy to partake in this festival of genius, the absence of Johnson could not but be wondered at and regretted. The only trace of him there was in the whimsical advertisement of a haberdasher, who sold *Shakesperian ribands* of various dyes; and, by way of illustrating their appropriation to the bard, introduced a line from the celebrated Prologue at the opening of Drury Lane Theatre :

'Each change of *many colour'd* life he drew.'

From Brighthelmstone Dr. Johnson wrote me the following letter, which they who may think that I ought to have suppressed, must have less ardent feelings than I have always avowed : [1]

---

[1] In the Preface to my *Account of Corsica*, published in 1768, I thus express myself :

'He who publishes a book affecting not to be an author, and professing an indifference for literary fame, may possibly impose upon many people such an idea of his consequence as he wishes may be received. For my part, I should be proud to be known as an author,

TO JAMES BOSWELL, ESQ.

'DEAR SIR,—Why do you charge me with unkindness? I
have omitted nothing that could do you good, or give you
pleasure, unless it be that I have forborne to tell you my
opinion of your *Account of Corsica.* I believe my opinion,
if you think well of my judgment, might have given you
pleasure; but when it is considered how much vanity is
excited by praise, I am not sure that it would have done you
good. Your History is like other histories, but your Journal
is in a very high degree curious and delightful. There is
between the History and the Journal that difference which
there will always be found between notions borrowed from
without, and notions generated within. Your History was
copied from books: your Journal rose out of your own experience and observation. You express images which operated
strongly upon yourself, and you have impressed them with
great force upon your readers. I know not whether I could
name any narrative by which curiosity is better excited or
better gratified.

'I am glad that you are going to be married; and as I wish
you well in things of less importance, wish you well with pro-
portionate ardour in this crisis of your life. What I can
contribute to your happiness I should be very unwilling to
withhold; for I have always loved and valued you, and shall
love you and value you still more, as you become more regular
and useful: effects which a happy marriage will hardly fail
to produce.

---

and I have an ardent ambition for literary fame; for, of all possessions
I should imagine literary fame to be the most valuable. A man who
has been able to furnish a book, which has been approved by the world,
has established himself as a respectable character in distant society,
without any danger of having that character lessened by the observation of his weaknesses. To preserve a uniform dignity among those
who see us every day is hardly possible; and to aim at it must put us
under the fetters of perpetual restraint. The author of an approved
book may allow his natural disposition an easy play, and yet indulge
the pride of superior genius, when he considers that by those who
know him only as an author he never ceases to be respected. Such an
author, when in his hours of gloom and discontent, may have the consolation to think that his writings are at that very time giving pleasure
to numbers; and such an author may cherish the hope of being remembered after death, which has been a great object to the noblest minds
in all ages.'

'I do not find that I am likely to come back very soon from this place. I shall, perhaps, stay a fortnight longer; and a fortnight is a long time to a lover absent from his mistress. Would a fortnight ever have an end?—I am, dear sir, your most affectionate humble servant,   SAM. JOHNSON.

'*Brighthelmstone,*
'*Sept.* 9, 1766.'

After his return to town we met frequently, and I continued the practice of making notes of his conversation, though not with so much assiduity as I wish I had done. At this time, indeed, I had a sufficient excuse for not being able to appropriate so much time to my journal; for General Paoli, after Corsica had been overpowered by the monarchy of France, was now no longer at the head of his brave countrymen, but having with difficulty escaped from his native island, had sought an asylum in Great Britain: and it was my duty, as well as my pleasure, to attend much upon him. Such particulars of Johnson's conversation at this period as I have committed to writing I shall here introduce, without any strict attention to methodical arrangement. Sometimes short notes of different days shall be blended together, and sometimes a day may seem important enough to be separately distinguished.

He said he would not have Sunday kept with rigid severity and gloom, but with a gravity and simplicity of behaviour.

I told him that David Hume had made a short collection of Scotticisms. 'I wonder,' said Johnson, ' that *he* should find them.' [1]

He would not admit the importance of the question

---

[1] [The first edition of Hume's *History of England* was full of Scotticisms, many of which he corrected in subsequent editions.—M.]

concerning the legality of general warrants. 'Such a power,' he observed, 'must be vested in every government, to answer particular cases of necessity; and there can be no just complaint but when it is abused, for which those who administer government must be answerable. It is a matter of such indifference, a matter about which the people care so very little, that were a man to be sent over Britain to offer them an exemption from it at a halfpenny apiece, very few would purchase it.' This was a specimen of that laxity of talking, which I had heard him fairly acknowledge; for, surely, while the power of granting general warrants was supposed to be legal, and the apprehension of them hung over our heads, we did not possess that security of freedom congenial to our happy constitution, and which, by the intrepid exertions of Mr. Wilkes, has been happily established.

He said : 'The duration of Parliament, whether for seven years or the life of the king, appears to me so immaterial, that I would not give half-a-crown to turn the scale one way or the other. The *habeas corpus* is the single advantage which our government has over that of other countries.'

On the 30th of September we dined together at the Mitre. I attempted to argue for the superior happiness of the savage life, upon the usual fanciful topics. JOHNSON : 'Sir, there can be nothing more false. The savages have no bodily advantages beyond those of civilised men. They have not better health; and as to care and mental uneasiness, they are not above it, but below it, like bears. No, sir, you are not to talk such paradox : let me have no more on 't. It cannot entertain, far less can it instruct. Lord Monboddo, one of your Scotch judges, talked a great deal of such nonsense. I suffered *him*; but I will not suffer *you.*' BOSWELL : 'But, sir, does not Rousseau talk such nonsense?' JOHNSON : 'True, sir, but Rousseau *knows* he is talking nonsense, and laughs at the world for staring at him.' BOSWELL : 'How so, sir?' JOHNSON : 'Why, sir, a man who talks nonsense so well, must know that he is talking nonsense. But I am *afraid* (chuckling and laughing), Monboddo does *not* know that he is talking nonsense.'[1] BOSWELL : 'Is it wrong then, sir, to affect singularity, in order to make people stare?' JOHNSON : 'Yes, if you do it by propagating error : and, indeed, it is wrong in any way. There is in human nature a general inclination to make people stare; and every wise man has himself to cure of it, and does cure himself. If you wish to make people stare by doing better than others, why, make them stare till they stare their eyes out. But consider how easy it is to make people stare, by being absurd. I may do it by going into a drawing-room without my shoes. You remember the gentleman in the *Spectator,* who had commission of lunacy taken out against him for his extreme singularity, such as never wearing a wig, but a night-cap. Now, sir, abstractedly, the night-cap was best; but, relatively, the advantage was overbalanced by his making the boys run after him.'

Talking of a London life, he said : 'The happiness

[1] His Lordship having frequently spoken in an abusive manner of Dr. Johnson, in my company, I on one occasion during the lifetime of my illustrious friend could not refrain from retaliation, and repeated to him this saying. He has since published I don't know how many pages in one of his curious books, attempting, in much anger, but with pitiful effect, to persuade mankind that my illustrious friend was not the great and good man which they esteemed and ever will esteem him to be.

of London is not to be conceived but by those who have been in it. I will venture to say, there is more learning and science within the circumference of ten miles from where we now sit, than in all the rest of the kingdom.' BOSWELL: 'The only disadvantage is the great distance at which people live from one another.' JOHNSON: 'Yes, sir; but that is occasioned by the largeness of it, which is the cause of all the other advantages.' BOSWELL: 'Sometimes I have been in the humour of wishing to retire to a desert.' JOHNSON: 'Sir, you have desert enough in Scotland.'

Although I had promised myself a great deal of instructive conversation with him on the conduct of the married state, of which I had then a near prospect, he did not say much upon that topic. Mr. Seward heard him once say, that 'a man has a very bad chance for happiness in that state, unless he marries a woman of very strong and fixed principles of religion.' He maintained to me, contrary to the common notion, that a woman would not be the worse wife for being learned; in which, from all that I have observed of *Artemisias*, I humbly differed from him. That a woman should be sensible and well informed, I allow to be a great advantage; and think that Sir Thomas Overbury,[1] in his rude versification, has very judiciously pointed out that degree of intelligence which is to be desired in a female companion:

> 'Give me, next *good*, an *understanding wife*,
>   By Nature *wise*, not *learned* by much art;
> Some *knowledge* on her side will all my life
>   More scope of conversation impart;
> Besides, her inborne virtue fortific;
>   They are most firmly good, who best know why.'

---

[1] 'A Wife,' a poem, 1614.

When I censured a gentleman of my acquaintance for marrying a second time, as it showed a disregard of his first wife, he said, 'Not at all, sir. On the contrary, were he not to marry again, it might be concluded that his first wife had given him a disgust to marriage; but by taking a second wife he pays the highest compliment to the first, by showing that she made him so happy as a married man, that he wishes to be so a second time.' So ingenious a turn did he give to this delicate question. And yet, on another occasion, he owned that he once had almost asked a promise of Mrs. Johnson that she would not marry again, but had checked himself. Indeed I cannot help thinking, that in his case the request would have been unreasonable; for if Mrs. Johnson forgot, or thought it no injury to the memory of her first love,—the husband of her youth and the father of her children, —to make a second marriage, why should she be precluded from the third, should she be so inclined? In Johnson's persevering fond appropriation of his *Tetty*, even after her decease, he seems totally to have overlooked the prior claim of the honest Birmingham trader. I presume that her having been married before had, at times, given him some uneasiness; for I remember his observing upon the marriage of one of our common friends, 'He has done a very foolish thing, sir; he has married a widow, when he might have had a maid.'

We drank tea with Mrs. Williams. I had last year the pleasure of seeing Mrs. Thrale at Dr. Johnson's one morning, and had conversation enough with her to admire her talents; and to show her that I was as Johnsonian as herself. Dr. Johnson had probably been

kind enough to speak well of me, for this evening he
delivered me a very polite card from Mr. Thrale and
her, inviting me to Streatham.

On the 6th of October I complied with this obliging
invitation, and found, at an elegant villa, six miles
from town, every circumstance that can make society
pleasing. Johnson, though quite at home, was yet
looked up to with an awe, tempered by affection, and
seemed to be equally the care of his host and hostess.
I rejoiced at seeing him so happy.

He played off his wit against Scotland with a good-
humoured pleasantry, which gave me, though no bigot
to national prejudices, an opportunity for a little contest with him. I having said that England was obliged
to us for gardeners, almost all their good gardeners
being Scotsmen. JOHNSON : 'Why, sir, that is because gardening is much more necessary amongst you
than with us, which makes so many of your people
learn it. It is *all* gardening with you. Things which
grow wild here must be cultivated with great care in
Scotland. Pray now (throwing himself back in his
chair, and laughing), are you ever able to bring the
sloe to perfection ?'

I boasted that we had the honour of being the first
to abolish the unhospitable, troublesome, and ungra-
cious custom of giving veils to servants. JOHNSON :
'Sir, you abolished veils because you were too poor to
be able to give them.'

Mrs. Thrale disputed with him on the merit of
Prior. He attacked him powerfully ; said he wrote
of love like a man who had never felt it : his love
verses were college verses ; and he repeated the song
'Alexis shunn'd his fellow swains,' etc., in so ludicrous

a manner, as to make us all wonder how any one could have been pleased with such fantastical stuff. Mrs. Thrale stood to her gun with great courage, in defence of amorous ditties, which Johnson despised, till he at last silenced her by saying, 'My dear lady, talk no more of this. Nonsense can be defended but by nonsense.'[1]

Mrs. Thrale then praised Garrick's talents for light, gay poetry; and, as a specimen, repeated his song in 'Florizel and Perdita,' and dwelt with peculiar pleasure on this line:

'I'd smile with the simple, and feed with the poor.'

JOHNSON: 'Nay, my dear Lady, this will never do. Poor David! Smile with the simple;—What folly is that? And who would feed with the poor that can help it? No, no; let me smile with the wise, and feed with the rich.' I repeated this sally to Garrick, and wondered to find his sensibility as a writer not a little irritated by it. To soothe him, I observed, that Johnson spared none of us; and I quoted the passage in Horace, in which he compares one who attacks his friends for the sake of a laugh, to a pushing ox, that is marked by a bunch of hay put upon his horns: *fœnum habet in cornu.* 'Ay (said Garrick vehemently), he has a whole *mow* of it.'

Talking of history, Johnson said: 'We may know historical facts to be true, as we may know facts in common life to be true. Motives are generally unknown. We cannot trust to the characters we find in history, unless when they are drawn by those who

---

[1] [As a set-off against this may be mentioned John Wesley's great appreciation of Prior's poetry. See his admirable *Essay on the Character and Writings of Mr. Prior. Works*, xiii. p. 380-7.—A. B.]

knew the persons; as those, for instance, by Sallust and by Lord Clarendon.'

He would not allow much merit to Whitefield's oratory. 'His popularity, sir (said he), is chiefly owing to the peculiarity of his manner. He would be followed by crowds were he to wear a night-cap in the pulpit, or were he to preach from a tree.'

I know not from what spirit of contradiction he burst out into a violent declamation against the Corsicans, of whose heroism I talked in high terms. 'Sir (said he), what is all this rout about the Corsicans? They have been at war with the Genoese for upwards of twenty years, and have never yet taken their forti-fied towns. They might have battered down their walls, and reduced them to powder in twenty years. They might have pulled the walls in pieces, and cracked the stones with their teeth in twenty years.' It was in vain to argue with him upon the want of artillery : he was not to be resisted for the moment.

On the evening of October 10, I presented Dr. Johnson to General Paoli. I had greatly wished that two men, for whom I had the highest esteem, should meet. They met with a manly ease, mutually conscious of their own abilities, and of the abilities of each other. The General spoke Italian, and Dr. Johnson English, and understood one another very well, with a little aid of interpretation from me, in which I compared myself to an isthmus which joins two great continents. Upon Johnson's approach, the General said, 'From what I have read of your works, sir, and from what Mr. Boswell has told me of you, I have long held you in great veneration.' The General talked of languages being formed on the particular notions and manners of a people, without knowing which we cannot know the language. We may know the direct signification of single words; but by these no beauty of expression, no sally of genius, no wit is conveyed to the mind. All this must be by allusion to other ideas. 'Sir (said Johnson), you talk of language as if you had never done anything else but study it, instead of governing a nation.' The General said, '*Questo è un troppo gran complimento*'; this is too great a compliment. Johnson answered, 'I should have thought so, sir, if I had not heard you talk.' The General asked him what he thought of the spirit of infidelity which was so prevalent? JOHNSON: 'Sir, this gloom of infidelity, I hope, is only a transient cloud passing through the hemisphere, which will soon be dissipated, and the sun break forth with his usual splendour.' 'You think, then (said the General), that they will change their principles like their clothes?' JOHNSON: 'Why, sir, if they bestow no more thought on principles than on dress, it must be so.' The General said, that ' a great part of the fashionable infidelity was owing to a desire of showing courage. Men who have no opportunities of showing it as to things in this life, take death and futurity as objects on which to display it.' JOHNSON: 'That is mighty foolish affectation. Fear is one of the passions of human nature, of which it is impossible to divest it. You remember that the Emperor Charles v. when he read upon the tombstone of a Spanish nobleman, "Here lies one who never knew fear," wittily said, "Then he never snuffed a candle with his fingers."'

He talked a few words of French to the General;

but finding he did not do it with facility he asked for pen, ink, and paper, and wrote the following note:

'*J'ai lu dans la géographie de Lucas de Linda un Pater-noster écrit dans une langue tout-à-fait différente de l'Italienne, et de toutes autres lesquelles se derivent du Latin. L'auteur l'appelle* linguam Corsicæ rusticam; *elle a peut-être passé, peu à peu; mais elle a certainement prevalue autrefois dans les montagnes et dans la campagne. Le même auteur dit la même chose en parlant de Sardaigne; qu'il y a deux langues dans l'Isle, une des villes, l'autre de la campagne.*'

The General immediately informed him that the *lingua rustica* was only in Sardinia.

Dr. Johnson went home with me, and drank tea till late in the night. He said: 'General Paoli had the loftiest port of any man he had ever seen.' He denied that military men were always the best-bred men. 'Perfect good breeding,' he observed, 'consists in having no particular mark of any profession, but a general elegance of manners; whereas, in a military man, you can commonly distinguish the *brand* of a soldier, *l'homme d'epée*.'

Dr. Johnson shunned to-night any discussion of the perplexed question of fate and free-will, which I attempted to agitate: 'Sir (said he), we *know* our will is free, and *there's* an end on't.'

He honoured me with his company at dinner on the 16th of October, at my lodgings in Old Bond Street, with Sir Joshua Reynolds, Mr. Garrick, Dr. Goldsmith, Mr. Murphy, Mr. Bickerstaff, and Mr. Thomas Davies. Garrick played round him with a fond vivacity, taking hold of the breasts of his coat, and looking up in his face with a lively archness, com-

plimented him on the good health which he seemed
then to enjoy; while the sage, shaking his head,
beheld him with a gentle complacency. One of the
company not being come at the appointed hour, I proposed, as usual upon such occasions, to order dinner
to be served; adding, 'Ought six people to be kept
waiting for one?' 'Why, yes (answered Johnson,
with a delicate humanity), if the one will suffer more
by your sitting down than the six will do by waiting.'
Goldsmith, to divert the tedious minutes, strutted
about, bragging of his dress, and I believe was seriously
vain of it, for his mind was wonderfully prone to such
impressions. 'Come, come (said Garrick), talk no
more of that.   You are, perhaps, the worst—eh, eh!'
—Goldsmith was eagerly attempting to interrupt him,
when Garrick went on, laughing ironically, 'Nay,
you will always *look* like a gentleman; but I am
talking of being well or *ill drest.*'   'Well, let me tell
you (said Goldsmith), when my tailor brought home
my bloom-coloured coat, he said, "Sir, I have a favour
to beg of you. When anybody asks you who made
your clothes, be pleased to mention John Filby, at the
Harrow, in Water Lane."' JOHNSON: 'Why, sir,
that was because he knew the strange colour would
attract crowds to gaze at it, and thus they might hear
of him, and see how well he could make a coat even
of so absurd a colour.'

After dinner our conversation first turned upon
Pope. Johnson said, his characters of men were
admirably drawn, those of women not so well. He
repeated to us, in his forcible melodious manner, the
concluding lines of the *Dunciad.* While he was talking loudly in praise of those lines one of the company

ventured to say, 'Too fine for such a poem :—a poem
on what?' JOHNSON (with a disdainful look) : 'Why,
on *dunces.* It was worth while being a dunce then.
Ah, sir, hadst *thou* lived in those days! It is not
worth while being a dunce now, when there are no
wits.' Bickerstaff observed, as a peculiar circumstance,
that Pope's fame was higher when he was alive than
it was then. Johnson said, his *Pastorals* were poor
things, though the versification was fine. He told us,
with high satisfaction, the anecdote of Pope's inquiring
who was the author of his *London,* and saying, he
will be soon *déterré.* He observed, that in Dryden's
poetry there were passages drawn from a profundity
which Pope could never reach. He repeated some
fine lines on love by the former (which I have now
forgotten), and gave great applause to the character
of Zimri. Goldsmith said that Pope's character of
Addison showed a deep knowledge of the human
heart. Johnson said, that the description of the
temple in *The Mourning Bride*[1] was the finest poetical
passage he had ever read ; he recollected none in
Shakespeare equal to it. 'But (said Garrick, all
alarmed for "the god of his idolatry"), we know
not the extent and variety of his powers. We are
to suppose there are such passages in his works.
Shakespeare must not suffer from the badness of our
memories.' Johnson, diverted by this enthusiastic
jealousy, went on with great ardour : 'No, sir ;
Congreve has *nature*' (smiling on the tragic eagerness
of Garrick); but composing himself, he added, 'Sir,
this is not comparing Congreve on the whole with

---

[1] [Act ii. sc. 3.—M.]

Shakespeare on the whole; but only maintaining that Congreve has one finer passage than any that can be found in Shakespeare. Sir, a man may have no more than ten guineas in the world, but he may have those ten guineas in one piece; and so may have a finer piece than a man who has ten thousand pound : but then he has only one ten-guinea piece. What I mean is, that you can show me no passage where there is simply a description of material objects, without any intermixture of moral notions, which produces such an effect.' Mr. Murphy mentioned Shakespeare's description of the night before the battle of Agincourt; but it was observed it had *men* in it. Mr. Davies suggested the speech of Juliet, in which she figures herself awaking in the tomb of her ancestors. Some one mentioned the description of Dover Cliff. JOHN-SON : 'No, sir; it should be all precipice,—all vacuum. The crows impede your fall. The diminished appearance of the boats, and other circumstances, are all very good description, but do not impress the mind at once with the horrible idea of immense height. The impression is divided; you pass on by computation from one stage of the tremendous space to another. Had the girl in *The Mourning Bride* said, she could not cast her shoe to the top of one of the pillars in the temple, it would not have aided the idea, but weakened it.'

Talking of a Barrister who had a bad utterance, some one (to rouse Johnson) wickedly said, that he was unfortunate in not having been taught oratory by Sheridan. JOHNSON : 'Nay, sir, if he had been taught by Sheridan he would have cleared the room.' GARRICK : 'Sheridan has too much vanity to be a good man.' We shall now see Johnson's mode of *defending* a man; taking him into his own hands, and discriminating. JOHNSON: 'No, sir. There is, to be sure, in Sheridan, something to reprehend and everything to laugh at; but, sir, he is not a bad man. No, sir; were mankind to be divided into good and bad, he would stand considerably within the ranks of good. And, sir, it must be allowed that Sheridan excels in plain declamation, though he can exhibit no character.'

I should, perhaps, have suppressed this disquisition concerning a person of whose merit and worth I think with respect, had he not attacked Johnson so outrageously in his *Life of Swift*, and, at the same time, treated us his admirers as a set of pigmies. He who has provoked the lash of wit cannot complain that he smarts from it.

Mrs. Montague, a lady distinguished for having written an Essay on Shakespeare, being mentioned;— REYNOLDS: 'I think that essay does her honour.' JOHNSON: 'Yes, sir; it does *her* honour, but it would do nobody else honour. I have, indeed, not read it all. But when I take up the end of a web, and find it pack-thread, I do not expect, by looking farther, to find embroidery. Sir, I will venture to say there is not one sentence of true criticism in her book.' GARRICK: 'But, sir, surely it shows how much Voltaire has mistaken Shakespeare, which nobody else has done.' JOHNSON: 'Sir, nobody else has thought it worth while. And what merit is there in that? You may as well praise a schoolmaster for whipping a boy who has construed ill. No, sir, there is no real criticism in it: none showing the beauty of thought, as formed on the workings of the human heart.'

The admirers of this Essay[1] may be offended at the slighting manner in which Johnson spoke of it; but let it be remembered that he gave his honest opinion unbiassed by any prejudice or any proud jealousy of a woman intruding herself into the chair of criticism; for Sir Joshua Reynolds has told me that when the Essay first came out, and it was not known who had written it, Johnson wondered how Sir Joshua could like it. At this time Sir Joshua himself had received no information concerning the author, except being assured by one of our most eminent literati, that it was clear its author did not know the Greek tragedies in the original. One day at Sir Joshua's table, when it was related that Mrs. Montague, in an excess of compliment to the author of a modern tragedy, had exclaimed, 'I tremble for Shakespeare'; Johnson said, 'When Shakespeare has got —— for his rival, and Mrs. Montague for his defender, he is in a poor state indeed.'

Johnson proceeded: 'The Scotsman[2] has taken the right method in his *Elements of Criticism.*' I do not mean that he has taught us anything; but he has told us old things in a new way.' MURPHY: 'He seems to have read a great deal of French criticism, and wants to make it his own; as if he had been for

---

[1] Of whom I acknowledge myself to be one, considering it as a piece of the secondary or comparative species of criticism, and not of that profound species which alone Dr. Johnson would allow to be 'real criticism.' It is, besides, clearly and elegantly expressed, and has done effectually what it professed to do, namely, vindicated Shakespeare from the misrepresentations of Voltaire; and considering how many young people were misled by his witty, though false observations, Mrs. Montague's Essay was of service to Shakespeare with a certain class of readers, and is, therefore, entitled to praise. Johnson, I am assured, allowed the merit which I have stated, saying (with reference to Voltaire), it is conclusive *ad hominem.*'

[2] Lord Kames.

years anatomising the heart of man, and peeping into every cranny of it.' GOLDSMITH : 'It is easier to write that book than to read it.' JOHNSON : 'We have an example of true criticism in Burke's *Essay on the Sublime and Beautiful*; and, if I recollect, there is also Du Bos ; and Bouhours, who shows all beauty to depend on truth. There is no great merit in telling how many plays have ghosts in them, and how this ghost is better than that. You must show how terror is impressed on the human heart. In the description of night in Macbeth, the beetle and the bat detract from the general idea of darkness — inspissated gloom.'

Politics being mentioned, he said : 'This petitioning is a new mode of distressing government, and a mighty easy one. I will undertake to get petitions either against quarter guineas or half guineas, with the help of a little hot wine. There must be no yielding to encourage this. The object is not important enough. We are not to blow up half a dozen palaces, because one cottage is burning.'

The conversation then took another turn. JOHNSON : 'It is amazing what ignorance of certain points one sometimes finds in men of eminence. A wit about town, who wrote Latin bawdy verses, asked me how it happened that England and Scotland, which were once two kingdoms, were now one ; and Sir Fletcher Norton did not seem to know that there were such publications as the Reviews.

'The ballad of Hardyknute has no great merit, if it be really ancient. People talk of nature. But mere obvious nature may be exhibited with very little power of mind.'

On Thursday, October 19, I passed the evening with him at his house. He advised me to complete a dictionary of words peculiar to Scotland, of which I showed him a specimen. 'Sir (said he), Ray has made a collection of north-country wòrds. By collecting those of your country, you will do a useful thing towards the history of the language.' He bade me also go on with collections which I was making upon the antiquities of Scotland. 'Make a large book; a folio.' BOSWELL: 'But of what use will it be, sir?' JOHNSON: 'Never mind the use; do it.'

I complained that he had not mentioned Garrick in his Preface to Shakespeare; and asked him if he did not admire him. JOHNSON: 'Yes, as "a poor player, who frets and struts his hour upon the stage"—as a shadow.' BOSWELL: 'But has he not brought Shakespeare into notice?' JOHNSON: 'Sir, to allow that would be to lampoon the age. Many of Shakespeare's plays are the worse for being acted: Macbeth, for instance.' BOSWELL: 'What, sir, is nothing gained by decoration and action? Indeed, I do wish that you had mentioned Garrick.' JOHNSON: 'My dear sir, had I mentioned him, I must have mentioned many more; Mrs. Pritchard, Mrs. Cibber,—nay, and Mr. Cibber too; he too altered Shakespeare.' BOSWELL: 'You have read his Apology, sir?' JOHNSON: 'Yes, it is very entertaining. But as for Cibber himself, taking from his conversation all that he ought not to have said, he was a poor creature. I remember when he brought me one of his Odes to have my opinion of it, I could not bear such nonsense, and would not let him read it to the end; so little respect had I for that great man! (laughing.) Yet I remember Richardson wondering that I could treat him with familiarity.'

I mentioned to him that I had seen the execution of several convicts at Tyburn, two days before, and that none of them seemed to be under any concern. JOHNSON : 'Most of them, sir, have never thought at all.' BOSWELL : 'But is not the fear of death natural to man ?' JOHNSON : 'So much so, sir, that the whole of life is but keeping away the thoughts of it.' He then, in a low and earnest tone, talked of his meditating upon the awful hour of his own dissolution, and in what manner he should conduct himself upon that occasion : 'I know not (said he) whether I should wish to have a friend by me, or have it all between God and myself.'

Talking of our feeling for the distresses of others— JOHNSON : 'Why, sir, there is much noise made about it, but it is greatly exaggerated. No, sir, we have a certain degree of feeling to prompt us to do good ; more than that, Providence does not intend. It would be misery to no purpose.' BOSWELL : 'But suppose now, sir, that one of your intimate friends were apprehended for an offence for which he might be hanged.' JOHNSON : 'I should do what I could to bail him, and give him any other assistance ; but if he were once fairly hanged, I should not suffer.' BOSWELL : 'Would you eat your dinner that day, sir ?' JOHNSON : 'Yes, sir, and eat it as if he were eating with me. Why, there's Baretti, who is to be tried for his life to-morrow, friends have risen up for him on every side ; yet if he should be hanged, none of them will eat a slice of plum-pudding the less. Sir, that sympathetic feeling goes a very little way in depressing the mind.'

I told him that I had dined lately at Foote's, who showed me a letter which he had received from Tom Davies, telling him that he had not been able to sleep from the concern he felt on account of '*this sad affair of Baretti,*' begging of him to try if he could suggest anything that might be of service; and, at the same time, recommending to him an industrious young man who kept a pickle-shop. JOHNSON: 'Ay, sir, here you have a specimen of human sympathy; a friend hanged and a cucumber pickled. We know not whether Baretti or the pickle-man has kept Davies from sleep: nor does he know himself. And as to his not sleeping, sir; Tom Davies is a very great man; Tom has been upon the stage, and knows how to do those things: I have not been upon the stage, and cannot do those things.' BOSWELL: 'I have often blamed myself, sir, for not feeling for others as sensibly as many say they do.' JOHNSON: 'Sir, don't be duped by them any more. You will find these very feeling people are not very ready to do you good. They *pay* you by *feeling.*'

BOSWELL: 'Foote has a great deal of humour.' JOHNSON: 'Yes, sir.' BOSWELL: 'He has a singular talent of exhibiting character.' JOHNSON: 'Sir, it is not a talent; it is a vice; it is what others abstain from. It is not comedy which exhibits the character of a species, as that of a miser gathered from many misers: it is farce which exhibits individuals.' BOSWELL: 'Did not he think of exhibiting you, sir?' JOHNSON: 'Sir, fear restrained him; he knew I would have broken his bones. I would have saved him the trouble of cutting off a leg; I would not have left him a leg to cut off.' BOSWELL: 'Pray, sir, is not Foote an infidel?' JOHNSON: 'I do not know, sir, that the fellow is an infidel; but if he be an infidel, he is an infidel as a dog is an infidel; that is to say, he has never thought upon the subject.'[1] BOSWELL: 'I suppose, sir, he has thought superficially, and seized the first notions which occurred to his mind.' JOHNSON: 'Why then, sir, still he is like a dog, that snatches the piece next him. Did you never observe that dogs have not the power of comparing? A dog will take a small bit of meat as readily as a large, when both are before him.'

'Buchanan (he observed) has fewer *centos* than any modern Latin poet. He has not only had great knowledge of the Latin language, but was a great poetical genius. Both the Scaligers praise him.'

He again talked of the passage in Congreve with high commendation, and said, 'Shakespeare never has six lines together without a fault. Perhaps you may find seven: but this does not refute my general assertion. If I come to an orchard and say there's no fruit here, and then comes a poring man who finds two apples and three pears, and tells me, "Sir, you are mistaken, I have found both apples and pears," I should laugh at him: what would that be to the purpose?'

---

[1] When Mr. Foote was at Edinburgh he thought fit to entertain a numerous Scotch company with a great deal of coarse jocularity, at the expense of Dr. Johnson, imagining it would be acceptable. I felt this as not civil to me; but sat very patiently till he had exhausted his merriment on that subject; and then observed that surely Johnson must be allowed to have some sterling wit, and that I heard him say a very good thing of Mr. Foote himself. 'Ah, my old friend Sam (cried Foote), no man says better things; do let us have it.' Upon which I told the above story, which produced a very loud laugh from the company. But I never saw Foote so disconcerted. He looked grave and angry, and entered into a serious refutation of the justice of the remark. 'What, sir (said he), talk thus of a man of liberal education:—a man who for years was at the University of Oxford:—a man who has added sixteen new characters to the English drama of his country!'

BOSWELL: 'What do you think of Dr. Young's *Night Thoughts*, sir?' JOHNSON: 'Why, sir, there are very fine things in them.' BOSWELL: 'Is there not less religion in the nation now, sir, than there was formerly?' JOHNSON: 'I don't know, sir, that there is.' BOSWELL: 'For instance, there used to be a chaplain in every great family, which we do not find now.' JOHNSON: 'Neither do you find any of the state servants which great families used formerly to have. There is a change of modes in the whole department of life.'

Next day, October 20, he appeared, for the only time I suppose in his life, as a witness in a Court of Justice, being called to give evidence to the character of Mr. Baretti, who having stabbed a man in the street, was arraigned at the Old Bailey for murder. Never did such a constellation of genius enlighten the awful Sessions House, emphatically called Justice Hall; Mr. Burke, Mr. Garrick, Mr. Beauclerk, and Dr. Johnson; and undoubtedly their favourable testimony had due weight with the Court and Jury. Johnson gave his evidence in a slow, deliberate, and distinct manner, which was uncommonly impressive. It is well known that Mr. Baretti was acquitted.

On the 26th of October we dined together at the Mitre tavern. I found fault with Foote for indulging his talent of ridicule at the expense of his visitors, which I colloquially termed making fools of his company. JOHNSON: 'Why, sir, when you go to see Foote you do not go to see a saint: you go to see a man who will be entertained at your house, and then bring you on a public stage; who will entertain you at his house for the very purpose of bringing you on a public stage. Sir, he does not make fools of his company; they whom he exposes are fools already; he only brings them into action.'

Talking of trade, he observed: 'It is a mistaken notion that a vast deal of money is brought into a nation by trade. It is not so. Commodities come from commodities; but trade produces no capital accession of wealth. However, though there should be little profit in money, there is a considerable profit in pleasure, as it gives to one nation the productions of another; as we have wines and fruits and many other foreign articles brought to us.' BOSWELL : 'Yes, sir, and there is a profit in pleasure by its furnishing occupation to such numbers of mankind.' JOHNSON : 'Why, sir, you cannot call that pleasure to which all are averse, and which none begin but with the hope of leaving off; a thing which men dislike before they have tried it, and when they have tried it.' BOSWELL : 'But, sir, the mind must be employed, and we grow weary when idle.' JOHNSON : 'That is, sir, because others being busy we want company; but if we were all idle there would be no growing weary; we should all entertain one another. There is, indeed, this in trade:—it gives men an opportunity of improving their situation. If there were no trade, many who are poor would always remain poor. But no man loves labour for itself.' BOSWELL : 'Yes, sir, I know a person who does. He is a very laborious judge, and he loves the labour.' JOHNSON : 'Sir, that is because he loves respect and distinction. Could he have them without labour he would like it less.' BOSWELL : 'He tells me he likes it for itself.'—'Why, sir, he fancies so, because he is not accustomed to abstract.

We went home to his house to tea. Mrs. Williams made it with sufficient dexterity, notwithstanding her blindness, though her manner of satisfying herself that the cups were full enough appeared to me a little awkward; for I fancied she put her finger down a certain way till she felt the tea touch it.[1] In my first elation at being allowed the privilege of attending Dr. Johnson at his late visits to this lady, which was like being *e secretioribus consiliis*, I willingly drank cup after cup, as if it had been the Heliconian spring. But as the charm of novelty went off I grew more fastidious; and besides, I discovered that she was of a peevish temper.

There was a pretty large circle this evening. Dr. Johnson was in very good humour, lively, and ready to talk upon all subjects. Mr. Fergusson, the self-taught philosopher, told him of a new-invented machine which went without horses: a man who sat in it turned a handle, which worked a spring that drove it forward. 'Then, sir (said Johnson), what is gained is, the man has his choice whether he will move himself alone, or himself and the machine too.' Dominicetti being mentioned, he would not allow him any merit. 'There is nothing in all this boasted system. No, sir; medicated baths can be no better than warm water: their only effect can be that of tepid moisture.' One of the company took the other side, maintaining that medicines of various sorts, and some too of most powerful effect, are introduced into

---

[1] I have since had reason to think that I was mistaken; for I have been informed by a lady, who was long intimate with her, and likely to be a more accurate observer of such matters, that she had acquired such a niceness of touch as to know, by the feeling on the outside of the cup, how near it was to being full.

the human frame by the medium of the pores; and, therefore, when warm water is impregnated with salutiferous substances, it may produce great effects as a bath. This appeared to me very satisfactory. Johnson did not answer it; but talking for victory, and determined to be master of the field, he had recourse to the device which Goldsmith imputed to him in the witty words of one of Cibber's comedies: 'There is no arguing with Johnson; for when his pistol misses fire, he knocks you down with the butt-end of it.' He turned to the gentleman, 'Well, sir, go to Dominicetti, and get thyself fumigated; but be sure that the steam be directed to thy *head*, for *that* is the *peccant part*.' This produced a triumphant roar of laughter from the motley assembly of philosophers, printers, and dependants, male and female.

I know not how so whimsical a thought came into my mind, but I asked, 'If, sir, you were shut up in a castle, and a new-born child with you, what would you do?' JOHNSON: 'Why, sir, I should not much like my company.' BOSWELL: 'But would you take the trouble of rearing it?' He seemed, as may be supposed, unwilling to pursue the subject: but upon my persevering in my question, replied, 'Why yes, sir, I would; but I must have all conveniences. If I had no garden, I would make a shed on the roof, and take it there for fresh air. I should feed it, and wash it much, and with warm water, to please it, not with cold water to give it pain.' BOSWELL: 'But, sir, does not heat relax?' JOHNSON: 'Sir, you are not to imagine the water is to be very hot. I would not *coddle* the child. No, sir, the hardy method of treating children does no good. I'll take you five children

from London, who shall cuff five Highland children.
· Sir, a man bred in London will carry a burden, or run,
or wrestle, as well as a man brought up in the hardest
manner in the country.' BOSWELL: 'Good living, I
suppose, makes the Londoners strong.' JOHNSON:
'Why, sir, I don't know that it does. Our chairmen
from Ireland, who are as strong men as any, have been
brought up upon potatoes. Quantity makes up for
quality.' BOSWELL: 'Would you teach this child that
I have furnished you with, anything?' JOHNSON:
'No, I should not be apt to teach it.' BOSWELL:
'Would not you have a pleasure in teaching it?'
JOHNSON: 'No, sir, I should *not* have a pleasure in
teaching it.' BOSWELL: 'Have you not a pleasure in
teaching men?—*There* I have you. You have the
same pleasure in teaching men, that I should have
in teaching children.' JOHNSON: 'Why, something
about that.'

BOSWELL: 'Do you think, sir, that what is called
natural affection is born with us? It seems to me to
be the effect of habit, or of gratitude for kindness.
No child has it for a parent, whom it has not seen.'
JOHNSON: 'Why, sir, I think there is an instinctive
natural affection in parents towards their children.'

Russia being mentioned as likely to become a great
empire by the rapid increase of population. JOHNSON:
'Why, sir, I see no prospect of their propagating more.
They can have no more children than they can get.
I know of no way to make them breed more than
they do. It is not from reason and prudence that
people marry, but from inclination. A man is poor;
he thinks, "I cannot be worse, and so I'll e'en take
Peggy."' BOSWELL: 'But have not nations been

more populous at one period than another?' JOHN-
SON: 'Yes, sir; but that has been owing to the people
being less thinned at one period than another, whether
by emigrations, war, or pestilence, not by their being
more or less prolific. Births at all times bear the
same proportion to the same number of people.'
BOSWELL: 'But, to consider the state of our own
country;—does not throwing a number of farms into
one hand hurt population?' JOHNSON: 'Why no,
sir; the same quantity of food being produced, will be
consumed by the same number of mouths, though the
people may be disposed of in different ways. We see,
if corn be dear, and butchers' meat cheap, the farmers
all apply themselves to the raising of corn, till it
becomes plentiful and cheap, and then butchers' meat
becomes dear; so that an equality is always preserved.
No, sir, let fanciful men do as they will, depend upon
it, it is difficult to disturb the system of life.' BOSWELL:
'But, sir, is it not a very bad thing for landlords to
oppress their tenants, by raising their rents?' JOHN-
SON: 'Very bad. But, sir, it never can have any
general influence; it may distress some individuals.
For, consider this: landlords cannot do without
tenants. Now tenants will not give more for land
than land is worth. If they can make more of their
money by keeping a shop, or any other way, they'll
do it, and so oblige landlords to let land come back to
a reasonable rent, in order that they may get tenants.
Land, in England, is an article of commerce. A
tenant who pays his landlord his rent, thinks himself
no more obliged to him than you think yourself
obliged to a man in whose shop you buy a piece of
goods. He knows the landlord does not let him have

his land for less than he can get from others, in the same manner as the shopkeeper sells his goods. No shopkeeper sells a yard of ribbon for sixpence when sevenpence is the current price.' BOSWELL : 'But, sir, is it not better that tenants should be dependent on landlords?' JOHNSON : 'Why, sir, as there are many more tenants than landlords, perhaps, strictly speaking, we should wish not. But if you please you may let your lands cheap, and so get the value, part in money, and part in homage. I should agree with you in that.' BOSWELL : 'So, sir, you laugh at schemes of political improvement.' JOHNSON : 'Why, sir, most schemes of political improvement are very laughable things.'

He observed : 'Providence has wisely ordered that the more numerous men are, the more difficult it is for them to agree in anything, and so they are governed. There is no doubt that if the poor should reason, "We'll be the poor no longer, we'll make the rich take their turn," they could easily do it, were it not that they can't agree. So the common soldiers, though so much more numerous than their officers, are governed by them for the same reason.'

He said : 'Mankind have a strong attachment to the habitations to which they have been accustomed. You see the inhabitants of Norway do not with one consent quit it, and go to some part of America, where there is a mild climate, and where they may have the same produce from land with the tenth part of the labour. No, sir ; their affection for their old dwellings, and the terror of a general change, keep them at home. Thus, we see many of the finest spots in the world thinly inhabited, and many rugged spots well inhabited.'

The *London Chronicle,* which was the only news-paper he constantly took in, being brought, the office of reading it aloud was assigned to me. I was diverted by his impatience. He made me pass over so many parts of it, that my task was very easy. He would not suffer one of the petitions to the King about the Middlesex election to be read.

I had hired a Bohemian as my servant while I re-mained in London, and being much pleased with him, I asked Dr. Johnson whether his being a Roman Catholic should prevent my taking him with me to Scotland? JOHNSON : 'Why no, sir. If *he* has no objection, you can have none.' BOSWELL : 'So, sir, you are no great enemy to the Roman Catholic re-ligion.' JOHNSON : 'No more, sir, than to the Pres-byterian religion.' BOSWELL : 'You are joking.' JOHNSON : 'No, sir, I really think so. Nay, sir, of the two, I prefer the Popish.' BOSWELL : 'How so, sir?' JOHNSON : 'Why, sir, the Presbyterians have no church, no apostolical ordination.' BOSWELL : 'And do you think that absolutely essential, sir?' JOHNSON : 'Why, sir, as it was an apostolic institution, I think it is dangerous to be without it. And, sir, the Presbyterians have no public worship : they have no form of prayer in which they know they are to join. They go to hear a man pray, and are to judge whether they will join with him.' BOSWELL : 'But, sir, their doctrine is the same with that of the Church of Eng-land. Their confession of faith, and the thirty-nine articles, contain the same points, even the doctrine of predestination.' JOHNSON : 'Why yes, sir ; predesti-nation was a part of the clamour of the times, so it is mentioned in our articles, but with as little positive-ness as could be.' Boswell: 'Is it necessary, sir, to believe all the thirty-nine articles?' Johnson: 'Why, sir, that is a question which has been much agitated. Some have thought it necessary that they should all be believed; others have considered them to be only articles of peace,[1] that is to say, you are not to preach against them.' Boswell: 'It appears to me, sir, that predestination, or what is equivalent to it, cannot be avoided, if we hold a universal prescience in the Deity.' Johnson: 'Why, sir, does not God every day see the things going on without preventing them?' Boswell: 'True, sir, but if a thing be *certainly* foreseen, it must be fixed, and cannot happen otherwise; and if we apply this consideration to the human mind, there is no free will, nor do I see how prayer can be of any avail.' He mentioned Dr. Clarke, and Bishop Bramhall on Liberty and Necessity, and bid me read South's Sermons on Prayer; but avoided the question which has excruciated philosophers and divines beyond any other. I did not press it further, when I perceived that he was displeased, and shrunk from any abridgment of an attribute usually ascribed to the divinity, however irreconcilable in its full extent with the grand system of moral government. His supposed

---

[1] [Dr. Simon Patrick (afterwards Bishop of Ely) thus expresses himself on this subject in a letter to the learned Dr. John Mapletoft, dated Feb. 8, 1682-3:

'I always took the Articles to be only articles of communion; and so Bishop Bramhall expressly maintains against the Bishop of Chalcedon; and I remember well that Bishop Sanderson, when the King was first restored, received the subscription of an acquaintance of mine, which he declared was not to them as articles of *faith*, but *peace*. I think you need make no scruple of the matter, because all that I know so understand the meaning of subscription, and upon other terms would not subscribe.' The above was printed some years ago in the *European Magazine*, from the original, now in the hands of Mr. Mapletoft, surgeon at Chertsey, grandson to Dr. John Mapletoft.—M.]

orthodoxy here cramped the vigorous powers of his
understanding. He was confined by a chain which
early imagination and long habit made him think
massy and strong, but which, had he ventured to try,
he could at once have snapped asunder.

I proceeded: 'What do you think, sir, of Purgatory,
as believed by the Roman Catholics?' JOHNSON:
'Why, sir, it is a very harmless doctrine. They are
of opinion that the generality of mankind are neither
so obstinately wicked as to deserve everlasting punishment, nor so good as to merit being admitted into the
society of blessed spirits ; and therefore that God is
graciously pleased to allow of a middle state, where
they may be purified by certain degrees of suffering.
You see, sir, there is nothing unreasonable in this.'
BOSWELL: 'But then, sir, their masses for the dead?'
JOHNSON: 'Why, sir, if it be once established that
there are souls in purgatory, it is as proper to pray for
them, as for our brethren of mankind who are yet
in this life.' BOSWELL: 'The idolatry of the Mass?'
JOHNSON: 'Sir, there is no idolatry in the Mass.
They believe God to be there, and they adore him.'
BOSWELL: 'The worship of Saints?' JOHNSON: 'Sir,
they do not worship saints ; they invoke them ; they
only ask their prayers. I am talking all this time of
the *doctrines* of the Church of Rome. I grant you that
in *practice*, Purgatory is made a lucrative imposition,
and that the people do become idolatrous as they
recommend themselves to the tutelary protection of
particular saints. I think their giving the sacrament
only in one kind is criminal, because it is contrary to
the express institution of Christ, and I wonder how
the Council of Trent admitted it.' BOSWELL: 'Con-

fession?' JOHNSON: 'Why, I don't know but that is a good thing. The Scripture says, "Confess your faults one to another," and the priests confess as well as the laity. Then it must be considered that their absolution is only upon repentance, and often upon penance also. You think your sins may be forgiven without penance, upon repentance alone.'

I thus ventured to mention all the common objections against the Roman Catholic Church, that I might hear so great a man upon them. What he said is here accurately recorded. But it is not improbable that if one had taken the other side, he might have reasoned differently.

I must however mention that he had a respect for *the old religion,* as the mild Melanchthon called that of the Roman Catholic Church, even while he was exerting himself for its reformation in some particulars. Sir William Scott informs me, that he heard Johnson say, ' A man who is converted from Protestantism to Popery, may be sincere: he parts with nothing; he is only superadding to what he already had. But a convert from Popery to Protestantism gives up so much of what he has held as sacred as anything that he retains ; there is so much *laceration of mind* in such a conversion, that it can hardly be sincere and lasting.' The truth of this reflection may be confirmed by many and eminent instances, some of which will occur to most of my readers.

When we were alone, I introduced the subject of death, and endeavoured to maintain that the fear of it might be got over. I told him that David Hume said to me, he was no more uneasy to think he should *not be* after his life, than that he *had not been* before he began to exist. JOHNSON: 'Sir, if he really thinks so, his perceptions are disturbed; he is mad; if he does not think so, he lies. He may tell you he holds his finger in the flame of a candle, without feeling pain; would you believe him? When he does, he at least gives up all he has.' BOSWELL: 'Foote, sir, told me that when he was very ill he was not afraid to die.' JOHNSON: 'It is not true, sir. Hold a pistol to Foote's breast, or to Hume's breast, and threaten to kill them, and you'll see how they behave.' BOSWELL: 'But may we not fortify our minds for the approach of death?' Here I am sensible I was in the wrong, to bring before his view what he ever looked upon with horror; for although when in a celestial frame of mind in his *Vanity of Human Wishes*, he has supposed death to be 'kind Nature's signal for retreat,' from his state of being to 'a happier seat,' his thoughts upon this awful change were in general full of dismal apprehensions. His mind resembled the vast amphitheatre, the Colosseum at Rome. In the centre stood his judgment, which, like a mighty gladiator, combated those apprehensions that, like the wild beasts of the arena, were all around in cells, ready to be let out upon him. After a conflict, he drives them back into their dens; but not killing them, they were still assailing him. To my question whether we might not fortify our minds for the approach of death, he answered, in a passion, 'No, sir, let it alone. It matters not how a man dies, but how he lives. The act of dying is not of importance, it lasts so short a time.' He added (with an earnest look), 'A man knows it must be so, and submits. It will do him no good to whine.'

I attempted to continue the conversation. He was

so provoked, that he said, 'Give us no more of this,' and was thrown into such a state of agitation, that he expressed himself in a way that alarmed and distressed me; showed an impatience that I should leave him, and when I was going away, called to me sternly, 'Don't let us meet to-morrow.'

I went home exceedingly uneasy. All the harsh observations which I had ever heard made upon his character crowded into my mind; and I seemed to myself like the man who had put his head into the lion's mouth a great many times with perfect safety, but at last had it bit off.

Next morning I sent him a note, stating that I might have been in the wrong, but it was not intentionally; he was therefore, I could not help thinking, too severe upon me. That notwithstanding our agreement not to meet that day I would call on him in my way to the city, and stay five minutes by my watch. 'You are (said I) in my mind, since last night, surrounded with cloud and storm. Let me have a glimpse of sunshine, and go about my affairs in serenity and cheerfulness.'

Upon entering his study I was glad that he was not alone, which would have made our meeting more awkward. There were with him Mr. Steevens and Mr. Tyers, both of whom I now saw for the first time. My note had, on his own reflection, softened him, for he received me very complacently; so that I unexpectedly found myself at ease; and joined in the conversation.

He said the critics had done too much honour to Sir Richard Blackmore, by writing so much against him. That in his *Creation* he had been helped by various wits, a line by Phillips and a line by Tickell; so that by their aid and that of others, the poem had been made out.

I defended Blackmore's supposed lines, which have been ridiculed as absolute nonsense:

> 'A painted vest Prince Voltiger had on,
> Which from a naked Pict his grandsire won.'[1]

I maintained it to be a poetical conceit. A Pict being painted, if he is slain in battle, and a vest is made of his skin, it is a painted vest won from him, though he was naked.

Johnson spoke unfavourably of a certain pretty voluminous author, saying, 'He used to write anonymous books, and then other books commending those books, in which there was something of rascality.'

I whispered him, 'Well, sir, you are now in good humour.' JOHNSON: 'Yes, sir.' I was going to leave him, and had got as far as the staircase. He

---

[1] An acute correspondent of the *European Magazine*, April 1792, has completely exposed a mistake which has been unaccountably frequent in ascribing these lines to Blackmore, notwithstanding that Sir Richard Steele, in that very popular work *The Spectator*, mentions them as written by the author of *The British Princes*, the Hon. Edward Howard. The correspondent above mentioned shows this mistake to be so inveterate, that not only *I* defended the lines as Blackmore's in the presence of Dr. Johnson without any contradiction or doubt of their authenticity, but that the Reverend Mr. Whitaker has asserted in print that he understands they were *suppressed* in the late edition or editions of Blackmore. 'After all (says this intelligent writer), it is not unworthy of particular observation that these lines so often quoted do not exist either in Blackmore or Howard.' In *The British Princes*, 8vo, 1669, now before me, p. 96, they stand thus:

> 'A vest as admired Voltiger had on,
> Which, from this Island's foes, his grandsire won,
> Whose artful colour pass'd the Tyrian dye,
> Obliged to triumph in this legacy.'

It is probable, I think, that some wag, in order to make Howard still more ridiculous than he really was, has formed the couplet as it now circulates.

stopped me, and smiling, said, 'Get you gone *in*,' a curious mode of inviting me to stay, which I accordingly did for some time longer.

This little incidental quarrel and reconciliation, which, perhaps, I may be thought to have detailed too minutely, must be esteemed as one of many proofs which his friends had, that though he might be charged with *bad humour* at times, he was always a *good-natured* man; and I have heard Sir Joshua Reynolds, a nice and delicate observer of manners, particularly remark, that when upon any occasion Johnson had been rough to any person in company he took the first opportunity of reconciliation, by drinking to him, or addressing his discourse to him; but if he found his dignified indirect overtures sullenly neglected, he was quite indifferent, and considered himself as having done all that he ought to do, and the other as now in the wrong.

Being to set out for Scotland on the 10th of November, I wrote to him at Streatham, begging that he would meet me in town on the 9th; but if this should be very inconvenient to him, I would go thither. His answer was as follows :

TO JAMES BOSWELL, ESQ.

'DEAR SIR,—Upon balancing the inconveniences of both parties, I find it will less incommode you to spend your night here, than me to come to town. I wish to see you, and am ordered by the lady of this house to invite you hither. Whether you can come or not I shall not have any occasion of writing to you again before your marriage, and therefore tell you now, that with great sincerity I wish you happiness. I am, dear sir, your most affectionate humble servant,

'SAM. JOHNSON.

'*Nov.* 9, 1769.

I was detained in town till it was too late on the ninth, so went to him early in the morning of the tenth of November. 'Now (said he), that you are going to marry, do not expect more from life than life will afford. You may often find yourself out of humour, and you may often think your wife not studious enough to please you ; and yet you may have reason to consider yourself as upon the whole very happily married.'

Talking of marriage in general, he observed : 'Our marriage service is too refined. It is calculated only for the best kind of marriages ; whereas, we should have a form for matches of convenience, of which there are many.' He agreed with me that there was no absolute necessity for having the marriage ceremony performed by a regular clergyman, for this was not commanded in Scripture.

I was volatile enough to repeat to him a little epigrammatic song of mine on matrimony, which Mr. Garrick had a few days before procured to be set to music by the very ingenious Mr. Dibdin :

A MATRIMONIAL THOUGHT

'In the blithe days of honey-moon,
  With Kate's allurements smitten,
I loved her late, I loved her soon,
  And call'd her dearest kitten.

But now my kitten 's grown a cat,
  And cross like other wives,
O ! by my soul, my honest Mat,
  I fear she has nine lives.'

My illustrious friend said, 'It is very well, sir ; but you should not swear.' Upon which I altered 'O ! by my soul,' to 'Alas, alas !'

He was so good as to accompany me to London, and see me into the post-chaise which was to carry me on my road to Scotland. And sure I am, that however inconsiderable many of the particulars recorded at this time may appear to some, they will be esteemed by the best part of my readers as genuine traits of his character, contributing together to give a full, fair, and distinct view of it.

In 1770 he published a political pamphlet, entitled *The False Alarm*, intended to justify the conduct of ministry and their majority in the House of Commons, for having virtually assumed it as an axiom, that the expulsion of a Member of Parliament was equivalent to exclusion, and thus having declared Colonel Lutterel to be duly elected for the county of Middlesex, notwithstanding Mr. Wilkes had a great majority of votes. This being justly considered as a gross violation of the right of election, an alarm for the constitution extended itself all over the kingdom. To prove this alarm to be false was the purpose of Johnson's pamphlet; but even his vast powers were inadequate to cope with constitutional truth and reason, and his argument failed of effect; and the House of Commons have since expunged the offensive resolution from their Journals. That the House of Commons might have expelled Mr. Wilkes repeatedly, and as often as he should be rechosen, was not denied; but incapacitation cannot be but an act of the whole legislature. It was wonderful to see how a prejudice in favour of government in general, and an aversion to popular clamour, could blind and contract such an understanding as Johnson's in this particular case;

yet the wit, the sarcasm, the eloquent vivacity which this pamphlet displayed, made it be read with great avidity at the time, and it will ever be read with plea-sure, for the sake of its composition. That it en-deavoured to infuse a narcotic indifference as to public concerns into the minds of the people, and that it broke out sometimes into an extreme coarseness of contemptuous abuse, is but too evident.

It must not, however, be omitted that when the storm of his violence subsides he takes a fair oppor-tunity to pay a grateful compliment to the King, who had rewarded his merit :

'These low-born rulers have endeavoured, surely without effect, to alienate the affections of the people from the only king who for almost a century has much appeared to desire, or much endeavoured to deserve them.'

And

'Every honest man must lament that the faction has been regarded with frigid neutrality by the Tories, who being long accustomed to signalise their principles by opposition to the court, do not yet consider that they have at last a king who knows not the name of party, and who wishes to be the common father of all his people.'

To this pamphlet, which was at once discovered to be Johnson's, several answers came out, in which care was taken to remind the public of his former attacks upon government, and of his now being a pensioner, without allowing for the honourable terms upon which Johnson's pension was granted and accepted, or the change of system which the British court had under-gone upon the accession of his present Majesty. He was, however, soothed in the highest strain of pan-

egyric in a poem, called 'The Remonstrance,' by the
Reverend Mr. Stockdale, to whom he was, upon many
occasions, a kind protector.

The following admirable minute made by him
describes so well his own state, and that of numbers
to whom self-examination is habitual, that I cannot
omit it:

'*June* 1, 1770.—Every man naturally persuades himself
that he can keep his resolutions, nor is he convinced of his
imbecility but by length of time and frequency of experiment.
This opinion of our own constancy is so prevalent that we
always despise him who suffers his general and settled purpose to be overpowered by an occasional desire. They, therefore, whom frequent failures have made desperate, cease to
form resolutions; and they who are become cunning do not
tell them. Those who do not make them are very few, but of
their effect little is perceived; for scarcely any man persists
in a course of life planned by choice, but as he is restrained
from deviation by some external power. He who may live
as he will, seldom lives long in the observation of his own
rules.'[1]

Of this year I have obtained the following letters:

TO THE REV. DR. FARMER, CAMBRIDGE

'SIR,—As no man ought to keep wholly to himself any
possession that may be useful to the public, I hope you will
not think me unreasonably intrusive, if I have recourse to you
for such information as you are more able to give me than any
other man.

'In support of an opinion which you have already placed
above the need of any more support, Mr. Steevens, a very
ingenious gentleman, lately of King's College, has collected
an account of all the translations which Shakespeare might
have seen and used. He wishes his catalogue to be perfect,
and therefore entreats that you will favour him by the inser-

---

[1] *Prayers and Meditations*, p. 95.

tion of such additions as the accuracy of your inquiries has enabled you to make. To this request I take the liberty of adding my own solicitation.

'We have no immediate use for this catalogue, and therefore do not desire that it should interrupt or hinder your more important employments. But it will be kind to let us know that you receive it.—I am, sir, etc.   SAM. JOHNSON.

'*Johnson's Court, Fleet Street,*
        '*March* 21, 1770.'

TO THE REV. MR. THOMAS WARTON

'DEAR SIR,—The readiness with which you were pleased to promise me some notes on Shakespeare was a new instance of your friendship. I shall not hurry you ; but am desired by Mr. Steevens, who helps me in this edition, to let you know that we shall print the tragedies first, and shall therefore want first the notes which belong to them. We think not to incommode the readers with a supplement ; and therefore, what we cannot put into its proper place, will do us no good. We shall not begin to print before the end of six weeks, perhaps not so soon.—I am, etc.   SAM. JOHNSON.

'*London, June* 23, 1770.'

TO THE REV. DR. JOSEPH WARTON

'DEAR SIR,—I am revising my edition of Shakespeare, and remember that I formerly misrepresented your opinion of Lear. Be pleased to write the paragraph as you would have it, and send it. If you have any remarks of your own upon that or any other play, I shall gladly receive them.

'Make my compliments to Mrs. Warton. I sometimes think of wandering for a few days to Winchester, but am apt to delay.—I am, sir, your most humble servant,

                                'SAM. JOHNSON.

'*Sept.* 27, 1770.'

TO MR. FRANCIS BARBER, AT MRS. CLAPP'S, BISHOP-STORTFORD, HERTFORDSHIRE

'DEAR FRANCIS,—I am at last sat down to write to you, and should very much blame myself for having neglected you so long, if I did not impute that and many other failings to want of health. I hope not to be so long silent again. I am very well satisfied with your progress, if you can really perform the exercises which you are set; and I hope Mr. Ellis does not suffer you to impose on him, or on yourself.

'Make my compliments to Mr. Ellis, and to Mrs. Clapp, and Mr. Smith.

'Let me know what English books you read for your entertainment. You can never be wise unless you love reading.

'Do not imagine that I shall forget or forsake you: for if, when I examine you, I find that you have not lost your time, you shall want no encouragement from yours affectionately,

'SAM. JOHNSON.

'*London, Sept. 25, 1770.*'

TO MR. FRANCIS BARBER

'DEAR FRANCIS,—I hope you mind your business. I design you shall stay with Mrs. Clapp these holidays. If you are invited out you may go, if Mr. Ellis gives leave. I have ordered you some clothes, which you will receive, I believe, next week. My compliments to Mrs. Clapp and to Mr. Ellis, and Mr. Smith, etc.—I am, your affectionate

'SAM. JOHNSON.

'*December 7, 1770.*'

During this year there was a total cessation of all correspondence between Dr. Johnson and me, without any coldness on either side, but merely from procrastination, continued from day to day; and as I was not in London, I had no opportunity of enjoying his company and recording his conversation. To supply this blank, I shall present my readers with some *Collectanea*, obligingly furnished to me by the Rev. Dr. Maxwell, of Falkland, in Ireland, some time assistant preacher at the Temple, and for many years the social friend of Johnson, who spoke of him with a very kind regard:

'My acquaintance with that great and venerable character commenced in the year 1754. I was introduced to him by Mr. Grierson,[1] his Majesty's printer at Dublin, a gentleman of uncommon learning, and great wit and vivacity. Mr. Grierson died in Germany, at the age of twenty-seven. Dr. Johnson highly respected his abilities, and often observed, that he possessed more extensive knowledge than any man of his years he had ever known. His industry was equal to his talents; and he particularly excelled in every species of philological learning, and was, perhaps, the best critic of the age he lived in.

'I must always remember with gratitude my obligation to Mr. Grierson, for the honour and happiness of Dr. Johnson's acquaintance and friendship, which continued uninterrupted and undiminished to his death : a connection, that was at once the pride and happiness of my life.

'What pity it is, that so much wit and good sense as he continually exhibited in conversation, should perish unrecorded ! Few persons quitted his company without perceiving themselves wiser and better than they were before. On serious subjects he flashed the most interesting conviction upon his auditors ; and upon lighter topics, you might have supposed—*Albano Musas de monte locutas.*

'Though I can hope to add but little to the celebrity of so exalted a character, by any communications I can furnish, yet out of pure respect to his memory, I will venture to transmit to you some anecdotes concerning him, which fell under my own observation. The very *minutiæ* of such a character must be interesting, and may be compared to the filings of diamonds.

'In politics he was deemed a Tory, but certainly was not so in the obnoxious or party sense of the term : for while he asserted the legal and salutary prerogatives of the crown, he no less respected the constitutional liberties of the people. Whiggism, at the time of the Revolution, he said, was accom-

---

[1] Son of the learned Mrs. Grierson, who was patronised by the late Lord Granville, and was the editor of several of the classics.

[Her edition of Tacitus, with the notes of Rychius, in three volumes, 8vo, 1730, was dedicated in very elegant Latin to John, Lord Carteret (afterwards Earl Granville), by whom she was patronised during his residence in Ireland as Lord Lieutenant between 1724 and 1730.—M.]

panied with certain principles; but latterly, as a mere party distinction under Walpole and the Pelhams, was no better than the politics of stock-jobbers, and the religion of infidels.

'He detested the idea of governing by parliamentary corruption, and asserted most strenuously, that a prince steadily and conspicuously pursuing the interests of his people, could not fail of parliamentary concurrence. A prince of ability, he contended, might and should be the directing soul and spirit of his own administration; in short, his own minister, and not the mere head of a party: and then, and not till then, would the royal dignity be sincerely respected.

'Johnson seemed to think, that a certain degree of crown influence over the Houses of Parliament (not meaning a corrupt and shameful dependence) was very salutary, nay, even necessary, in our mixed government. "For (said he), if the members were under no crown influence, and disqualified from receiving any gratification from court, and resembled, as they possibly might, Pym and Haslerig, and other stubborn and sturdy members of the Long Parliament, the wheels of government would be totally obstructed. Such men would oppose, merely to show their power, from envy, jealousy, and perversity of disposition: and not gaining themselves, would hate and oppose all who did: not loving the person of the prince, and conceiving they owed him little gratitude, from the mere spirit of insolence and contradiction, they would oppose and thwart him upon all occasions."

'The inseparable imperfection annexed to all human governments, consisted, he said, in not being able to create a sufficient fund of virtue and principle to carry the laws into due and effectual execution. Wisdom might plan, but virtue alone could execute. And where could sufficient virtue be found? A variety of delegated, and often discretionary, powers, must be intrusted somewhere; which, if not governed by integrity and conscience, would necessarily be abused, till at last the constable would sell his for a shilling.

'This excellent person was sometimes charged with abetting slavish and arbitrary principles of government. Nothing in my opinion could be a grosser calumny and misrepresentation; for how can it be rationally supposed, that he should adopt such pernicious and absurd opinions, who supported his philosophical character with so much dignity, was extremely jealous of his personal liberty and independence, and could not brook the smallest appearance of neglect or insult, even from the highest personages ?

'But let us view him in some instances of more familiar life.

'His general mode of life during my acquaintance, seemed to be pretty uniform. About twelve o'clock I commonly visited him, and frequently found him in bed, or declaiming over his tea, which he drank very plentifully. He generally had a levee of morning visitors, chiefly men of letters; Hawkesworth, Goldsmith, Murphy, Langton, Steevens, Beauclerk, etc. etc., and sometimes learned ladies; particularly I remember a French lady of wit and fashion doing him the honour of a visit. He seemed to me to be considered as a kind of public oracle, whom everybody thought they had a right to visit and consult; and doubtless they were well rewarded. I never could discover how he found time for his compositions. He declaimed all the morning, then went to dinner at a tavern, where he commonly stayed late, and then drank his tea at some friend's house, over which he loitered a great while, but seldom took supper. I fancy he must have read and wrote chiefly in the night, for I can scarcely recollect that he ever refused going with me to a tavern, and he often went to Ranelagh, which he deemed a place of innocent recreation.

'He frequently gave all the silver in his pocket to the poor, who watched him between his house and the tavern where he dined. He walked the streets at all hours, and said he was never robbed, for the rogues knew he had little money, nor had the appearance of having much.

'Though the most accessible and communicative man alive, yet when he suspected he was invited to be exhibited, he constantly spurned the invitation.

'Two young women from Staffordshire visited him when I was present, to consult him on the subject of Methodism, to which they were inclined. "Come (said he), you pretty fools, dine with Maxwell and me at the Mitre, and we will talk over that subject"; which they did, and after dinner he took one of them upon his knee, and fondled her for half an hour together.

'Upon a visit to me at a country lodging near Twickenham, he asked what sort of society I had there. I told him: But indifferent; as they chiefly consisted of opulent traders, retired from business. He said he never much liked that class of people; "for, sir (said he), they have lost the civility of tradesmen, without acquiring the manners of gentlemen."

'Johnson was much attached to London: he observed that a man stored his mind better there than anywhere else; and that in remote situations a man's body might be feasted, but his mind was starved, and his faculties apt to degenerate, from want of exercise and competition. No place (he said) cured a man's vanity or arrogance so well as London; for as no man was either great or good *per se*, but as compared with others not so good or great, he was sure to find in the metropolis many his equals, and some his superiors. He observed, that a man in London was in less danger of falling in love indiscreetly, than anywhere else; for there the difficulty of deciding between the conflicting pretensions of a vast variety of objects, kept him safe. He told me that he had frequently been offered country preferment, if he would consent to take orders; but he could not leave the improved society of the capital, or consent to exchange the exhilarating joys and splendid decorations of public life, for the obscurity, insipidity, and uniformity of remote situations.

'Speaking of Mr. Harte, Canon of Windsor, and writer of *The History of Gustavus Adolphus*, he much commended him as a scholar, and a man of the most companionable talents he had ever known. He said, the defects in his history proceeded not from imbecility, but from foppery.

'He loved, he said, the old blackletter books; they were rich in matter, though their style was inelegant; wonderfully so, considering how conversant the writers were with the best models of antiquity.

'Burton's *Anatomy of Melancholy*, he said, was the only book that ever took him out of bed two hours sooner than he wished to rise.[1]

'He frequently exhorted me to set about writing a History

---

[1] [This is perhaps the most frequently reprinted *dictum* of the Doctor. Every second-hand bookseller who has a copy of the *Anatomy* to sell prints it in his catalogue.—A. B.]

of Ireland, and archly remarked, there had been some good Irish writers, and that one Irishman might at least aspire to be equal to another. He had great compassion for the miseries and distresses of the Irish nation, particularly the Papists; and severely reprobated the barbarous debilitating policy of the British government, which, he said, was the most detestable mode of persecution. To a gentleman, who hinted such policy might be necessary to support the authority of the English government, he replied by saying, "Let the authority of the English government perish rather than be maintained by iniquity. Better would it be to restrain the turbulence of the natives by the authority of the sword, and to make them amenable to law and justice by an effectual and vigorous police, than to grind them to powder by all manner of disabilities and incapacities. Better (said he) to hang or drown people at once, than by an unrelenting persecution to beggar and starve them." The moderation and humanity of the present times have, in some measure, justified the wisdom of his observations.

'Dr. Johnson was often accused of prejudices, nay, antipathy, with regard to the natives of Scotland. Surely, so illiberal a prejudice never entered his mind: and it is well known, many natives of that respectable country possessed a large share in his esteem: nor were any of them ever excluded from his good offices, as far as opportunity permitted. True it is, he considered the Scotch, nationally, as a crafty, designing people, eagerly attentive to their own interest, and too apt to overlook the claims and pretensions of other people. "While they confine their benevolence, in a manner, exclusively to those of their own country, they expect to share in the good offices of other people. Now (said Johnson) this principle is either right or wrong ; if right, we should do well to imitate such conduct; if wrong, we cannot too much detest it."

'Being solicited to compose a funeral sermon for the daughter of a tradesman, he naturally inquired into the character of the deceased ; and being told she was remarkable for her humility and condescension to inferiors, he observed that those were very laudable qualities, but it might not be so easy to discover who the lady's inferiors were.

'Of a certain player he remarked that his conversation usually threatened and announced more than it performed; that he fed you with a continual renovation of hope, to end in a constant succession of disappointment.

'When exasperated by contradiction, he was apt to treat his opponents with too much acrimony: as, "Sir, you don't see your way through that question":—"Sir, you talk the language of ignorance." On my observing to him that a certain gentleman had remained silent the whole evening, in the midst of a very brilliant and learned society, "Sir," said he, "the conversation overflowed, and drowned him."

'His philosophy, though austere and solemn, was by no means morose and cynical, and never blunted the laudable sensibilities of his character, or exempted him from the influence of the tender passions. Want of tenderness, he always alleged, was want of parts, and was no less a proof of stupidity than depravity.

'Speaking of Mr. Hanway, who published *An Eight Days' Journey from London to Portsmouth*, "Jonas (said he) acquired some reputation by travelling abroad, but lost it all by travelling at home."

'Of the passion of love he remarked that its violence and ill effects were much exaggerated; for who knows any real sufferings on that head, more than from the exorbitancy of any other passion?

'He much commended Law's *Serious Call*, which, he said, was the finest piece of hortatory theology in any language. "Law (said he) fell latterly into the reveries of Jacob Behmen, whom Law alleged to have been somewhat in the same state with St. Paul, and to have seen *unutterable things*. Were it even so (said Johnson), Jacob would have resembled St. Paul still more, by not attempting to utter them."

'He observed that the established clergy in general did not preach plain enough; and that polished periods and glittering sentences flew over the heads of the common people, without any impression upon their hearts. Something might be necessary, he observed, to excite the affections of the common people, who were sunk in languor and lethargy, and therefore he supposed that the new concomitants of Methodism might probably produce so desirable an effect. The mind, like the body, he observed, delighted in change and novelty, and even in religion itself courted new appearances and modifications. Whatever might be thought of some Methodist teachers, he said, he could scarcely doubt the sincerity of that man, who travelled nine hundred miles in the month, and preached twelve times a week; for no adequate reward, merely temporal, could be given for such indefatigable labour.

'Of Dr. Priestley's theological works, he remarked that they tended to unsettle everything, and yet settled nothing.

'He was much affected by the death of his mother, and wrote to me to come and assist him to compose his mind, which indeed I found extremely agitated. He lamented that all serious and religious conversation was banished from the society of men, and yet great advantages might be derived from it. All acknowledged, he said, what hardly anybody practised, the obligations we were under of making the concerns of eternity the governing principles of our lives. Every man, he observed, at last wishes for retreat: he sees his expectations frustrated in the world, and begins to wean himself from it, and to prepare for everlasting separation.

'He observed that the influence of London now extended everywhere, and that from all manner of communication being opened, there shortly would be no remains of the ancient simplicity, or places of cheap retreat to be found.

'He was no admirer of blank verse, and said it always failed, unless sustained by the dignity of the subject. In blank verse, he said, the language suffered more distortion, to keep it out of prose, than any inconvenience or limitation to be apprehended from the shackles and circumspection of rhyme.

'He reproved me once for saying grace without mention of the name of our Lord Jesus Christ, and hoped in future I would be more mindful of the apostolical injunction.

'He refused to go out of a room before me at Mr. Langton's house, saying he hoped he knew his rank better than to presume to take place of a Doctor in Divinity. I mention such little anecdotes merely to show the peculiar turn and habit of his mind.

'He used frequently to observe that there was more to be

endured than enjoyed in the general condition of human life ; and frequently quoted those lines of Dryden :

"Strange cozenage ! none would live past years again,
    Yet all hope pleasure from what still remain."

For his part, he said, he never passed that week in his life which he would wish to repeat, were an angel to make the proposal to him.

'He was of opinion that the English nation cultivated both their soil and their reason better than any other people ; but admitted that the French, though not the highest, perhaps, in any department of literature, yet in every department were very high. Intellectual pre-eminence, he observed, was the highest superiority ; and that every nation derived their highest reputation from the splendour and dignity of their writers. Voltaire, he said, was a good narrator, and that his principal merit consisted in a happy selection and arrangement of circumstances.

'Speaking of the French novels, compared with Richardson's, he said, they might be pretty baubles, but a wren was not an eagle.

'In a Latin conversation with the Pere Boscovitch, at the house of Mrs. Cholmondeley, I heard him maintain the superiority of Sir Isaac Newton over all foreign philosophers,[1] with a dignity and eloquence that surprised that learned foreigner. It being observed to him that a rage for everything English prevailed much in France after Lord Chatham's glorious war, he said he did not wonder at it, for that we had drubbed those fellows into a proper reverence for us, and that their national petulance required periodical chastisement.

'Lord Lyttelton's *Dialogues* he deemed a nugatory performance. "That man (said he) sat down to write a book, to tell the world what the world had all his life been telling him."

'Somebody observing that the Scotch Highlanders in the year 1745 had made surprising efforts, considering their

---

[1] [In a Discourse by Sir William Jones, addressed to the Asiatic Society, Feb. 24, 1785, is the following passage : 'One of the most sagacious men in this age who continues, I hope, to improve and adorn it, Samuel Johnson, remarked in my hearing, that if Newton had flourished in ancient Greece he would have been worshipped as a Divinity.'—M.]

numerous wants and disadvantages: "Yes, sir (said he), their wants were numerous; but you have not mentioned the greatest of them all,—the want of law."

'Speaking of the *inward light*, to which some Methodists pretended, he said it was a principle utterly incompatible with social or civil security. "If a man (said he) pretends to a principle of action of which I can know nothing, nay, not so much as that he has it, but only that he pretends to it, how can I tell what that person may be prompted to do? When a person professes to be governed by a written ascertained law, I can then know where to find him."

'The poem of Fingal, he said, was a mere unconnected rhapsody, a tiresome repetition of the same images. "In vain shall we look for the *lucidus ordo*, where there is neither end nor object, design or moral, *nec certa recurrit imago.*"

' Being asked by a young nobleman what was become of the gallantry and military spirit of the old English nobility, he replied, "Why, my Lord, I'll tell you what has become of it: it is gone into the city to look for a fortune."

'Speaking of a dull, tiresome fellow, whom he chanced to meet, he said, "That fellow seems to me to possess but one idea, and that is a wrong one."

'Much inquiry having been made concerning a gentleman who had quitted a company where Johnson was, and no information being obtained; at last Johnson observed that "he did not care to speak ill of any man behind his back, but he believed the gentleman was an *attorney.*"

'He spoke with much contempt of the notice taken of Woodhouse, the political shoemaker. He said, it was all vanity and childishness: and that such objects were, to those who patronised them, mere mirrors of their own superiority. "They had better (said he) furnish the man with good implements for his trade, than raise subscriptions for his poems. He may make an excellent shoemaker, but can never make a good poet. A schoolboy's exercise may be a pretty thing for a schoolboy; but it is no treat for a man."

'Speaking of Boetius, who was the favourite writer of the middle ages, he said it was very surprising, that upon such a subject, and in such a situation, he should be *magis philosophus quam Christianus.*

'Speaking of Arthur Murphy, whom he very much loved, "I don't know (said he), that Arthur can be classed with the very first dramatic writers; yet at present I doubt much whether we have anything superior to Arthur."

'Speaking of the national debt, he said, it was an idle dream to suppose that the country could sink under it. Let the public creditors be ever so clamorous, the interest of millions must ever prevail over that of thousands.

'Of Dr. Kennicott's *Collations*, he observed, that though the text should not be much mended thereby, yet it was no small advantage to know that we had as good a text as the most consummate industry and diligence could procure.

'Johnson observed that so many objections might be made to everything, that nothing could overcome them but the necessity of doing something. No man would be of any profession, as simply opposed to not being of it: but every one must do something.

'He remarked that a London parish was a very comfortless thing; for the clergyman seldom knew the face of one out of ten parishioners.

'Of the late Mr. Mallet he spoke with no great respect: said, he was ready for any dirty job; that he had wrote against Byng at the instigation of the ministry, and was equally ready to write for him, provided he found his account in it.

'A gentleman who had been very unhappy in marriage, married immediately after his wife died; Johnson said it was the triumph of hope over experience.

'He observed that a man of sense and education should meet a suitable companion in a wife. It was a miserable thing when the conversation could only be such as, whether the mutton should be boiled or roasted, and probably a dispute about that.

'He did not approve of late marriages, observing that more was lost in point of time, than compensated for by any possible advantages. Even ill-assorted marriages were preferable to cheerless celibacy.

'Of old Sheridan he remarked, that he neither wanted parts nor literature; but that his vanity and Quixotism obscured his merits.

'He said foppery was never cured; it was the bad stamina of the mind, which, like those of the body, were never rectified; once a coxcomb, and always a coxcomb.

'Being told that Gilbert Cowper called him the Caliban of literature: "Well (said he), I must dub him the Punchinello."

'Speaking of the old Earl of Cork and Orrery, he said, "That man spent his life in catching at an object [literary eminence], which he had not power to grasp."

'To find a substitution for violated morality, he said, was the leading feature in all perversions of religion.

'He often used to quote, with great pathos, those fine lines of Virgil:[1]

'"*Optima quæque dies miseris mortalibus ævi*
Prima fugit; subeunt morbi, tristisque senectus,
Et labor, et duræ rapit inclementia mortis."

'Speaking of Homer, whom he venerated as the prince of poets, Johnson remarked that the advice given to Diomed[2] by his father, when he sent him to the Trojan war, was the noblest exhortation that could be instanced in any heathen writer, and comprised in a single line:

Αἰὲν ἀριστεύειν καὶ ὑπείροχον ἔμμεναι ἄλλων:

which, if I recollect well, is translated by Dr. Clarke thus: *semper appetere præstantissima, et omnibus aliis antecellere.*

'He observed, "It was a most mortifying reflection for any man to consider, *what he had done*, compared with what *he might have done.*"

'He said few people had intellectual resources sufficient to forego the pleasures of wine. They could not otherwise contrive how to fill the interval between dinner and supper.

'He went with me one Sunday to hear my old Master, Gregory Sharpe, preach at the Temple.—In the prefatory prayer, Sharpe ranted about *Liberty*, as a blessing most fervently to be implored, and its continuance prayed for. John-

---

[1] *Georg.* iii. 66.
[2] [Glaucus is the person who received this counsel: and Clarke's translation of the passage (*Il.* vi. 208), is as follows:
' Ut semper fortissime rem gererem, et superior virtute essem aliis.']

son observed that our *liberty* was in no sort of danger :—he would have done much better to pray against our *licentiousness*.

'One evening at Mrs. Montagu's, where a splendid company was assembled, consisting of the most eminent literary characters, I thought he seemed highly pleased with the respect and attention that were shown him, and asked him on our return home, if he was not highly *gratified* by his visit: "No, sir (said he), not highly *gratified*; yet I do not recollect to have passed many evenings *with fewer objections*."

'Though of no high extraction himself, he had much respect for birth and family, especially among ladies. He said, "Adventitious accomplishments may be possessed by all ranks; but one may easily distinguish the *born gentlewoman*."

'He said, "The poor in England were better provided for than in any other country of the same extent: he did not mean little Cantons, or petty Republics. Where a great proportion of the people (said he) are suffered to languish in helpless misery, that country must be ill policed, and wretchedly governed: a decent provision for the poor is the true test of civilisation.—Gentlemen of Education, he observed, were pretty much the same in all countries; the condition of the lower orders, the poor especially, was the true mark of national discrimination."

'When the Corn Laws were in agitation in Ireland, by which that country has been enabled not only to feed itself, but to export corn to a large amount, Sir Thomas Robinson observed that those laws might be prejudicial to the corn trade of England. "Sir Thomas (said he), you talk the language of a savage: what, sir, would you prevent any people from feeding themselves, if by any honest means they can do it?"

'It being mentioned that Garrick assisted Dr. Brown, the author of the *Estimate*,[1] in some dramatic composition, "No, sir (said Johnson), he would no more suffer Garrick to write a

---

1 [The *Inestimable Estimate* of Brown enjoyed at the date of its publication (1756) a greater popularity than was awarded in our own time to the late Dr. Pearson's glowing book, *National Life and Character*. Dr. Brown's forebodings of decadence received their answer in the expansion of England under Chatham's administration. It is an interesting book.—A. B.]

line in his play, than he would suffer him to mount his
pulpit."

'Speaking of Burke, he said, "It was commonly observed
he spoke too often in Parliament; but nobody could say he
did not speak well, though too frequently and too familiarly."

'Speaking of economy, he remarked, it was hardly worth
while to save anxiously twenty pounds a year. If a man
could save to that degree, so as to enable him to assume a
different rank in society, then, indeed, it might answer some
purpose.

' He observed, a principal source of erroneous judgment was,
viewing things partially and only on *one side*—as, for instance,
fortune-hunters, when they contemplated the fortunes *singly*
and *separately*, it was a dazzling and tempting object; but
when they came to possess the wives and their fortunes
together, they began to suspect they had not made quite so
good a bargain.

'Speaking of the late Duke of Northumberland living very
magnificently when Lord Lieutenant of Ireland, somebody
remarked, it would be difficult to find a suitable successor to
him : then, exclaimed Johnson, *he is only fit to succeed himself*.

'He advised me, if possible, to have a good orchard. He
knew, he said, a clergyman of small income, who brought up
a family very reputably, which he chiefly fed with apple
dumplings.

'He said he had known several good scholars among the
Irish gentlemen, but scarcely any of them correct in *quantity*.
He extended the same observation to Scotland.

'Speaking of a certain prelate, who exerted himself very
laudably in building churches and parsonage-houses : "However (said he), I do not find that he is esteemed a man of much
professional learning, or a liberal patron of it; yet, it is well
where a man possesses any strong positive excellence. Few
have all kinds of merit belonging to their character. We must
not examine matters too deeply. No, sir, a *fallible being will
fail somewhere*."

'Talking of the Irish clergy, he said, Swift was a man of
great parts, and the instrument of much good to his country.
Berkeley was a profound scholar, as well as a man of fine

imagination; but Usher, he said, was the great luminary of the Irish Church; and a greater, he added, no church could boast of, at least in modern times.

'We dined *tête-à-tête* at the Mitre, as I was preparing to return to Ireland, after an absence of many years. I regretted much leaving London, where I had formed many agreeable connections: "Sir (said he), I don't wonder at it; no man, fond of letters, leaves London without regret. But remember, sir, you have seen and enjoyed a great deal; you have seen life in its highest decorations, and the world has nothing new to exhibit. No man is so well qualified to leave public life as he who has long tried it and known it well. We are always hankering after untried situations, and imagining greater felicity from them than they can afford. No, sir, knowledge and virtue may be acquired in all countries, and your local consequence will make you some amends for the intellectual gratifications you relinquish." Then he quoted the following lines with great pathos:

> ' "He who has early known the pomps of state
> (For things unknown, 'tis ignorance to condemn);
> And after having viewed the gaudy bait,
> Can boldly say, the trifle I contemn;
> With such a one contented could I live,
> Contented could I die." [1]

---

[1] [Being desirous to trace these verses to the fountain-head, after having in vain turned over several of our elder poets with the hope of lighting on them, I applied to Dr. Maxwell, now resident at Bath, for the purpose of ascertaining their author; but that gentleman could furnish no aid on this occasion. At length the lines having been discovered by the author's second son, Mr. James Boswell, in the *London Magazine* for July 1732, where they form part of a poem on 'Retirement,' there published anonymously, and doubtless for the first time; and they exhibit another proof of what has been elsewhere observed by the author of the work before us, that Johnson retained in his memory fragments of very obscure poetic writers. In quoting verses of that description, he appears by a slight variation to have sometimes given them a moral turn, and to have dexterously adapted them to his own sentiments, where the original had a very different tendency. Thus, in the present instance (as Mr. J. Boswell observes to me), 'the author of the poem above mentioned exhibits himself as having retired to the country, to avoid the vain follies of a town life—ambition, avarice, and the pursuit of pleasure, contrasted with the enjoyments of the country, and the delightful conversation that the brooks, etc., furnish; which he holds to be infinitely more pleasing and instructive than any which

'He then took a most affecting leave of me; said he knew it was a point of *duty* that called me away. "We shall all be sorry to lose you," said he: "*laudo tamen.*"'

In 1771 he published another political pamphlet entitled *Thoughts on the late Transactions respecting Falkland's Islands,* in which, upon materials furnished to him by ministry, and upon general topics expanded in his rich style, he successfully endeavoured to per-

---

towns afford. He is then led to consider the weakness of the human mind, and after lamenting that he (the writer) who is neither enslaved by avarice, ambition, or pleasure, has yet made himself a slave to *love,* he thus proceeds:

'"If this dire passion never will be done,
    If beauty always must my heart enthral,
O, rather let me be enslaved by *one,*
    Than madly thus become a slave to all:

One *who has early known the pomp of state,*
    For things unknown, 'tis ignorance to condemn,
And, after having viewed the gaudy bait,
    Can coldly say, *the trifle I contemn;*

In her blest arms *contented could I live,*
    Contented could I die. But, O my mind,
Imaginary scenes of bliss deceive
    With hopes of joys impossible to find."'

Another instance of Johnson's retaining in his memory verses of obscure authors is given in Mr. Boswell's *Tour to the Hebrides,* where, in consequence of hearing a girl spinning in a chamber over that in which he was sitting, he repeated these lines, which he said were written by one Gifford, a clergyman; but the poem in which they are introduced has hitherto been undiscovered:

'Verse sweetens toil, however rude the sound:
    All at her work the village maiden sings;
Nor while she turns the giddy wheel around,
    Revolves the sad vicissitude of things.'

[Johnson did not give the second line accurately, though his version is the better. See 'Contemplation,' a poem printed by Dodsley in 1753. Its author was the Rev. Richard Gifford of Balliol College, Oxon.— A. B.]

In the autumn of 1782, when he was at Brighthelmstone, he frequently accompanied Mr. Philip Metcalfe in his chaise, to take the air; and the conversation in one of their excursions happening to turn on a celebrated historian, since deceased, he repeated with great precision some verses, as very characteristic of that gentleman. These furnish another proof of what has been above observed, for they are found in a very obscure quarter, among some anonymous poems appended to the second volume

suade the nation that it was wise and laudable to suffer
the question of right to remain undecided, rather than
involve our country in another war.   It has been
suggested by some, with what truth I shall not take
upon me to decide, that he rated the consequence of
those islands to Great Britain too low.   But however
this may be, every humane mind must surely applaud
the earnestness with which he averted the calamity of
war ; calamity so dreadful, that it is astonishing how
civilised—nay, Christian nations, can deliberately continue to renew it.   His description of its miseries in
this pamphlet is one of the finest pieces of eloquence
in the English language.   Upon this occasion, too, we
find Johnson lashing the party in opposition with un-
bounded severity, and making the fullest use of what
he ever reckoned a most effectual argumentative
instrument—contempt.   His character of their very
able, mysterious champion, Junius, is executed with
all the force of his genius, and finished with the highest
care.   He seems to have exulted in sallying forth to
single combat against the boasted and formidable hero,

---

of a collection frequently printed by Lintot, under the title of Pope's
Miscellanies :

'See how the wand'ring Danube flows,
  Realms and religions parting ;
A friend to all true Christian foes,
  To Peter, Jack, and Martin.

Now Protestant, and Papist now,
  Not constant long to either,
At length an infidel does grow,
  And ends his journey neither.

Thus many a youth I 've known set out,
  Half Protestant, half Papist,
And rambling long the world about,
  Turn infidel or atheist.'

In reciting these verses I have no doubt that Johnson substituted
some word for *infidel* in the second stanza, to avoid the disagreeable
repetition of the same expression.—M.]

who bade defiance to 'principalities and powers, and
the rulers of this world.'

This pamphlet, it is observable, was softened in one
particular, after the first edition; for the conclusion
of Mr. George Grenville's character stood thus : ' Let
him not, however, be depreciated in his grave. He
had powers not universally possessed : could he have
enforced payment of the Manilla ransom, *he could have
counted it.*' Which, instead of retaining its sly sharp
point, was reduced to a mere flat unmeaning expression, or, if I may use the word—*truism* : ' He had
powers not universally possessed ; and if he sometimes
erred, he was likewise sometimes right.'

TO BENNET LANGTON, ESQ.

'Dear Sir,—After much lingering of my own, and much
of the ministry, I have at length got out my paper.[1] But
delay is not yet at an end. Not many had been dispersed,
before Lord North ordered the sale to stop. His reasons I do
not distinctly know. You may try to find them in the perusal.[2]
Before his order, a sufficient number were dispersed to do all
the mischief, though perhaps, not to make all the sport that
might be expected from it.

'Soon after your departure, I had the pleasure of finding all
the danger past with which your navigation was threatened.
I hope nothing happens at home to abate your satisfaction ;
but that Lady Rothes, and Mrs. Langton, and the young
ladies, are all well.

'I was last night at the Club. Dr. Percy has written a long
ballad in many *fits* ; it is pretty enough. He has printed, and
will soon publish it. Goldsmith is at Bath with Lord Clare.

---

[1] *Thoughts on the late Transactions respecting Falkland's Islands.*
[2] By comparing the first with the subsequent editions, this curious
circumstance of ministerial authorship may be discovered.
[It can only be discovered (as Mr. Bindley observes to me) by him
who possesses a copy of the first edition issued out before the sale was
stopped.—M.]

At Mr. Thrale's, where I am now writing, all are well.—I am, dear sir, your most humble servant, SAM. JOHNSON.
'*March* 20, 1771.'

Mr. Strahan, the printer, who had been long in intimacy with Johnson in the course of his literary labours, who was at once his friendly agent in receiving his pension for him, and his banker in supplying him with money when he wanted it ; who was himself now a member of Parliament, and who loved much to be employed in political negotiation ; thought he should do eminent service, both to Government and Johnson, if he could be the means of his getting a seat in the House of Commons. With this view, he wrote a letter to one of the secretaries of the Treasury, of which he gave me a copy in his own handwriting, which is as follows :

'SIR,—You will easily recollect, when I had the honour of waiting upon you some time ago, I took the liberty to observe to you that Dr. Johnson would make an excellent figure in the House of Commons, and heartily wished he had a seat there. My reasons are briefly these :

'I know his perfect good affection to his Majesty, and his government, which I am certain he wishes to support by every means in his power.

'He possesses a great share of manly, nervous, and ready eloquence ; is quick in discerning the strength and weakness of an argument, can express himself with clearness and precision, and fears the face of no man alive.

'His known character as a man of extraordinary sense and unimpeached virtue, would secure him the attention of the House, and could not fail to give him a proper weight there.

'He is capable of the greatest application, and can undergo any degree of labour where he sees it necessary, and where his heart and affections are strongly engaged. His Majesty's ministers might therefore securely depend on his doing, upon every proper occasion, the utmost that could be expected from

him. They would find him ready to vindicate such measures
as tended to promote the stability of government, and resolute
and steady in carrying them into execution. Nor is anything
to be apprehended from the supposed impetuosity of his temper.
To the friends of the King you will find him a lamb, to his
enemies a lion.

'For these reasons I humbly apprehend that he would be a
very able and useful member. And I will venture to say, the
employment would not be disagreeable to him ; and knowing,
as I do, his strong affection to the King, his ability to serve
him in that capacity, and the extreme ardour with which I am
convinced he would engage in that service, I must repeat, that
I wish most heartily to see him in the House.

'If you think this worthy of attention, you will be pleased to
take a convenient opportunity of mentioning it to Lord North.
If his Lordship should happily approve of it, I shall have the
satisfaction of having been, in some degree, the humble instrument of doing my country, in my opinion, a very essential
service. I know your good nature, and your zeal for the
public welfare, will plead my excuse for giving you this trouble.
—I am, with the greatest respect, sir, your most obedient and
humble servant,   WILLIAM STRAHAN.

'*New Street, March* 30, 1771.'

This recommendation, we know, was not effectual ;
but how, or for what reason, can only be conjectured.
It is not to be believed that Mr. Strahan would have
applied, unless Johnson had approved of it. I never
heard him mention the subject ; but at a later period
of his life, when Sir Joshua Reynolds told him that
Mr. Edmund Burke had said, that if he had come
early into Parliament, he certainly would have been
the greatest speaker that ever was there, Johnson
exclaimed, 'I should like to try my hand now.'

It has been much agitated among his friends and
others, whether he would have been a powerful speaker
in Parliament, had he been brought in when advanced

in life. I am inclined to think that his extensive knowledge, his quickness and force of mind, his vivacity and richness of expression, his wit and humour, and above all, his poignancy of sarcasm, would have had great effect in a popular assembly; and that the magnitude of his figure, and striking peculiarity of his manner, would have aided the effect. But I remember it was observed by Mr. Flood, that Johnson having been long used to sententious brevity and the short flights of conversation, might have failed in that continued and expanded kind of argument, which is requisite in stating complicated matters in public speaking; and as a proof of this he mentioned the supposed speeches in Parliament written by him for the magazine, none of which, in his opinion, were at all like real debates. The opinion of one who was himself so eminent an orator, must be allowed to have great weight. It was confirmed by Sir William Scott, who mentioned that Johnson had told him, that he had several times tried to speak in the Society of Arts and Sciences, but 'had found he could not get on.' From Mr. William Gerrard Hamilton I have heard that Johnson, when observing to him that it was prudent for a man who had not been accustomed to speak in public to begin his speech in as simple a manner as possible, acknowledged that he rose in that society to deliver a speech which he had prepared; 'but (said he) all my flowers of oratory forsook me.' I however cannot help wishing that he *had* 'tried his hand' in Parliament; and I wonder that ministry did not make the experiment.

I at length renewed a correspondence which had been too long discontinued :

TO DR. JOHNSON

'*Edinburgh, April* 18, 1771.

'My dear Sir,—I can now fully understand those intervals of silence in your correspondence with me, which have often given me anxiety and uneasiness ; for although I am conscious that my veneration and love for Mr. Johnson have never in the least abated, yet I have deferred for almost a year and a half to write to him.' . . .

In the subsequent part of this letter, I gave him an account of my comfortable life as a married man, and a lawyer in practice at the Scotch bar : invited him to Scotland, and promised to attend him to the Highlands and Hebrides.

TO JAMES BOSWELL, ESQ.

'Dear Sir,—If you are now able to comprehend that I might neglect to write without diminution of affection, you have taught me, likewise, how that neglect may be uneasily felt without resentment. I wished for your letter a long time, and when it came, it amply recompensed the delay. I never was so much pleased as now with your account of yourself ; and sincerely hope that between public business, improving studies, and domestic pleasures, neither melancholy nor caprice will find any place for entrance. Whatever philosophy may determine of material nature, it is certainly true of intellectual nature, that it *abhors a vacuum* : our minds cannot be empty ; and evil will break in upon them, if they are not pre-occupied by good. My dear sir, mind your studies, mind your business, make your lady happy, and be a good Christian. After this,

> . . . " *tristitiam et metus*
> *Trades protervis in mare Creticum*
> *Portare ventis.*" [1]

---

[1] Horat. *Odes* i. 26.

'If we perform our duty, we shall be safe and steady, "*Sive per*," etc., whether we climb the Highlands, or are tossed among the Hebrides; and I hope the time will come when we may try our powers both with cliffs and water. I see but little of Lord Elibank, I know not why; perhaps by my own fault. I am this day going into Staffordshire and Derbyshire for six weeks.—I am, dear sir, your most affectionate and most humble servant,   SAM. JOHNSON.

'*London, June* 20, 1771.'

TO SIR JOSHUA REYNOLDS IN LEICESTER FIELDS

'DEAR SIR,—When I came to Lichfield, I found that my portrait had been much visited and much admired. Every man has a lurking wish to appear considerable in his native place; and I was pleased with the dignity conferred by such a testimony of your regard.

'Be pleased, therefore, to accept the thanks of, sir, your most obliged and most humble servant,   SAM. JOHNSON.

'*Ashbourn in Derbyshire,*
      July 17, 1771.
'Compliments to Miss Reynolds.'

TO DR. JOHNSON

'*Edinburgh, July* 27, 1771.
'MY DEAR SIR,—The bearer of this, Mr. Beattie, Professor of Moral Philosophy at Aberdeen, is desirous of being introduced to your acquaintance. His genius and learning, and labours in the service of virtue and religion, render him very worthy of it; and as he has a high esteem of your character, I hope you will give him a favourable reception.—I ever am, etc.,   JAMES BOSWELL.'

TO BENNET LANGTON, ESQ., AT LANGTON, NEAR SPILSBY, LINCOLNSHIRE

'DEAR SIR,—I am lately returned from Staffordshire and Derbyshire. The last letter mentions two others which you have written to me since you received my pamphlet. Of these two I never had but one, in which you mentioned a design of

visiting Scotland, and, by consequence, put my journey to
Langton out of my thoughts.   My summer wanderings are
now over, and I am engaging in a very great work, the revision of my *Dictionary*; from which I know not, at present,
how to get loose.

'If you have observed, or been told, any errors or omissions,
you will do me a great favour by letting me know them.

'Lady Rothes, I find, has disappointed you and herself.
Ladies will have these tricks. The Queen and Mrs. Thrale,
both ladies of experience, yet both missed their reckoning
this summer.   I hope a few months will recompense your
uneasiness.

'Please to tell Lady Rothes how highly I value the honour
of her invitation, which it is my purpose to obey as soon as I
have disengaged myself.   In the meantime I shall hope to
hear often of her ladyship, and every day better news and
better, till I hear that you have both the happiness, which to
both is very sincerely wished, by, sir, your most affectionate
and most humble servant,   SAM. JOHNSON.

'*August* 29, 1771.'

In October I again wrote to him, thanking him for
his last letter, and his obliging reception of Mr.
Beattie; informing him that I had been at Alnwick
lately, and had good accounts of him from Dr. Percy.

In his religious record of this year we observe that
he was better than usual, both in body and mind, and
better satisfied with the regularity of his conduct.
But he is still 'trying his ways' too rigorously. He
charges himself with not rising early enough; yet he
mentions what was surely a sufficient excuse for this,
supposing it to be a duty seriously required, as he all
his life appears to have thought it.   'One great
hindrance is want of rest; my nocturnal complaints
grow less troublesome towards morning; and I am
tempted to repair the deficiencies of the night.'[1]

---

[1] *Prayers and Meditations*, p. 101.

Alas! how hard would it be if this indulgence were to be imputed to a sick man as a crime. In his retrospect on the following Easter eve, he says, 'When I review the last year, I am able to recollect so little done, that shame and sorrow, though perhaps too weakly, come upon me.' Had he been judging of any one else in the same circumstances, how clear would he have been on the favourable side. How very difficult, and in my opinion, almost constitutionally impossible it was for him to be raised early, even by the strongest resolutions, appears from a note in one of his little paper-books (containing words arranged for his *Dictionary*), written, I suppose, about 1753: 'I do not remember that since I left Oxford I ever rose early by mere choice, but once or twice at Edial, and two or three times for the *Rambler*.' I think he had fair ground enough to have quieted his mind on the subject, by concluding that he was physically incapable of what is at best but a commodious regulation.

END OF VOL. II

Printed by T. and A. CONSTABLE, Printers to Her Majesty at the Edinburgh University Press

www.ingramcontent.com/pod-product-compliance
Lightning Source LLC
Chambersburg PA
CBHW020900020726
47497CB00005B/1497